The Widowmaker

"Heat of The Night"

I0598049

A John Roméo Novel

by

Gene Cartwright

First Edition Softcover

Gene Cartwright

The Widowmaker (Heat of the Night)
Gene Cartwright - 1st Edition p.cm

ISBN: 978-0-9649756-3-7

1. Title
10 9 8 7 6 5 4 3 2 1

GMW

CA-TX-DC

Published by Falcon Creek Publishing Company - January 2009, 2016
My Shoelace Books, Falcon Books are imprints of Falcon Creek Publishing Co.

Book Design, cover, artwork by Gene Cartwright © 2008, 2016 Gene Cartwright All rights reserved. falconcreekbooks.com I ifogo.com

Printed in the United States of America

Thanks.

Special thanks to my great friend, Florinda Johnson, co-founder of Sistalic Book Club of San Diego. Flo, your sharp mind, sharp editor's eye, and intense interest in this work was invaluable in helping make it the best possible. My continued prayers and best wishes for you, Bub, your entire family.

The Women of Sistalic Founders:
Felita Johnson-Joy, Florinda Johnson, and Stephanie Johnson, (sisters)

Members:
Taryn Clarke, Elaine Howard, Thomas Howard, Merdis Jackson-Maurice, Florinda Johnson, Samantha Spears.

I am also grateful for the love and support of my few real friends, for the kindness of strangers and pets, and the forbearance of reptiles.

Novels & Books by Gene Cartwright

I Never Played Catch With My Father
Half Moon, Full Heart
A Family Gathering
Fire Night
Quietkill
Dying for Love
The Promise Road
Still Dreaming (visual poetry
The Drammen Code (3/17)
The Value of Small Things (non-fiction)

Coming Novels by Gene Cartwright:

Nowhere, Texas
Twelfth Night of The August Moon
Alone Again
Harold

The Widowmaker

"Heat of The Night"

"John Roméo has an eye for beauty, and a nose for murder."

A John Roméo Novel

A Poem

How Long You Gon' Be Dead?

When did the last note of promise
    fade from your heart's song?
    When did the final thread of hope
    unravel from the tapestry of your life?
    When did faith in your dreams
    turn to hopelessness and despair?
    Tell me, when did you die,
    and how long you gon' be dead?

When did the light in your eyes
    grow dim, your gaze lose its aim?
    When did your belief in tomorrow
    lose itself forever in yesterday?
    When did your hunger for success
    melt like last winter's snow?
    Tell me, when did you die,
    and how long you gon' be dead?

When did you consign your thinking to the corrupting minds of others?
When did fear consume your soul, wilt your fiery desire and passion?
What words sowed seeds of doubt, crushing your boundless ambition?
Tell me, when did you die, and how long you gon' be dead?

When did your soul lose its vision,
    your flame become merely a flicker?
    How did your step become uncertain,
    your joy and laughter disappear?
    When did your spirit fail to lift you,
    to restore you, to arm you as before?
    In other words, when did you die,
    and how long you gon' be dead?

Now, ain't the time for fluttering hearts.
Gaze into your mirror and see hope
resurrected in your eyes, your faith reborn.
Turn a deaf ear to the voices of those
who only take pleasure in your failing.
Seize every thread of possibility,
Devour every crumb of inspiration.
Rise and walk. You ain't dead yet!

The Widowmaker

"Heat of The Night"

Don't skip this, alright?

The name is Roméo, not Romeo. Got it?

I'm not afraid of dying; it's living that scares me shitless.

The former is inescapable; the latter, unpredictable. I'm a cop. I *was* a cop. Hell, I am still a cop. And notwithstanding my hard-nosed, take no prisoner's facade, I am subject to the same fears, frailties and foibles as most mortals.

My obligatory vow to *Protect and Serve* sprang not so much from saccharin-laced altruism, as from overvalued ego, coupled with a desire to curry favor with my late father. To secure reasonable expectations of physical and emotional survival, I made my own Faustian deal with the devil. The devil won. That should come as no surprise.

I confess it has taken a long time for me to come to grips with the maelstrom that engulfed me a few years ago. The *officially* concluded serial murder investigation I headed was a bitch—a pain in the ass, in more ways than I can count.

In the aftermath, I have found myself immersed in self-appraisal; undertaking amateur self-analysis, grappling with the psychological trauma my professional experiences have inflicted upon me.

Murder is an ugly business; investigating it takes its toll. Do not be misled by television shows and films depicting the most complex murders being solved in an hour or two. It ain't so. And once the case is done, it is not easy to compartmentalize and simply move on. But we do...move on, carrying with us whatever ill effects attain.

Serial murder cases are even more frustrating. They can drive you mad in an anguished search for answers, while the body count climbs. The pressure to solve grows daily. Each succeeding murder denotes a greater failing than the previous. Often, the psychopath seems to delight in exhibiting deeper and deeper levels of depravity. This case I dub the *Widowmaker* was such a case.

If I never see another mutilated stiff sliced or blown to hell and lying in bloody chunks before my jaded eyes again, that will be fine with me. After thirteen years in LAPD Homicide, I've had more than my fill of gory images, the clinging stench of decaying human flesh.

However, I confess to having a morbid fascination with the depravity of many of my fellow beings. I am not being melodramatic. There is something about savage acts perpetrated by so-called human beings that can savage one's sensibilities. Disturbingly, I find myself requiring a greater and greater degree of savagery in order to be fazed or repulsed; that bothers me.

However, I still cringe whenever I recall the Glazer case. Rachel Glazer was a 23 year-old mother-to-be in her late third trimester. On November 23, 1993, she was brutally raped, her brains scattered over the walls and floors of her Laurel Canyon home, her fetus ripped from her womb by some sadistic maniac of the extreme sort.

The sick bastard left semen deposits on the carpet next to the mutilated body, having apparently masturbated before or after his murderous orgy. I still regret having to enter that murder scene. Half a dozen seasoned detectives, including me, broke down that day.

The memory is searing, numbing, an image forever imprinted upon my psyche. It took us eight months to nail the monster: a former hospital orderly from Riverside. At the conclusion of a two-hour freeway chase ending near what is now Ontario Mills—a sprawling shopping mall on I-10—he stuck a .45 in his mouth and blew his brains out. Score one for taxpayers.

Four fetuses were later found in the suspect's rented home. They were preserved in glass containers filled with formaldehyde and locked in a large, red and white Igloo cooler. I later disposed of an identical one I owned. I wanted no reminder. To this day, we have no idea if the Glazer fetus was among them. Anthony Glazer, the husband and father, declined DNA matching analysis.

I sometimes have flash dreams about the Glazer death scene. All the self-important, all-knowing, tree-hugging psychologists in the world cannot erase crap like that from my mind. The deepest sleep offers little refuge. And the last thing I want to hear from some glib-tongued, bleeding-heart apologist is that the poor psychotic bastard had an abusive childhood. Screw him and his entire dysfunctional family.

My solution: Give me one minute alone with any of these antisocial pricks. And I'm a card-carrying liberal. I even have a faded tattoo of Big Mama Thornton on my black ass. I voted for Michael Dukakis. So do not color me as some heartless, compassionless, law and order, ultra right-wing nut who never had a mother, let alone anyone else with whom to bond. I have a habit of reserving my compassion for victims. I am weird, that way.

Presently, I welcome a chance to get back to the womb-like environs of home, back to my Macintosh, back to my cocoon. I relish immersing myself in my own *escapist reality*—my writing.

Yet, even now, I am loath to confess what I realize I must inevitably confess. I come late to this decision, after much agony, deep introspection, and the boisterous objections of that persistent inner voice that is my ego, not my conscience. The latter often speaks to me in much lower decibels. And though not easily heard, it is much more persistent, even nagging—ever nudging me toward truth. I know it sounds like bullshit but I am serious.

There is little doubt those who have always longed for my scalp will delight in the more titillating revelations that follow. They will likely get off on it—blow some juice. I know how the game is played. I don't mean to sound so pissed, but to hell with my detractors and assorted critics. As far as I am concerned, they can kiss my ebony ass, particularly some of my former associates.

And I can imagine some of you hissing at my use of a few expletives—cuss words, for my brothers in the 'hood. My publisher probably will not like it either. In fact, we have had some very spirited discussions about it, and other aspects of this book. They were a little queasy about my frank portrayal of certain members of the LAPD.

It is not that I dislike LAPD cops, just specific ones. I still find, as I did when I was an active officer, that while most cops are dedicated, honest people, a few are low-life, egomaniacal scum buckets with guns. Some others could use a damn spine transplant. As in any organization, they should be rooted out.

My publisher was also concerned I would come off as having too much edge; that I needed to soften my self-portrayal. The concern was that some women readers would be turned off by a hard-edged persona. Are you kidding me? My response was to assure them I would simply be honest. I am not perfect. The truth is, before I became a cop, I was two credits shy of a Masters Degree in pacifism. You will definitely see my warts, weaknesses, and imperfections. You cannot do what I do and come off like Bishop Tutu or Mister Rogers.

Others have also raised well-meaning questions regarding my edge and my anger, as they put it. *"What are you running away from? What are you trying to mask,"* they ask. My answer? I have seen enough gore and depravity to put an edge on the Pope. And I am not attempting to mask anything. I admit I am beset by my own demons that are not easily banished.

Still, I do have a soft side. I am really a lamb at heart. Perhaps, by the end of this book, you will recognize that fact. But remember: This is not a *Bridges of Madison County* story. We are talking murder, here.

Forgive my manners. My name is Roméo, John Roméo, pronounced *Ro-may-o, alright?* I have always insisted on that pronunciation. Doing so has not always been easy. For most of my childhood, I was a frail, shy, introverted, stuttering, dyslexic kid who seldom spoke above a whisper and rarely got angry. I still have to work hard to overcome the stuttering and dyslexia.

My 'boys' back in my Harlem hood did not give a damn about medical problems with fancy names. All they knew was, your ass 'was' different; that you were 'flicted. So you tried to hide that shit... pretend all those little twitches and screwed up expressions were being done on purpose.

As if that were not enough, I had to put up with the crap I received because of my last name: Roméo. Besides the endless questions regarding the whereabouts of Juliet, there was the attitude that black folks were not suppose to have names like Roméo. Hell, truth be told, Africans on the Middle Passage did not have names like John, Bruce, Kashonda, Leroy or Lamont, either.

And my face was a disaster zone. I was nearly twenty-one before I finally rid myself of oozing zits and blackheads with attitude. Guys who say those things do not concern them are liars. My biggest challenge growing up was coping with the innate cruelty of other kids.

One day, during my junior year in high school, having endured as much teasing about my stuttering, my zits and my last name as I could take, I jammed an annoying classmate into a row of wall lockers outside Mrs. Washington's room. I then crunched him with a hard right that left his nose bleeding, and a left hook that closed his right eye. He was in pain but /was in shock. This was not who I was, or was it?

All the suppressed rage I had always locked away, one day suddenly erupted like Mt. Vesuvius onto this unfortunate kid. Thomas Arceneaux was his name. I often wonder whatever happened to Thomas. He really was not a bad kid, just stupid. Today, boys treated similarly to me tend to react much more violently towards those perceived as oppressors.

Following my violent outburst, I was suddenly popular with fellow students who never had two words for me before the incident. But I did not want their friendship, and let them know it. Truth was, I respected

Thomas more than I did them. The two of us became good friends and remained so until the day we graduated and went our separate ways.

Immediately following the incident, I told my mother that from that day on, my last name would be pronounced Ro-may-o. No more *"Hey Romeo! Where forth is Juliet"* crap. Mother smiled lovingly, shook her head, dried her hands on her favorite, handmade, red plaid, white lace-trimmed apron and said sternly:

"Take out that trash, finish cleaning that filthy room like I told you this morning, and do your homework. By the way, I got an urgent call from Mrs. Washington. You just wait."

My mother, a 5'-3," chocolate dynamo with a disarming smile and laser wit, had a way of cutting through the bullshit and going straight for the aorta. Had my father been alive, he likely would have toasted my decking of Thomas Arceneaux by hoisting a beer. My attempts at subterfuge and deflection seldom worked with mother. I never raised the subject of changing my name again, at least not in *Sweet Caroline's* presence.

Those days now seem an eternity ago. Whatever difficulties existed then; whatever trials I endured then, pale when contrasted to my adult life, particularly my career with the LAPD. And what of all those years—years that gave me the highest highs and the lowest lows? How did I arrive at this moment in my life?

Keep Reading

For thirteen eventful years, I was an LAPD cop with middle class lifestyle; a postgraduate education; a blue-collar, New York attitude; love for the music of Miles Davis, Otis Redding, Nancy Wilson; and a taste for pork rinds chased with Pabst Blue Ribbon beer years past its prime. Go figure.

I ate, slept, bled, and crapped blue. All this represented a baffling dichotomy to those familiar with my more liberal lineage and penchant for quiet moments spent watching sunsets and writing poetry.

I spent eleven of those years in Homicide where I discovered I was more than well suited. And if I may be permitted a smidgen of immodesty, I was not just good at what I did, I was damn good. Still am. Even my enemies concede this fact, though grudgingly. They say I have an eye for beauty and a nose for murder—a sixth sense.

That is why whenever Homicide slams into a brick wall and cannot navigate their way through, around or over it, they call me. I am flattered by their confidence in me. Do not misunderstand, the nearly eighty members of LAPD Robbery/Homicide, and especially those in Sections 1 and 2 are some of the best detectives anywhere. My working these cases without the constraints afflicting permanent officers gives me distinct advantages. For one, I am not looking for a promotion or in need of a job.

Still many are not enamored of the arrangement. I am sensitive to their sensibilities. Some think I am cocky and brash. I am just self-assured and quick to recognize God-given gifts, even if they reside within me.

More often than not, I accept these "special, off the book assignments" without rubbing my detractors' collective noses in it. I happily confess I had nothing to do with the O.J. Simpson case. As far as the LAPD is concerned, it is and was never a mystery. Publicly, the Department and the DA's office expressed little doubt concerning whodunit. That was not the first or last mistake they made. I know they privately acknowledged serious concerns about the quality of certain aspects of their own scientific investigations. But hell, that's history now.

Lately, I have been less willing to tear myself away from my real work, my passion: writing. I do find time to travel extensively in Europe, Africa, the Far East, and recently South America. When not at my Beverly Hills digs, I can be found ensconced at my villa in the South of France, the Tudor in the pastoral English countryside or my condo on

Maui. The travel reinvigorates and inspires me. It is my elixir. It is also tax-deductible.

Realizing that lesser minds will be eager to pounce on any perceived inaccuracies, I want to be precise. I lease the villa and the mansion when I'm traveling in Europe. However, I do own the Beverly Hills Estate and the condo. I never actively seek special assignments from Homicide; I do not have to. The real difficulty is avoiding them. Sometimes I feel stupid after accepting them. After all, one of the reasons I retired was to put that chapter of my life behind me.

But it's hard to say no to Captain C.E. 'Bear' Nicholson—head of Robbery/Homicide Division; a 6'-4" hard-ass, square-jawed ex-marine with a dragon exterior and the heart of a teddy bear. Every one of his guys would follow wherever he led. While giving orders is in part what leaders do, Nick would rather show than tell.

Perhaps what is most endearing about Captain Nick is the fact he still identifies so intensely with the 'street cop.' He remains one at heart. And his role as head of RHD has not changed him. What is more, he has no desire to move beyond P.A.B's 3rd floor.

So, when I get his call, I know it heralds a challenge. And honestly, I find it easier to walk on hot coals than resist a worthy challenge. Yet, I have no scarcity of obligations that could more than justify a *no* to the good Captain. He is one persuasive man. He reminds me of my dear, late father—an iron-willed, ex-Bronx cop with an acid tongue and a marshmallow heart.

About my father, he spent more than twenty-eight callous-building years strapped to the 41st precinct, known as Fort Apache, located in the south Bronx at Simpson Street between East 167th Street and Westchester Avenue. For some reason, that is where he wanted to be. It became a decadent symbol of all things wanton, lawless, and evil. The "Fort," a crucible that tested the mettle of every decent cop there, on a daily basis, especially in the 60's and most of the 70's, made mincemeat of lesser men, but not Alexander Roméo.

My father's boundless love for my mother, and his desire to please her and provide us all the best life he could, was always clear. I miss him and my mother more than I can say. My only regret is that I have no sisters, and only one brother.

I get a bit emotional speaking about my family. Had fate not intervened so tragically, I would have two sisters and a second brother, each older than me. It was not until I was eleven years old, that mother revealed my sisters had been stillborn, three years apart; and my older brother had died from SIDS *(sudden infant death syndrome)* at age three months. Of course, back in the day, we had no idea what the hell SIDS was.

My mother and father had all but given up on having more children, until I was, admittedly, accidentally conceived six years later. The following nine months were filled with torturous anxiety for both of them. Even after I was born, and until nearly four, my mother hardly permitted me out of her sight. Father would call home from the precinct several times a day to see if I was alright.

After all the heartbreak my parents suffered, I was their "miracle child." It was a burden I did not relish then or now. It made me feel that every step I took was weighted with imagining that my parents' very lives—their happiness either rose or fell on whatever I did.

What should have been normal, anticipated childhood diseases for me became causes for alarm. My folks' exaggerated reactions burdened me so, that by the time I was 7 or 8 years old, I began concealing the slightest scrape or injury. I seldom told them when I felt bad. The danger in my decision is obvious, but that was how I found relief from their exaggerated concerns. I swore to never go through the torment of losing children as my parents had, vowing if I ever had children, I would adopt them. Let's change the subject. I can't afford to get emotional this early in the book.

Six years ago, at the tender age of thirty-three, with degrees in criminology and psychology, and having always fancied myself a man of letters, I wrote my first novel: *Shadow of Death.* It earned millions, in hard and soft-covers; the top spot on the New York Times Best Sellers list for months, and a ridiculously lucrative movie deal. I also wrote the screenplay, while enduring the *"Who the hell do you think you are insisting we tell your story the way you wrote it,"* attitude of more than a few nauseating studio twits.

However, I did insist, within reasonable limits. The movie grossed 248 million dollars, worldwide, before video release. It did not take a nanosecond to decide what the hell I was going to do, from that point on. The know-it-all, pseudo-sophisticates in Hollywood, who had earlier whispered when I passed, and cast snotty glances, were now bowing, scraping and kissing my suddenly genius posterior. It was clear they only wanted *more*—more of the same, always more of the same.

While most of my fellow cops gave me congratulatory back slaps, and expressed toothy congratulations, there were a few dickheads who viewed me as an opportunist. Several accused me of unfairly using my LAPD experiences as grist for the literary mill; of selling my shield for a few lousy millions. I lost no sleep over these accusations by those who would have gladly traded places with me.

Now, after one of the most bizarre serial murder cases ever in Los Angeles or anywhere else, I now, in this account, explain my role in helping investigate it. Here, I have set about to tell what I personally know and have learned from: notes, diaries, threats, forced confessions, snitches, books, newspapers, audio tapes, video tapes, rap sheets, victims, pimps, whores, the Farmer's Almanac and, of course, the Department.

This story is not linear—not a straight-line progression; murder investigations seldom are. This account is based, primarily, on substantive aspects of an actual case. The names of some individuals, excluding my own, have been changed to protect my net worth.

It may surprise some I spare myself no embarrassment. I have always said when the time comes, I will write my own tell all book which exposes me from *my* perspective. To date, my darling ex-wife, Claire, has not attempted to preempt me. I am not proud of some of my actions herein revealed. However, I am prepared to suffer the consequences.

At the insistence of my agent and my publisher, I agreed to work with author, Michael Manstar. Everyone felt I was and am too close to these events to author the book alone, notwithstanding the degree of fictionalization. Actually, having a writing partner gives me plausible deniability, regarding parts of the story. I have no objections and will provide all the information, facts and a major portion of the writing. This proves I *am* capable of setting aside my much-maligned ego for the greater good.

To the extent possible, I have tried hard to remain objective. Have I succeeded? Who knows? I tried. I confess that, where first, second, or third-hand information is not available, I have taken liberty to draw upon my deep reservoir of experience. At times, I provide what I call logical *extensions* of known facts.

Do not be so surprised. That is the way it is often done. I have the chutzpah to tell you. You are free to believe whatever you like and draw whatever conclusions you feel bound to draw. I have no desire to create a monolithic view of my work or of myself. Simply judge me on the facts.

My only obligation is to be as honest as I can. I cannot be burdened by some phony attempt to be sensitive to everyone—to be politically correct. If you are squeamish, are offended by my frankness or my language, I am sorry. You have the option of continuing or stopping here. I have no doubt some will think me egotistical and self-centered. Nonsense, I am simply a self-assured individual with a penchant for telling the unadorned truth. Some find truth unpalatable.

Are you still reading?

The L.A.P.D.—

*They don't want John Roméo,
but they sure as hell need him.*

One
The Deadpool

"Talk dirty to you?"

Modesty be damned.

Computer software magnate Colin Sumner had little use for it. He always got what he wanted, lucky bastard. Wealth and pleasure were not only his obsessions; he judged them his birthright, and indulged himself without constraint.

When the board of San Jose based Sumner Technologies bounced him as Chairman and CEO in 2004, he cashed in his chips, took his genius, his patents and his money, left Silicon Valley and returned to his southern California playground. Six months later, he launched a much-anticipated tech venture, issBroadband.com, while the stock value of his former company plummeted to single digits. Sumner was savoring the sweet taste of revenge.

His was no geek physique. At 43, six feet, clean-shaven, wearing only his tan skin, Sumner stood on the deck of his heated indoor pool, with its monogrammed bottom, sipping his winery's newest Chardonnay and admiring Lisa bob up and down in the *Aqua-Velva* water. She made a point of rising high enough to expose her bulbous 38'dds, before submerging again with a splash.

Colin felt his pulsating erection growing faster than the trade deficit. Lisa, a former Hustler model and would-be actress he met at a Larry Flynt Christmas party in '02, took note and moved closer.

"You gonna just stand there?" She asked in a sultry *'come and get it* 'voice.

Colin drew another sip, eased onto the deck and set his drink aside. He sat at pool's edge, his 'runners' legs planted in the water. Lisa stopped three feet away, gazed at him. Her smile evaporated, her bottom lip quivered, as it always did whenever anticipation seized her.

"Colin," she purred.

Sumner had no doubt where the conversation was headed.

"Water's fine. You coming back in, or do you just plan to sit there and watch me?"

"In a minute. I love watching you."

Colin stared at his lover's distorted image visible below the water line. Lisa hesitated then swam away toward the far end of the pool. She climbed out, sat on the rose-colored concrete deck facing Colin over the wet expanse. An Everett Harp CD oozed rousing but soothing saxophone riffs from the phalanx of ceiling-mounted speakers suspended above them.

For the longest time, neither spoke. The lovers sat like statues, staring at each other, playing some silly cat and mouse game, waiting for the other to shatter the silence. The only light poured in from a full moon, visible through the half dozen rectangular skylight panels. The silvery illumination bathed the pool in a soft glow, accented by perimeter lights mounted just below water level. Colin Sumner's palatial, Pacific Palisades home, featured a month earlier in *Architectural Digest,* was exactly what one would expect a man worth an estimated 860 million dollars to own.

Colin eyed Lisa, feeling every bit the master of all he surveyed, including her. He knew he could have Lisa whenever, wherever,   and however he wanted. She was the kind of woman he would never marry, even if he were single. But she was the best screw he had ever had. Lisa could do things with her body pretzels never dreamed. Sumner loved his women part lady, part whore. Lisa was all that. All he had to do to keep her hanging on was to keep her believing he would someday divorce his wife for her. No way in hell

Minutes passed. Lisa swam closer, climbed from the pool, and sat on the deck adjacent to her lover. She leaned back onto her forearms, riveted her eyes on Colin then parted her legs slowly, revealing herself completely. Her taut, sculpted bottom hardly lost its curves, even pressed against the unforgiving concrete. Colin, taking in every inch of her curvaceous form, sipped the last of his drink.

Lisa thrust her head backwards, began caressing both breasts with her right hand, raking her tongue repeatedly across her painted lips. Colin's breathing deepened. He watched, determined to constrain reaction, save the one over which he had no control.

Rocking gently from side to side, Lisa eased her hand along the length of her supple body, past her navel, drew circles atop her curly patch, coming to rest between her baby smooth thighs. Seizing herself firmly, she clamped her legs tightly then released, repeating the motion again and again.

Less than five minutes elapsed. Lisa again slipped into the pool and swam toward her lover. Colin, exuding an air of indifference, folded his arms and waited. Momentarily she was a foot away, peering up at him, both hands clutching the lip of the deck.

Just as Colin started to speak, Lisa submerged herself, lingered for almost twenty seconds then shot straight up. Water cascaded from her auburn hair, down her neck, streamed between her buoyed breasts. She tossed her head to one side, stared pointedly at him.

"I know what you're thinking," said Colin.

"And you should."

Colin shook his head in mild disgust. His reaction angered Lisa.

"What does *that* mean?" She asked.

"Nothing. Let's not ruin the moment," Colin answered with a half smile.

"The moment? You're concerned about the moment, I'm concerned about our future."

"Can't we talk about this later? We'll have dinner, some wine..."

"No. Let's not talk later. I think I have a right to know if all you want to do is pool-fuck me while Diane wears your name and sleeps in your damn bed."

"That's uncalled for."

Lisa pushed off and swam away. A playful Colin, determined to not let the atmosphere turn too serious, leaped into the pool in quick pursuit. Near the middle, he caught her from behind, pulled her under. Lisa sprang up instantly, flailing her arms—frantic to free herself.

Overpowered, Lisa surrendered. The two suddenly found themselves locked in a long kiss and a passionate embrace. Colin's rock-rigid erection bridged the distance between them.

"I'm sorry," he said softly, "There're some legal matters I have to attend to first. I explained that before. I plan to end it once and for all. I promise."

"When?"

"Do you really want to spend our night together talking about...?"

"When?" Lisa's voice echoed loudly. Colin drew a deep breath, turned away briefly.

"When Diane gets back from Paris. I'll tell her then."

Lisa shook her head, conveying disbelief.

Again, Colin threw his arms around her and kissed her firmly. Her tongue darted into his eager mouth. She had not driven twenty miles in a cramped Cooper Mini to ruin the evening with talk of Colin's wife, and resisting his insatiable desire for sex. The talking would have to wait for later in the evening. In Lisa's mind, if not her heart, *she* was the woman of this house.

Although weary of playing the *other woman*, Lisa hoped it was just a matter of time before she became the new Mrs. Sumner. Colin often complained of Diane's disinterest in sex; her rabid fear of losing her youth and beauty. At that very moment she was again in France, chasing down scant evidence some French doctor had discovered a promising anti-aging drug.

Lisa surrendered completely, as Colin eased his probing fingers between her thighs and captured her. He held her waist and guided her gently toward the edge of the pool. Lisa closed her eyes in anticipation, clinging to Colin's neck with both arms.

"What are you gonna do to me?" She whispered.

"What do you think?"

"Tell me. You know I like to hear you say it."

"Talk dirty to you?"

"Yes. What are you going to do to me?"

Colin smiled. "What do you think?"

"I don't want to think anymore. Tell me."

Colin reached the edge of the pool, throbbing fiercely. He pressed his lips to Lisa's ear, whispered the words she craved. She reached down, wrapped her right hand firmly around him. He lifted her slightly and pressed forward. Lisa threw both arms around his neck again, eagerly accommodating his every move.

Neither needed foreplay. Tilting back, Lisa raised her right leg, locked it firmly around the back of Colin's upper thigh, drawing him closer. He shut his eyes, raised her just so, lowered himself, gripped her beneath the curve of her ass, slipped inside her and quickly found her spot. Lisa gasped, winced, and urged him on. Colin felt himself surge even deeper, slowly withdrew then slipped further into her.

Amid loud, uninhibited groans, the two welded themselves to each other, sending pool water sloshing and churning like turbine backwash. Colin retreated gently, then returned, then retreated to return again, probing and massaging her every inner surface. Lisa winced again, clenched her teeth; dug her fingers into his back, forcing him to her deepest part.

Colin opened then sealed his eyes shut again; he eased forward. Now fully inside Lisa now, he could feel a rhythmic gripping—an inviting, massaging sensation that captured him. He loosed a loud, guttural groan—a primal sound soon masked by Lisa's sudden and sustained high-pitched scream.

Inspired by Lisa's explicit, raw verbal language urging him on, Colin grasped the deck with both hands and pulled himself forward, and upward, hoisting her on his firmness.

Colin loved the fact Lisa was a screamer. It made him even more aroused and steeled. He stood on his toes, forcing his full length inside her, gripping her sculptured bottom with a force that always left their mark on her. Lisa wanted more, more than even the endowed Colin was able to give her. Soon, both were lost in the pulsing rhythm of the night.

Just then a loud pop. The sound crackled, filling the air, amplified by the water, the acoustics. Colin's head shot back violently—a deformed mass. A second pop. A goulash of streaking bloodlets; fractured bone and brain tissue splattered, filling Lisa's face, her eyes, her mouth. Colin's gaze locked. His blood-filled mouth froze open, yielding a staccato gurgle.

A shocked Lisa could scarcely react. In a split second, she started to turn. A third round tore into the back of her head, thrusting her forward into the water against Colin's lifeless form. Blood geysered from their wounds. A crimson pool foamed and swirled. In a gasp, the couple's watery playground became a *deadpool.* As if on cue, the music stopped. There was silence. Dead silence.

Just then, from deep shadows near poolside, a handful of computer discs were ceremoniously tossed into the air. Several landed near pool's edge; others danced across the discolored, foaming water. The surreality was heightened by moonlight that cast an eerie glow upon the naked, disfigured, partly submerged bodies floating face down in the water.

Nothing moved, only stillness—eerie stillness, a stillness and the unmistakable presence of death. The killer or killers remained cloaked in darkness, content to survey the carnage from a distance. Then, out of the blackness, a blinding light flared then vanished.

Two
Love-fest

"I don't usually take shit from writers."

"Goddamn!

I love it, John. Great piece of work you got here. I now see why you get the big bucks. You deserve every damn penny. Look, you know my reputation. I don't usually open up like this, especially to writers. But what the hell, this is good stuff. I confess to having misgivings before. I was a doubter but I was wrong—dead wrong. Congratulations!"

Movie producer Peter Blaine's effusive words of praise only fetched a cold stare from his handsome visitor slouched in the oversized chair in front of his desk. It was nearly 7pm. After a day on the set that saw a leading man decked by his female co-star, Blaine was hoping to end on an upbeat note. That was before John Roméo—all six-foot-four, short-cropped hair, dressed in a black Armani and white silk T-shirt—entered his office.

"Bullshit," John scoffed. "It's commercial. That *is* the operative word, isn't it? You don't have to blow cigar smoke up my ass. I agree it is commercial, but it ain't great. *Casablanca* is great. *Citizen Kane, Gone*

With The Wind are great. Of course, you were just engaging in a little hyperbole, right? A little verbal masturbation, huh? We sure as hell need more of that, don't we?"

John was in one of his foul, venom-spewing moods. Good thing his new screenplay, a political/sex thriller entitled *Messiah: The Embodiment*, was not being criticized. After all, following a record-setting bidding war that had tongues in Hollywood and New York wagging like a sheep dog's tail, he had been paid $7,000,000 for hard and soft cover rights to the book, and nearly $2,000,000 for his first draft screenplay. John's caustic reaction to the man with his hand on the production purse strings did not go down well. Peter Blaine was not one to suffer indignities with grace.

"Look, you're on my turf now. A little humility goes a long way. In case you don't know, I ain't exactly a can of Spam around this town. Didn't call you here for you to give me the damn *high hat*. I got that from Miller's Crossing...love that damn movie. Look, I know you're a homicide genius, turn multi-millionaire, and *your* shit don't stink but still..."

"I tailor my conversations for the company I'm in. If you're insulted..."

"Say what you want, John Romeo..."

"It's *Romayo.* "

"You pronounce it the way you want. I'll pronounce it the way it spells: R-O-M-E-O. Romeo." Blaine, leaned back in his chair, wagged his finger.

John turned purple. "When I'm not around, I don't give a shit how you pronounce my name. But when you're talking to me, you'll say it the way I want or not at all. What's unreasonable about that?"

"Look, John..."

"No, you look. I didn't come in here for this trivial crap. I thought you wanted a serious discussion."

"You're a friggin' riot, John. But I refuse to be insulted. You're not gonna pee on my shoes today. I'm immune to all negativity. 'Course, tomorrow may be a different story, so don't push it. Besides, I thought we were friends."

Peter Blaine, a tree stump, beach ball of a man, forced a grin and leaned back in the plush comfort of his Italian leather executive chair. He took a long drag on his $25 Cuban cigar contraband, released a plume of smoke, spat out a piece of tobacco and stared, first at John, then the screenplay on his desk. In contrast to John's dour expression, a look of immense satisfaction covered Peter's scraggly, 'salt and pepper' bearded face.

The two men, normally civil to each other, had just finished watching action excerpts from *Midnight City,* the blockbuster movie from John's most recent screenplay. John was steamed by Peter's insistence the Mega-buck script he was presently completing be as violent and laced with sex as *Midnight City.* John felt Peter and the premiere studio he was currently milking, which had not had a major hit in three years, should be happy to have *Messiah*. John had also agreed to give them first crack at his new novel.

Today, he just happened to be in a deep-blue funk and found Blaine particularly irksome. He was sure it was the beard, and probably the stinking cigar stuck between his tobacco-stained teeth.

"Like I said. Great stuff, John."

John said nothing.

"Of course, I'm an action kind 'a guy, you know that," Peter continued, champing vigorously on his half-smoked stogie. A tiny brown stream of tobacco juice trailed down the right corner of Blaine's mouth, into his beard. He wiped it away with the back of his hand and droned on.

"Regardless of your hoity-toity attitude, I love *Midnight City*. And that's exactly what I want from the one you're finishing. Name of the game is box office, babe. And we did *Midnight City* without a Schwarzenegger, a Snipes, a Segal, a Smith or a Stallone. Okay? 'Course one is a 'Guvna now,' and two are a little long in the tooth. Hey, I just realized something. All these guys' last names start with '*S.* 'What's with that shit?"

"Anybody can do crash and burn and beaver banging," said John. "Let's agree on that. I want to write..."

"Spare me!" Peter interrupted, pounding his fist on the desk so hard his cigar flipped out of his mouth. He stuffed it back between his teeth, without missing a beat. "I know what the hell you want. You want *Fried Green Tomatoes, Bridges of Madison County*, right? That artsy-fartsy, touchy-feely crap, that's what you want."

"That's not what I'm saying, but what's wrong with that?"

"John! John! Look baby. I thought we had an understanding, you and me. Who's the damn genius here? I give people what they want. It's that simple. If I want to see schlock like that, I'll rent the damn' DVDs. Hello! Talk to me."

"Schlock? I have some idea what people want, too. Besides, I've given you four *blood and guts, tits and asses* already."

"Yeah, yeah. You have for a fact. And what are you bitchin' about? I don't believe you! You set this town on its nose with the money you just got for a damn first draft. This studio spent that money because of the real life elements—the politics, the blood and guts and beaver-banging, as you put it—that *you* wove into the story. I only made some... some strong suggestions. You wrote the story. It's your story, John. So stop bitching!"

"I'm not bitching. Look. I'm just..."

"No, no wait! You look. You're forgetting your little Beverly Hills estate, the French villa, the mansion in England, the Hawaii condo, the Ferarri Fiorano, the Mercedes, the Range Rover, the Chris Craft, the... the women."

"You got it all figured. Right?"

Blaine folded his beefy arms across his protruding paunch. "Hey! Me producer, you writer. That's what I figure, John. Look, if it ain't broke, leave it the *blank* alone."

"Blank?"

"Yeah. See, I'm trying to stop using the "F" word. My wife says I say *fuck* too much. Oops! That one slipped. But I am making sense. Right? You have to admit I'm making sense here."

Before John could respond, his phone chimed. The interruption visibly annoyed him. He yanked the phone from his jacket and punched the send button.

"Roméo. Yeah, Nick."

John listened with growing impatience, while Blaine thumbed through pages of the script for the fifth time.

"C'mon! I'm in a meeting, then I'm heading home," John explained to Homicide Captain, C.E. Nicholson. "Alright, ten... fifteen minutes tops. I'll be there."

John tucked the phone away, stood and turned to leave. Peter pushed away from the desk, bounded to his feet and followed—both hands stuffed in his pockets. The cigar hung loosely from the corner of his mouth.

"You were a great cop, John," Blaine yelled. "You got a thousand war stories, I only need one. I'm not lookin' for a *friggin'* Academy Award here. Just finish the *blankety* script. If the damn ratings board even thinks of *dickin'* us with an NC-17, somebody up there is gonna get their ass kicked, or worse. Besides, what if every play, every movie, every book, every work of art had the same Mary Poppins theme?"

An expressionless John headed for the door.

"Two damn weeks!" Peter yelled. And...and what's with the black... always black. What you got against colors, John?

John shook his head defiantly. "What you got against black?" He shot his middle finger into the air and kept walking...never looked back.

"I said two weeks, John... two fuckin' weeks. Damn! See there. You made me say a bad word. Hey! You know, I don't usually take shit from writers."

Three
Corpus Delecti

"Circumstantial my ass."

Assistant County Coroner,

Tom Blankley stood with arms folded, draped in an ill-fitting white lab coat. An unlit cigarette dangled precariously from the left corner of his mouth, as he hovered passively between Roméo and Captain Nicholson. The Captain was a tall, burly, ex-marine whose midsection revealed his penchant for Budweisers and Big Macs. It was clear it had been many moons since this Leatherneck stormed a beach wearing full battle gear.

Wearing protective latex gloves and stern expressions, all three stared silently at the bloated, ash-grey male and female corpses laid out atop two stainless steel slabs. Minutes earlier, both post-autopsy cadavers had been wheeled from a less than tidy 40° freezer filled to overflowing. Such was the increasingly sorry state of conditions at the L.A. County morgue. Too many people were dying—getting killed. Gurneys often lined the corridors like cars at In-&-Out Burgers.

Blankley was a lanky, frail, gaunt, Ichabod Crane-type with horn-rimmed glasses covering bulging eyes that twitched nervously. Each time he chomped on the cigarette, John glared at him. The wiry fellow took a couple of unsteady steps backward, nodded to John and the Captain then exited. Nicholson waited until he had gone before turning to John.

"Meet Mr. Colin Sumner... bigtime software tycoon."

"Damn!" John grimaced.

"Ugly, huh?"

More than a quarter of Sumner's head and brain were gone; same was true of Lisa. He could see the large metal staples the coroner had used to close the chest wound, and the autopsy invasion of the chest cavity.

"I use his software. Guy's worth millions."

"Not anymore... and female companion, not his wife. Fished 'em both butt-naked out of his indoor pool last night. Somebody caught 'em doing more than backstroking."

"How do you know?"

"They had no clothes on, John."

"May all be circumstantial."

"Circumstantial my ass."

"I'm just playing DA."

"Devil's advocate. I know. And you make a good one. Be my guest," said Nicholson with grudging admiration.

"As I said, circumstantial, though an arguably reasonable assumption. How do you know they weren't stripped, wasted then dumped in the pool? Was she examined for semen?"

"Semen? No reason to. She didn't die from a dick overdose, 'dawg,' she was shot to death."

John chuckled. "Good one, good one. That's good. Dick overdose... dawg? Damn, Captain. I see you've been hanging out with the brothers, honing your ability to deliver a rapid, urban-flavored rejoinder, no less."

Nicholson shrugged his shoulders and glanced away briefly. John was thoroughly amused, found it almost impossible to not laugh aloud.

"Probably wouldn't have found a damn thing anyway." Nicholson continued. "There was no evidence anyone other than Sumner had boned her. The pool water probably performed a rinse cycle anyway." All the while, John surveyed the cadavers from every angle, including the back of Lisa's head as her rigid neck rested on a curved wooden block. He carefully examined the extremities: fingers, toes, nails on same, even the ears. He saw what appeared to be teeth prints on Lisa's right ear lobe, a deep bruise or love bite on the left side of her neck. Her fuscia-colored nails, now partially recessed into her puffy fingertips, appeared freshly done.

Roméo observed the absence of contrasting skin color or indentation on Colin's ring finger. He noted completely clipped nails on only the middle fingers of both hands; he drew two conclusions before turning to the wounds.

First, Colin had apparently prepared for a night of lovemaking. Secondly, he had not worn his wedding ring for some time. Admittedly, neither fact was of great moment. Although John had witnessed autopsies and post-autopsy cadavers dozens of times, he was noticeably affected by what he saw. He kept thinking these were the remains of once living, loving, breathing individuals. These images were something he had never grown accustomed to. He prayed he never would.

"What do you think?"

John folded his arms, shook his head a bit. "Someone wanted to make damn sure these two were very dead. Although there's horrendous damage here, looks like a dead center shot on impact," said John, examining what remained of Colin's deformed head, his exposed remaining skull. "Once the round's in the cranial cavity, even the exploding bone fragments become missiles. Shock waves turn brain matter into gelatin... damn Jello. The velocity, yawing, angulation... I'd say, looking at the damage, most likely a .357 or .44 Magnum. My guess would be the .44 with hollows, at least 1200 'fips' or better... upwards of 250 to 300 grain rounds. This sucker was not playing games."

"We found .44s. And we recovered significant bone fragments, bio matter from both victims when we strained Sumner's pool," the Captain explained.

John nodded. "From the female's frontal exit wound, she took a hell of a round in back of the head," he noted, assuming a new position. "A huge chunk of her right frontal skull mass is gone. Rounds were apparently fired from short range. What a waste."

Nicholson moved closer. "Officers at the scene figured the killer fired from a position on the deck surrounding the pool—most likely the area adjacent to the dressing rooms."

"Damn. Accurate head shots with a handgun, from damn near any appreciable distance, is tough." John noted. "Could have used a scope, though. Some hunters use .44s with scopes."

"I know. He took one between his eyes, one in his chest. Part of his lungs flew out of his mouth. Pretty gross sight. Coroner removed it. It's over there if you want to see it." Nicholson's expression was unchanged. He pointed to a capped jar atop a nearby table. John turned to his friend.

"I see your knack for understatement is still intact. Who discovered the bodies?"

"The maid... about ten this morning. She upchucked all over the deck when she saw the carnage."

"Can't really blame her for that," said John. "Let me guess. The revenge of an angry wife?"

Nicholson shook his head no. "Don't think so. She's traveling. Maid says she's in London... was in Paris for more than two weeks."

"I see. Wife's in Paris, so he has a pool party for two. How'd the girlfriend get up to the house?"

"Drove. We impounded a red, late model Cooper Mini registered to her.
It'll be checked out by S.I.D."

"What's her name?"

"Lisa. Lisa Halladay, 26. Lived in Thousand Oaks."

"What about examination of the estate's exterior?" Asked John, while still examining the cadavers.

"What do you mean?"

"Front door, rear door, side doors, windows, the grounds, garages, the driveway... all the way to the street. Was it all checked out?"

"Lt. Foster managed the scene. Said there were no signs of forced entry. I have to assume he did the right things... the basic things."

"Hell, it's the basic stuff that usually gets skipped or screwed up."

"The work on this one is just getting started," said Nicholson.

"What about security systems. He must have had a hell of a system."

"That's what's strange. The system was quite elaborate: doors and windows protected, motion detectors, you name it."

"And?"

"And none of it worked. I mean, it works, but apparently it wasn't activated that night."

"Hmm, maybe," John mused. "I'm sure there's more than a single maid. Anyone talk to the rest of the hired help yet?"

"Only briefly. They saw nothing, heard nothing. There's a staff of three, including the maid. They live in separate quarters... away from the main house."

"So Captain, if you can rule out the wife, staff, and barring evidence implicating business competitors, you saying this one's like the other three?"

"That's not the question. Question is who and why."

"Questions *are*," said John, correcting the Captain's grammar.

"Say what?" Nicholson aimed his patented stare.

"Sorry, never mind. Go on."

"Listen, my friend," the Captain snarled, "I'm not paid to be grammatically correct. I'm paid to solve homicides."

John smiled, mumbled something unintelligible, and continued examining the victims. A long, stony silence followed before Nicholson continued.

"Could be a business deal gone sour, but I doubt it. No signs of forced entry. Nothing. Damn m.o. is practically identical, except..."

"Except what?"

"Forget it."

John wasn't ready to forget it. "Forget what? You were about to make a comparison to the other three cases, right?"

"I said forget it,"

"Why don't you admit it?"

"Admit what?"

Nicholson reacted defensively, getting in John's face, forcing a steady gaze.

"You guys have a serial killer on your hands. Face it! Nearly every paper from Maine to Alaska has been covering these killings."

"We're not using that word... least not yet."

"Which word, Maine or Alaska? Okay. So what's this I hear about some similar cases in Pittsburgh?"

"We got a call from Pittsburgh PD three months ago. Three cases, all wealthy men... m.o. looks similar, except the choice of weapons and other details vary. Same thing in Atlanta...two there. Dallas...another two cases. Even Arizona...one case more than a month and a half ago. All occurred less than a month apart. FBI's all over it. Not sure if there's some maniac traveling west on some killing spree. Our first case here was nearly two months ago."

"Is there an identifiable suspect? Do we know who they're chasing?"

"Not really. They don't know for sure. A male, we know that. A Pittsburgh witness described seeing some guy—white male, six feet—wearing a ninja outfit, jumping the perimeter fence of the estate where the first victim, a university president, was killed. A fifteen year-old provided a similar description in the killing of a prominent city councilman in Atlanta."

"What weapon was used?"

"A nine millimeter... in all the suspected cases. And there're other differences between their guy and ours."

Nicholson seemed anxious to draw distinctions between *his* unacknowledged serial killer and the one belonging to the FBI. John thought it peculiar and insightful.

"I still think you're dealing with a serial killer here," John repeated.

"We're not using the "s" word around here," said the Captain, emphatically, his brows rising on his furrowed forehead.

"Doesn't change the facts. Listen, you say you've got a task force on this..."

"A small one."

"A task force, FBI, Ouija boards, the old Psychic Network. What the hell you need me for?"

Nicholson clenched his teeth, took a few steps away then turned back to John, now only inches from his face. "'Cause you love this shit, John Roméo. You eat it up. It intrigues you. And though it pains me to say it, you're the best and we need help. Okay? That what you wanna' hear? And what about your book? We found another one at the Sumner death scene, on the deck... blood splattered all over the damn jacket cover."

John let the Captain's words resonate a few beats, then wheeled toward the door. Nicholson followed. Both stopped near a metal table piled with empty body bags. John removed his gloves and tossed them into the bio-waste container. "Wait a sec," he said. "You mentioned my book. If they were killed in the pool, how did blood splatter onto the book? They weren't reading in the pool, were they? Has the blood on the book been matched to the victims? Was it fresh splatter?"

"I don't know," Nicholson acknowledged frankly. "And you already knew I didn't know."

"C'mon. Don't hate me 'cause I'm retired."

Nicholson was not amused. "Cut the stand-up. People are dying here. What's with you? Ever since you and Claire broke up, you've been... different. It's like I don't know you. The John Roméo I used to know was still a tough, self-assured guy, but he was also low-key, even self-effacing, sometimes. He let his *actions* speak for him. Now you're...

different. And I don't think it's because of all the money you make. It's something else. I think you're covering up something. This isn't you. I want the old John Roméo back, damnit! Is what happened to Keith Langhorne still haunting you?"

"I don't want to talk about that. Ever!"

"I'm no shrink, but maybe you should."

"With all due respect, Captain, he was my partner, not yours. I'll decide if I want to talk about him or not."

"You can't run away forever, Roméo."

"You called *me* here for other reasons, Captain. Remember? I was headed home to a hot bath, a glass of wine, a warm bed and an even warmer woman. So if you..."

"Excuse me."

"Nick. My hands are full. I don't have time to take on the case."

"Bullshit."

"I'm busy as hell."

"Well, whatever. I ain't gonna kiss your rich black ass, not this time. Just do the right thing. That's all I'm saying. Do the right thing."

John stepped closer, pointedly stared into Nicholson's squinting eyes. Nicholson frowned. "Why the hell you looking at me like that?"

"I'm disappointed," said John, feigning sincerity.

The Captain grew exasperated. "Could at least think about it. I know you, Roméo. And I can't believe you'd pass up another chance to show us all how dumb and inept we are."

"You're cruel."

"No, no. I'm brutally frank. Remember? You've said so often enough. And you know me better than most. "

"True."

Roméo knew the Captain was in no mood for a stand-up routine. "Listen, Captain, I know you wouldn't ask if you weren't in a bind. So, I'll think about it. I promise. I'll be in London for a week, in Bahrain for a couple of days and I'm back."

"We can't wait that long."

"I'll be thinking about this all the time. I promise."

Nicholson responded with a faint head bob. John saluted and left without looking back. Nicholson stared grimly toward the empty doorway with arms folded, shaking his head with mild disgust. A weak smile crept across his leathery face. There was no way John could turn him down, he thought. His ego wouldn't let him.

After leaving the good Captain Nick, my smile and swagger disappeared almost the instant I breached the doorway. I knew he was not as pissed as he wanted me to think. This kind of exchange was not new for us. I admit I was not unaffected. On the way to my car, I was suddenly assaulted by my own demons—demons that had long ago trespassed, inhabiting a corner of my most secret place—my mind soul. My private demons had dogged me from my very first homicide case, but especially after the case that led to the brutal and horrible death of my partner and friend, Keith Langhorne, a celebrated homicide detective. I retired exactly one year later, to the day.

This night, I fought to not let the indelible memory of that fateful day seep into my consciousness. I clenched my teeth, squeezed my eyes shut, struggled to banish the images. I thought about Nicholson's proposition. Even thoughts of those disfigured cadavers were preferable to the horrid recollections of what had happened to Keith.

The magnetic, nearly irresistible notion of solving one more unsolvable case more than intrigued me; it was seducing me. And with the seduction came the psycho-baggage born of all the carnage and inhumanity I once witnessed. At some level, it was never far away, dogging me like some tenacious pit bull.

Suddenly, my cautionary inner voice launched a plaintive counterattack, warning me in ominous tones of the resurrection of dark inner secrets known only to my deepest inner self. Just thinking about it all would most certainly insure another episode of *the dream,* as well as the fleeting image of Keith I keep seeing in shadows. But I would confront it the way I always did. I had no choice. After all, what would Alexander Roméo say?

Forgive me for personalizing and stepping out of character here. I promised to keep my third person perspective. Sorry. I'll try and do better from here on. Meanwhile, I'm heading to 'The Station,' wondering what's serious enough to get Skeeter out of bed.

Four
The Station

Five Minutes Later - *"I used to be somebody, too!"*

John's red Ferarri Fiorano

slipped past a half-empty RTD bus pasted with gang graffiti. He made a point of driving the car at least two or three times a month. This just happened to be one of those days. He had purchased the month-old exotic machine from a well-known action-movie producer 'down on his credit.' In hindsight, the car was much too flashy for him. He preferred one of his half dozen 70's muscle cars to both the Ferrari and the Mercedes.

Changing lanes, John inadvertently cut off a multicolored low-rider sedan. Two male teens, hanging halfway out of the car, shot him the finger and yelled a vulgar epithet, suggesting he have an incestuous relationship with his mother. John ignored them and continued on his iPhone. His 'Bluetooth' was in his briefcase. He seldom used it, although hands-free was the law. Roméo refused to have some device stuck in his ear.

"Skeeter?"

The scruffy voice on the other end was barely audible. John pressed the phone to his ear "It's only eight. Take off the bottom-flap pjs and meet me at the station. I need to talk. I'll owe you one."

Twenty minutes later, John eased into a *no-parking* zone, directly in front of the cavernous old Union Amtrak station on Alameda.

"Watch this for me," he said with a wink and nod to a security guard standing at the curb. The man was draped around a young woman dressed in cutoffs and a halter-top. John ripped a fifty-dollar bill in half and gave it to the guard. The man nodded. John walked on.

Inside the dimly lit landmark facility, a location for many old movies and still home to Amtrak, John strode through the nearly deserted lobby with its high ceilings, dark shadows and ghosts of travelers past. His footsteps reverberated loudly and eerily on the concrete floor. John liked the sound. Any minute he expected to see Humphrey Bogart emerge from the shadows, half a cigarette angling from loosely pursed lips.

From nowhere, a beggar, in a flea-bitten sport coat and dirt-blackened jeans, approached with right hand extended. Without breaking stride, John handed him a dollar bill. The man scowled at what he felt was a paltry sum. Then, with an expletive insulting John's mother, the homeless man tossed the bill to the floor. John wheeled around, retrieved the dollar. He resisted telling the man to go to hell, realizing it was pointless; the guy was already there.

"I use to be somebody, too!" The man yelled. "Five bucks wouldn't hurt you, mister. Takes money to live in L.A.!"

John quickened his pace, eyes scanning left and right. Finally, he strolled past a bench where Skeeter, a thin, wispy man, was seated far from the aisle, closeted in near darkness.

Skeeter's hair was nearly solid white; his narrow face weathered, wrinkled, shaped by his years and his penchant for frowning and scowling. He could still do a hundred push-ups in two and a half minutes; run a sub-six minute mile, and collar any bad guy.

By force of personality, Skeeter projected a stature much larger than his "5-9' frame. He wore faded jeans and a dark blue sweatshirt.

LAPD, in bold type, leaped from his chest. Skeeter, a.k.a. Jake Mecham, was salty and rough edged. He was the type who would set sail aboard a leaky boat, in a storm, rather than yield to outside forces, including God Almighty. Once the crusty veteran made up his mind to do something, nothing stopped him.

The only person who could make him melt like butter on a hot knife was Emily, *Emmy* to her friends, his childhood sweetheart and wife of thirty-eight years. Both had grown up near Coos Bay, Oregon. It was just the two of them, now. The couple lost their only child, Jason, a 35 year-old orthopedist, in 1993. It happened in a violent act of road rage on the 134 Freeway near the Brand and Central exit, only minutes from their Glendale home. Jason's wedding was less than a month away. In a way, Skeeter and Emmy lost both a son and a daughter.

Sherri, Jason's fiancée, moved back to Maine shortly after the tragedy. Skeeter says she still calls, though infrequently, and is married. She and her husband have a son she named Jason. While meant to be an act of respect and love, it actually brought more grieving to Skeeter and Emmy.

Their loss dramatically changed the couple. Skeeter seemed to age and gray overnight. The entire department closed ranks, embracing them. Yet, Emmy withdrew. Even now, she seldom ventured out, except in the immediate neighborhood, avoiding freeways, crowds, social gatherings.

"John!"

John wheeled toward the sound. "Skeeter! Almost didn't see you. What are you doing lurking here in the shadows?"

"Got my reasons."

John nodded, plopped down next to him, let loose a heavy sigh. "How've you been? How's Emmy?"

"We're alive. She misses you. You haven't been over in months. Em hasn't cooked one of her famous spaghetti dinners since the last time you and Claire were over...just before your divorce. I don't get the same meals when you're not stopping by. Get my drift? I like you and all, you're like a son. So get your butt over sometime, so I can eat like I should."

"I will...promise. I miss her too. Give her my best."

"Done. And I'm really sorry about you and Claire. Wish things had worked out for both of you."

"Me too."

"It's like I lost a daughter-in-law, again. Listen, I don't mean to sound like some self-pitying old geezer. Listen, you okay and every-thing? I know you're a tough guy and all, but living takes things out of you...robs you of things only the grave gives back. Like peace and quiet, no creditors or telemarketers calling at the dinner hour."

"I'm fine." John sounded less than convincing.

"Glad to hear it, even though I know you're feeding me a load. Look, I know what you want to talk about," said Skeeter, leveling a pointed gaze at his friend. The salty old Sarge never did place stock in pleasantries.

"Doesn't surprise me. You and my 'old man could always read empty minds. How's Stalag Thirteen?"

Skeeter grew animated. His demeanor clearly demonstrated un-happiness with what was still going on at the LAPD. "Gone to hell. Just be glad you're out. Sonsabitches. Good folks get screwed, bad ones promoted. Tell ya' one damn thing, three more years and I'm haulin' ass...moving back to Oregon, back to God's country."

"Can't blame you. You deserve it. Emmy does too."

Skeeter momentarily buried his face in his hands then raised his head, tossed it so far back his vertebrae crackled, yielding a resounding pop.

"Nicholson wants you on those killings," he warned in a stern, fatherly manner. "It's a shit detail. Sonsabitches ain't got a clue. But that's not the worst."

John leaned closer. "Don't hold back, Skeeter. "

Skeeter leaned even closer, as if there was someone within three city blocks with a snowball's chance of overhearing him. "I don't think the killer's a civie. Could be a cop."

"A cop? Wait, you don't think this FBI thing about some spree kill-er heading west has any validity?"

"Spree my ass. This ain't the work of some Andrew Cunanan wan-nabe. Like I said, I think he could even be a cop."

John's ears perked; his eyes widened. "Thought that's what you said. You know something?"

"You damn right, I know something. I know the jobs are too damn clean...immaculate."

"That it?"

"I also know four years ago a cop, Sergeant Steve Bolen—the sono-fabitch you tracked and busted, worked out of Rampart—executed six prostitutes. Shot them in the head after banging them and, according to him, making them read the 23rd Psalms. He then stuffed their damn panties in their mouths. Asshole even left the Bible next to the bod-ies."

"How could I forget? Wish I could, but I can't."

"Nobody should forget it. Said he was only exacting God's retri-bution, self-righteous bastard. We ignored a mountain of evidence; I'm talkin' about the dicks above our pay grade. Shoulda' nailed his squirrelly ass sooner than we did. Hadn't been for you, the prick would probably still be out there killing in the name of God and some warped sense of law and order."

"I didn't nail him alone."

"Damn near. But here's the real sad shit. Even though this dick-head was committing murder, some still threw up a blue wall to pro-tect his ass, you know. Hell, *they*—meaning a few line cops and even some brass—weren't that happy with you for bagging him. They want-ed to look the other way. Accused you of burning a cop for a half dozen garden-variety street whores. Even the goddamn DA didn't seek the death penalty, at first. No way that would have happened with a civie. You didn't say anything, but I knew you were aware of what was being whispered."

"I heard things."

"We all heard things. Son, you know me. I am as blue as they come. In fact, if you cut me, I don't just bleed blue, I bleed LAPD blue. But I am tired of it...tired of rotten cops making it hard for the good ones; tired of the good ones being too damn afraid to speak out. I'm tired of little kids looking at me on the street like I'm some damn boogey man. What happened at Rampart, years ago, was just the tip of the damn iceberg; it's everywhere. Not just in LA either, and not just California. You can find this crap in almost any PD." Skeeter took a needed breath. "Hey, if I sound like I'm pissed it's because I am. You see, Bolen was just a symptom, not the entire disease. Long after they shove the needle in that cocksucker's arm, the disease will still be around."

Skeeter took another well-deserved breath.

"He was a member of the White Aryan Resistance, too," John recalled.

"Right. Bastards still want a race war. And there's more of 'em inside the department, like that prick... what's his face?"

"Dennis. Sergeant David Dennis."

"Yeah, your nemesis. Guy's a card-carrying fool. He and Bolen were friends, you know. I still believe he was involved, too. If he didn't do any of the killing, I believe he knew what Bolen was doing."

"You could be right. And he knows you suspected him."

"I made no secret of it. But forget about me. Just watch your ass. I don't know why you keep taking these damn assignments. Your success hasn't exactly endeared you to many of your old comrades, you know."

"I know."

"You think you do. Call this a hunch, if you like. I don't think the killer is a civie. And another thing: beware Delilah. Keep your dick in your pants. World's full of damn Delilahs. Don't become the hunted, son."

John looked confused. "What do you mean?"

Skeeter stood slowly, grimaced, rubbed his stomach. Seconds later, the pain appeared to subside.

"I'm just ranting. Just wait 'til you get old, you rant a lot. It's part of the job description of a senior citizen. Ranting. You get fined if you don't rant."

"You're not ranting; you're venting."

No, I'm rantin,' alright. Wait 'til you get old. It is your job to rant. And run like hell, when they send that damn AARP card and shit. And never order from any senior's menu. First time you do, you'll sage ten years on the damn spot, swear to god. And they serve you smaller portions, like you're not supposed to notice."

"That's funny."

"Whatever. Look, they *want* you and they *don't* want you. With you on board, no one—especially the press—can accuse us of not pulling out all the stops. I've got a hunch the pressure to solve this case is driven more by the fact these primary vics are rich and famous, and by upcoming elections, than by a desire to solve these damn crimes. I'm not talking about RHD or the Section guys, or even the sixth floor. I'm talking about these fat-ass, potbellied elected types. The problem is, they lean on us so we can make them look good. We just want to be left to do our jobs the way we're supposed to do them."

"I agree. That's one reason I wanted to ask you about what's going on so far. I talked to the Captain tonight."

"I know."

"How?"

"You're... you're asking me how I know things? You met him at the morgue."

"You amaze me. I forget there's little you don't know."

"I'm not saying all that. I just know what I know. And I know it's a shit detail. Did I say that already? Look, they want a damn Messiah: You. They want you to lead them to the promise land on this thing. But they want you to do it in a heartbeat. Just watch. And one more thing, don't expect a ready admission that the war is on again with the FBI, but it is."

"What's the problem now?"

"It goes way back to the last millennium, back to the O.J. Simpson thing. Some in IAS and SID said some unkind things about the Feds and their lab guys. They got pissed. It's a pissing war. It's a battle about who's got the biggest dong. Now even some of the FBI Behavioral Science guys are into it. I don't know all the details, except it's a piss-poor way for both sides to be behaving. Anyway, forget this so-called *Westbound Killer* shit."

Skeeter grabbed his stomach again and winced.

"What's wrong? You okay?"

"Yeah, think so. Soon as I get back to my Maalox, my bathroom and my bed."

"In that order, I hope. Let's go,"

"Good," Skeeter groaned. "I'm okay, though."

"I hope so. I love you, but I ain't cleaning you if you dump on yourself. We can grab some coffee...talk some more," said John.

"I'm not *that* okay. Maybe next time. Just call me at a decent hour. All law-abiding, God-fearing people oughta be in bed by eight o'clock."

"That's because you're always up by four."

John and Skeeter stood, both unaware of a shadowy figure cloaked in the darkness some distance away. The concealed figure cranked off a dozen 35mm telephoto shots and watched the two old friends head toward the front entrance.

Five
A Cry for Help

A week following the Sumner murder,

the entire tech-world remained in shock, even as it appeared to adjust to the reality of Sumner's death. Every major newspaper, business news publication and cable news network served up extensive coverage of the tragedy, referencing the unsolved LA murders now being linked by the media.

Much of the coverage bordered on the obscene. One major cable news network, offered instant polls asking whether viewers suspected industry competitors were responsible for the murder. Diane Sumner, the bereaved wife, had been hounded on two continents. She was now in seclusion. Few could blame her for delaying her return to the States.

Then, as it always does, the nation's attention refocused. Los Angeles appeared to quickly absorb the shock like just one more 3.0 tremor, moving on to the next event—the next *story du jour.*

From fifteen hundred feet up, the downtown Los Angeles skyline loomed like an endless urban Stonehenge. Below, a sea of sparkling lights offered scant illumination of hapless souls inhabiting the cruel surface below. The night offered cover, granting them license to trespass into the daytime domain of the captains of commerce.

In the dead of night, amidst the howls of sirens and the stench of discarded humanity, the dispossessed ruled without challenge, but only 'till morning. By then, the human garbage was expected to retreat to human landfills—anywhere, as long as they were not seen or heard.

Above the dark, dank milieu, the air was crisp and invigorating, thanks to three straight days of wimpy Los Angeles rain. The news chopper crisscrossed above crowded freeways, moved with scalpel-like precision between sleek, towering skyscrapers shimmering in the moonlight.

The 'blue mushroom,' —the Staple Center—glowed like a neon Frisbee. From this perch, Los Angeles presented a deceptive beauty, concealing its harsh realities.

Aboard the chopper, as the CBS Radio Network newscast ended, the distant, yet distinct baritone voice of local radio personality, Steve Dayner, rose on the cockpit's am-radio speaker:

> "It's a gorgeous night here in the City of Angels at 8:05. Sixty-one degrees going down to forty-eight overnight. I'm Steve Dayner. L.A. Police continue to release very little information regarding last week's brutal double slaying of multimillionaire computer software magnate, Colin Sumner, and a still unidentified female companion. Sumner's friends and even competitors are still expressing shock and disbelief.
>
> "Tonight, Microsoft Chairman, Bill Gates said: "He was a friend as well as a business competitor. My heart goes out to his wife and surviving family." Mrs. Sumner, believed to be in Paris at the time of the killing, remains in seclusion.

"This is the fourth double slaying, under similar circumstances, in the past three months. However, police, under fire from several members of the City Council, still refuse to draw parallels. They are also refusing comment on speculation that former homicide detective JOHN ROMÉO will soon join the investigation. Roméo, now a best-selling author and screenwriter, has been unavailable for comment.

"All this comes even as we are learning the FBI is tracking what some say is a spree killer, believed to have murdered the first of more than ten victims, all wealthy men, in Pittsburgh, Pennsylvania. The LAPD has refused to comment on that case. The trail, that has left victims in Atlanta, Dallas and Phoenix, appears to be leading to California.

"In other news tonight, Arnold Schwarzenegger and Whoopi Goldberg have announced they are planning to..."

Inside the sleek, 865 Figueroa Avenue skyscraper, and halfway down a dimly lit 30th floor corridor, faint rays of light spilled from underneath the closed doors of an office suite. The brass nameplate read: Dr. Diane Deauville. Beyond the door, carefully placed floor and table lamps softly lighted the posh, spacious office. Recessed, perimeter ceiling-lights cast a continuous wave pattern only inches below and up to the union of wall and ceiling.

Dr. Deauville, 35, a sculpted 5'-7,"and single, was arrestingly beautiful. Her shoulder-length blonde hair bounced like a sun-warmed silk mane. Descriptions of her always fell short of the reality. She possessed the presence of an intellectual; the charm and poise of a model, and exuded self-confidence in an easy manner. Dr. Deauville displayed no hint of pretense, despite her Yale, ivy-league undergrad, and Johns-Hopkins University Masters and Ph.D. degrees.

From her large Fellini leather chair, Dr. Deauville peered at Mrs. Catherine Douglas Jeffries. The latter, less than relaxed, sat on a contoured recliner, shading her brow with her left hand. Mrs. Jeffries, a youthful 59, slightly grey, elegantly dressed, reeked of affluence. Her English bearing was evident. She closed her eyes and heaved a long, agony-ridden sigh. Dr. Deauville, her long shapely legs crossed, her arms resting on the arms of the chair, waited for her patient to resume emptying her heart and soul.

Diane Elizabeth Deauville was well aware she was at the pinnacle of her profession. With great effort, she had learned to moderate her immodesty, accept success. It had not been easy. After years of educating and establishing herself, professionally, she enjoyed national stature for her tireless work with battered and abused women. She always made two points: battery and abuse are both physical and psychological. The epidemic demanded holistic solutions.

Because of her outspokenness on women's issues, and the phenomenal success of her critically acclaimed books, the doctor was always in great demand, both as lecturer and talk show expert. Her frequent appearances on Oprah had garnered her international acclaim, and sold millions of her five books currently in print.

However, Diane's passion involved reaching out and affecting the lives of her patients in one-on-one settings. She often found herself declining speaking engagements, opting instead to devote more time to her patients. Lately, she had come to realize her intense dedication to her profession had not been without a heavy personal price. Never married, Dr. Deauville had all but given up on marriage and children. During the early years, *that* was not a consideration to contemplate. Of late, her views had undergone radical transformation

In many respects, Diane's own life was not the storybook, Pollyannaish existence so many imagined. And even as such thoughts struggled to the fore of her consciousness, she effectively held them in check.

Dr. Deauville glanced at Catherine Jeffries and resumed shuffling four black & white, 8"x10" glossies she held in her lap. The ghastly photos were of the double-murder crime scenes being investigated by the LAPD. The most recent was that of Colin Sumner and Lisa Richter, taken before and after their removal from the pool.

Except for the Sumner photos, the pictures showed victims sprawled in bed, in place, executed while in the act of making love. The savage detail was muted only by the absence of full color. Still, the stark black and white was vivid enough to turn any stomach. What a horrible marriage of pleasure and pain, Diane thought, shaking her head with disgust and resignation, then tossing the photos back onto a nearby lamp table.

Catherine finally opened her eyes, folded her arms across her chest and tossed her head to one side. She always found these probing sessions difficult to reconcile with her long-held love of privacy. Worse, she felt obliged to quietly endure a personal and embarrassing marital problem. But here she was, pouring her lonely heart out in bits and pieces. It had finally come to this.

"The important thing is you're finally facing up to reality. That's crucial, if we're to have any success here," Dr. Deauville assured her.

"Perhaps." Catherine's voice resonated with the ring of defeat.

"Trust me. Nothing is more important than facing the truth."

"I know, but it's so...painful."

"It has to be. But in the long run, not facing it is even more painful. It's like knowing you have a terrible disease but refusing treatment because you feel fine on any given day. Then, suddenly, you learn it's too late."

"I know you're right, I wish I didn't know what I know. Like they say: What you don't know can't hurt you."

"But you *do* know. You do know. How long have you known about all this?"

Catherine, in her aristocratic English accent, chose her words carefully and with difficulty. The words did not come easily.

"I suppose I knew from the beginning...fifteen years ago. There were signs. There were always signs. I refused to accept them. I could not bring myself to accept the obvious. I blocked it all out. I would say to myself:

Catherine, don't be silly. He loves you. Reason this out. He would not have married you; he would not be here if he didn't love you. Besides, he repeated the vows. He said the words with such fervor and passion. You heard him with your very own ears. So, what are you going to believe, his emotional, tear-filled pledge of eternal love and fidelity, or your own eyes?

Well, he's been unfaithful from the first. And I've been tolerating it, like a fool. I feel so...so stupid."

"There's no need for self-flagellation."

"I'm being honest."

"I understand. But I don't want to hear anymore of this self-blame. Enough."

"I hate myself for loving him, and for not having the strength to leave him."

The truth was out. Dr. Deauville had been unable to get her to open up during earlier sessions. Catherine had suffered alone in silence long enough. She began sobbing again. Dr. Deauville consciously suppressed her desire to immediately respond. Instead, she watched and listened.

Catherine's reserve gave way to a tide of frustration and guilt, guilt at not being able to solve her own problems. She felt weak for not confronting her husband with the determination and resolve she had always possessed.

The doctor retrieved a box of tissue from her desk, returned, handed it to Catherine; she dabbed her eyes. Dr. Deauville walked to the wet bar and poured a glass of water for her. She sipped the water and leaned back, both hands wrapped tightly around the glass.

"Is that really what you want to do, Mrs. Jeffries? Leave him?"

"I'm not really...I'm not sure," Catherine's resolve appeared to falter. "Yes. Yes, I do."

"You seem unsure. But, if that's true then tell me what's stopping you?"

Catherine sat forward. "Actually, I'd love to kill him."

"Kill him?"

Dr. Deauville sat back; her eyes widened with surprise.

"If I had the nerve, I'd end his lying, his cheating."

Dr. Deauville focused on Catherine but did not speak. It was clear a deep well of emotion was bubbling inside her patient. The doctor wanted her to proceed at her own pace, unpressured.

"I've had it," Catherine blurted out, choking back tears. "And I realize it's never going to get any better. And I can't tolerate it getting worse." A brief silence was broken by Catherine's deep sigh. "Would you like to know about last Saturday?" Catherine's grip on the glass tightened with every word.

"Would you like to tell me?"

Twiddling her fingers nervously, Catherine lowered her eyes. "It's not easy."

"Take your time."

"I'm sure I'll go insane, if I don't."

Catherine's voice revealed more hurt than anger. Dr. Deauville laced her fingers underneath her chin and waited.

"Last Saturday, he went to Palm Springs to play golf. Naturally, I was left at home with the servants."

"You say naturally. Why? Does he force you to stay at home?"

Catherine pursed her lips, stared blankly at the ceiling for what seemed an eternity. "Well, no. Not really. I just..."

Dr. Deauville seemed annoyed. "Please. Just go on."

"He doesn't actually force me."

"Tell me what happened."

Even as she defended an obvious failing, Catherine knew her submissive role in her marriage only deepened her emotional crisis. Yet, she found it impossible to alter her behavior. Her resolve always vanished in her husband's overpowering presence. A crestfallen Catherine reacted as if she had been chastised by the doctor's reprimanding tone. She hesitated.

Meanwhile, unable to shut them out of her mind, Dr. Deauville retrieved the four photos and scanned them again. The awful images seared into her brain like a branding iron. Their macabre magnetism drew her back to them again and again. She was thankful they were not in color.

Catherine finally began speaking again. Her voice rose with a surge of short-lived defiance. "After he left, I noticed a case-file he'd left on the nightstand the night before. I took it downstairs to the study to place it in his briefcase on the desk. I opened it to put the file inside and...I don't know why but I looked in the pockets. I wish I hadn't."

"Why?"

"Because, folded very neatly inside was a pair of black bikini panties, size six. I was devastated. It was obviously one of his trophies—a spoil of some sort. What was worse, even from a foot away, her scent was still evident."

"Her scent?"

"Yes, her scent. The filthy, lying sonofabitch; he probably had oral sex with her, too."

Dr. Deauville's gaze sharpened; she tried to moderate her incredulity, and her surprise at Catherine's frank language. "Of course, you chose not to confront him."

"Yes."

"Meaning you did or you didn't?"

"I did not confront him. You don't have to say it. I know I should have. I simply put them in a plastic bag and hid them."

"What was that supposed to do?"

"He had to have known. He had to have missed them later. I'm sure of it. But he never said anything or asked how the file got inside his briefcase."

"Come on, now. Did you really expect he would?"

"I don't know what I expected."

"And you never brought up the subject."

"No, I didn't."

"Mrs. Jeffries, I assure you your actions are not atypical. But tell me, what is it that keeps you there? It couldn't be wealth; you were a very wealthy woman when you married your husband."

"I love him."

"You love him?"

"Yes. I know that's my undoing."

"You say you love him. But is it love, great sex, his prominence, fear of being alone? Why do you continue to tolerate his behavior—a behavior that demeans and trivializes you and your feelings? You're an intelligent, thinking woman. What is it?"

"I honestly don't know."

"You don't know? What does your heart tell you? What does your rational mind tell you?"

"I just... I just wish I had the nerve to blow his lying brains out."

Catherine's emotional words were uttered with eerie calm. They were not the incoherent ramblings of an unstable woman with some distorted, irrational mind. It was apparent she had reached the end of her rope.

Dr. Deauville let Catherine's words settle, before reacting. "Why wouldn't you just leave... or, hell just tell *him* to? That's twice you've mentioned killing him."

"I know."

"Killing is an irreversible act. Perhaps you were only speaking figuratively. You really think you're capable of such a violent act?"

Catherine clenched her jaws tightly. Her eyes flared. "Yes, I do. Under the right circumstances, we're all capable, aren't we? After all, part of *me* is dead anyway."

Dr. Deauville was taken aback by Catherine's resoluteness. She stared pointedly, during a long silence. Catherine dabbed her eyes, took a long sip of water, emptying the glass. Dr. Deauville took the glass and filled it again. When she returned, Catherine was up and walking slowly about the room. She suddenly stopped at the large window and stared blankly out over the city below. Sirens wailed in the distance then faded into silence.

Catherine Jeffries was part of the upper crust of Los Angeles society—a woman of considerable stature. Her family had long been revered throughout the United States. In 1978, John Wadsworth Douglas—Catherine's father and an old-line, eastern establishment industrialist—died in a yachting accident. He reportedly left her an estate of eight hundred million dollars, give or take a few million. Her six siblings, residing in New York, and no fewer than a dozen charities, had received an equal or greater sum.

Additionally, in 1988, Catherine sold controlling interest in a cosmetics conglomerate for considerably more than five hundred million dollars cash and an undisclosed amount of stock. Money was not one of her problems. Dr. Deauville hoped to help her face her realities and do something about them. She was aware the defiance and the bravado Catherine exhibited in her office always dissipated when she found herself facing her powerful, charismatic husband.

Momentarily, she wondered just how serious Catherine Jeffries really was, regarding wishing her husband dead. Given the prospect that in a California divorce, her husband would likely be awarded alimony and a large share of her fortune, it made economical sense, setting aside the moral question. However, Dr. Deauville knew Catherine was not one to make impulsive statements. Still, she did not press the matter further.

Suddenly, and without a single word, Catherine Jeffries bounded to her feet, grabbed her purse and stormed from the room. Dr. Deauville watched in stunned silence, as her patient all but ran to the door. She never looked back.

Six
Rendezvous

One Week Later — *"C'mon, baby. Don't go soft now."*

The splashy front entrance

of the luxury condominium complex resembled a posh five-star hotel. The sleek off-white facade of sculpted masonry and glass was accented in low lumen, metal-halide light. The structure jutted skyward like some tall, sterile, innocuous monument to the god, Hedon.

Nearby, trendy Westwood provided a fitting setting for the stratospheric price tags of the condos featured recently in a glitzy Los Angeles magazine. In the covered, semicircular driveway, two spry young valets, with well-flossed teeth and store-bought smiles, stood at the ready. Many residents chose to drive themselves past the cut stone driveway and onto the drive leading into the gated underground parking facility.

Spewing black diesel exhaust, an aging Mercedes sedan pulled up to the self-service gate and waited for it to retract. Idling roughly and badly in need of cleaning, a silver, late model BMW 7-series sedan pulled behind it. The Mercedes finally pulled past the gate, followed closely by the BMW that entered before the gate closed.

Inside a darkened condo bedroom, oblivious to the outside world, a slightly balding man of sixty, and an energetic, nubile young woman were caught up in torrid lovemaking. Their sweaty, glistening bodies were tangled like human pretzels. Primal sounds and explicit love-language filled the love-laden air.

The man, greying but fit, raised himself rhythmically, gasping, eyelids fluttering. He wrapped an arm around his frenetic partner and, without withdrawing, rolled gently onto his back. The endowed young woman of 25, moved passionately astride him, raising and lowering herself onto his rock-rigid member with locomotive zeal.

Looking like an artist's sculptures, her perspiration covered, melon-like breasts, succulent nipples pointing, glistened in the low light. Hungrily seizing her taut, tan buttocks with both hands, the man fell back against several crumpled pillows. He drew the woman to him, thrusting upward in sync to meet her. Wincing and groaning, the young woman tossed her head back, thrust herself down onto him, then up again, repeatedly.

Grimacing, the man loosed a symphony of grunts in low guttural tones, while the young woman rose and descended with no sign of slowing. Her hair flailed like a palomino's mane. Their tumultuous cacophony grew louder, blending into a strange sounding duet which neither heard.

"That's it," she blurted, shedding all inhibition. "Right there! Stay right there! Oh, god. Don't stop," she commanded, arms extended onto the bed on either side of her lover's head. She braced herself, forcing his hardness against her spot.

The lovers' faces contorted; the rush of adrenaline exploded like geysers. Now drenched with salty perspiration, the man began thrusting even more forcefully. The young woman met him with equal force, exhorting him, daring him, pleading. The two seemed bent on mutual destruction.

With hair flailing, the young woman tossed her head back then forward, flicked her tongue over her pouty lips. Beads of perspiration fell onto her lover's face and mouth. The couple's strained voices blended in a shrill, sustained crescendo. The flailing and moans mounted; the large bed creaked and bounced. Then, with animal-like shrieks, both reached violent climax, and proceeded with only slightly declining intensity.

The woman's face glistened with perspiration; she slowed and leaned forward, staring intently at her fatigued partner. Beads of love-sweat dripped steadily onto his upper torso. The man's eyes closed, momentarily. His exhausted body was spent, but his erection still pulsated deep inside her.

"Baby, baby," she whispered, "You're still up. I still feel you. I can't believe you're still hard. You sure you're sixty?"

"Parts of me are," the man quipped. "I got this in a transplant from an eighteen year-old."

Both laughed then fought to catch their breaths. The man slowly lifted his hands, seized the woman's breasts, began caressing them. She smiled, pressed his hands firmly to her body, forced her smooth, sculpted thighs against him. She raised herself slightly, then peered down, determined to see where the two of them remained joined.

Seconds later, the young woman slowly retreated toward the foot of the bed, exposing her lover's still firm, glistening pride. She leaned down, grasped him firmly in her right hand, while raking her tongue across her lips in hungry anticipation.

Then, shock gripped her lover's face like a steel claw. The man stared past her; his mouth fell open. A contorted expression seized him, the woman felt him suddenly go limp in her hand.

"C'mon, baby! Don't go soft now," she implored, massaging him gently.

A loud pop punctuated the air, thrusting the man's head back with violent force. A hole instantly filled his brow. His eyes locked in a death stare, as he slumped to one side. Blood spilled from the ugly opening.

The powerful, tumbling exit of the round blew brain tissue and chunks of skull onto once white pillows.

Horrified, the poor woman froze solid; her lips parted in a silent scream. A second pop. She never heard it. In a beat, she slumped forward onto her lover, fatally wounded. Her curvaceous, once vibrant young body quivered for several seconds, then fell still.

Gripping a .44 Magnum fitted with silencer, a stealthy male-like figure dressed in black, including gloves, slowly lowered his right hand. A black fedora sat firmly in place. The killer stood shrouded in a trench coat with dangling belt. With surprising calm, he removed the silencer, placed it and the gun into the coat pocket. He approached the bed and stood gazing at the two bloody, distorted, lifeless bodies.

With only minor difficulty, the shooter rolled the woman aside and stood glaring at the man whose upper torso was covered with her blood. A bloody circle enveloped the two, soaking the top and bottom sheets. The killer calmly eased a gloved hand into his left coat pocket then withdrew it. Clutching a pair of black bikini panties, which he raised above his head, he released them, allowing them to float down onto the man's body.

With no apparent remorse, the brazen killer removed a pair of scissors and a clear, plastic bag. He cut a handful of the woman's hair, stuffed it into the bag, and thrust the bag into yet another pocket. His actions appeared well-rehearsed. Showing no eagerness to leave, the killer removed a paperback novel from his coat and placed it on the blood-soaked bed. The book jacket read: "John Roméo's Curse of The Gods." The author's once bearded likeness graced the jacket. 'Curse' was Roméo's most recent, and most controversial novel.

Still unhurried, the killer produced a digital camera and began taking photos of his victims. His cold, ruthless behavior was almost ritualistic. He moved to the stereo on a far wall, turned it on and inserted a CD into the player. Seconds later, the late Sam Cooke's *Frankie And Johnny* began playing.

The song's lyrics detailed the tragic fate of a man showered with love and treasure by his woman. Later, she caught him cheating and dispatched him to hell with a .44, as he and his lover sat in a café. As 'Johnny' lay dying on the floor, he vainly tried to explain to 'Frankie' that things were not as they seemed.

Twisted and sick, is the only description the killer's use of this song to make some apparent point about infidelity. However, the parallels were clear and unmistakable.

The shooter soon returned to the foot of the bed and stood, for an interminable period, ogling the two bodies with morbid fixation. He turned his head from side to side, clearly admiring his gruesome handiwork.

After a full twenty minutes, the murderer finally moved away from the bed and toward the open bedroom door. He paused, turned and stared once more at the carnage. Seconds later, he crossed the sprawling living room, joined an accomplice—a hulking figure, likewise outfitted in black. The two exited the condominium, gently closing the door behind them.

Seven

The Return - Next Day - Police Administration Bldg (P.A.B.), DOWNTOWN

Next, he was done with the sexist and racist behavior of assholes...

Nicholson was busy working the telephone,

in his characteristically brusque style. His office was a potpourri of Marine Corps and LAPD memorabilia. The walls strained under countless framed certificates from charity groups, and organizations as varied as the Heritage Foundation and the NAACP.

The Captain sat with his back to the door, facing a credenza with framed pictures of his wife of thirty-three years, and his twenty-five year-old twin sons. A dark-stained, knurled-wood nameplate graced the front edge of his desk. The name 'Captain C.E. 'Bear' Nicholson was carved into it.

"It's about time you came home. Now, don't make me beg, Roméo. It's not befitting a man in my position. We'll work things the way we always have," he bellowed. "And please don't give me that 'I'm *busy* crap.' You're always busy. Haven't you made enough money?"

The Captain wheeled around in his chair, toying with the already tangled telephone cord as he listened to John's response. "The department needs help. I tried to convince you of that the last time I called. You owe us, if for no other reason than to explain why your novel keeps showing up at our crime scenes. I've been reading this last one. Got any ideas to share with me?"

There was no answer. "Listen, this call's just between you and me," Nicholson continued. "If you decide to stop being selfish and help out, call me. But hurry the hell up. The old man is starting to chew on my ass. For some reason, he thinks I have some influence with you."

Nicholson pounded the receiver in his open palm, hung up then glanced at the stack of folders piled atop his desk. His attention was quickly drawn to four crime scene photographs. He carefully re-examined them, turning each to the light, just so. They were prints of the four, glossy, black and white photos Dr. Deauville viewed in her office. Each depicted nude, savagely murdered bodies of a man and woman.

Curiously, each murder scene photo showed objects next to each couple: in one, a large screwdriver; in another, a surgical glove; a bible, and a CD. The Captain's guess—shared by others in the department— was that this was the killer's warped, demented way of associating the male victims with their jobs or professions. The men were, respectively: a hardware chain CEO; a prominent heart surgeon; a famous mega-evangelist and his homosexual lover, and a computer software magnate—Colin Sumner.

Glaring at the photos, his brow deeply furrowed, the Captain shook his head in disgust then tossed the photos back onto his desk next to a stack of audio CDs. He grabbed a disc, placed it into a well-used player atop his desk and pressed play. Sam Cooke's Frankie and Johnny began pouring from the speaker. The high volume sent Nicholson fumbling for the control knob.

The Captain now found himself in an unenviable position. He had to quickly answer a growing chorus of critics, in and out of the department, for failure to make progress in the investigations. Having his ass planted squarely on the burner was not a predicament he relished. Recently, the Department had been severely battered, and was in need of successes and positive press. Nicholson had little doubt Roméo would join the investigation. It was tailor-made for him and his uncanny sixth sense. What more could he want? There was sex, murder, intrigue and a baffled LAPD.

With minor exceptions, the Captain viewed his relationship with Roméo as both friendly and professional. Although they had not always seen eye to eye, he respected John's refusal to subordinate his views and positions for short-term expediency. In many ways, the two were ideological soul mates.

For six months, prior to John's retirement from the Department, Nicholson tried to convince him to stay on. John's one concession was to remain until he completed one of the most difficult, and potentially explosive, murder cases in the history of Los Angeles: the "Sheraton Murders."

Five wealthy Arab Sheiks visiting Los Angeles were poisoned to death in their hotel suite. Several conditions made the case extremely difficult to crack. The Sheiks had reserved an entire floor for their extensive entourages and provided their own security. Following the deaths, their associates steadfastly insisted on no outside involvement in the case. Of course, such a request could not be honored.

Members of the group were convinced a radical Jewish group was responsible. They said so, loudly and often. The resulting rhetoric proved incendiary. Prior to the murders, the LAPD accepted a limited security role, but had been restricted to areas beyond the limits of the hotel.

At first, the case threatened to evolve into a major international incident. It remained unsolved for several weeks, until John was assigned the lead role. After less than a month of rigorous investigation, and a great deal of luck, he turned up a strong lead. It led to the wife of an exiled former ambassador from the subject Arab State. She happened to be an opponent of the ruling family represented by the Sheiks.

The Department and Roméo received little help from the FBI and other federal agencies. According to some LAPD brass, and even lower level officers, the FBI could be real dicks, when they wanted to be. As it turned out, unknown to the Sheiks, the company, owned by he former ambassador's wife, had been contracted to provide entertainment for the unsuspecting visitors. The 'entertainment' was in the form of several young women.

However, one of the 'entertainers' had been hired to provide more than pure entertainment. Her primary role was to poison the food and drink of the visiting royalty. She succeeded but was, herself, eliminated. Her murder was contracted out to a former Mafia hit man, hired by the ambassador's wife to cover her own tracks. The murder was murdered.

The wife was later taken into custody, as a result of information provided by a member of John's legion of informants. As it turned out, the informant had been hired to eliminate the former Mafia hit man. The suspect's motive? Revenge for the removal of her husband from his ambassadorial post.

Roméo's work on the case only enhanced his already legendary reputation both inside and outside the Department. His decision to leave the Department, Captain Nicholson's pleas notwithstanding, was more a matter of conscience. He would have left, with or without the literary success.

First, he was fed up with the LAPD hierarchy's tolerance of political interference. Roméo felt the Chief lacked the balls to tell the Mayor, and other such sycophants, to go the hell. Next, he was done with the sexist and racist behavior of assholes allowed to get away with such crap. The very idea rednecks and Neo-Nazi wannabes found sanctuary for their hateful garbage was shameful. John felt it only served to weaken and destroy the Department. Some called him a bleeding-heart liberal. He regaled in the verbal abuse.

A year before he left, John Roméo took his concerns over the heads of his superiors, straight to the Chief. He was assured corrective action would be taken. However, that very evening, he witnessed the Chief respond to a television reporter inquiring about alleged racism within the department. In his defensive response, the Chief characterized the allegations, by a group of women and black officers, as completely unfounded. He asserted this was likely a case of "sour grapes on the part of a few officers with connections to *'certain organizations.'*"There were other important reasons for John's decision to leave the LAPD. Chief among these was the fact he was making real money, and was no longer obliged to suffer fools. Yet, as free as he now was to control his own life, John was on a collision course. On this day, he would meet his match in the person of a vivacious young woman named Krystal Knight. The outcome would surprise even him.

Eight
Showtime.

John Roméo had little use for Daytime Talk-TV.

He felt all trash belonged at curbside in closed containers. But today would be different in ways neither he nor millions would soon forget.

Backstage, the top-rated, nationally syndicated talk show, the KRYSTAL KNIGHT SHOW, featuring thirty-three year-old, Emmy Award winning host, Krystal Knight, was only minutes from air. There was a buzz of frenzied activity, as show personnel, assistant producers, and techno rats scurried to make their final equipment and personnel checks.

The controversial show, normally taped in and aired from Chicago, was originating live from Los Angeles. Although the five feet-seven, natural-blonde was enthusiastically committed to doing live shows, periodically, she was having serious second thoughts regarding taking to the road at this time. Krystal's grip on first place in the ratings was rock solid. She did not need the risks that often attend live shows. That was especially true in media centers like New York and Los Angeles. Most of her competitors were eating her dust.

Staring straight ahead, an antsy Krystal, thirty-three, vivacious and attractive, made her way past a cluster of busy technicians. She was trailed by an assistant, Colleen, a homely-looking young producer in desperate need of a fashion makeover. The latter struggled to keep up, as she filled Krystal in on last minute disasters and mini-uprisings amongst the troops. Krystal was well aware of the young woman's penchant for drowning in minutia.

"I think we're all *go*, except for the doctor's mike. Rick's busy changing it out now," Colleen said.

"Good," said Krystal. "I don't need screw ups today."

"And our two mallards are all in a row." Colleen was referring to the two male guests. "But our friend, Rose, still insists she won't answer any questions about prison."

Krystal came to a halt; her eyes flared. "What do you mean she won't..."

"Doesn't want to talk about it."

"We'll see about that," Krystal continued walking. Her gait quickened. Colleen raced to keep up.

"She's dead serious."

A seething Krystal stopped again, and wheeled around to face Colleen.

"What?" She scowled. "She says she doesn't..."

"Why the hell she agree to come on? She didn't tell Cynthia, or Melanie, or me that crap when we spoke with her during three interviews."

"I know. Please don't go off," Colleen pleaded.

"Listen, I don't want to hear it. Understood?" Krystal continued walking. Colleen knew Krystal could be blustery and short-fused, with or without reason. She wisely allowed her to vent, then continued. "She says she just doesn't want to dwell on it."

"Guests don't decide how I conduct this show."

"I know."

"I know many of them would like to, but that's not the way it works. You guys have to make sure they understand that. I shouldn't have to deal with this kind of crap."

"Well, she's threatening to walk, if you push the issue."

"Let the dyke walk, if she wants," snapped Krystal then cupped her hand to her mouth. At the same time, a young production assistant, Stephanie, approached with clipboard in hand. A pained expression covered her face.

"You didn't hear me say that," said Krystal.

"I didn't hear it," Colleen agreed, pressing her hands to her ears.

"But listen," Krystal insisted, "her going to prison is central to her story. If I'd wanted a saint, I would've booked a Mother Teresa."

Colleen did a three-sixty. Krystal thrust one hand to her forehead briefly and mumbled something under her breath.

"How do I look?" She asked. Colleen gave her the once over.

"The truth," Krystal insisted, "Your job is secure."

"You look fine."

"Listen, don't worry. I'll do the setup... talk to her at the top of the segment. She wants to walk; we'll have her story down. How're we on time? And where the hell is Alicia? I need more gloss, more powder. I swear, I'm perspiring like a fu..." Krystal turned to Stephanie. "Hold on Steph."

Colleen checked her watch, as Krystal took note of Stephanie waiting patiently for her.

"There's plenty of time," Colleen assured her. "We've got fifteen to camera. You're on in five, and I'll get Alicia."

Colleen dashed away; Krystal started to walk on. Stephanie calmly stepped in front of her, blocking her advance.

"Steph, what is it? Do I have to do everything, huh?"

Stephanie's wounded expression was obvious. Krystal placed a hand on her shoulder. "Listen, I'm sorry," Krystal apologized. Stephanie forced a thin smile.

"You've seen me like this before. These live shows are a bitch. But when you preempt two of the hottest soaps on TV, you'd better have your *you know what* together."

"I understand."

Nine
What is That Thing?

John's Ferarri sat just off the cobblestone motor court,

beyond the plant-festooned, gated, white-columned entry, and in front of the detached, red-tile roofed 'Autohaus.' It sported the personalized license plate: ROMEO-1. Next to it set a black, S600 Mercedes; a coral blue, 1971 Olds 442, a 1966 Shelby-GT Mustang, and a 1957 Chevrolet BelAir—John's pride and joy.

The main residence was a sprawling, white, two-story masonry structure set on a meticulously manicured, four and one-half acres. Inside the home's chandeliered entry lay an expansive interior. A spiral staircase with a white marble railing was trimmed with a faint gold-leaf stream.

The lush, subtly sculpted white carpet stretched endlessly throughout the twelve thousand square foot main house, except for occasional Italian marble and English oak flooring in the right places. The exquisitely decorated surroundings appeared even more expansive, thanks to the seemingly seamless mirrored wall to the right of the entry. It extended the full length of the formal living room.

John was 41, 6'-3,' clean-shaven, trimly athletic, and electively bald. He had choirboy looks and oozed charm whenever he wanted. Several movie producers had tried to convince him to accept acting roles...develop an acting career. "You look 25, have the eyes and charm of a young Sidney Poitier, the sex appeal of George Clooney, and the swagger of a youthful Clint Eastwood," they said. John ignored the entreaties. He saw none of those guys in his mirror.

He approached the stairs in his bare feet, carrying a bottle of Dom Perignon and a wineglass. Wearing only black jockey briefs and a thin smile, he bounded energetically up the stairs, down an 'S' shaped hallway and into a vaulted study.

John reached his Mac G6 computer with 30 inch, flat screen monitor, all atop a two-inch thick, beveled crystal table. He plopped down, filled his glass, sat staring at the screenplay and sipped his wine. Momentarily, he placed the glass on the table and resumed working.

It was now one o'clock in the afternoon. Having started at six that morning, John had been working for six hours. Pressure was mounting from Peter Blaine to complete rewrites of the long-awaited screenplay rewrite. He was also pushed hard to make several changes to a new book manuscript.

Twenty minutes earlier, John had received a curious e-mail that managed to get past his spam filter. The body of the message read: *Roses are red then they die.* That was it. John tried replying to the sender but kept getting an error indicating a mail server problem. While it was not the weirdest message he'd ever received, it was stuck in his head like gum to a whorehouse bedpost.

John was fully absorbed. Hidden from his view, near an interior doorway, a lone figure slipped slowly and stealthily toward him. The apparent intruder paused intuitively, slinking behind furniture whenever John turned around. Seconds passed. The shadowy figure again moved forward, easing to a stop just behind him, arms outstretched. John sensed a presence. He stopped. Froze.

Suddenly, Aimee Jardin, 28, thrust both arms around his neck. The dark auburn-haired, French-Somalian beauty—long one the world's top fashion models—leaned her tempting 5'-9" body over his right shoulder and planted a moist kiss on his cheek.

"You taste good," she whispered.

"You have very good taste," John answered, in his low, rumbling baritone.

Aimee, clothed only in an unbuttoned, long-sleeve silk shirt and a pair of red bikini panties, pressed closer. Her right breast lay poised on John's shoulder. He closed his eyes, turned and kissed it softly, gently caressing it with his left hand. Aimee moaned. John pressed more firmly.

"John," she purred, in her arresting French accent then tossed her head back; she grasped the sides of John's head with both hands, wheeled him around, and buried his face between her warm breasts. He kissed them, hungrily suckled her nipples gently, and repeatedly. Aimee responded with a stream of gasps and shuttered eyes; her right hand pressing him firmly against her. John grasped her waist, gently guided her to him, easing her onto his lap. Her leggy frame straddled him easily. Ravishing her lips, he pushed away from the desk.

Fully aroused, John leaned back and stared at the gorgeous woman planted atop him, He swelled even more. Aimee returned his gaze, determined to not allow him to spend all day hunkered over his computer. She knew how difficult that would be, once his inspiration was flowing. She had seen days when John would spend 16 hours writing.

There was no denying the depth of John and Aimee's love for each other. Still there was an unresolved tension that lay just beneath the surface. Both were aware of it, though it was never openly discussed. Each wondered if the other sensed it, too.

Following his recent divorce from first wife, Claire, John was aware the last thing he needed was a new relationship. He had denied himself the space and time needed to reflect upon the emotional trauma inherent in any divorce. He struggled to force those thoughts aside now.

Aimee gripped John's shoulders with both hands; a hot charge raced the length of her body. She felt his hot breath on her breasts; felt moisture seeping from inside her. No one ever made her so wet, so easily, and for so long. The thought of it turned her on even more.

"Umm," John groaned, flicking his tongue rapidly over her firm, pointed nipples. Aimee moaned aloud. With her left nipple between his lips, John pressed down lightly then gently, repeatedly, suckling while rotating his tongue. A flash raced through her body, just as he released, seized her right nipple gently between his teeth, while caressing her left. Again he pressed lightly, alternately stroking her nipple with his flicking tongue. Aimee reacted even more wildly. For some reason, her right nipple always produced a greater erogenous rush.

John gazed up at her and smiled.

"Now, tell me. How am I sup- posed to work when you keep presenting me with such delicious dis- tractions?"

"Don't," said Aimee, smiling.

"Yeah, sure. I've got a rewrite on this screenplay; a publisher who's having a cardiac, all because I'm a lousy three days late uploading a final draft. You think maybe it's 'cause they've already paid me?"

"No more work, John. Please! You've been at it all day, Cherie. Your mind can't be on your work now."

"Is that right?"

"Yes," Aimee slipped the shirt from her shoulders.

"And why is that?"

"I just know. But you can lie to me and say it's not. Okay?"

John loosed a loud laugh.

"I'm serious. Stop laughing."

John kissed her then tried to force her to stand. Aimee playfully resisted, forcing herself back onto his lap.

"Okay," John relented. "You're right, sweetheart."

"Don't patronize me."

"You think I'm patronizing you?"

"You're still planning to work, aren't you?"

"Doesn't mean I'm being patronizing. I've got one more scene and I'll stop. Promise. Scout'shonor."

"You never told me you were a Boy Scout," said a skeptical Aimee.

"Alright, be picky. I was a Cub Scout."

"Liar," said Aimee, feigning a punch at him.

"It's true. And once a scout, always a scout."

"I don't believe you."

"I was. Anyway, you can watch me finish this scene. It won't take long," John insisted, with a twinkle.

"No. Please! In two weeks, I'll be back in Paris. You won't see me, or make love to me for a whole month. Besides, I want to drain you, so you'll still be able to say no to Claire."

"What?" John feigned indignation. "What's my ex-wife got to do with this?"

"You know exactly what I'm talking about."

"That's cute, real cute. You could've gone all day without saying that."

"Well, she is very persistent and very beautiful too. And she keeps calling you. Why does she keep calling you? She called just yesterday... even left you a message. The woman has no shame. None!"

"I don't want to talk about it."

John had heard these snipes before, but this one had a sharper edge to it. He had never acknowledged it angered him to hear disparaging remarks about Claire. It was becoming more and more difficult to not defend her.

John kissed Aimee's left ear, knowing how it always drove her up the wall. She shuddered, straddled him again, began grinding in his lap. John's erection turned granite. Aimee felt it boring against her, and in the perfect spot.

"What *is* that thing?" She joked. "A tumor? I'm not sure."

"You didn't have any doubt last night."

"I was faking."

"So was I."

"Liar. Men can't fake it. That's the difference," Aimee said, poking him playfully in the ribs with a finger. "You can't fake it."

Aimee continued gyrating. "This is for me, oui? Don't tease me, John."

"Sweetheart, I assure you I'm not teasing."

Facing him, Aimee drew her long legs around John and crossed them. They kissed long and deep. While still joined, John leaned forward, fumbled for the mouse then clicked to save the document. He stood, with Aimee in his arms, and carefully made his way across the room, toward the interior doorway, and down the hallway to the master bedroom. Aimee rested her head on his shoulder, arms draped around his neck.

Near, the bedroom doorway, John stumbled. That brought a yelp and a quick caution from Aimee.

"Don't drop me."

"Don't worry. If I do, we'll make love right here on the floor."

"As long as I don't get carpet burns on my butt," Aimee joked.

John took a couple of more steps. "Oh, by the way, this may not be the right time to say this, but...I don't want any more messages from Roger, okay?"

"You're right. This is definitely not the right moment. Besides, that doesn't make sense. The least you could do is talk to him.

"No more," John repeated.

"You can't be this way. He needs you."

The telephone rang.

"He needs a shrink; that's what he needs."

The phone rang again.

"It never fails," John mumbled.

The phone rang a third time. John lowered Aimee and hurried to the phone set on a nightstand next to the bed. Aimee watched from the doorway. John reached the phone on the fourth ring, lifted the receiver.

"Hello," he barked. No reply. "Hello!" John repeated. There was a faint voice. "What was that?" He asked, straining to hear. Nothing more. He slammed the phone down and returned to Aimee.

"What was all that?"

"Same as the others. I spend thirteen years on the force and not one death threat in all that time. I'm retired three years and I get three in four days. Go figure."

"What's happening?"

John glanced back at the phone, then at Aimee. "I'm sure it's just some nut. Next week they'll probably be harassing someone else. I don't know what I was thinking. I should've let the message center answer." John eased closer to Aimee.

"What are you hiding from me? What are you working on that's got somebody threatening to kill you?"

"Where were we?" John asked, ignoring Aimee's question. A smile crept across his face.

"John?"

"I have absolutely no idea. I don't know what the call was about. I'm working on a book and another script. That's it. That's it!"

Aimee stared disbelievingly, then began gently seizing his crotch. John returned the favor. She crossed her legs, trapping his hand. She squeezed tightly and released. He lifted her in his arms again, and made his way across the room to the bed.

With a slight grunt, John tossed Aimee toward the middle of the large bed. She landed on her stomach, arms outstretched, clutched the pillows in front of her. Aimee lay there, revealing her bare back and the red thong cinched tightly between her taut cheeks.

John took in the lovely sight, throbbing, ready to burst through his briefs. He climbed slowly onto the bed from behind Aimee and, poised on his knees, began gently kissing her calves, her legs, behind her knees, slowly inching upward to the back of her thighs.

Rhythmically tensing and releasing her curvaceous posterior, Aimee began writhing, reacting to every kiss, every touch. John eased both palms slowly onto her taut buttocks, squeezing and massaging them in a gentle but firm, counter-circular motion. Aimee winced; began grinding against the mattress beneath her; arching her back slightly, fingers dug deeper into the pillows. She felt warm moisture seep from deep inside her. A tingle raced up her spine.

John moved slowly upward, until he leaned down and kissed the back of her neck. She went wild, feeling the sensation of his warm, pulsating cock pressed against her, on her split. He held it there. Aimee placed her right hand behind her, desperate to touch him, to pull him to her.

Then, guiding her gently onto her back, and with her knees raised, John rested his head on Aimee's stomach and sent a long stream of warm breath cascading downward. She rose off the bed, clinching the sheets in her hands. John eased himself forward, causing the full length of his firmness to press solidly against her mound. Aimee grasped his forearms and held on, briefly.

Now resting lightly atop her, John could feel Aimee's warm wetness seeping through her panties. His hands reached for her breasts. Aimee again arched her back, forcing them skyward.

The telephone rang.

John continued a few seconds then paused. He sighed disgustedly, but gave no sign he intended to answer it. It kept ringing, only louder it seemed. The message center was set to pick up on the fourth ring. The ringing continued. Four, five rings. John pounded the bed.

"Aren't you going to answer?"

"Hell no. The center is supposed to get it."

"Apparently not. Could be important."

"Nothing's that important."

"I agree but..."

More ringing.

"It's probably the same clown that called earlier," John guessed.

"Answer or disconnect it, sweetheart."

"You trying to get rid of me?"

"Don't be silly."

The ringing stopped. John laughed and had just rested his head on Aimee's stomach when the phone rang again.

Ten
The Show

KCBC-TV — *"So the guys are P-whipped and the women are shrews."*

The enthusiastic studio audience

Buzzed with conversation. Guests were in place; the warm-up was done. The silence sign flashed. A refreshed Krystal stood poised, clutching a hand-held mike, and facing the camera as *on-air* time neared. Across America, from Maine to Alaska, millions were in front of their TV sets.

Krystal, with piercing blue eyes, took a deep breath, smiled, and was cued. Viewers at home heard theme music and saw the opening graphic montage. In the studio, the bespectacled woman producer folded down fingers on one hand to a raised fist. The graphic trailed, the music ended in a flourish, and the show was on.

Krystal beamed, flashed a wide, infectious smile, and held the mic to her lips. Her ador- ing audience continued applauding, as she faced the camera and Tele-PrompTer. She was resplendent, as always, in another designer original. This one was a cleavage-revealing, soft yellow, two-piece suit with a skirt that ended just above the knees.

Krystal's adrenaline was in full flow. Buoyed by the enthusiastic audience reaction, she soon forgot her pre-show jitters. She was 'on.'

"Thank you!" Krystal belted amid tumultuous applause that tapered as she spoke. "Thank you, and hello, America! Welcome to the show. We are live here in Los Angeles today and tomorrow, and I want to take a second to thank the local ABC station personnel for the hospitality they've shown me, my staff and our guests. And thanks to all of you here in southern California and Los AN-GE-LES!" She screamed.

Krystal punctuated her words with a clenched fist thrust high into the air. The audience responded with wild applause. Feeding off them, Krystal felt the electricity surge through her.

"Great!" She screamed, "It's great to be here. Chicago is still my home, but it's great to be in L.A." Wild applause erupted all over again.

Krystal raised her hand to settle the audience.

"Thank you! Thank you, thank you! I promise you an exciting, controversial topic and, most importantly, an informative show today. If you're married or contemplating marriage, I hope you'll stay tuned. Let's get started.

"Recent statistics reveal that fully sixty-five to seventy percent of all married men either have cheated, or will cheat on their wives, at some point during their marriage. That's an amazing statistic.

"Now, before you men get upset and start sending me hate e-mails, let me say...I know many wives cheat too, but that's another show. We're dealing with you men, today. We'll do our best to examine this emotional issue of male infidelity, as we look at *Husbands who cheat and the wives who still love them, "*today, on the Krystal Knight Show."

Bumper music rose to enthusiastic audience applause. A bank of control room monitors showed Krystal awaiting her post credits cue, chatting briefly with nearby audience members. Seconds later, the show resumed.

"Please help me welcome my guests today. They are, from my far left, Ann and Harold Rheem. Harold admits that for seven years he has been hopelessly addicted to extramarital affairs."

"Was. I was addicted," Harold corrected her. "I'm in treatment now."

A groan rose from the mostly female audience.

"Okay," said Krystal. "According to Harold, he *was* addicted to extramarital affairs which began..." Krystal hesitated briefly, as she stared at the TelePrompTer with genuine incredulity.

"Which began on his wedding night? Am I reading that right? Ann, is that true? And if it is, how in the world did you find out? That's what I'm dying to know."

Ann started to reply, but Krystal halted her in mid sentence.

"Wait! Just tell us if it's true. We'll get to the juicy stuff later."

Oohs and aahs erupted. Harold dropped his head sheepishly and squeezed Ann's hand affectionately.

"It is true," Ann confirmed, "But we are still together and we're working it out. I know that sounds strange, and I'm sure many of you probably won't understand."

The audience responded cynically. Krystal cleared her throat loudly and pressed Ann further. "You say you're working it out. Right?"

"That's right."

"Don't get me wrong, I'm happy for both of you, but does that mean you still love him...you forgive him?"

"Yes, I do. I love him and I forgive him. I know many in your audience won't understand that..."

"You're right," Krystal agreed.

"And I'm not offering a prescription for anyone else. I had a decision to make and I made it for me."

"I see," said Krystal.

"She's crazy," a woman blurted out.

Krystal scurried toward the middle of the audience, and motioned the woman to stand. The woman was suddenly reluctant.

"Stand up," Krystal insisted. "I saw you making faces and screaming over here. Why do you say she's crazy? What makes *you* so smart? Stand up!"

The animated young woman stood, reached for the mic. Krystal held on to it, extending it to her.

"She's nuts. I mean, how can she trust him again?"

"She says she loves him," Krystal pointed out.

The woman was not persuaded. "She's gonna always be expecting or wondering if he's gonna do it again. I know I wouldn't trust him."

The audience agreed.

"Are you married?" Krystal asked the woman. She shook her head *no*. The audience reacted with some amusement. Krystal started back toward her panel of guests.

"Hold on now, Ann. I promise I'll give you a chance to explain further in a minute. You folks are merciless," Krystal grinned and raised her hand to calm her audience. "I'll give you another chance, Ann. Seated next to Ann and Harold, is Philip Farrar. Philip and his wife of eleven years, Annette, who is not here, are presently separated. And I understand she has filed for divorce. Hmm, I wonder why."

Krystal's quip brought more laughter, as she stepped toward a smiling, cocky Philip. He was an arguably good-looking man, late thirties, tan, thinning hair, dressed in a sport coat, slacks and banded-collar shirt.

Krystal stepped closer then turned to the TelePrompTer. "Philip says his wife knew, when she married him, that he loved women—heavy emphasis on the love part. He claims she married him then tried to change him. He insists she was the one who needed changing."

Philip gazed with contempt at the audience. Krystal continued. "He also says considering all the women there are, it's ridiculous to imagine any real man could be happy with just one. According to Philip, if God made anything better, he must've kept it for himself." Krystal hesitated before reading further. "I refuse to read this last line here."

Philip chuckled. Krystal waited for the audience to settle down.

"C'mon, drop the self righteousness," he lectured. "What I said is true. And the few men I see in the audience know damn well I'm right. But they won't admit it here in this den of screaming shrews."

The women reacted angrily. Krystal reacted with indignation. "Hold on a second, I take offense at your characterization of this audience, or my show, as a den of shrews."

Philip waved his arms and fired back. "Your indignation is noted. My point is, that on most of these kinds of shows, you get this patronizing of female audiences. That's a fact. The men in the audiences at these shows come with their wives or girlfriends and they're scared to death they'll get cut off at home if they react honestly."

"So the guys are P-whipped and the women are shrews."

"Damn right. The guys here know if they were alone with a sexy broad, and she showcased her goods in front of them, they'd bone her in a New York minute. That's what happened to a former president. He got thonged and he bit. Or she bit, right? Whatever. He lost his head over a piece of tail. Women do it too. It's true. Look at 'em. These guys can't keep a straight face. You women turn to your husbands and boyfriends and look at them right now. Go on. Look! I dare you. At the top of the show you pointed out the statistics. Seven out of ten of you married guys are fu... I mean messing around. Case closed."

The men in the audience were visibly uncomfortable. One man's wife nudged him. He lowered his head and grinned, sheepishly.

Krystal waited for calm. "Did you say 'broad,' a second ago?" Philip did not respond. Krystal gave him a menacing look and moved on. "You've made your point. We'll get back to Philip in a moment. Seated next to Philip is Dr. Diane Deauville, a clinical psychologist, therapist, and marriage counselor.

"Dr. Deauville says that for many unfaithful men, it's a matter of sexual insecurity and a lousy self-image. She believes many of these men are not the great lovers they perceive themselves to be. They tend to have a constant need to blame and victimize women for their own shortcomings, no pun intended."

Krystal's statement evoked a loud laughter. Dr. Deauville tried to conceal her own smile. "Welcome Doctor. I'm glad you're here to help us make sense of all this."

Dr. Deauville nodded. "Thanks. Glad to be here, Krystal."

"What do you make of all this?"

"First of all, I want to say I'm not here to bash men. The fact is, I find a number of unfaithful men do indeed feel sexually inadequate, and invariably blame their spouses for not fulfilling their requisites for gratification; some are justified. Many of their problems are traceable to negative childhood experiences, as well as early manifestations of an identity crisis."

"So it often does begin in childhood," said Krystal.

"Correct. Perhaps many of them observed marital problems between parents...perhaps infidelity. And to be blunt, for many, the problem is testosterone, period."

"Testosterone?" Krystal asked.

"I mean that in an anthropological sense. Men are wired to engage in sex...to grow the 'tribe'; to further the species. Now, I do not suggest this inherent urge provides justification. We all have to live within the moral code. Being male does not excuse the behavior I have heard described here. Sometimes, believe it or not, another factor is impotency."

Krystal looked puzzled. "I'm afraid you've lost me"

"Most people understand impotency as a man's inability to perform the conventional sex act. You know, penis-vagina."

"I think we know, doctor," Krystal joked.

"You never know these days. Anyway, in many cases, men who find they cannot get it *up* to perform with their wives, find no such problem with other women. I see some of the men out there are smiling."

Krystal pivoted quickly to face the audience.

"Which ones? Seriously, I've never heard this point made before."

"It's not that rare."

"Let see if I understand this," said Krystal. "We've got an unfaithful husband who can't get it up at home, but he has no problem performing on the road. Do I have that right?"

"Correct." The audience roared. "It is a curious psychosexual dysfunction. But this is not true of all men who cheat."

"I would think not," said Krystal.

"And there's one more thing. And I don't mean to cover all men with the same fig leaf. But I must point out that numerous studies show a significant percentage of male cheaters are not happy with the size of their penises."

Krystal made a face and turned toward the audience. Raucous laughter drowned out the doctor. Krystal motioned for silence.

Eleven
'Krystalus Interruptus'

"Sixty seconds should be long enough. You need more time?"

A few miles away from the KCBC studios,

in a spartan, immaculate, but dimly lit bedroom with polished wood floors, and an antique four-poster bed with white linen canopy, a 50's era black and white console television set was tuned to Krystal's show. The washed out images from the old set were reflected in the mirror of a 1930's era triple dresser lined with small, black and white photos arranged around its perimeter.

A white cat of some indeterminable breed lay on the bed, nearly lost against the snow-white comforter. A stoic, barely visible male figure, dressed in an ankle length white lace dress with choker collar, and wearing white lace gloves, sat across the room in a deep cushioned upholstered chair that all but swallowed her. Dr. Deauville continued.

"Most men would like to have them larger. At least that is a common assumption. While that may be true of the general male population, the percentage appears higher among cheaters. It's perhaps a Napoleon complex with a sexual twist, if you will. Of course, we know that while size is interesting and has both esoteric and functional value, it is not the most important factor. Imagination, attention to detail and physical dexterity are critically important to a woman's pleasure quotient. I call it rigid flexibility."

Krystal stifled her own laughter, and turned to look at an audience near hysterics. "I know we're laughing here, but infidelity is a very serious subject, often with serious, and sometimes even deadly consequences." A quiet descended. "That's certainly true in the case of my next guest, Rose Henley."

Krystal moved toward Rose, a stern-faced, sturdy, jean-clad woman in her forties. She had spiked blonde hair, wore ostrich cowboy boots, a red rose pinned to her white, western-style shirt.

The Krystal Knight show filled the large plasma screen TV set. John and Aimee lay quietly in bed. Only a sheet covered them. John's fingers were laced behind his head, as he rested on several large pillows and stared up at the Fresco ceiling. Aimee's eyes were riveted on the set.

John glanced over and nudged her. "This isn't what I had in mind." His words broke Aimee's concentration on Krystal's show. "I'm crushed," he groaned.

"Shh! Watch," said Aimee, frowning.

"My ego is devastated. Besides, why should I watch this crap? Krystal Knight's show is nothing but a platform for male bashing. And those guys are stupid for showing up to be pilloried like that. There's no way I'd agree to go on any of these shows. It's masochistic. If a guy shows up, you know right away he's stupid as hell."

Aimee pretended to ignore John. Krystal's soft-spoken introduction of Rose Elizabeth Henley continued. Rose remained emotionless.

"Thanks for joining us today, Rose."

Rose nodded.

"Rose is the bestselling author of a new book which is number three on the New York Times best-seller list," said Krystal.

"Number two," Rose corrected.

"Excuse me, number two. The book's entitled: The Enemy Within. And you'll understand that title in a moment. Rose was married for... how long, Rose?"

John turned to Aimee. "I could've been working," he said. She frowned, placed a silencing index finger to her lips.

Rose shifted in her chair. "Eighteen years. One month shy of eighteen years."

Krystal stepped up onto the riser where the guests were seated. Rose gazed down and laced her fingers.

"I'm going to ask you to tell us your story, in your own words," Krystal informed her in warm tones, then reversed herself. "No, we'll take a break now, so you won't be interrupted. Back in a moment."

Energetic bumper music rose, signaling a commercial break. Krystal walked over to Rose and whispered.

"I thought I'd let you tell your story right up front. Of course, I'll have some questions, just to keep things moving and to fill in any blanks."

Rose nodded yes.

Meantime, Harold and an animated Philip exchanged muffled comments, followed by thigh-slapping laughter. The audience remained attentive, listening to a producer and poised to begin their applause on cue.

While commercials filled the screen, Aimee leaned over to plant a kiss on John's forehead. He turned away, shielded his face. She pursued him.

"C'mon John."

"I could've been writing. You lured me in here under false pretenses. We both know it."

"I'll make it up to you, darling... whatever your heart desires. You can tie me up with wet noodles and do wild, warm, wicked things to me. I won't resist."

"But only during the commercials, right?"

"Sixty seconds should be long enough. You need more time?"

John was not amused; he tossed a pillow at her. Aimee ducked, then tossed her own. The show returned. She quickly signaled *time-out*, and John started to climb from bed. Aimee grabbed his underwear and pulled him down, exposing his rear end. She relinquished her grip, snapping the elastic band with a pop.

Twelve
A Rose

"Welcome back.

Once again, we're discussing 'Husbands Who Cheat and the Wives Who Still Love Them.' Continuing with author Rose Henley. Please, go ahead, Rose."

Rose shifted uncomfortably in her chair. "As I said, I was married for eighteen years."

"How old were you when you married him?"

"Twenty-four. He was thirty."

"Was it the first marriage for both of you?"

"My first, his third. I loved him very much, and I honestly believed he loved me. But two years after we were married, I found he was cheating."

"How? Did someone tell you or did you find out on your own?"

"I just knew. But later on, of course, it seemed everyone I knew confessed they had known all along. After I suspected him, I didn't say anything about it for a whole year."

"Wait," Krystal interrupted, "I just don't think I could do that. I'm sorry but I'd be all over him like a cheap suit."

"That is not unusual," Dr. Deauville offered. "In fact, more often than not women suffer silently in bad relationships for long periods. It happens in rape cases... cases of sexual harassment, and abuse as well. It is not uncommon for women in these situations to even maintain cordial relations with the offending men. It's really a power paradigm for these men."

Krystal signaled Rose to continue."

"During that time, my suspicions persisted. By then, other signs surfaced. For example, it became harder and harder for me to satisfy him, sexually. He would criticize me at every opportunity. I could do nothing right. Nothing. I'd cook his favorite meal but all of a sudden, he didn't like it. He also began pressuring me to do things I'd never been asked to do before."

"What things?" Asked Krystal.

"I suppose I can say this on national television," said Rose.

"Just don't you get me canceled or end my career," Krystal   joked. The audience voiced approval. Rose continued.

"For one thing, he wanted me to perform oral sex. And that had never been on the menu before. So...."

"How did you respond?"

"I told him, hell no. With apologies to the good doctor, my husband did not have a *Napoleon* penis complex. I made it clear that I choke on a toothbrush. There was no way I was going to let him put a log in my mouth." Uproarious laughter exploded. "Besides, he was running around...sticking his log in every hole he could find. There was no way."

Krystal covered her mouth. Philip folded his arms and glanced up at the ceiling. Krystal signaled for quiet.

Inside the dimly lit bedroom, as Krystal's show continued, the shapely, gloved woman, still concealed by the near darkness, walked slowly to the dresser. She paused briefly, before lifting a bald, anatomically correct female doll from the dresser top. She held it close, turning it in her gloved right hand, observing it from several angles before placing it back onto the dresser.

She next lifted a clear plastic bag, removed a handful of auburn hair and a small white bottle containing a liquid substance. With precise movements, she applied the adhesive to the doll's head then gently layered strands of hair into place.

For a brief time, she stood still. The doll remained upright, hair falling unevenly along the sides of her face. The woman suddenly threw open the top middle dresser drawer, reached inside, removed a pair of scissors and began trimming the doll's hair.

In The Studio...

"Please folks. Let's allow Rose to finish. Rose."

"I'll try and hurry," a grim-faced Rose promised. "One day, I finally confronted him and, of course, he denied it. Ironically, it was that denial that made me convinced. He couldn't look me in the eye, and became irate. But, in spite of that, I stayed with him. Like Ann there, I felt we could work things out. I really did."

Rose's voice grew shaky. It was the first sign of emotion in her otherwise dispassionate discourse. She quickly rid herself of it.

"But you found you just couldn't work it out. And you had no children. Correct?"

"He couldn't keep it home long enough for children."

Krystal moved toward the first row with a hand-held mike held tightly. The audience sat gripped, as the impact of Rose's words sank in.

"Actually, he began to flaunt it," she resumed. "It was like he didn't care whether I knew or not. But I tolerated it for sixteen more hellish years... something I would not advise any woman to do.

"How did you do it?"

"I don't know. Actually, it was in the last year of our so-called marriage that everything came apart for me. My mother died in an auto accident, and my father died of cancer six months later. After my father's funeral—and I'm talking the day of my dad's funeral, which my husband did not attend—I came home and found him..." Rose's voice broke..." in my bed with this bitch, screwing her brains out."

Krystal shook her head. Her audience groaned.

"What did you do?"

"I freaked...came apart. The pain and anguish of the previous eighteen years flooded my mind. That's all I could see and feel... all I could think about. So, I ran to the den, grabbed his .44 magnum he kept in a desk drawer, returned to the bedroom and shot him... once, at first."

Krystal grimaced. "What did he do after you shot him the first time? The first shot wasn't fatal. Right?"

"No. I was trying to hold the gun with both hands, but it's so powerful. The first shot barely nicked him in the shoulder. He was bleeding, but he turned toward me... jumped from the bed and came at me... yelling: *You crazy bitch! I'll kill you! I'll kill you!* So I shot him twice more. He fell to the floor face first...dead."

A heavy silence followed. The hush was broken by Krystal's subdued voice. "My God. What happened then? You must have been absolutely..."

"I stared at him. Then I covered him with a sheet, called the police and waited. I was... I was numb. It was like I wasn't really there, like I was dreaming or something."

"I'm curious. What happened to the woman?"

Rose snapped back in her chair; her eyes narrowed. "She tore her ass out and flat out ran naked down the driveway, 'round the corner. I recognized the bitch, but I didn't shoot her. I mean, I started to, but I'm glad I didn't. I'm not sure I would've hit her though. She was hauling butt, especially after that second shot."

Rose's voice was rife with venom. Krystal searched for some levity. "I'd like to ask who she was, but I won't. You were convicted of murder... served time in prison. Are you remorseful? I ask because you sound bitter and..."

Rose appeared annoyed by Krystal's inference. She bit her lip, hesitated before answering. "Goddamn right, I'm bitter. But I regret the circumstances that led me to take a life. That's something I'll have to live with."

"I understand."

"I served twelve years in prison for second degree murder. I was released last year."

"Second degree. Was that because the shooting was not ruled premeditated?"

Rose nodded yes.

"What about present and future relationships with men? And what do you hope to accomplish? What are you saying to women in your new book?"

"Well, for one thing, I'm not talking exclusively to women. If there is a message, it must be heard by men as well. And I haven't become a lesbian, if that's what you're asking. You either are or you aren't. I still like men. It's just that I find I can live a very full life without them. I date, on occasion. And as far as sex is concerned, that's my business."

Krystal was surprised. "I wasn't suggesting you'd become a lesbian. I don't believe one 'becomes' a lesbian. But be that as it may. Please, go on."

"About the last part of your question, I suppose what I'm saying is, men do what they do, because women are all too often our own worst enemies. We allow them to get away with it. When men cheat, it's excused or explained away as boys being boys. If a woman cheats, she' s a slut...a whore. We women take a lot of crap. And when we do speak out, nobody believes us, especially if the man has stature and position. What's even more amazing is the fact other women don't believe us. Figure that one out."

The audience erupted in sustained applause. Philip was livid. He began yelling and waving an arm frantically, extending it high above his head.

"That's crap! Pure crap!" He shouted.

"What's crap?" Asked Krystal.

"What I'm hearing on this show. This is classic male-bashing. Your audience and this ex-con are saying it's okay for women to cheat 'cause they're poor little victims. Right? That's crap! And if things are as bad as they claim, why do they wait so long to complain?"

"Philip," I don't think that's what Rose is..."

"That's not what I'm saying," Rose blasted. "And I think this dumb bastard knows it."

"Look, butch!"

"Butch?" An incensed Rose stood and started toward Philip."

"Please folks!" Krystal stepped between them and gently guided Rose back to her seat.

"You heard me," Philip fired angrily. "You want to call names, I can do that too."

Philip and Rose exchanged more fiery words, prompting Krystal to interrupt. However, the audience made it clear it supported Rose.

"Okay, folks," urged Krystal. "Let's calm down. Please. And let's watch the language. We are on live."

Rose insisted on making a point in her own defense.

"It's as wrong for women to cheat as it is for men. What I'm saying is, there is a double standard here, as in other things when it comes to men. You can't honestly deny that. And that shouldn't be. I'm not telling women out there to do what I did. I did what I did in my own circumstances. Period."

"You're on a damn crusade!" Charged Philip. "Every time I turn on the TV, there you are hawking your damn book."

Rose glared at Philip. "Listen you prick, I am not on a crusade. But I will tell you, and the women will bear me out on this, there are millions of women out there who are trapped in much the same situation as I was. And the potential for many of the men out there to suffer my husband's fate is very high. Believe me. You could be next!"

Philip was boiling mad. Krystal turned to the audience and tossed up both hands.

"Philip! I won't have any more insults. One more and you're history. Let me get the audience involved here, before I have to get gloves for you two, and a brand new career for myself." Krystal turned to her audience "Hang on there. I'm coming to you," she called out to a woman sitting in the fourth row middle section.

By now, John was watching the show as intently as Aimee. She glanced at him obliquely and smiled. He was so engrossed he never noticed her observing him.

Krystal reached the young woman still seated in the audience.

"Stand up please," Krystal insisted. "You have to stand up to talk on my show. You all should know that by now. Up! Up!"

The woman stood reluctantly, clutching her chest with one hand, obviously nervous.

"Don't die on me here," joked Krystal.

"I'm just nervous," the woman explained.

"Don't be. Settle down. What do you think about all this?"

"First of all, Krystal, I love your show. I watch you all the time. You look even better in person."

"Thank you."

"I'd like to go back to what Ann said before we had the break. She said she still loves her husband and decided to stay with him and all that. I see Ann is nodding yes. And I understand he's seeing a therapist. So I was wondering, what happens when he falls off the wagon? Does he sneak out in the middle of the night and get a little piece and crawl back into bed? I mean, he makes it sound like AA or Weight Watchers or something."

The question brought a laugh and a surprised look from Krystal .

"My God! Where are we getting these audiences? Ann? Harold?" Krystal offered them a chance to respond. Harold deferred to Ann.

"I understand where she's coming from," she said. "Believe me, this is not a piece of cake. I got married because I loved Harold and I believed in the institution of marriage. I took my vows seriously, even if Harold did not. As I said, he cheated on our wedding night with my maid of honor." Everyone responded with incredulity.

"That's right, my maid of honor," Ann continued, "who had, unbeknownst to me, taken a room in the same hotel we were honeymooning in. She later told me herself, just to try and break us up. She and Harold had become bitter enemies by the time she told me all this."

The audience's boos were deafening.

"We've been married ten years. We were married five years when my sister, over my objections, told me Harold was cheating.

"What did you do?" Asked Krystal.

"I didn't want to believe it. I simply didn't believe it. And for a long time, afterwards, I refused to even speak to my sister. I even accused her of trying to break us up so she could have him. That was really stupid, because she and Harold never did hit it off.

"Perhaps she saw something I didn't.. I was in love; I was also in total denial. Then, I found love letters, credit card invoices for hotels and other stuff I couldn't ignore. So, one day I confronted him, after having all his things shipped to a homeless shelter with a note to distribute them to the needy."

The audience hooted and applauded.

"I'm glad she did confront me," Harold confessed. "Because that forced me to face the truth. I had a serious addiction. And that's exactly what it was. Of course this isn't the kind of illness a man wants to own up too. It's not considered a macho thing to do.

"You see, women tend to discuss their problems with each other... support each other. It's a different thing with men. Men are constantly competing, even with very close friends. Women discuss their feelings with each other in an intimate way. Men, on the other hand, talk about their jobs, politics, sports... non-personal things."

"He's absolutely correct," Dr. Deauville agreed.

"It's easy for all of you to sit out there and make snap judgments. But an addiction is an addiction," said Harold.

"An addiction, doctor?" Krystal asked.

"Of course, I can't speak for Harold," Dr. Deauville answered. "But for many men, that is indeed the case. In fact, I was reading author, John Roméo's most recent novel, *Curse of The Gods*."

John's eyes and ears suddenly perked up. He and Aimee glanced at each other in shocked surprise.

"I know it's fictional," Dr. Deauville continued, "But it does point up something very real. In the book, the most tragic character is a man who feels cursed by his insatiable sexual appetite. He fantasizes about having sex with almost every woman he sees. He rates every woman by whether he would or would not want to have sex with her. It's a twenty-four hour a day obsession with him that drives him to a horrible end."

"But that's fiction, doctor," said Krystal.

"True. That's true. However, this depiction, though caricatured, does have considerable basis in fact. It is very real."

"I understand," Krystal conceded.

Aimee glanced again at John. By now, the show had his undivided attention. In the studio, Krystal nodded for Harold to add his response.

"For me, cheating was something I felt I had just had to do. Sex was my fix, just like a drug addict. And I didn't want it only from my wife. I needed the thrill of experiencing sex anew—experimenting with a different partner. There was no pressure to perform in a way that satisfied the need of some permanent relationship. I knew that after I'd done my number, I didn't have to see the woman again, if I didn't want to," he explained.

"Afterwards, I would have this tremendous remorse and guilt. I'm not talking about the normal remorse a man feels immediately after ejaculation, whether he's cheating or not. You men know what I'm talking about. This was like crashing down off some enormous drug high. I had to get help. And I did. And I've been faithful to my wife for three years," Harold concluded.

There was a smattering of applause. Krystal interrupted. "When we return, maybe we'll get some of the men to speak. Back in a moment."

The bumper music rose again and the audience applauded. Krystal returned to the short riser at the guest platform. She whispered a stern admonishment to both Philip and Rose about offensive language.

Philip nodded and leaned back with arms folded. A smug smile crept across his face.

By now, John was hooked. He found himself unable to stop watching the show. Already, he had formed opinions about each guest; imagined they could even be neighbors, people he passed in the grocery store or at the mall. There was an electric quality—a tension that permeated every exchange. But John also sensed an inexplicable feeling of foreboding that seized his attention. He couldn't explain it, but he knew it was real.

Thirteen
No Love Lost

Ensconced in a small office

in the Behavioral Sciences Building, and surrounded by a sterile, benign, minimal atmosphere, Special Agent Tom Merker, mid-forties and balding slightly, sat staring at an open file folder spread before him. He clutched a phone in one hand, and periodically sipped coffee with the other.

At the other end of the line was Captain Nicholson, whose attention was split between his conversation with Merker, and the Krystal Knight show, now in commercial break.

"We'll get this off to you by overnight courier," said Merker. "I won't bother faxing a synopsis. You should see the entire profile. I will say there are some similarities between this one and the one related to the killer we're tracking west. The dates of the killings do lend to the possibility they could be the same. But we're not making that call yet." The furrows in Nicholson's brow deepened. "What about the forensic workups?" He asked.

"You should talk to the lab guys. Takes a little time. I hear you guys didn't send them the quality specimens you usually do. What happened? Another earthquake? Human error... or maybe that commercial lab you guys sent the bulk of the prime swatches to fucked up again? You can't send us shit and expect caviar back, you know."

The Captain's nostrils flared; he leaned forward. "Guess we're not perfect android wind-ups like you guys," he shot back.

Merker was keen to realize his caustic dig had detonated a nuclear warhead under Nicholson's chair. He took a deep breath. "The scuttlebutt is you guys have a profiler already. But if you like, Captain, I could set up a video conference with Newman. She's one of the best we have on serials, especially ones involving male victims. 'Course, it'd be better if you could send your people here."

"If this... this Newman person is such an expert, send her to L.A. You guys have a bigger budget than we do."

"No can do. You'd have to wait a month or two... maybe even longer. She's got her hands full."

"You telling me with all the FBI's manpower and resources, you can't spare one damn skirt for a few days? What's her real job anyway?"

Merker clenched his teeth tightly and leaned back in his chair. "Every now and then, Captain, I hear that kind of sexist crap around here too. Look, take a pill or something. I'll get this off to you," Merker mouthed the word *sonofabitch*.

Nicholson started to respond, when he heard the phone slam down in his ear. Merker slapped the folder shut, tossed it aside and resumed sipping his coffee. This was only the most recent example of the often-strained relationship between the FBI and the LAPD. Lately, it had become the rule rather than the exception. On some cases, the LAPD had elected to not consult the FBI at all.

These tiffs were taking place much too often, considering both organizations presumably shared the same objectives. Previous negative revelations about the FBI lab in Washington had not helped matters. Neither had a recent DUI arrest of a Bureau agent in Hollywood. The

twenty-year veteran agent was not shown any of the customary professional courtesies. He was given a field sobriety test, which he failed,
and was arrested. Adding further embarrassment, he was detained at
the scene until TV news cameras arrived.

Presently, the antipathy posed a real danger. People were being
murdered. Professionalism and decency demanded everyone concerned do the jobs they swore to do. Seconds after hanging up, the Captain regretted his tone with Merker, for about a minute. He thought of
calling back and apologizing but did not.

Fourteen
Neo-"Nutzi" Vermin

RAMPART DETECTIVE'S BUREAU - *"If he's stupid," Gerald whispered.*

Homicide Detective,

Sergeant. Gerald K. Li (GK), 6'-5", 42, a powerful but gentle man with a ready smile, sat working at his pea-green government surplus desk. The UCLA economics grad found himself surrounded by USC alums, but was a forgiving sort.

Li would never admit it, but he felt out of place there, viewed with suspicion by some. Not because he was not an honest, straight-laced cop who believed in the oath he took, but *because* he was all those things. There were others like him, but they tended to look the other way.

The busy, cramped, Homicide Detectives quarters at Rampart Division was a hellhole—a madhouse. It wasn't as bad as it once was but it was not state of the art either. Aesthetically, the facility looked much better from the outside. The effects of the scandal that had wracked the division in '99 were evident in the conversations of good cops who felt betrayed by rogue officers. Despite encouraging comments by those in the immediate community, it was clear, all had been tarred by the same brush.

Sergeant Li loved his work at Rampart. He had been there almost five years. About 360 police personnel protected and served nearly 400,000 inhabitants in an area roughly eight square miles. That's a density that about equals Manhattan Island. Few denied it was one of the busiest police stations in the country. Even into the new millennium, other adjectives were being used.

Inside the station, citizens, officers, suspects and lawyers formed an eclectic processional, all engaged in a strange social dance set to an even stranger symphony of voices, telephones, footsteps and slamming doors. Elsewhere, this would be bedlam. Here, it was routine.

Detective Sergeant Li was an experienced, dedicated officer... father of two. Like most good cops, he had worked hard to get where he was. A thoughtful and intensely private man, Li managed to erect a wall between his professional and private lives. He had few friends, and liked it that way. One exception was John Roméo, with whom he had enjoyed a genuine friendship for seven years. John's departure from the LAPD had not lessened that friendship.

Gerald lifted his phone's receiver and began dialing. Jake Brandt, a fellow detective—outfitted in his customary frumpy beige suit with coffee-stained Dallas Cowboy necktie, loose at the collar— approached with a manila folder. He reached Gerald's desk, looked around cautiously, slipped it under a stack of papers atop his desk.

Gerald glanced up, winked, and completed dialing. He waited for an answer, cupping his right hand over the mouthpiece as Brandt leaned forward.

"I know he's watching me give this to you. I'll bet you five seconds after I walk away, he'll be over here to give you a hard time," he whispered.

"If he's stupid," Gerald replied.

"He is."

Gerald grinned. Brandt walked away.

Inside John's bedroom, the phone rang again. He frowned and snatched it from the lamp table. Aimee, still in her thong, returned to the room with a silver platter, laden with snacks and soft drinks.

"Roméo," John answered.

"Did I get you out of bed?" Asked Gerald.

John turned to sit on the edge of the bed. "C'mon. Is it really that obvious?"

"Aimee, right?"

"I'm impressed. You must be a detective or something. What's on your feeble brain, besides the obvious?"

Gerald hesitated, as a thin, ghost-white, pimpled, freckled-faced detective approached, wearing a smirk, and with a wad of chewing gum bulging in his jaw. He plopped down onto the corner of Gerald's desk, stared pointedly at him and began rifling the stack of folders on the desk. Gerald's jaws clenched. He turned eggplant-purple.

"Hold on!" Gerald told John, then covered the phone with one hand and turned to face the detective.

"What the hell can I do for you, Dennis?"

Sergeant Dennis flashed a twisted smile and glanced around, as if soliciting the attention and approval of those watching.

"I was sitting over there doing honest work and was distracted by the glare on your forehead," said Dennis. "Thought I'd come over to see what it was... see what's in that folder Jake slipped to you," he chuckled, again glancing around for approval.

Gerald, 240 pounds of muscle, was not amused. He uncovered the receiver and stood slowly, towering over the still seated Sergeant.

"Listen John, I'll get back to you."

Gerald eased the receiver into its cradle then moved toward Dennis. With officers and others looking on, he shoved him off the desk, onto the floor then stood astride him, pointing down angrily. Two other detectives rushed forward to restrain him and plead for calm. Gerald wheeled to face them. His menacing stare stopped them in their tracks.

"Keep your Aryan ass out of my space," he warned Dennis, in a cool, deliberate voice that belied his rage. "I'm not taking anymore shit from you or anyone else around here."

A hush fell over the entire area. Work came to a halt; conversations fell silent. Others rushed to the room for a better look, as Gerald stalked past them and down the hallway. Fellow officers gazed, with drooped jaws, at an embarrassed Dennis who struggled to his feet.

Fifteen
Rage: She Vs. He

"There you go with that victim crap,"

Deep frowns scarred John's brow.

His thoughts were divided between Aimee, the show, and Nicholson's impassioned pleas for help. He was not being coy or playing hard to get. Despite his flippant demeanor, the gory images of Sumner and his mistress still filled his head... had even crept into his sleep. John still was not sure he had the stomach for a long, protracted murder case just now, despite the challenge.

Aimee sensed John's preoccupation was with more than Peter Blaine's demands. She had not yet voiced concern but knew the man she loved would likely be drawn into a high profile murder case that could last for months.

Although she had only known John as a former detective, Aimee had little doubt their relationship would be seriously impacted. She had no desire to see him immerse himself, body and soul in the assignment.

Back at KCBC, a new segment had already started. The audience was responding derisively to hostile comments from Philip. By now, he had begun to grate on everyone, including the crew.

"I've listened to this crap," he railed. "It's hypocrisy. Like you said at the top of the show, my wife knew when she married me that I..."

"Excuse me!" Krystal interrupted, "I was only repeating what you'd said in pre-show interviews. But go on."

Krystal moved to within a few feet of Philip and stood with arms folded.

"And it's true," Philip went on, his voice rising. "She knew I loved women. In fact, I was in a relationship that I left for her. And I wasn't the kind of guy who would be with his wife and pretend not to look when a good-looking woman walked by. I got a good look!"

"But your problem wasn't...looking, or you wouldn't be here."

"I admit that."

"So what was it? Tell us the whole truth, Philip."

"Alright. The truth is my wife couldn't satisfy me. She knew I had other women on the side before I married her. I'm being honest."

"She knew about other women?"

"Right. And she never complained."

An angry woman in the audience yelled out at Philip. Krystal dashed up to hand her a microphone.

"Hold on. They can't hear you. Wait a sec."

Krystal reached the woman, who was standing, fuming, angrily pointing her finger.

"This guy's a jerk," she said. "Your problem is, all your thinking is done by the worm in your pants and not the brain in your head."

The audience hooted.

"That's what I was talking about before," Phillip yelled at the woman. "You don't know me or my wife. You jump up like some damn idiot, without knowing what the hell you're talking about."

"Philip!" Krystal yelled, determined to take control.

"Let me finish!" Philip yelled back, "I'm honest enough to sit here and tell all of you there was no way my wife didn't know. In fact, I think she got off on it. She knew she couldn't satisfy me, and she also knew I was going to get satisfaction. Her problem was she thought she could change me. You women do that. You bring it on yourselves. Face it!"

"Easy for you to sit here and paint this picture of your wife," said Krystal, "when she can't give us the other side. It's obvious to me your wife was a victim."

Philip threw up his hands and rolled his eyes. "There you go with that *victim* crap," he yelled. "You women would be lost without that word. My wife made herself a victim; she loved being a victim. It gave her something to feel sorry for herself about. It was something she could cry in her tea about, along with her fellow victims during their bitching sessions."

Krystal shook her head, with disgust. Suddenly, a petite, solemn-faced, woman in the fifth row stood up. Tears cascaded down her face. Philip's jaw dropped; he stared at the woman, his mouth agape.

Krystal moved toward her. "Yes. You wanted to say..."

The woman struggled to find her voice. "I'm... Annette, Philip's wife," she said weakly.

Krystal and her audience were dumbstruck. She turned toward the audience, then to Philip, then back to his wife, Annette. "You're Annette? Philip's wife?"

"Yes, I am. But I've filed for divorce," she said in a quivering voice. Philip's sudden silence was deafening.

Krystal turned toward him then back to the audience. "Please," she pleaded. "I had no idea this would happen. This is not a setup, and Annette, you will confirm this."

"Yes," Annette answered, weakly.

"This is completely unexpected," Krystal insisted. "We did contact Annette...asked if she would appear as a guest. She was very cordial, but declined." Annette nodded yes.

"Well, since you're here, would you like to tell us your side of the story?"

Annette began timidly, "I... I just," she faltered, dabbing her eyes with a white handkerchief. Philip raked both hands down his face.

"Take your time," Krystal said.

"I don't know... where to start, except to say that most of what Philip has said is a complete lie. That's the first thing."

"You're the liar," charged Philip.

"I suffered every form of humiliation during our marriage, but, I truly loved Philip. And I endured it, hoping things would change."

"That's a crock!" Philip shouted. "And I believe this *was* a setup!"

"Believe whatever you like," Krystal fired back then turned to Annette, placed an arm on her shoulder. "How long were you married, and when did Philip's infidelity begin?"

"Why don't you just ask her a *real* leading question?" Philip screamed.

"Stuff it or else!" Krystal warned.

The audience cheered, while Annette took a measured breath. She appeared even more nervous.

"We've been married eleven years. Philip began cheating, almost from the beginning. He was good to me before we were married."

"I was good to you afterwards, too. I tolerated your sick, neurotic behavior, your rampant paranoia, your damn frigidity, your phobias. I was damn good to you. I tolerated your lousy lovemaking too."

Tears filled Annette's eyes.

"How's that for being a devoted husband?" Philip continued. "And where's the broad that yelled at me? I want to make sure she understands this, and the rest of you, too."

Damning boos were unleashed. A visibly shaken Annette struggled to steady herself. Krystal tried to console her then leveled another caution. "Philip, if you don't mind, I believe this is still my show."

"And this is my life!" Philip fired back. "You invited *me* here, now let me talk. Without me you got no show, today."

"I beg your pardon?"

"And you should. My love loves this victim's role she's playing. Look at her! She's anorexic, too...maybe worse. It's just another way of getting attention and sympathy. And it works! You all are suckers for this crap."

Annette was in tears. "This man not only cheated on me, he was physically abusive and sadistic. He...."

"Liar!" Philip screamed. The veins in his neck popped out. "Tell the damn truth! It was your father who sexually abused you. It was your father who made you a frigid wreck unable to satisfy any real man."

"Philip!" Krystal shouted.

Philip ignored her. "Your old man! He's the one you should be directing your poison toward, not me, darling. That's why your mother left him. And don't start in with the damn tears! I've got tears too. All God's children's got tears," Philip screamed.

Philip's verbal barrage was brutal and unrelenting. Tears cascaded down Annette's face; she thrust both hands to her forehead. One man in the audience blurted out profanity at Philip. A defiant Philip grinned and waved his fist, mockingly.

With her head bowed, Annette slumped to her seat and collapsed her head into her lap, angered by Philip's outburst.

"You've said enough, Philip. We need a break here," Krystal said, turning toward the camera. "When we come back, we'll hear from the men in the audience, provided we can get them to talk."

Krystal had barely completed her sentence, when she was interrupted. A distraught Annette, who had appeared to it, suddenly leaped to her feet, clutching a chrome-plated .25 automatic. A chorus of screams erupted. Staff and audience dove for cover. Guests bolted, scrambling over furniture. In fractured seconds that followed, Annette grasped the gun with both hands, aimed at Philip. He sat frozen in place, transfixed, his lips parted to form some never spoken word. She squeezed, even as she closed her eyes, releasing a stream of bullets that tore into his forehead, his neck, his chest. Blood splattered. The rounds forced him backward, overturning his chair leaving him sprawled on the floor.

Chaos reigned. A chorus of screams reverberated. Krystal lay prone on the floor in the middle aisle, partially covered by a male guest who had shoved her down. Guests, technicians, cameramen bolted for cover. Annette emptied the clip and stood marbleized in the firing position—her arms fully extended, a look of disbelief registered on her face. Suddenly, a man from the audience leaped over three rows and grabbed her from behind, securing her in a bear hug. Uniformed security soon joined him. Two remote cameras had captured the entire event.

Seconds passed. A dazed Krystal was helped to her feet. A man identifying himself as a medical Doctor, dashed to the stage and examined Philip's motionless body. He was dead. The second bullet had ripped through his jugular. In the rear of the studio, stunned audience guests and panel members, were being escorted out by a reinforced contingent of security guards.

In John's bedroom, he and Aimee sat rock-still—rendered mute. Stunned, they sat on the edge of the bed facing the television. Aimee trembled; her eyes filled with tears that began streaming down her face. Just then, there was a cutaway to the newsroom of the local ABC affiliate. A shaken male and female news team had clearly rushed to get on air.

"Ladies and gentlemen, I'm Jan Steele along with Bruce Behren. If you were just watching the nationally syndicated Krystal Knight Show, along with millions of other Americans, we don't have to tell you what we have witnessed here—just a horrible, horrible tragedy." Jan struggled to compose herself. Bruce, in shirt-sleeves and open collar, was breathing heavily, struggling to project calm and professionalism.

John embraced Aimee. He could feel her tears streaming onto his shoulder. Her chest heaved with every sob. Soon, video replay of the incident appeared on the television screen. John quickly located the remote and switched it off.

Aimee tried to gather herself. She closed her eyes and covered her face with both hands. "I can't believe it," she whispered. John stroked her face gently. "I know," John whispered.

Aimee lay still, staring at the ceiling, tears still spilling. John grabbed a handful of tissues from the nightstand, dabbed her cheeks then lay quietly beside her, with her head nestled against his chest.

Sixteen
Requiem For a Fool

KCBC-TV 7PM - *".. here comes the Exalted Grand Dragon."*

From the elevated rear of the studio,

it hardly seemed possible that only a few hours earlier, a scene of panic and death was witnessed by tens of millions. At the front, near the middle of the second row, John and Gerald sat talking in subdued tones. They were all that remained of homicide investigators, the coroner's team, and a horde of media. Several feet away, three khaki-clad studio employees were busy trying to remove blood from the carpet where Philip had fallen.

John was in jeans, T-shirt and sneakers, both feet supported on the rear of the chair in front of him. Gerald was slouched next to him, fingers laced under his chin. After the shooting, Gerald called his friend again, and asked him to meet him at the studio.

"How's Aimee?" He asked.

"Still upset. I finally got her to fall asleep before I left. She's in shambles. She takes everything to heart... stray dogs, cats, wounded birds, the homeless, plight of the manatees. That's the way she is."

"Something like this was bound to happen," said Gerald. "Still, I don't understand how a gun got past the metal detectors."

A long silence: The two watched the workers' desperate attempt to remove the bloodstains. It was not working.

"The way this happened kinda reminds me of what my ol' man once told me about that day Ruby shot Oswald in Dallas," Gerald said. "Ruby came out of nowhere and...kaboom! That was it. I've only seen the old, grainy black and white film."

Less than an hour after the shooting, and against her attorney's advice, Krystal spoke with KCBC anchor Bruce Behren. She expressed horror and shock, and reiterated her denial that the confrontation had been staged. Already, media critics were attacking like sharks smelling blood, blasting Krystal, specifically, and talk shows in general.

Cursing aloud, the two workers covered the carpet with a thick pink liquid poured from a large plastic jug. They resumed running the power scrubber over the affected areas. Yet, despite their efforts, the stubborn stains remained visible from where John and Gerald sat.

"As heated as some of these shows get, you had to wonder where the edge was," said Gerald.

"What are you and Dennis doing on this one?" John asked.

"Dennis?"

"Your buddy."

Gerald looked at his friend with a pained expression.

"What the hell is there to do? The asshole was supposed to be here an hour ago. We've got the videotape; we've got a more than probable suspect... few million witnesses. The whole world's seen the replay at least a hundred times already, and the dead guy's balls are probably still warm. Even Dennis can figure this one out."

Gerald's tone regarding Sergeant Dennis came as no surprise to John. He was aware of Dennis' talent for making enemies.

"He still knawing on your ass every chance he gets?" Asked John."

"I don't think he wants to chew on this black ass any more. As for this case, he requested the lead on it. I should say...begged for it, He saw it was a slam-dunk, sucked some ass. You know how he is."

"I know," said John. "What's his problem?"

"Who knows? Some think he went south, after that Times story came out, two years ago about him being adopted."

"And that his biological father is of German-Jewish descent."

"Right. According to the story, was never told he was adopted. The whole story grew out of rumors that there was a small clique of neo-Nazi sympathizers and wannabes within the department."

"Yeah, rumor."

"I noticed the Chief stayed out the whole thing. Never answered a single question about his nephew...actually, his adopted nephew."

"Can you blame him?"

"Hell, no." Both laughed.

The remaining workers gathered their buckets, brushes, the rickety shampooer and left.

"What about you?" Gerald asked?

"What about me?"

"Two years from now, am I gonna be paying eight dollars to watch some movie you've written about this crap?"

"I doubt it. I'm more curious about these double murder cases you guys are banging your heads against," said John.

"Look, there's something I've been meaning to say."

John turned to face his friend squarely. "Since when are you reluctant to say anything to me?"

"It's about your..."

"My divorce?"

"I wasn't sure about the right time to bring it up."

"Any time's as good as any other."

"Sorry the two of you couldn't work things out. You seemed... so perfect. You two belonged together just like..."

"Like Romeo and Juliet?" John chuckled. Gerald grinned.

"We both know it's tough on wives, being married to cops, but you had already walked away from all this crap."

"It was more than that. It's hard to explain. We still have a hard time understanding what went wrong. But we both came to realize it wasn't working. We still cared deeply for each other but it wasn't working. I sometimes wonder if we gave up too quickly. That's the thing about divorce. Afterwards, depending on the kind of marriage you had, you wonder if you gave up too quickly. You wonder if perhaps you should have tried even harder to make things work."

"You think you did... give up too quickly?"

"I don't know."

"You guys still love each other?"

"I don't allow myself to ask that question. One thing though: Claire always wanted kids. And you know why that was not something I wanted to deal with. We talked about it before we were married and I felt we agreed. But after a few years, and the closer she got to forty, Claire suddenly had this burning desire to be a mother—to give birth."

"That's not unnatural. In fact it's very natural."

"I know. And I wasn't against being a parent. I just didn't want to... father any children. I wanted to adopt."

"You told her?"

"Yeah. We talked about it. We even made the right contacts and everything. Then, she changed her mind. But don't get me wrong; I don't think this thing about kids was the deciding factor in our break-up. I'm still trying to figure it all out."

"Claire alright?"

"She's alright. We still talk. It's only been three and a half months."

"What about Aimee?"

"She's fine... goes through changes whenever Claire calls but she deals with it. I sometimes feel I jumped into that relationship too soon. Should have waited a while... let the emotions swirling around my divorce settle down."

"What now?"

"This may shock you."

"Shock me."

"I'm still thinking about adopting. Not right away, though. Maybe in a year or so."

"You're serious?"

"I want to be a father. And I think I would make a very good father."

"You still spend time with Benjy."

"When I can. It's hard to go see the little guy, then leave him—drive away. He stands there looking at me like... like I'm never coming back. I reassure him, but it's hard on both of us. Here's a recent picture."

John took out his wallet and handed a photo to Gerald. The picture was of a 6 year-old with smiling eyes, a missing front tooth, and wearing a Dodger baseball uniform. John beamed like a proud father.

"Handsome guy, huh?" He said, boastfully.

Benjamin Robinson, a six year old foster child lived with a wonderful, elderly foster couple in South, L.A.. Three years earlier, Benjy's parents were both killed leaving a New Year's Eve Party in Compton. Benjamin's extended family was either unable or unwilling to care for him.

The case was never solved. John vowed he would find the killer or killers whether he was on the force or not, and no matter how long it took. He still maintained that vow. He renewed it every time he visited Benjy, who would begin first grade in September. John became visibly moved, every time he talked about him. Today was no different.

"Benjy's a great kid. You two look like father and son. I've been meaning to tell you that. You plan on getting married again?"

"No way. No time soon. But that doesn't keep me from adopting a son."

"I know. It's just that... what about Aimee?"

"I care a lot for Aimee. And I'm not misleading her. We give each other what we want and need right now. Neither of us has made any promises. I'm thinking long-term... about my life, where I want it to go. I want a son. And it has nothing to do with some male ego about progeny. I love kids. That's why I'm involved with Boys and Girls Club, Scouting, visit Juvenile Hall, all that. I feel I have something to offer. And as much as Benjy needs me, I think I need him even more."

"I agree with all that."

"Hey! What are we doing?" Asked John.

"What do you mean?"

"I mean, we're sitting here relating, discussing marriage, family, kids, emotions, and there's not a woman in sight. Men don't talk about these kinds of things. That's what they say, and certainly not to other men, right?"

"I know. Where are Krystal and Oprah when you need 'em?"

Several times during their far-ranging conversation, Gerald thought to ask his friend how he was coping with the tragic death of his longtime partner, Keith Langhorne. He struggled to find the suitable moment but decided to not ask.

For a cop, losing a partner often meant a lifetime of self-blame, anger and even shame. Despite the fact Gerald knew John Roméo to be a resilient person, there was little doubt his friend was confronting some, if not all those inescapable emotions.

The double doors at the rear of the studio flew open. Gerald turned to see Sergeant Dennis, and a uniformed officer; he nudged John.

"Don't look now, but here comes the Exalted Grand Dragon."

"You mean, Ze Furhrer."

"Either one. Only thing missing is the hood," Gerald joked.

John glanced over his shoulder and turned back with a grin.

"We're up to eight stiffs now," said Gerald. "Four men, four women... m.o. is almost identical in all of them. Personally, I think it's a single shooter. The heat's building 'cause the men were all well-known, well-connected... big names. Truth is, we're not making much headway. It's frustrating as hell. Task force members are bitching 'mongst them- selves. 'Course you know 'bout all that intramural bullshit. Anyway, we haven't produced any clear results yet. You've probably already talked to Nicholson, right?"

John didn't answer. The conversation abruptly halted, as Sgt. Dennis and the officer reached them. Dennis had a weasel smile plastered across his pockmarked face, both hands dug into the pockets.

"Well, well. Sergeant Li and homicide detective emeritus, John "John" Roméo," Dennis said, sarcastically, "Can't stay away from my crime scenes, huh Roméo?"

John lowered his feet and leaned forward, stretching both arms across the back of the chair in front of him. "To be honest, I wanted the rare experience of being present at the scene of a crime you may actually have a snowball's chance of solving. I even postponed sex for this."

Dennis' smile evaporated; his eyes narrowed. John knew he had drawn blood. The officer accompanying Dennis appeared shocked, yet amused; he suppressed a grin. Sergeant. Dennis swallowed hard and turned red.

"Postponed sex? I'm sorry to keep your mother waiting."

John sprang forward, grabbed Dennis' neck with both hands, began choking him, flailing him like a rope. Dennis' eyes bulged, he chortled, struggled to breathe. Gerald moved to intervene, though less than forcefully. He had never seen his friend so angry. He pleaded with him, finally persuaded him to release his death grip. Dennis gasped, coughed violently, massaged his throat as he struggled to breathe.

"You crazy... crazy, damn sonofabitch," he managed. "John's mother is dead, you dumb ass," said Gerald.

John glared at Dennis, surprised that he hadn't drawn his 9mm and shot the bastard instead. "Now I understand why your wife left your redneck ass for another woman," he said. "After living with a pussy like you all these years, she decided she wanted the real thing."

Dennis' nostrils flared; his eyes squinted. "I expected you to be down at lockup, shoving a contract in front of the suspect for rights to her story," he sniped, too stupid to quit while he still had a chance.

Gerald was thoroughly enjoying the verbal jousting, despite his mild protests to the contrary. John glared at Dennis before turning to walk away. He stepped into the aisle, brushed past Dennis without looking at him. Dennis was livid.

"I'm outta here. See you in district four tomorrow, after my class," John told Gerald.

Their camaraderie angered a fuming Dennis. He wheeled around to watch John's departure. "You...you...you think you're some goddamn bigshot... some fuckin' prima donna. The LAPD doesn't need you to solve a goddamn thing! You're overrated Romeo. You hear me?"

John thrust his right middle finger into the air; never turned around, never broke stride.

Dennis lost it. "We don't need a damn outsider," he yelled, spewing spit. "You ain't all that, you know." Dennis kicked a nearby chair anchored to the floor. Gerald doubled over laughing, as the Sergeant hobbled in pain. The uniformed cop even snickered. Gerald called out for John to wait, and started after him. Neither had any idea the day would get even more bizarre.

Seventeen
The Beauty in Black – 'Bootylicious'

"Wesley Snipes never looked this good."

Rizzo's Sports Bar was filled with music, hot bodies,

and raucous laughter. John and Gerald sat at the horseshoe-shaped bar downing Dos Equis beer and verbally abusing Dennis in his absence. John's cell kept going off. He checked the number, didn't recognize the sender. After the fourth call, he turned the phone off. The Bartender and owner Phil Rizzo—a burly former LAPD hopeful, in his late for-ties—set new rounds in front of his two friends.

"So what's the big case?" Asked Phil.

"What big case?" Gerald stared him down.

"Alright, don't make me get the rubber hose," Phil joked. "When-ever 'youse' two show up together, I know something big is brewing."

Gerald and John laughed off Rizzo's suggestion; Phil moved on. The killing at KCBC consumed most of the pair's conversation. Not far from where they sat, a blonde—dressed in a black dress, black hat, black lace gloves, and a thin, black veil—sat watching them   intently.

She inched closer and closer, eyes riveted. Both noticed her. The woman's gaze fixed on John.

"You were saying," Gerald prompted.

"I forgot."

The woman stood and started toward them. Just then, a news story on the bar TV caught their attention.

"Turn that up, Phil," said Gerald. Phil cranked up the volume.

A middle-aged man in black suit and cleric collar was at a bank of microphones in front of LA City Hall. The graphic identified him as the Reverend Thomas Baswell, a media-labeled 'kook' unassociated with any religion anyone could determine. Gerald and John recognized him. He once attempted to start a defense fund for Sergeant Bolen. His influence in the white supremacist movement, was owed to his ability to raise money, and to garner public attention.

"I have made no secret of my abhorrence of the role government, especially the federal government, plays in our lives. But this is different. I also believe in the strict interpretation of Judaeo-Christian principles. To that end, I must say that no tears should be shed for those who violate the sanctity of marriage and commit adultery. The wages of sin are death."

"What about murder?" Shouted a questioner.

"Are you talking about abortionists?"

"I'm talking about those who murder in violation of the law. The last I looked abortion was legal."

"You sound like an advocate."

"I'm asking a question. Will you answer it?"

"I thought I did. I'll repeat myself for those of you who are apparently hearing-challenged. The wages of sin are death. Adultery is sin. That's not Thomas Baswell's words, the Bible says so...the Christian Bible. And if anyone is ever arrested and charged for upholding God's word, we will, as usual, provide both legal and financial assistance."

"You support serial murder?" Someone yelled from off-camera. Baswell ignored the question. The reporter repeated the question. Baswell turned and walked away.

The anchor overrode the field report, concluding the segment. Phil lowered the volume. Gerald turned to John. "We owe him a visit," he said. John nodded.

"Excuse me," the veiled woman said, after taking the seat next to John and waiting for an opening. She had watched the news segment and was again focused on him. "You're Wesley Snipes, aren't you?"

Gerald loosed one of his patented belly laughs. John was taken off guard. "You're kidding!" He said. "Wesley Snipes is shorter, far less sexy, and has never looked this good. Who're you and what's with the veil? You been to a funeral or something?"

"Or something," the woman answered. "But, that's not fair. I asked your name first. What's your name?"

"Gerald Li."

Gerald flinched, pounded John's shoulder with his fist.

"What's *your* name?" John repeated.

"Call me Elizabeth."

"As in... Taylor?"

"No, as in Queen."

John and Gerald exchanged quick glances.

"You look very married, Gerald," the woman leaned closer to John and frowned. What are you doing here in a place like this? You should be at home with your wife."

"Excuse me?"

"You should be home with your wife, instead of in some bar trying to pick up strange women. I'm going to pray for you... pray that you atone for your sins," she said.

John was both amused and puzzled.

"Good-bye, Gerald," the woman stood, and left as abruptly as she had appeared. John riveted his eyes on the woman's swaying rear end as she disappeared into the crowd.

Gerald's mouth was wide open. "What the hell was that?"

John shrugged. Both gulped the rest of their drinks and tried to figure out which sanitarium the woman had escaped from. Still, something about her, other than her body, caught John's eye. Despite   the veil, he could see she was very attractive, mysterious, and definitely strange. But what the hell, this was L.A.

Gerald stood, got Phil's attention. "Phil. That woman with the veil... you see her in here before?"

Phil stepped closer. She's been in here three or four times before tonight...always with the veil. She sits at the bar for a couple of hours, nurses two Wild Turkeys and Coke; never moves. She's a heavy tipper, though. Guys try to pick her up, but she never gives 'em two seconds. Tonight is the first time she's made a move on somebody. Guess she's got a thing for cops."

"Like she knew we were cops," said Gerald.

"Everybody here knows you guys are cops," Phil said, laughing. "It's your aftershave and cheap suits."

Eighteen
First Glance

John's heart raced; he could not keep his eyes off her.

Aimee, wearing a black silk negligee,

sat brushing her nearly shoulder-length hair. Music streamed from the recessed, ceiling speakers. She gazed into the mirror, lost in thought, staring, searching for something. Her solemn mood was in sharp contrast to the playful one exhibited earlier. Now, she wished John had convinced her not to watch Krystal's show.

Aimee glanced into the mirror again and smiled. John entered the room with one hand held behind his back. He approached her, leaned forward, kissed the nape of her neck.

"Close your eyes," he whispered.

Aimee closed her eyes. John lifted his right hand, clutching a diamond-cluster, heart pendant necklace, and placed it around her neck.

"Open your eyes."

Aimee did so, and gasped. She wheeled around, grasping the necklace.

"John. It's beautiful."

"Not as beautiful as you," he whispered.

Aimee blushed, covered her face with both hands. John kissed her neck again. She stood, thrust both arms around him, and they embraced and kissed. John's thoughts turned to the first time the two met.

It was in France, on a postcard-summer day, a little over six months earlier. John sat under an umbrella, sipping wine at a sidewalk cafe, just off the Rue De Flandre in Paris. He had gone to France to get away, clear his head and maybe do a little research for a new book. A year earlier, he and Claire had separated. Aimee and several female, and male friends sat at a short distance away. Their eyes met; they exchanged fleeting smiles.

And both may have been content to leave it at that. However, moments later, John looked up to see her peering at him through the lens of a small camera. He saw the flash go off and began striking contorted faces. Aimee broke up but continued snapping until the last exposure. Then, to the consternation of a young man seated next to her, Aimee rose and started for John's table. As she approached, he took in her loveliness, savoring the sight of her, and wondering what would happen next. She had to be a model, he thought. Her poise, her beauty, her grace were striking. John's heart raced; he could not keep his eyes off her. He glanced over his shoulder, thinking it possible her attention had been focused elsewhere. He feared making a colossal ass of himself.

Aimee reached John's table, asked if she could join him. He said yes. "You owe me a roll of film," she said. He laughed. She continued, declaring it was his irresistible charm that had seduced her. Further, she explained she had used all her film on him. John found her argument persuasive and agreed to amends. It was the least he could do.

Over the next three days, Aimee joined him at his villa, as did a number of her friends. It was the most excitement the place had seen ever. As fate would have it, both were scheduled to take the Concorde to New York the following week, on Bastille Day. Aimee had a major fashion show, and John was scheduled to appear on the   Today Show to promote his latest novel. The two spent a week together in The 'Big Apple.' Three months later, John and Claire's divorce was final. He and Aimee had been together ever since.

John was certain his relationship with Aimee was not a result of some 'rebound' from his divorce; she was not a quick and needed replacement for the emptiness Claire left. He could not deny he still cared deeply for Claire. But Aimee was more than an arresting beauty with a killer body wrapped in youthful exuberance. She possessed unassuming grace, extraordinary intellect and incorruptible honesty.

John found Aimee physically and emotionally stimulating in a way he had not known before. Modeling was by no means her sole interest. Her love of photography and her talent as a photographer were evident. The photo-art community recognized the gallery quality of her work. Much of her work adorned John's home. Theirs was not a passing moment.

Nineteen
Holes in Two

Two Days Later — *"Sure you can take it?"*

The full moon cast a platinum glow.

For a brief moment, all seemed well with the world. John and Aimee were on the second floor balcony, sharing a love-lounger, sipping a Chardonnay, basking in the moonlight, and listening to jazz CDs. Following two earlier annoying calls from Peter Blaine, John tossed his bedroom phone into the closet. However, before Blaine's interruptions, two new anonymous calls followed an established pattern.

Two nights earlier, after leaving Rizzo's, John told Gerald about the calls. Gerald suggested a phone tap. "Skeeter could take care of it," he suggested. John, first cool to the idea, was now seriously considering it. Something in his gut told him someone had the long knives out, and he was clearly the target.

Less than ten minutes away from John's balcony retreat, several luxury cars lined the entry leading into the posh Hillcrest Country Club, near Beverly Hills. Inside the lavishly appointed dining area, members and guests savored their dinners and the ambiance. The sanguine music, rendered by an *almost* live band, flowed through and beyond the main facility.

Far from the main country club complex, Mike Gregg, 30, dressed in a hounds-tooth sport coat and dark slacks, walked hand-in-hand with Mia, a young vixen with obvious assets. She was breathtaking, all bound up in a skintight, dark green leather mini-dress, three inch heels, and a tan leather waist-jacket.

Mia was bubbly and effervescent. Her infectious laughter split the night air, as the two made their way toward the second green. Mike had no idea where he was headed, but was determined to follow Mia.

The main building was still visible; the music could be heard, though only faintly. Mia was having difficulty with her heels sinking into the turf, but was undaunted. She released Mike's hand and moved ahead of him, backpedaling and beckoning playfully. She removed her shoes and dangled one in each hand.

"You're crazy," Mike laughed.

"Lana would never dream of doing this with you, right?"

"You had to mention her name."

A discussion of his wife was not what Mike had in mind. All he wanted was Mia's legs in the air and her bikini panties past her ankles; that is if she were wearing any.

"C'mon. Loosen up. Don't be so stuffy. You're with me, baby."

Mia's voice was purring and sultry; she tugged upward on her skirt, revealing her bikini panties. Mike was already throbbing. Mia broke into a fast walk; he hurried to catch up. Both soon reached the green. Mike drew her to him, seized her; embraced her passionately. They kissed wildly. Darting tongues alternately filled the other's mouth. Mia's purse slipped from her shoulder to the ground. The two groped each other feverishly. Mia backed away.

"You're crazy," said Mike, panting.

"Yeah, I am...and you love it."

"Damn right." Both were breathing heavily.

"I know I'm crazy."

"You look so sexy in moonlight."

"Let's stop talking. I'm already wet," said Mia. "Do me, Mikie. Do me. Do me."

The two began stripping, tossing their clothes in a heap onto the green. The air was cool but neither noticed nor cared. Mia grabbed both Mike's hands and led him to the middle of the green, near the cup. He quickly retrieved his jacket and rejoined her. Mike looked on as Mia lowered herself onto the jacket and eased onto her back.

"Ooh!"

"Cold?"

"Yeah. I need some fire."

Mike ripped off his boxer shorts and dropped to his knees in front of her.

"Show me how much you want me," she whispered, reaching for him. " Show me... show me, baby. Hmm... awww."

"Sure you can take it?" Asked Mike, pausing, touching her with his fullness, backing away, teasing her before slipping easily inside her. He immediately felt a warm wet, suctioning, a irresistible drawing-in that urged him on.

"Is it mine, Mikie? Tell me it's mine. Tell me!"

"Mike could only groan. He slipped both hands underneath Mia, forcing her upward. She clung to him like Velcro. Awareness of their surroundings evaporated.

Just then, a silhouetted figure in dark clothing looked on, waiting just off the green, near the rough. In near darkness, he slipped his left hand slowly down to his crotch and began massaging himself as he looked on. Moments later, he began a steady, stealthy approach toward the green.

Sounds of uninhibited lovemaking grew louder. Mike and Mia were lost in each other; nothing else mattered. She wrapped both legs around his back, rose rhythmically with his repeated thrusts. The silent stalker paused briefly then moved closer, stopping nearly halfway to the hole.

The lovemaking grew more intense; the vivid love language more explicit.

Mike responded with even more powerful thrusts. He gasped for breath, eyes shut. Both were steamy with perspiration. The stalker raised his right hand, gripping the .44 Magnum.

Mike felt himself explode inside Mia, even as she dug her fingers into his butt, forcing him deeper. Her nails sank into his skin but he felt no pain. He forced himself on, despite his emotional plunge.

The stalker took a deep breath. An audible pop. A vicious recoil. Mike collapsed forward. His dead weight crushed against his lover.

"Mike?" Mia mumbled, startled by his sudden stillness.

The killer stepped forward, as a puzzled Mia struggled to rise, to free herself. A second blast ripped into her forehead, slamming her backwards. Then silence, except for the eerie strain of music streaming from the Hillcrest Country Club.

Twenty
Hall of Infamy

Two uniformed LAPD officers

held a boisterous contingent of media at bay. The gaggle was unrelenting, insisting upon access to the golf course. At the head of the pack, a KCBC TV news reporter vainly pleaded her case.

"Why don't you let us in? Ever hear of freedom of the press?"

The young officer struggled to stay calm. "We've got strict orders to keep everyone out," he explained. "The Lieutenant will give the word when he's ready. I'll pass it on to all of you. You all know how this works. Those folks out there are going to be dead for quite a while."

John arrived in his restored, blue and white, 1957 Chevy. 'Fifties Oldies' poured from the radio. He noticed the throng and eased to a stop a short distance from the Country Club entrance. Wearing a jogging suit and well-worn sneakers, he leaped from the car, dashed toward the police lines, and was quickly ushered through. He continued past a group of detectives, SID (Scientific Investigations Division) investigators and a team from the Coroner's office. When he reached the green, he stepped underneath the barricade tape and was confronted by Detective Dennis.

"Hold it, Romeo. Where the hell you think you're going?"

John gazed past his nemesis at the covered corpses lying on the green. Several uniformed officers and investigators were methodically gathering clothing, tagging each piece, securing them in evidence bags.

"I expected to see Lt. Medrano here. You worm your way onto this case too?" Asked John.

"Never mind the small talk. What are you doing here?"

John stepped to within a few inches of Dennis face. "Listen, I'm not the enemy, you asshole. What's your problem? You can pull this crap on Sergeant Li 'cause he's a nice guy. He has a high tolerance for bullshit. I, on the other hand, will shoot your ass."

Before Dennis could respond, John moved past him toward Lieutenant Paul Medrano. The tall, lanky, affable 55 year-old stood several yards away. Dennis looked on with contempt.

"John. Good to see you," said Medrano. "Hope you haven't had breakfast. If you have, you're gonna' lose it."

"What the hell have we got here, Paul?"

Lieutenant Medrano, a tall, thin, fit, well groomed man with short hair, graying sides, and not an ounce of visible body-fat, had a slight tic that frequently caused his top lip to twitch.

A product of East, Los Angeles, Lieutenant Medrano had the unconditional respect of top brass and street cops. He had a reputation for being soft-spoken but firm. Everyone paid attention whenever he spoke.

Medrano pointed toward the covered victims lying side by side on the green. Darkened blood appeared in two large, distinct areas. He and John approached. Medrano retracted the heavy zippers on the thick plastic body bags, allowing John to examine the victims.

"Damn dirty business," said Medrano.

"That's an understatement."

"No, I mean dirtier than when you left us, if you can believe that."

"Is that possible?"

"More than possible. It's a reality. You recognize this guy?" Asked Medrano, folding back the plastic cover even farther. "Of course the exit took out most of his frontal. Shot came from behind him somewhere over there." Lieutenant Medrano pointed toward the edge of the green, several yards away.

"Damn."

"Had one head buried in her, the other one blown to hell," said Medrano.

"I guess.   What we got... .44 again?"

"Yeah. We found one round, so far," said Medrano. "Probably used a silencer. No one inside the main building, or in the area, reported hearing anything. But we're still interviewing. We're also trying to get a list of patrons who were here last night."

"Good luck."

"You think you've seen it all then wham, reality check."

John nodded.

"Guess who," said Medrano.

"Don't have a clue."

John took another look at the man, a long gaze at the woman. He stood, shook his head. The Coroner's team began transferring Mia's body to the van.

Medrano moved closer to John. "Mike Gregg. The guy's Mike Gregg. Ain't that a bitch?"

"Mike Gregg? The Mike Gregg...the baseball player?"

"The one and only," said Medrano. "The media's gonna go nuts."

"Gregg? You're kidding."

Medrano shook his head no. "Wish the hell I was."

The two turned away from the area to tour the perimeter of the murder scene. Medrano stopped suddenly, knelt to examine an obscure object embedded in the grass. He picked it up, stood, examined the broken tee and tossed it.

"Guy's a cinch for the hall of fame," said Medrano.

"You mean, he was," John corrected him.

"Best pure hitter I ever saw. Lifetime .319... vacuum cleaner at 3rd base, five-time golden glove, top RBI man, clutch hitter to any part of the field. He was born and raised in Van Nuys. Only spent a year in AAA ball. He had the gift. He sure as hell had the gift. Damn shame!"

"What the hell was he doing in L.A. screwing some bimbo in the middle of a golf course? His team in town this week?"

"Yeah. They open a three game series with the Angels tomorrow night. The girl was either a, a damn hooker... girlfriend or something," Medrano speculated. "I didn't know people did things like this on golf courses. I must be getting old. I've been married thirty years. When me and my wife were dating, the most adventurous we got was stealing kisses in a dark theater."

"Right. By the way, it's, 'sex-worker,' not hooker. It's demeaning now. And isn't he married?"

"Yeah, he is. So? The word's demeaning"

"I seem to remember something about an affair he had a few years ago. It made all the newspapers... talk shows," said John.

"I remember that. The wife's the one I feel for—her and their two kids. This is gruesome crap, ol' buddy. And, like I said, when the media gets a hold of this in a few minutes, they're gonna go bonkers. They like this kinda stuff. They've been raising hell all morning... wanted to get in here before the bodies stopped twitching."

"Anything leap out at you?"

"Keep this under your hat. There was a wig and a fake womb broom. Apparently Gregg was wearing it to disguise himself. You figure if a guy has to do all that, bells should go off in his head. You gotta know you're doing some wrong shit."

"Anything else? The usual?"

"Pretty much, including a copy of one of your paperbacks. We also found a baseball and a CD. We'll listen to the CD later, but based on the other cases, I think I know what's on it."

"A baseball? CD?"

Medrano nodded yes, turned toward Dennis and beckoned, as the coroner's vehicles pulled away.

"This guy's a real suck ass," Medrano whispered, as Dennis approached.

"I know."

Dennis reached them and positioned himself squarely between the two, his back turned to John.

"Yessir, Lieutenant," said Dennis. John snickered. "Open the gates for the news hounds," said Medrano.

Dennis nodded, grabbed a two-way from a uniformed officer and hurried away.

"Why all the inside scoop?" Asked John.

"I figured since you're back on the payroll, I might as well..."

"You've lost me."

"Cute, John. I talk to the Captain every day. We need your help on this one. Our nuts are in the microwave and this just might push the *roast* button. Captain wants you to help us out... perform some of your magic."

"I'm no Houdini, right? Besides, timing is bad. I'm busy as hell. I've got..."

"What about your civic pride, all for one, Semper Fi?"

"What's that got to do with anything? You guys haven't had very good press lately. I'm not sure I want to risk my hard-won, stellar reputation," John said with a wink.

"You putting us down?"

"Seriously, I've got a full plate."

"You know how persuasive the Captain can be. Lookit, I'd better wrap this up. I'll talk to you," said Medrano, with a slap on the back. He excused himself.

Sgt. Dennis stood a few feet away, speaking with a uniformed officer. John's cell phone rang. Dennis turned toward him. It was Nicholson.

Dennis' eyes bulged, his ears perked. He stared, as John started away and headed toward his car. Several yards away, he watched Roméo pass the oncoming herd of media. The throng unleashed a barrage of questions at him. He waved them off and kept walking.

Twenty-one
All Aboard?

Nicholson sat scowling.

John was slumped in a chair in front of him. The Captain wore his *game face* but John had seen it before. Nicholson dragged his hands over his face, slurped his coffee, lowered the mug with a thud.

"We've got to get a handle on this...progress we can point to quickly, like in three weeks."

"What does that mean? Sounds like a public relations problem. That's not my game. I go where the trail leads, that's it."

"It's not my game either."

"Right. I forget you're just a part of the pipeline. Right?"

"Right. Wish I could separate my division from the political crap that goes on around here. I really do."

"Then do it."

"Wish I could. But the goal is to have some progress to report. And don't worry about the task force," said Nicholson.

"What about the task force?"

"I only mention it to let you know you'll have complete access to them and their files. But you won't cross swords in any way. We'll do it the way we always have. I promise."

John gave Nicholson a curious look.

"Why are you looking at me like I'm just sitting here pissing in the wind?" Asked Nicholson.

There was plenty John wanted to say but he held back. Aimee would have been proud.

"You think it's a lone killer?" John shifted the conversation.

"We don't know that."

"You must have some clue."

"Of course, we've got clues...more hunches than clues. Some of them point in that direction, as you'll see. The problem is a lack of suspects."

"What about the FBI's theory that it could be the so-called *Westbound killer*. You given up on that one?"

"I never embraced that crap. But I can't give up on anything. What bothers me is the fact that after the guy was tracked to Phoenix, there have been no more killings with the same m.o., not like those before. Of course, I'm basing that on what little we've gotten from the FBI. I'm no forensic psychologist, but I can't see a serial killer changing his m.o. based on what state he's in. But then, Sam Talon and his mistress are whacked. I have to admit the timeline is not in conflict. What is in conflict...is the fact the m.o. is very different. I ask myself why that is."

"Your answer?"

"I don't got one."

"The pressure must be on to find one."

"True. But. I'm a Captain, not Commander In Chief. To the brain-trusts upstairs, I'm just another stinkin' turd in the sewer. I know that, and I do what I have to do. It's called a survivor mode. The problem is there's an election in six months. And these cases are an albatross around our collective necks. They're tougher than anything we've seen since the 'Nightstalker case, eons ago."

"Which means..."

"You tell me."

"Fine," John answered. "Which means, it'll be necessary to use methods we may not have used before. I don't want to make waves... don't want to step on any toes, but I refuse to have my hands tied by politics. I don't give a damn about some tight-ass, penny-loafer wearing, pencil-pushing, baby ass-kissing politician. I'll do things my own way."

"You always did. And I insist you do just that," Nicholson assured him.

"Good. You guys know what you're getting when you call me in on these cases. I haven't changed since the last one."

"Does this mean you're aboard?"

"If I wasn't, I'd be gone by now. But I'm in on my terms. Period."

"You're a real sweetheart, Roméo. You're free to use whatever personnel or equipment you think you need."

"I've got an unlimited budget? That what you're saying?"

"Let's not get carried away. We'll provide files, computers, gofers—you name it. You can even take Li or Dennis or whomever you want to help you on this...if you want a partner at all. Everything's been blessed by the *gods* upstairs."

"They set the time limit too?"

"I'm a lowly Captain. I admit I'm in the pipeline but I'm downstream. So you know what the hell that means," said Nicholson.

"I'll take Sergeant Li," said John. "Dennis is a..."

"I know. He's a suck ass twit... not worth a cup of warm spit, but he's the old man's nephew."

Nicholson planted himself on the edge of his desk, drew a deep breath. "I'll get Medrano to brief you," he said. "He's a damn good man. Doesn't have an ego problem, doesn't bullshit."

"I know him well."

"One more thing. You'll be working closely with a new outside shrink we've brought in. She's putting together profiles for us. Name's Deauville—Dr. Diane Deauville. "

"I'm sure Dr. Kern is pleased about that."

Nicholson laughed. "Kern doesn't care for outsiders, but it's not his call. He can't cut it like he used to. Anyway, he's got his hands full already with all that Commission-mandated, psychological testing crap. If you ask me, we can save 'em a lot of money, by just admitting we're all crazy. Why else would we want to be cops?"

"Good point," John agreed.

"We also received a profile from the FBI's Behavioral Science boys but I'm not sold on it," said Nicholson. "I want a second opinion. At least, the old man tells me I do."

"Why?"

"Can't talk about it, right now. Don't press me on this one. Okay?"

"Well, I guess a trip to Quantico is out," said John. "You say the doctor's name is what?"

"Deauville. Dr. Diane Deauville. You know her?"

"Saw her yesterday, on the Krystal Knight show."

"Right. Terrible. Then this Mike Gregg thing this morning. And it's not nine o'clock yet," Nicholson groaned. "They'll be talking about this one forever. Damn shame."

"Don't hold back on me," said John.

"Have I ever?"

"No. But the politics are constantly fluxing around here and I just don't want to be fluxed with."

"I'm on your side," the Captain assured.

"If this *is* a serial case, I'll need to call in a friend of mine from the University of Minnesota; he's an expert in serials. He can help us a lot. But if I get any crap from anybody, I'm walking."

"Nobody's going to give you any crap. They do, I cut off their goddamn balls and stuff 'em up their asses. Just let me know whatever you need."

"I will."

"And... Li is a good man," said Nicholson. "I know you two already know each other. I've got a feeling he'll be happy to take a break from Rampart. As for the doctor, be careful."

"What do you mean?"

"She's hot. The first time I met her, she gave me bulges I hadn't had since I was eighteen. She has a kind of...of aura about her that... hell, I can't explain it," said Nicholson.

"You sound positively smitten."

"Call it whatever you like. I confess to it."

"Thanks for the warning. I'll be sure and control my libido. Besides, I never mix work and play."

"Sure," Nicholson chuckled. "She's due to stop by the office in a few. Stick around... meet her."

"Can't. You're a dirty 'ol man, Captain; things have changed. You can't regard women as sex objects anymore. It's not fair. And it's not politically correct. You'll get sued."

"It's still okay to think dirty, huh? They haven't taken that away from us, have they?"

John stood to leave. Nicholson rose and walked around to the front of his desk then suddenly remembered something. "These crime photos and CDs I showed you will be in a special, classified evidence room," he said. "You can get a good look whenever you're ready. Remember, three weeks. I just need to buy a little time."

Nicholson held up three fingers. John shook his head defiantly, never cracked a smile. After he left, the Captain returned to his desk, collapsed into his chair, and retrieved the ghastly crime scene photos.

John was halfway down the busy 3rd floor corridor when he spotted Gerald and Skeeter moving briskly in his direction. The three greeted each other, paused and moved to one side of the hallway.

"Figured I'd find you here," said Gerald.

"How'd you know? Skeeter reading minds again?"

"Wasn't hard. I know the Captain and I know you. He can't take no for an answer, and you can't resist a damn challenge. Simple as that."

"You got me. You said it yourself. I like challenges."

"Homicide's been on this for months. You won't solve these cases in an hour and go home. I don't have to tell you this ain't Law and Order."

"Right, I won't. WE will. Now, don't bitch, I could've gotten Dennis but I didn't want somebody who got in here on a one-man affirmative action plan."

The sight of an approaching Dr. Deauville suddenly halted the snappy repartee. She was accompanied by a nattily dressed lawyer-type in a blue suit and a Jerry Garcia tie. The three stopped talking and watched as the pair neared.

"You don't think we're gawking, do you?" Asked Skeeter. Gerald and John both replied in unison: "Who cares?"

Dr. Deauville passed, clearly aware of the attention she was getting. "Good morning, gentlemen."

The three simultaneously returned her greeting, and turned heads to follow. The doctor glanced back over her shoulder, briefly. John was riveted.

"Watch it, Sampson," Skeeter warned.

"What did he mean?" Gerald asked. No answer. He turned serious. "Moving right along. Seeing as how we only have three weeks, you got a minute?"

John looked at his watch. "I've got a class. What've you got in mind?"

"Since you're here, I should brief you. Every minute counts. Meet me in Lt. Medrano' office in five."

Gerald turned and walked on. John started down the corridor in the opposite direction. Skeeter interrupted him.

"The way me and GK figure it, you've actually been on the case ever since the Captain spoke to you about it. That stuff about London and Bahrain was to clear out some space and keep the phone from ringing. Am I right?"

"I told you you're just like my 'ol man," John grinned.

"I'll take that as a yes. So if I'm right, that means you've alerted your network of CIs, street urchins, the internet; you've hit Lexis-Nexis for every story about this you can find, combed through Hoovers On-Line, and checked sources only you and God know about."

"Well, you taught me most of what I know." John patted Skeeter on the shoulder.

"Not really, but you're making me blush anyway. Li told me about the phone calls. I would have thought you'd tell me yourself. I can handle the tap for you. We'll have to make it legal, though...work it out with Nick on the QT. Won't take long."

John nodded yes. "With the following conditions: I get the tapes... all the originals, whenever this goes away, or whenever I say it's over. And you decide who does the monitoring."

"Right. By the way, Emmy says anytime you want to stop by with your "lady friend,"—she calls her your lady friend—the door still works."

John smiled and bobbed his head.

Dr. Deauville had just floated down onto a seat in front of Nicholson's desk. The Captain was about to plop, when John sauntered in.

Nicholson looked quite surprised. "Thought you'd left the damn building."

Dr. Deauville turned and smiled as John approached. "Think I left something."

Nicholson reacted with raised brows. "What?"

"My pen."

John was unconvincing. Nicholson grinned. "Your pen?"

"A Mont Blanc. You know, the big one... it's black, has a white dot on top.

"Hmm, haven't seen it. But since you're here, let me introduce you to Dr. Diane Deauville. I mentioned she's doing psych profiles on your case."

John stepped forward, right hand extended. "Please to meet you. I'm John Roméo."

The doctor looked him up and down. "I know. I've read all your books. You're one of my favorite writers."

John swallowed hard, smiled faintly. " I'm... happy to hear that." He and the doctor exchanged lingering glances. "I wish I could stay," said John.

"Why don't you? I'm sure Dr. Deauville wouldn't mind. You two have to get together anyway."

"I'd consider it an honor," Dr. Deauville agreed.

"I'd love to but I've got classes this morning. However, I will be calling to arrange a meeting with you."

"I look forward to that."

John nodded, backed away toward the door. Nicholson looked on with amusement. "By the way," he said, tossing John a yellow Bic pen, "Use this until we find your... your Mont Blanc."

John flashed a faint smile, stuffed the pen in his pocket, and left. Halfway down the corridor, John stopped...did a three-sixty. What the hell had he gotten himself into, he thought. He had enough work to last until the tercentennial. It wasn't the meager obligatory fee he was to be paid; and the last place he wanted to be was center-ring in the LAPD/City politics circus.

"Damn!"

Twenty-two
Curse of The Gods

The flickering flames created a choreography of eerie light patterns...

The dank, unkempt bedroom

was lit by a dim lamp set atop a rickety dresser. A dented lamp shade, with yellowing plastic protector, lay skewed to one side. An eerie ambiance filled the musty environs. Peeling wallpaper clung to mildewed walls.

Two velveteen posters of some unknown Spanish Conquistadors adorned the wall above the antique, Queen Anne bed. Black and white posters of Madonna, David Bowie, Mick Jagger and Grace Jones, respectively, graced an adjacent wall. A curious gallery.

The musty room was further illuminated by the ghostly glow of dozens of partially-burned white candles arrayed in a large semi-circle at the foot of the massive, wood framed bed. Dozens of rose petals lay sprinkled on the floor amidst the candles. A second gallery—even more curious—was arrayed on a wall directly opposite the first: Joseph McCarthy, J. Edgar Hoover, Richard Nixon, and Dick Cheney.

A hodgepodge of items lay atop the cluttered dresser: rusting scissors; clipped newspaper articles on the murders; a jar with clumps of hair, a collection of matchbooks; a faded photo of a middle-age man with a 5 year-old girl in his arms; a copy of John Roméo's novel, *Curse Of The Gods;* and Rose Henley's book, *The Enemy Within.*

The room door creaked open. A broad shaft of hallway light invaded the space briefly then disappeared with a loud clunk as the door closed shut. Almost immediately, the raspy sound of heavy breathing pierced the silence. A lone male figure, bathed in shadows, stood a few steps away from the candles.

The flickering flames produced a choreographed dance of light patterns that fell erratically upon the oversized photos, causing them to appear to move. The stilted figure moved forward, knelt on both knees, raised sleeved arms and gloved hands above the candles, and passed them back and forth in a rhythmic, ritualistic manner.

A sustained, low-level alto hum—a barely audible chant—rose slowly. Then, as if in answer to some depraved prayer, the room was filled with the spiking crescendo of flapping wings—a crushing, nearly deafening sound as of a thousand birds suddenly taking flight. And all was contained within the consciousness of this lone figure now sitting, immobile, a worshiper before the altar of dying candles.

Twenty-three
Curse of The Gods

"Bullshit."

Inside Lt. Medrano' P.A.B. office,

Gerald sat hunched over a long table stacked with folders, a computer, CDs, crime photos, and a small CD player with a pair of mini-speakers. A carafe of coffee and a half empty box of bear claws were within hand's reach.

John was propped on the edge of the desk near an erasable marker board. Large, block numerals 1, 2, 3 and 4 were underlined in a heading across the top. He clutched a black marker pen, while staring intently at data filling the board. Victim photos covered a nearby wall; detailed data cards were attached underneath each. On the wall, just to the left of the door, and nearest John, was a large-scale map of Los Angeles County. It was dotted with red pins marking murder sites.

"We know .44 hollow points were used...probably with silencer," Gerald managed between munches and slurps. "The male deceased were all well known, prominent married men."

John stepped to the board...quickly made notes, repeating the details aloud. "44's, a silencer, most likely...ah, an audio CD, some articles on or near male deceased, times of all deaths between 11pm and 2am... and ah, hair taken from females, right?

"Right."

"What about forensics: fiber and blood analysis, latent prints?"

Gerald tossed up both hands. "Zip."

"Zip? What about the CD, prints, special coding—anything."

"Nothing, so far. That's what we're getting from SID and IAS. We've checked everything for prints; done fiber tests; soil tests on the carpet; checked doors, mirrors for prints. It's all a big fat zero. I mean, this guy, if it's a guy—leaves more stuff than Santa Claus, and it's all clean. How the hell does he do that?"

"Clean? As in clean?"

"As in clean."

"Can we determine source of any of the items...store brands, maybe; limited production runs on specific SKUs, if any; or if any of the items left were only available locally... regionally?"

"We've checked into a lot of that. There's more to do. But, basically, it's common stuff. Could have been purchased anywhere and by anyone. Could've been purchased over the Internet. I'm wondering if there's anyway of knowing what kind of device...brand...whatever was used to produce the CDs. "

"Good question. Look into it. What about serology?"

"We were hoping to find a bloody glove, maybe some Bruno Magli footprints or something, but no luck. S.I.D. made dozens of swatches from the blood found at each scene. So far RFLP tests reveal all blood samples match those of the victims. More elaborate DNA tests will take a little longer to conclude. We'll just have to wait."

"What about Luminol tests in principal and ancillary areas of the crime scenes?"

"Reliability isn't that great, but we've been there, done that. Still zip."

"D.O.J. involved?"

John was referring to the California Department of Justice.

"Yeah. But we're on the back burner. The Crandon case has everybody stretched to the limit. We don't expect even preliminary results back from D.O.J for another full month... maybe two."

"From the first case?"

"Right. We've also been forced to send blood samples to a secondary commercial lab in Minnesota. Our primary commercial lab, Hematech, in Boston, is working round the clock on the Crandon case and a half dozen others. We ain't got much going here."

John was getting the picture.

"And what about your book?" Asked Gerald. "I don't understand why the killer keeps leaving a copy of your book at the murder scenes."

"I don't know. It's strange. It's not the way I want to see my book promoted. Publisher's happy, though. Sales have spiked. Maybe the killer is drawing some parallel between himself and Wayne."

Gerald looked confused. "Who the hell is Wayne?"

"The sex-obsessed character in the book. He's impotent, slightly deranged, fantasizes about having sex with every woman he sees. He can't escape his powerful sexual thoughts."

"Sounds like a college roommate I had once."

"He desperately wants to find a way to stop the thoughts, the fantasies, but can't. Feels cursed. He develops intense hatred for men who seem to have their way with women; comes to hate the women as well."

Gerald returned his bear claw to the carton and leaned forward. "So, does he go off the deep end?"

"Worse. One night, while on a cocaine and alcohol binge, he tried to castrate himself."

"Don't tell me anymore."

"He didn't realize castration wouldn't affect his sexual urges, unless you remove the testicles—the source of testosterone—and maybe even a part of the brain. Whacking off the penis and leaving the balls only eliminates your ability to have conventional sex with ejaculation.

Meanwhile, while he was on the verge of psychological meltdown. He lashed out."

"Is that it?"

"No. But, you'll have to read the book to find out how it ends."

"Apparently, the killer's read it already...doesn't leave home without it. You have to admit the similarities are there," said Gerald.

"On the surface, maybe. But not in the details I see here."

"We've determined one thing about these books. They aren't being purchased from some bookstore. No evidence of store markers or telltale UPCs... Barnes And Noble, Borders, Wal-Mart or codes other retailers use."

"What does that tell you?" Asked John.

"Well, most likely, they're being bought over the Internet; Amazon, Barnes and Noble or something."

"Probably. If so, they're likely using credit cards. Which means there's a trail. But, here's the good and bad of it. The book's a huge seller. And without prints on the ones being left, it's a dead end. Maybe it could be determined if a single buyer is purchasing repeated copies in a relatively short time. But, what would that tell us? The problem is finding some link that takes us to any part of that trail. It's a long shot. Tell me about the usual suspects: wives, girlfriends, boyfriends," said John.

"They're all on our *A list*. We've attempted to question the wives of each victim."

"Attempted?"

"In each case, attorneys representing them have declined to have their clients sit down with us. "

"So what are we doing?"

"We've been told that we may submit written questions for review by the respective attorneys. They'll decide what gets passed on for answers."

"That's bullshit."

"That's the way we all feel. We keep trying to arrange for in-person interviews. None are real suspects right now. That could   change.

I don't expect it will, though. Of course, you always look at spouses," said Gerald.

"We've got to find a way to get these wives to talk," said John. "I want to find out what shape these marriages were in before these guys got whacked. We'll probably have to get down in the dirt a little. Skeeter knows how to get that done."

"My professional, wild guess is, the victims' marital status is coincidental," said Gerald.

"I'll give you 10 to 1 it's critical," John disagreed. "What about boyfriends...significant others related to the women victims?"

"We're still investigating that. "Bollinger and Kimball—task force members we pulled from Central—are on that. The one we've talked to—the boyfriend of the girl in the Sam Talon case—didn't raise any red flags."

"Wives whose husbands are murdered while literally screwing around on them won't talk to us? Interesting," said John, returning to the point.

While Gerald pondered the rhetorical question, his friend took a long look at the marker board then walked over, slumped into the chair next to him.

"I hope what you said about their marital status is true," he said.

"And if it's not?" Asked Gerald.

"If it's not, we could have a nut out there trying to stamp out infidelity, one adulterer at a time. Just look at the board."

"I'm looking."

"What do you see?"

Gerald stared at the chalkboard and took a long swig of coffee. Just then, Sergeant Dennis barged into the room. The two stopped talking and turned to face him. A smirk covered Dennis' face.

"Now, this is what I call commanding attention," he said with a grin. He sat down a few feet away. "Not all of us have that kind of presence. At ease, gentlemen. I'll just sit in on the meeting, toss in a few ideas here and there... keep things moving along. I've got a lot to offer, you know."

"We appreciate your selfless desire to be of assistance, but that won't be necessary. Thanks anyway," said John.

A pregnant moment passed. Dennis' smile evaporated. Gerald resumed slurping his coffee. Dennis hesitated a moment longer, stood and started for the door. He turned back to level a parting shot. "By the way Sergeant Li. I understand there's a problem with missing drug evidence in a case you and Jake handled a couple of years ago. Anyone contact you on that yet?"

Gerald aimed a cold stare at him. "Screw you."

Dennis smirked. "Don't get pissed at me. There's a missing evidence checkout log sheet too."

"Good-bye Sergeant," John whispered.

Dennis paused at the door and turned back to John.

"Poof," he said, mimicking an explosion, thrusting both arms in the air.

John rose, took a step toward Dennis. He flinched.

Gerald stepped in front. "This asshole ain't worth it," he said. Dennis slammed the door shut. John broke into a head-shaking grin.

Twenty-four
The Briefing

"C'mon John. Don't make me answer that."

"Where the hell were we?" Gerald asked.

"I think I would've killed him," said John. "I knew a guy like him when I first joined the department. He was killed in a drug buy. Somebody tipped the dealer off, and a reception party was waiting. We never found out who set him up. Some say it was an inside deal."

Gerald refreshed his coffee and took a long sip. John returned to the board and picked up the marker.

"You were talking about the info on the board," Gerald said. "I was asking what you saw."

"Looking at this, I feel safe in saying there's one shooter, except for one little thing. And I know we haven't had time to discuss ballistics reports or anything."

"What about them?"

"They show each victim was shot with a different .44."

"All of them?"

"All of them."

"Damn."

"But I still say it's one shooter," said Gerald.

"Why? I thought you said each pair of victims was killed with different guns. How do you reconcile that?"

"Chances are, if I'm right, he's trying to confuse us by switching guns. It's part of the asshole's calculations. I admit it's more cunning than usual but..."

"Switching guns. Hmm," John mused.

"I know that appears far-fetched on the surface. But if it's true, you have to admit it's pretty damn smart," Gerald continued. "That's the point I tried hard to make before. It was the one possibility I felt was not being addressed."

"It's certainly possible," John conceded. "Who'd you make the point to? What did they say?"

"Foster, Dennis, Emory—all of them."

"What happened?"

"C'mon John. Don't make me answer that."

"Tell me."

"Nobody listened. That's what happened. What the hell do I know, right? Foster and Emory keep insisting we've got one original killer and three copycats. To them, that's the only possibility. It's bullshit!"

"If they're right, then the Gregg case makes copycat number four."

"I heard about that. Don't know all the details though," Gerald admitted.

"If they were copycats, that could account for different .44's."

"Maybe. The problem is," said Gerald, "the killer's a little too exacting. The possibility several others could commit the same acts in the very same way is unlikely. Copycats would have to know exactly what we know, in every single detail. And they'd have to duplicate it. However, since we haven't released information on those details, how would they know?"

"Good question. Our job is to collect the facts and put it all on the table. Everything else will take care of itself," said John.

"You mentioned the Gregg case."

"They found a baseball, an audio CD, and evidence a .44 was fired at fairly close range" John explained. "I'm curious about the fact the killer's using a .44 magnum. It's not exactly the choice of weapons for most serial killers, and certainly not women. The recoil has been known to snap a few wrists."

"So he's not perfect," said Gerald.

"And no book was left this time. Why?"

"Nevertheless, I don't think anything this guy does is arbitrary. He's got this whole thing planned right down to the last detail."

"Too detailed."

Gerald didn't ask John what he meant. "What we really need is some plain ol' luck," he lamented. "We haven't found a damn thing. No fibers, no prints. Nothing. One thing's for sure. Whoever the sonofabitch is, he has to be familiar with the victims, to know their haunts and habits. Not to mention being able to show up at such an intimate moment, right on cue."

"Makes sense," John agreed.

"Think about it. He's damn good. We haven't found a single sign of forced entry. There's no way the victims are randomly selected. They're carefully chosen then probably stalked—a felony, in this state. All this is a bit too calculating for me."

"I admit it makes you wonder how he knows when to be there. But how long does it take to get the scoop on somebody these days, especially a public personality? You read the paper, watch TV, follow them, tap their phones, read their e-mail," John said. "It's easy. Too damn easy."

"Sounds like an argument for more privacy rights."

"True, but you're a cop, and cops aren't suppose to think like that, right? Don't answer that. Look, I take it you don't place much stock in the notion this could be the work of the *Westbound Killer,* "said John.

"All I know is that the Feds have come up with this catchy little name for some guy who has supposedly killed wealthy men from Pittsburgh to Phoenix. Other than that, we hardly know more than the average guy on the street. If I had to bet, I'd say there's no connection. I can give you all of my reasons."

"Do it later. Gotta go," said John. "This is my last class before summer. I don't want to be late. We'll get into more details: coroner's reports, crime scene reports, ballistics. There must be clues...something. I'll also want to tour the murder scenes myself...read the reports."

Gerald informed him he was interviewing Rose Henley later, then heading over to Annette Farrar's arraignment later. "See you later in D-4 after your class. When do you plan to talk to the doctor?" He asked.

"Don't know yet. I'll have to make an appointment or something—see if she can squeeze me in this afternoon. If not, maybe tonight. She's doing profiles."

"Hmm. Never knew you to depend on local profilers before. What's changed?"

"Nothing. The Captain says to work with her, so I will."

"What do you think about all this?" Gerald asked. "I can see your antennae is up; your mind's going a hundred miles an hour."

"We got computers around here? I only see this one on the table," said John.

"Not enough to go around," Gerald said. "Out in the divisions, we're mostly stuck with either dated systems that often don't work right; typewriters with broken keys; radios that fail, and a too few state-of-the-art cell phones.

"To answer your question, HQ has computers, but too much of our data is still logged and maintained the old fashioned way. And this is a new millennium. It's changing, but not fast enough. What's new is the communications center behind us. It's a major leap forward. Wish we would fully update everything else."

John listened, shook his head with disappointment. "What about the murder books?"

John was referring to the detailed case books kept on each murder. "Some are pretty complete, others are shells," said Gerald, frankly.

"I'll need several things," said John. "First I want to review the *books*, transcribed interviews, the reports I mentioned. I also want scaled layouts of the murder scenes. If possible, we can obtain phone records of the victims, especially during the months immediately before their deaths. There's more, but we'll get to that. My thinking is that if we concentrate on *one* of these cases, we may solve them all."

"Domino theory. You sure that'll get us started?" Gerald teased. He knew John's penchant for detail.

"It's a start. Ideally, I'd like financial records of the victims and their spouses. But that's a little dicey. That's usually where you start getting lawyers objecting, real quick. Financial records can be very revealing, though. When possible, follow the money. Gotta go. Later."

"It's good to be working with an expert again," said Gerald.

John was almost out the door when he turned back and grinned. "Expert? Most of this stuff is just ball-breaking work and experience. But a great deal is just plain ol' luck, you know that. Sometimes, events sweep me toward a solution before I've even exhausted my leads or hunches. It amazes me sometimes."

Gerald nodded. John left, closed the door behind him and disappeared. Gerald poured more coffee, grabbed another bear claw, dumped it back into the box and stood staring at the board.

Twenty-five
The Other Romeo

The downtown morning

traffic crush had subsided. John stepped from the city bus, wearing a hooded jogging suit, a pair of funky Nikes, and sunglasses. Dozens of homeless men and women lined the sidewalk leading into the Mission. Inside the aging two-story structure, men, women and children of all ages swarmed the overcrowded main room. Dozens sat hunched at long tables eagerly devouring their breakfast.

John spotted his friend, Pastor Harrison James, a cherub-faced, twinkle-eyed, robust man in his late sixties. He was in his usual garb: short-sleeves, slacks and an apron. From where he stood in the serving line, he spotted John and started toward him. Pastor James's face beamed. The subdued expression John had observed seconds earlier had magically disappeared.

"John, m'boy. Over here!" Pastor James called out, in his booming tenor. His voice carried like a public address system.

"They got you slinging hash this morning?" John asked, as the two embraced warmly. Pastor patted him firmly, rattling him down to his Nikes. He hugged him again and stepped back to get a better look.

"I had a feeling in my 'ol bones you'd show up here this morning. I truly did," he declared.

"That right?"

"For a fact. These ol' bones are getting to be like radar, you know. Yesterday I could swear I picked up KISS-FM in my left shoulder," he added with a belly laugh. "You're looking good, son. And still doing good, too. I hear things."

"I'm doing okay."

"You're far too modest. God's been good to you. I read the trades."

"How're things here?" Asked John, casting a sweeping glance around the crowded room and the line that spilled out the door.

Pastor's expression suddenly turned downward. "What can I say? There's never enough of anything around here except nothing. I know things are better for some people, but... we're still serving folks in record numbers. Fact is, often we find ourselves turning people away in greater and greater numbers. You can see how crowded we are this morning already."

"I had no idea it was as bad as it is," John confessed.

"Families too. We do our best and pray a lot. Look at those faces."

"I know how it weighs on your heart. Thank God for people like you. This is great work you do here."

"John, were it not for people like you, we'd be turning away more folk than we do now. You're a Godsend."

John was embarrassed by the compliment. He stepped closer, reached into his Jacket and handed Pastor James a check.

The Pastor held it to his face, stared at it with bulging eyes, cupped one hand to his mouth. "My God! This is a twenty thousand dollar check!" He stammered.

"This is between you and me," John whispered.

"I'll honor your desire for anonymity, my son. I respect you for it. God bless you. You're as generous a man as I've ever seen."

"Keep that quiet. I have a reputation to maintain."

And thanks, for all of them here," the Reverend said, pointing.

John embraced Pastor Harrison again and started for the door. Pastor watched with the check clutched to his chest.

Despite the donation, John still felt guilty. He gave generously and often to charities and urged his friends to do so. Yet he realized that in part, his involvement was probably superficial—an attempt to soothe his conscience in the face of conspicuous personal consumption.

Even as he stood inside the Mission, he recognized his impatience to leave. He was anxious to get the hell out—away from vivid reminders of the stark difference between people like himself and *them*. John didn't like being there. He didn't like inhaling the foul stench of urine and feces covered clothing. He didn't like staring into the doleful eyes of hungry children with grubby little fingers; they made him feel dirty and privileged—part of the pampered dominant class.

John's donations allowed him to bask in a fleeting redemptive afterglow. He somehow felt cleansed, if only for a day or two. Yet he found himself going back and forth with this endless mental jousting—a point-counterpoint—in an ongoing encounter with his *other self.*

The balancing argument in his mind was the realization he *was* making the effort, trying to make a difference, regardless of the motive. There was no rational reason to feel guilty for being successful. That was the way of the world. Some have and some have not; some rule and some are ruled. But why was he going through all of this mental masturbation?

The truth is, John had never really accepted he was deserving of his success. In the recesses of his mind, he had this overriding fear that any minute he would be exposed as an imposter. Any moment, he would find himself cowering naked in the middle of a jeering crowd. He had dreams about it.

Guilt consumed John each time he paused outside P.A.B. and stared at the memorial to fallen LAPD officers. He often asked himself why and how *he* had escaped to the world he now inhabited, and they had not. He thought about his late partner and friend, Keith Langhorne, and fought back the tears.

Twenty-six
The Big One

Inside the large Criminal Justice Building amphitheater,

an attractive, mini-skirted Kharla Appel, with bulging cleavage and dancing eyes, sat in the front row. John, in a black suit jacket, jeans, white shirt, and cowboy boots, was well into his lecture.

"I know everyone's still talking about what happened on the Krystal Knight show. Since we've only got a few minutes left, I'll open it up for discussion."

Kharla raised her hand eagerly, drawing derisive laughter from two female students sitting near her.

"Mr. Roméo, I was wondering if you think most men who cheat really do have small penises."

Despite the hoots and laughter, Kharla appeared oblivious to the reaction. John was sympathetic. "Kharla, I...I have no opinion on that. I did hear the comment the psychologist made." He pointed to a male student a few rows back. "Yes, you have a question?"

"Yes, Do you think it's an open and shut case?"

"What do you think?"

"Kinda hard for her to claim she didn't do it."

"I'm no lawyer," said John. "But it's dangerous to assume any case is open and shut. Her arraignment is this morning. Already, her attorney is giving hints of things to come. There're a lot of exotic defenses floating around.

John was about to recognize another student when the door opened. He turned and was surprised to see a animated Gerald Li beckon. He excused himself and rushed to the door.

"Hope your class is about over," Gerald said, with foreboding. "You need to come with me. There's been another one. A big one."

"A big one?"

"Yeah, big," Gerald repeated.

John dashed back to his lectern. "Sorry, class. Gotta run. We're almost out of time, anyway. Have a great summer and perhaps I'll see you in the fall." John grabbed his attaché and started for the door.

The class stood and yelled in unison: "Fade to black!"

John smiled, gave the thumbs up, and he joined Gerald. The two had barely entered the hallway, when Kharla followed them out.

"Mr. Roméo, may I call you sometimes? I'm an excellent reader... and listener. You could test some of your script ideas on me. I give great ear. I really do."

John fumbled for a suitable response. "I'll keep your offer in mind. Thanks."

Kharla smiled. John and Gerald hurried on. The latter gave her a long parting look. Seconds later they were through the exit, onto the sidewalk.

"Okay. Who's the big one?" Asked John, as they turned the corner and headed toward State University Drive. "And don't tell me it's the mayor."

Gerald was somber. "It's Jeffries, The Honorable Judge Hunter Jeffries."

John stopped in his tracks. "Jeffries?"

Gerald nodded yes. "Mr. Conservative, himself."

"Jeffries? You're kidding me. Wasn't he being considered for the State Supreme Court?"

"*Was* is right. I was in his court this morning after the Farrar arraignment. He never showed. No wonder."

"Damn. He presided over the Bolen case."

"You're right! I forgot."

The two dashed across State, toward the faculty parking lot east of the Foundation Building.

"How'd you find out?"

"When he didn't show for the prelim on the Reuben case, everybody got antsy. I talked to Rosa, his clerk. She was all upset and nervous. Normally, she's like a glacier." John nodded. Gerald continued. "Anyway, she told me they couldn't locate him at home. Then his wife called the court looking for him... said she hadn't seen him since two evenings previous. That did it."

"Where are we headed?"

"Parking lot."

"I meant where are you taking me?"

"High-rise condo complex on Wilshire, near Westwood somewhere. I've got the address in my pocket. Can't remember the name. Anyway..."

"Is that where it happened?"

"Yeah. Rosa had a second... a secret address for the judge. She was told it was a small office he leased."

"Told by whom? The Judge?"

"That would be my guess."

"Only it's not an office."

"Correcto. Quite the contrary. It's a luxury condo complex. Some of the units go for up to five mill. I didn't think judges made that kind of money."

"They don't," John said, cynically. "His wife's loaded."

"That's one way to get rich."

"Whoa, did you just cut one loose," asked John, reacting to a loud air blast.

"Just a mild touch of flatulence," Gerald explained. "It's those damn bear claws and coffee... and real cream."

"Whew! We got somebody at the scene?" John asked.

"Foster and Emory are there now with a special forensic team."

"Whose idea was the special team?"

"I talked to Medrano about it a week ago," Gerald said. "I've been concerned evidence was possibly being compromised during normal crime scene investigations. So I said something about it."

"Good for you."

The two reached Gerald's unmarked vehicle. "You'll have to drive me back here to my car," said John. "No problem. Toss that junk in the back."

Twenty-seven
Death Sentence

"I don't need a lecture from some free-lance sleuth..."

After storming past the media horde,

and past the police barricade, John and Gerald exited the elevator on the tenth floor of Cologne Gardens, the Wilshire Boulevard luxury condo complex. Two uniformed LAPD officers stood in the corridor, just outside the door to the Judge's condo. Gerald flashed his badge; the officer waved them through. The two stepped inside, but halted, giving way to the coroner's crew transporting two victims in body bags. John stopped them.

"The victims?"

"Yessir," answered one of the men, "Detective Sergeant Foster cleared us to leave."

"Hold on," said John, motioning the men to lower the litters. They did so, reluctantly. One man, wearing latex gloves, unzipped the bags. John and Gerald braced themselves. The male victim's upper torso was caked with congealed blood; his disfigured head lay to one side. Biological matter—brain tissue, bone frags—were visible on the same side. Small amounts of a dark, purplish grey fluid oozed from around the forehead entry wound. Apparently the bullet had flattened after impacting at an odd angle.

John was pissed. He thought he had established that victims were not to be moved, let alone transported, until after he had arrived and viewed the scene. However, he took a deep breath, opting to not start a war over it... this time.

The woman's wounds were not as visibly unsettling as those of her lover. The obvious exit wound in her forehead, though more than 4.5 centimeters in diameter, was fairly clean. Gerald pointed to a small, rose tattoo just above her right breast. A large spot of dried blood almost obscured it. John stared at the two bodies for a long minute then motioned the attendants to proceed. He was not happy.

When they entered the condo, John and Gerald observed S.I.D. still searching for, and collecting evidence. "Tell me something," John whispered. "If the killer's after the men, why are they capping the women, too?"

"No witnesses. That's the way it is in your book."

"Thanks."

'No problem."

The pair moved farther into posh residence, into the cavernous living room, and virtually unnoticed.

"Look at this place," said Gerald, "Damn! This is a condo? This thing's bigger than my damn house...my neighborhood."

The condo was crawling with investigators in white latex gloves. The pair took note of the surroundings, moved cautiously toward the master bedroom, where most of the activity was concentrated.

Lieutenant Frank Foster, a bespectacled man in his fifties with a reputation for ultra right-wing politics, and extreme self-righteousness, made his way toward them. He wore a determined expression. Foster was so far right, he viewed the far right Heritage Foundation as a cabal of milquetoast pretenders. The joke around the department was that he had the left pockets of all his trousers sewn shut.

"Roméo," Foster called out. "Heard you'd been brought in to help on this mess. Good to have you," he beamed, without looking John directly in the eyes.

John considered Foster a hypocrite. And Frank Foster hated John's gut. Foster smiled broadly, handed John and Gerald a pair of latex gloves.

"Regulation, you know. Can't take any chances."

An officer near the bloodied bed, several feet away, glanced over, resumed examining the scene, as John and Gerald donned the gloves and approached.

"What've we got?" John asked.

"Same as the others," said Foster, "I'm afraid only the names are changing."

The trio moved closer, careful to avoid areas being examined by the forensic team.

"I hear we've got a big fish this time," said John.

Foster was visibly angered. Judge Jeffries was a man Foster had long admired.

"It's His honor. The honorable Hunter Jeffries and a female companion," Foster said, "They were in...in bed. Both were taken out by a .44 magnum... close range, maybe six, seven feet. Awful sight, as you can imagine."

"We took a quick look," said John. "Would have preferred to see the scene in its virgin state."

John and Lt. Foster moved to another angle; Gerald stepped away to view the deathbed up close, note pad in hand.

"Both were head shots, hair taken from the woman?" Asked John. Foster nodded yes. "We found parts of the judge's skull and brain matter splattered on those pillows over there," he said, pointing. "A sizable fragment of the girl's skull was just lying there, on the bed... on the edge where you see the fold in the sheet. We've recovered both rounds... .44 hollow points, fully jacketed."

Foster turned, stepped closer to the brass bed; he pointed to a large bloodstained area one of four large pillows.

"We've already bagged recoverable tissue and..."

"That's fine," John interrupted. "How'd the shooter get inside? Any idea? What do we know?"

"Best we can figure, he or she either had a key or was perhaps otherwise granted entry. No sign of forced entry."

"Granted entry while they were having sex? Are you suggesting a threesome?"

"No, no. Okay, either the killer had a key or the door was left unlocked. Like I said, There were no signs of forced entry... door was locked when we got here. The balcony was still secured from the inside. That's about it. Housekeeper discovered the bodies when she arrived."

"What time was that?"

Foster scanned his notes. "About 11:30"

"Anyone speak to her at length? We know how long she's worked here? If the key she has was ever misplaced...ever out of her possession?"

"Not yet. She's available later for detailed questioning."

"When was she last here?"

"Day before last. She comes every other day," Foster answered curtly. He was beginning to feel like some rookie officer.

"Anything more regarding how the killer may have entered?"

"Nothing," said Foster.

"There's got to be more," John insisted. "This is a secure building; there's a guard on duty...cameras, monitors."

Foster agreed, sullenly. "I'm telling you what we know. You got some other ideas, let's hear 'em, Sergeant. Emory spoke to the guard and, according to him, the Judge always came in through the garage access, like most of the residents who self-park. There's a camera out there in the lobby. Says he observed nothing unusual...left when his shift was over at six."

"PM?"

"Right. Another guard came on at five. They overlapped about an hour or so. He won't be here until this evening. I'll get someone back here to talk to him."

"Or out to wherever he lives," said John.

"That's possible."

John leaned over to get a closer look at the large spots of blood on the bed. Some of it had soaked through to the mattress.

"What about the female vic?" He asked.

"Got a positive i.d. from her license. Name's Karen Stone—an assistant DA The guard said she lived here."

John held his right hand up, palm out. "Whoa, whoa! Assistant DA? She lived here...here in the complex or...?"

"In this unit," said Foster. "Although we're sure the Judge owns the place. It seems they were unusually open about their relationship, here, that is."

"Damn. Was she married? Anybody here know her?" Asked John. Foster took a deep breath. "I met her once, two years ago... the Wes Umbro case. Not sure if she was married."

"We can verify all that later," John said.

Foster continued walking John through the scene, even as their conversation grew more strained.

"What about the videotaping system here?" John asked. "It record or just monitor?"

"Both. But the guard thinks it was only monitoring over the past twenty-four hours. Says it's arbitrary as to when they actually tape."

John turned to face Foster squarely. "Even so, I think we should find out if we can get tapes from whatever days they *were* taping. Hopefully, they save them. We'll get an order, if we have to. What do you think?"

"I think that's a good idea. I was getting to that."

"Then, I agree with you, Lieutenant."

Just then, Gerald called out from his position near the entertainment center. John and Foster hurried over. "There's a CD wound in the player and the stereo's on," Gerald said.

"Play it," said John.

Gerald pressed rewind and waited.

Meanwhile, Sgt. Emory joined them, carrying a small plastic bag with black bikini panties inside. John and Gerald swapped glances.

"Far as we can tell, these are brand new, size tens," Emory informed them. "The girl had a pair of sixes. We found hers at the foot of the bed, buried under the sheets, and a third pair lying on the judge's chest."

"On his chest?" Asked Gerald. "Where did you find the pair in the bag?"

Emory hesitated, gazed at Foster, then back at Gerald. It was clear the former would rather not answer. He loosed a long, audible breath.

"The... the judge had one leg in them," said Emory.

John cleared his throat, while suppressing a chuckle.

"It's possible the killer put them on him...as a joke or something. It could happen," a defensive Foster insisted.

"Right," John mumbled.

Gerald pressed play on the CD player. As expected, Sam Cooke's *Frankie and Johnny* started. After a few bars, Gerald tapped the stop button, removed the CD and handed it to Emory. He placed it in a plastic evidence bag and turned to Foster.

"Sergeant, we've lifted solid prints from all over the place," said Emory. They most likely belonged to both deceased."

"We'll see," said Foster. "Shame about the Judge. Sure wish he'd been a damn liberal instead."

John and Gerald exchanged deadpan expressions. The former stepped to within a foot of Foster. All pretense of cordiality was about to disappear.

"Sergeant, I've got a problem with what's going on here."

Foster's eyes flared. "In what way?"

Gerald looked on, preparing himself for the fireworks.

"I'll be blunt," said John. "There're too many people in here. Looks like a damn *Men In Black* convention."

"What the hell do you mean?" Foster clenched his teeth, sucked in a deep nasal breath. "These men are doing a job...damn good job. There's no party going on here."

"I'm sure they're doing their jobs. However, in the future, I think we should limit the number of on-scene personnel to what is minimally necessary." John spoke calmly.

"Every man here..." Foster started.

John interrupted. "My point is this: it's very easy to trash evidence, compromise crime scenes, even under the best circumstances. The more people we have trampling around, the more likely a compromise will occur. There's soil, fiber, footprints. I'll show you what I mean."

John motioned them all toward the living room, winking as he passed Gerald, who was struggling to contain himself. By now, Foster's face was tomato red. John stopped in the middle of the living room, turned back to him.

"This is short nap, soft pile carpet... very impressionable. Chances are the killer would've taken this route in and out of the bedroom, if he entered through the front door. So, this path should've been protected until everything in the immediate vicinity was surveyed... catalogued. That includes even keeping the coroner out for as long as necessary. Once the victims are dead, they won't be getting any deader."

Foster scowled, glanced away then turned back. "You finished?" He asked, brusquely.

John continued, ignoring Foster's question. "There may have been unusual footprints in this soft carpet as well. There may have been prints that don't match the shoe sizes of the victims or the maid's, or any of the staff in the complex. Of course, we'll never know. Here's a suggestion. In the future, everyone's expected to cover both hands and feet, before entering a scene. No one met us at the door to make sure we were ready to enter. We should have been given booties... whatever. We tag and collect them for later examination. Everybody signs in and out of the scene. No one signed Detective Li or me into this scene, Sergeant. By the way, was the outside of the front door dusted before anyone entered?"

Foster eyed Emory. The latter shook his head. John heaved a loud sigh and turned away, briefly. "Sergeant, we all make mistakes, but I'm sure you realize the crime scene starts at the front door," said John, smiling.

Foster had reached the boiling point. "Roméo. I don't know what rank they give you when you take these special assignments, so I can't formally address you."

"Say what you have to say," John said, coolly.

"I know my fucking job, okay? I'm twenty years doing this shit... and without complaints, I might add. I headed this damn task force before the Captain brought you in on this. We know our jobs. I don't need a lecture from some free-lance sleuth who thinks he's got all the damn answers. Besides, I don't particularly like you... never have. And its got nothing to do with your money, fame, or the fact you're black."

John toyed with his chin, as he listened and waited. This was not the John Roméo Gerald knew so well. "Black? I'm... I'm black? Someone should've told me. All this time, I thought I was just 'colored.' Now you have to go hurt my feelings," John mocked. His smile quickly faded. "Look, Sergeant, I assume everyone knows his or her job, until I see different. And I'm afraid I see different. And it's got nothing to do with the fact you're a... how can I say this? A bigot."

Before Foster could respond, John noticed a small object on the floor near the edge of the horseshoe-shaped sofa. He walked over, removed a tweezers from a small, leather-bound evidence kit he carried in his pocket, and picked it up.

"Rose petal," he announced. "I'd say... American beauty, couple of days old." John sniffed the petal, placed it in the small plastic envelope then signaled to Emory. Sergeant Emory placed it inside a larger, clear plastic bag and marked the label. John then took Emory aside and spoke to him in quiet tones.

"I want you to do another look through. I am particularly interested in anything that looks like bank statements, financial records, deeds, telephone records, personal letters, computer disks, anything along those lines."

Emory seemed a little reticent."

"Question?" Asked John.

"I just... I just wondered if we need... a warrant or anything?"

"Who would we serve it on? The owner and only residents are deceased. We're doing a double homicide investigation."

"Gotcha."

John walked back toward Gerald and Foster. Foster was livid; the veins in his neck seemed ready to pop. He stood with both hands on his hips, nearly hyperventilating. John and Gerald took another long look around the scene, removed their gloves, deposited them in a bio-bag and headed for the door.

Once downstairs, the two exited the elevator and started straight for the center of the lobby.

"You're off to a flying start. Haven't changed a bit," said Gerald.

"I don't mean to ruffle feathers. Just doing my job. I hate to impose on you further, but I've got another stop before we head back."

"Where to? You buying lunch?"

"Hold on I want to check with this guy," John said, referring to the guard at the lobby desk. They reached the man seated at a multi-monitor console.

"Hi there, LAPD," said John, flashing his shield. "This where you monitor everything?"

"Yessir," said the guard, rising from his chair. "You all investigating the murders, too?"

"What's your procedure for admitting visitors?"

"Well sir, if someone walks in, I ask them who they're here to see. We buzz the resident to notify them...verify they're expecting the party. The resident can acknowledge by simply pressing a second button on a keypad in their units. Then, we clear the guest to proceed."

While they spoke to the guard, John carefully observed the monitors. Several cars entered the underground garage on a single card entry. He also noticed several individuals, presumably residents, approach and enter the garage elevator on foot.

"Thanks a lot," Gerald told the guard.

"Oh, one more thing," said John. "Yessir."

"Are delivery men required to check in here first?"

"Yessir. We log them into the computer."

"Great. Would you check and see if any floral delivery was made to the Jeffries unit any day this week?"

"No problem."

The man leaned over the keyboard, entered several strokes, and brought up a new screen. He entered a date range in the search block, pressed return and waited. A second data window opened. Seconds later, he returned.

"Nothing, sir."

He and John then started for the door. John stayed mum until they passed through the large double doors and stepped into the warm sun. The news gaggle was nearly twice its earlier size. Ignoring questions and microphones thrust into their faces, the two forged a path toward Gerald's vehicle.

"Anyone who piggy-backed in on a resident entering the garage could've gained entry easily," said John.

"Probably," Gerald agreed.

"Not probably. I was checking the monitors. Several cars entered while we were talking. He never saw them."

"So, with distractions inside, getting in this place unnoticed through the garage would be a piece of cake," Gerald concluded.

"Looks that way. Head for Santa Monica. And later, I want to make sure any evidence moved from the condo gets to Medrano's office, only"

Gerald wheeled hard onto Wilshire Boulevard and headed west toward Santa Monica.

"What a hypocrite," John muttered. "How do you figure it?"

"Figure what?"

"Damn judge. This guy's claim to fame was his constant railing about family values. Loved to point out the failings of liberalism; loved to call names, make moral judgments. He practically had the Ten Commandments tattooed on his forehead. And he ends up with his brains blown out, humping some Assistant D.A. cutie while he's wearing women's underwear. What's wrong with this picture? Wanna bet she never lost a case in his court room?"

For John, the most baffling aspect of the murder scene was the question of how the killer could gain entry and escape without detection. If investigators were lucky, the video system may provide clues.

The duo briefly continued musing over the Judge's apparent penchant for wearing women's underwear. While that in itself was not a hanging offense, it was illuminating. And it made necessary a determination regarding whether or not sexual proclivities of the judge may have played a part in his murder.

If the killer remained consistent, his next male victim —and John was sure there would be another—would almost certainly be someone well known, and someone involved in an extramarital relationship. The pool of potential victims, even if limited to southern California, was too enormous to contemplate.

By now, that one inescapable fact was being thoroughly discussed in the press. Anyone fitting that description—who had not been in solitary for the past several months—would have been wise to take a time-out. But there was no chance of that. Victims were always TOGs—"The Other Guys."

Twenty-eight
Real Love Never Dies; It just Throws Up On You Every Now and Then.

"Brevity always was your best and worst quality."

John and Gerald both

suffered from bulging eyes and swollen crotches, as each stood inside Claire's Santa Monica bikini store, gaping at hot female models, and listening to pulsing music. Her swimwear fashion show was in high gear.

"Thanks for the invitation," said Gerald. "This is real tough work but, hey..."

"Yeah, somebody's gotta do it. Stop drooling," said John.

The pair were fully engrossed, when a strikingly beautiful woman, 35, 5'-7," tan, resplendent in a white business suit, stepped in front of them. She stood on her tiptoes, kissed John on the lips, smiled at Gerald. "Thanks for coming, sweetheart. "Who's the hunk you brought with you?"

Gerald blushed. John groaned. "Hunk?"

"Hi, Gerald," said Claire, kissing him on the cheek. "It's been forever."

"Claire. If I had known about your new business, I would've come a lot sooner, and often."

"While you're here, you can buy a couple of bikinis for Laura. Hope you're enjoying the show. From the looks of the log in John's pants, *he's* having a great time. I've got shows in all fifteen stores today. I'm worn out and the day's only half over." Claire aimed her unblinking gaze at John.

"Aimee said you'd called," he said.

Claire heard him but didn't respond. Instead, her expression fell; she rolled her eyes, half-seriously.

"Aimee. Such a sweet child. I *do* want to talk to you. Please, excuse us, Gerald."

"Can't we talk here?" John asked.

Gerald, we'll be in my office for a while. Enjoy," answered Claire.

Gerald nodded and moved closer for a better look. Claire started for her office; John followed, eyes trained on Claire's gorgeous posterior.

"You look great," he said.

"You're right, I always look great, darling. Even when we were married, I always looked fantastic. But thanks. You don't look too bad yourself. How's the new book; the new screenplay, the new... whatever? Are you on another case? How's Roger? And I've got a follow-up," she said, facetiously.

Inside her spacious but decoratively cluttered office, Claire pointed toward a seat filled with bikinis and other beachwear. A full-sized female mannequin, in a red thong-bikini, hovered next to her desk.

John cleared the items from the chair and plopped down. The music and intermittent applause could still be heard. Claire leaned against the edge of her desk and stared at her ex-husband.

"Everything's fine," John said, calmly.

Claire grinned and waited. "Brevity always was your best and worst quality. But so is consistency, my dear. The world needs consistency."

"Gee, thanks. Why'd you want to see me today?"

"Baby, you can dispense with the cop persona. It's me, okay? You tell me. I'll give you one guess. Grand prize is a Barry White Greatest hits CD and a weekend for two in Shangri-La," Claire said, slowly brushing her right leg against John's.

"Alright. You're near ovulation and you want an answer."

"Bingo!" Claire flashed a wide grin. Just as quickly, her expression turned solemn. "But you *should* know that. We were officially divorced only three months ago. Seems more like three days. I thought we'd be together forever. I'm such a romantic. I've got my practical side but I'm a hopeless romantic. But why am I telling you?"

John and Claire's relationship had endured the tough early years of his police career. In the end, it could not survive their individual successes. It was a strange and inexplicable irony. Both still loved and cared for the other.

"The National Insider says our divorce was a big publicity stunt," said Claire. "Some stunt, huh? And I'm still getting calls. Over the past three days, ever since the article, I've had three."

"What kinda phone calls?"

Claire was surprised by the tone of John's reaction. "The caller asked if I knew what my husband was doing and with whom he was doing it."

"What did you say?"

"Nothing. I hung up. Why do you ask?"

John smoothed his wrinkled brow, tried to downplay his concern. "Just curious, that's all."

He was lying. John immediately thought of the threatening phone calls *he* had received.

"You're still concerned about me?" Claire asked, playfully.

John didn't answer. Claire lifted her right leg, removed her shoe, placed her right foot in John's lap, and pressed her toes against his crotch. He gently lifted her foot.

"Don't worry, I wouldn't hurt it."

"Claire, you can't be serious about this."

"Why not?"

"We're not married anymore."

"I'm sure I realize that more than you."

"Why would I impregnate you?"

"Impregnate? You're talking like an author. Talk like a lover. Why would you fuck me and make me pregnant? Because I asked nicely, like a good little girl. And because I'd make you feel good in the process." John shook his head and rose to his feet. "C'mon, babe. You have to admit that, at the very least, the idea strokes your ego. Be honest."

"This has nothing to do with ego-stroking."

"Not entirely, that's true. Actually, I want a baby, I don't want a husband, and I don't want child support. I'll even give up the alimony. How's that?"

"This is ridiculous. If you want a baby, adopt one; go to a sperm bank."

Claire, feigning indignation, sprang to her feet, walked over to John and stood with both hands on her hips.

"Buy a sperm, buy a vowel? You make it sound like *Wheel of Fortune* or something. Why would I buy generic sperm? I'm more selective. A sperm bank? Hell, I want a direct deposit. Besides, think of the fun you'll have. Or have you purged those memories already? Have you forgotten how good that part of our marriage was? That was the one part that worked. Too bad we couldn't screw twenty-four hours a day. We'd either still be married or dead by now."

John appeared embarrassed; he took a deep breath and looked away. "This is all very flattering, but I've got to go."

Claire pretended to pout. She lowered her head and wiped her eyes. John started for the door then turned back.

"I'm not trying to flatter you. I'm serious," said Claire. "Here. Feel my nipples. You remember how hard they get when I'm...serious, and horny."

"Claire."

"You always did love to call my name in that sultry baritone with the slight tremor. You use to whisper it in my ear, releasing a soft stream of hot breath. My nipples would get hard, and I'd start coming before you even touched me. Remember?" John remained mute. "If you can't say yes to my request, then don't say no. There's always next month. I know I'm making a fool of myself this way but I'm not asking for a favor. Just consider it one of those many things you promised and never found time to do."

"You make it sound like negotiating the end of a lease, or a contract. We talked about this many times, even before we were married. You understood I didn't mind adopting, but did not want to father children," said John.

"Yeah, but I thought...hoped you would change your mind. Besides, you never talked about a vasectomy, so I figured there was a chance. I always wanted to have children. I know I should have made that absolutely clear all along but I wanted our marriage to work. I felt because we loved each other we would grow to feel the same about children, about family."

John stepped to within inches of Claire. She gazed into his eyes. He returned her gaze then looked away.

"You're not happy," she said. "I can see it in your eyes. I always could. You're still searching."

"Wrong."

"With all your successes, you're still searching."

"I'm fine."

"You've reached your mountaintop, but it's not what you expected. You don't have to tell me. That's why you drive yourself so. I was the best thing that ever happened to you and you drove me too—away."

"The top of my mountain is just fine, thank you. And I didn't drive you away. We just grew apart. You said it yourself."

"What are you trying to prove?" Claire peered into John's eyes. "You're driving yourself like some madman. It's like you're out to prove something to yourself... to the world."

"I appreciate the concern. I really do. I admit I'm a workaholic sometimes but I'm fine."

"You aren't taking care of yourself. And I know little Aimee isn't helping...in that department. She can hardly take care of herself. Don't get me wrong, darling, I'm sure she's a good lay, but that's about it."

"Claire..."

"Tell me, John. What was it? The French accent, her nymphomania, the way her wet lips glide over the head of your..."

John turned to leave. Claire grabbed his arm. "I'm sorry, kinda. I'll change the subject. Have you had more angina? And don't lie."

"No."

"Liar! Dr. Greenberg says you missed your appointment with him two months ago, and you never rescheduled. You also missed your prostate exam. They don't always *have* to do the digital exam, you know."

"You called my doctor?"

"And I made another appointment for you for two weeks from today. And there's one more thing."

"I'm not surprised."

"Who's Dr. Oliver Tarnower?"

"Why?" John's eyes narrowed.

"Answer my question. Do you know him?"

"I might."

"Such uncharacteristic imprecision. I found a check you wrote to him. He's a well-known psychiatrist. Look, you endured so much stress for so long, one can understand the need for occasional therapy. I tried to convince you of that after Keith's death."

"Claire."

"Okay. I'm done with it."

John turned to leave. Claire grabbed his arm and stood facing him. She lifted her head and kissed him. Neither spoke. John turned away and started for the door.

"John!"

Gerald was entranced and did not see his partner until the latter was standing in front of him, waving his arms, motioning him toward the door. A reluctant Gerald followed, suggesting they grab lunch. Food was the last thing on John's mind. Claire's voice reverberated in his head. He kept thinking of what the two of them were like before they were married.

They met as grad students at UCLA and fell into immediate dislike. Claire thought John was opinionated and cocky; he felt the same way about her. The only direction their relationship could move was up, and it did.

Both found themselves going out of their way to cross paths. John began asking her to help him with his Psychology studies. Soon, they were taking frequent trips to Catalina, Palm Springs, Santa Barbara, Las Vegas, San Francisco, and elsewhere.

Before either realized it, they were inseparable. John remembered those days and longed for that kind of innocence—that feeling of palpable excitement. He now found himself in a relationship with Aimee, a beautiful, vibrant woman for whom he cared deeply and sincerely.

Twenty-nine
The Widowmaker. Gotta Be A Better Way

"Was shooting him in the head with a .44 magnum on the list?"

Fatburgers was John's suggestion.

Gerald reacted with alarm. John thought his friend had lost it. "What are you talking about?" He asked.

Gerald was nearly freaking out. "Tradition! You're blowing tradition. You're gonna screw up everything, jinx the whole investigation. We always do Pink's when we start a case. Change now and there's no telling what will happen."

John shook his head and laughed aloud. "Damn, alright, already. It's Pink's, if the line isn't wrapped around the block. Didn't know you were that superstitious."

"It's tradition. There's a difference."

It took less than twenty minutes to arrive at the famous hot-dog eatery on LaBrea, near Melrose. As John had predicted, the line to the sidewalk walk-up window stretched north to the corner. It was worth the wait. Once they reached the counter, the cashier—longtime employee, Bonita Vasquez—recognized them both.

"Lieutenant Romeo... Sergeant Li, you're back."

"Ro-me-o?" Gerald snickered. Bonita, you're the only one in L.A. who can get away with that." John grinned.

"You two stay away too long. You eating at Fatburgers, now?"

"No way."

"Ah-ha! You on a new case, right?" Must be. You come here first, when you start a new case, yes?"

John shushed her and quickly placed his order.

With a fistful of napkins clutched in his left hand, John swiped at the clump of chili clinging to the corner of his mouth. A single 'dog' remained on his tray. Gerald was working on two Polish, cheese dogs with spiced onions and relish, along with a shared mountain of chili-cheese fries.

"Jeezus! Doesn't Laura feed you anymore?" John asked.

"She'd kill me if she saw this. She's into calorie counting, health food, twigs and leaves... won't let me eat anything without checking fat and cholesterol."

"Guess she must love your big butt, or something."

Hell, yeah. What's not to love? Look at all this."

En route to CSULB, the conversation quickly returned to the murder of Judge Jeffries and Assistant DA Stone. John scribbled a page of 'To Dos.' Amongst other things, he wanted a printout of the Judge's most controversial rulings over the past ten years, in addition to the Bolen case. There was always the possibility his murder was related to a previous ruling.

John and Gerald agreed Foster and Emory should break the news to Catherine Jeffries, and attempt to interview her. Both hoped the press would not get to her first. "I'd be surprised if her attorney doesn't move to prevent any interview at all," John offered.

Gerald volunteered to secure a copy of the interview report and have it ready for review. He also promised a transcript of his brief conversation with Rose Henley. The two met at P.A.B., shortly after   John left for his CSLUB class. Gerald felt Rose might provide some insight, regarding women who kill their husbands.

John tuned the radio to an all-news station in time to hear reports of the murders of Judge Jeffries and DA Stone. An AP story erroneously reported LAPD investigators had discovered multiple bullet wounds, and sexual mutilation on both victims. The report also wrongly reported DA Stone had been partially scalped.

During the drive to Cal State Long Beach, via the 405 freeway, it soon became clear the effects of the dogs, fries, and a last minute pineapple malt had taken its toll on Gerald. Something in his gut was not sitting right, and it showed. John hoped it wouldn't get worse.

Minutes later, the two stood in the Foundation Building parking lot, near John's car, mapping strategy for *pushing* the investigation.

"I'm meeting with the good doctor tonight," John said. "I called her before class. Aimee and I are going out to dinner afterwards. So, unless something major comes up, I'll meet you at P.C. in the morning, about eightish. I want to go over more files, ballistics... Foster's report."

Gerald nodded. "Rose gave me an autographed copy of her book," he remembered. "You should read it. There's a chapter on networking. In it, she talks about how women network...pass along info on all kinds of things, especially through the Internet. One chapter is entitled *Fifty Ways To Leave Your Husband.* Real cute. It's a takeoff on the old Paul Simon hit from the 70's."

"Was shooting him in the head with a .44 Magnum on the list?"

Gerald laughed and shook his head, *no.* "But being the cynic I am, I also wondered if some of that networking info could be..."

"A solicitation tool for women looking to 'off' their husbands?" Asked John.

"Something like that...an underground connection or something. Look, I'm not saying definitely, but if Soldier of Fortune Magazine could do it..."

"Forty-four magnum's are cropping up everywhere," said John. "Coincidence?"

"There are few coincidences in this business. Get someone on the task force to begin checking gun stores, pawnshops for .44 Mag sales. Could have gotten them from gun shows, though. Those would be hard to track."

"Gotta try, though."

"What's Nicholson's problem with the FBI profile?" John quizzed. "He says he disagrees with it, but didn't want to talk about it... flat out refused to discuss it."

Gerald massaged his stomach and burped. "Sorry. The problem is, the FBI report strongly suggests the killer may have a military or law enforcement background."

John remembered his conversation with Skeeter. "Why?" Gerald hesitated, shrugged. He seemed reluctant to speculate. "Never mind," John went on, "I'll read the report."

"The Captain is not the one sitting on the report," Gerald added. "It's the 6th floor. That's why they're anxious for a second opinion. They hope that opinion will counter the FBI report, or at least omit the military or law enforcement suggestion."

"Why?"

"Bunker mentality. The brass doesn't want to hear anything that could even remotely cast a negative light on the Department."

"I don't like this," John said, emphatically. "I won't have anything to do with cooking the damn books. The chips will fall wherever they will or they can have this case."

"My feelings exactly."

Thirty
Aimee, Ooh, La La

"I don't want to talk about it."

John stood rock-still,

as the warm water cascaded over his body in massaging torrents. A thousand thoughts churned in his head. He tried sorting them out; tried to concoct some strategy for approaching the case. At the rate the murders were now occurring, the count could number more than a dozen in no time.

The evidence tumbled around in his mind. He hoped one little thing would stand out above all else. It did not. He thought about his upcoming meeting with Dr. Deauville; his brief encounter with her, and Nicholson's earlier description. It fascinated him. He knew Nick was not one to exaggerate.

It was the first time he could remember the Captain referring to any woman in such a manner. That aside, John fixed his mind on the job at hand. Some nut, apparently with an axe to grind, was killing people in a remarkably consistent way. And now, he was being trusted to stop him.

Suddenly, the shower door swung open, revealing Aimee, standing there, clutching a large bath towel. John killed the water and climbed out. He kissed Aimee, softly and repeatedly, as water dripped to the floor. Their eyes locked in a hypnotic gaze. She took the towel, began slowly and teasingly drying him. Taking it all in, John stood with one foot on the closed toilet cover and watched as Aimee lowered herself to her knees and continued drying him.

"Your turn tomorrow," she whispered.

"Why not tonight?" John eased his fingers through her hair. "Why not right now?"

Aimee stood, slipped the towel between John's legs, passing it through. She reached around him, grabbed the other end and began sawing it gently, back and forth.

"I'd better finish this myself," he said.

Aimee released the towel, smiled and turned to leave. John watched her. She reached the door, stopped and lifted her dress, exposing her smooth, tan, nude bottom.

John's erection was instant. "That's not fair," he yelled. Moments later, he entered the bedroom and found Aimee on the bed, resting against the bank of a half dozen pillows. Both her legs were drawn—knees to her chest, revealing all.

"It's five o'clock," she said. "Our dinner reservations are for eight."

John nodded and continued dressing. Aimee's eyes followed his every move, as he sat on the edge of the bed to put on his shoes.

"She's very, very pretty," she said. "And she reads your books."

"Fortunately for me, a lot of people read my books, or I'd be in serious trouble."

"Yes. But not all of them are so pretty or on your evening schedule. And not all of them refer to you and your book on national television. I heard how she said your name. *John Ro-may-o*," Aimee mimicked.

John went to her, grasped her chin with one hand, lifted her head back, slightly, gazed into her eyes. "You're jealous."

"No. I'm just... "

"Just what?"

"Nothing. You're trying to change the subject," said Aimee. "I have no reason to be jealous of you. You love me and I'm sure no sexy, silky-voiced psychologist could make you forget that for a second."

John selected a suit from the closet and returned to the bed. Aimee removed the hanger and handed him the trousers. He smiled, kissed her forehead and continued dressing.

"Roger called again," Aimee said, reluctantly.

"When?"

"Don't get angry. He sounded really scared."

"I don't want to talk about it."

"But..."

"No buts!"

Aimee relented but it took a short while for John's rebuff to wear off. "So when should I expect you?"

"Nine."

John was certain there was more Aimee wanted to talk about. He was not sure he wanted to begin a conversation he did not have time to finish. He said little more.

"What was wrong last night? You tossed badly," said Aimee slipping onto the edge of the bed. John secured the belt on his trousers.

"I slept fine."

"Hardly. You startled me awake, at one point. You were tossing and flailing. At one point you sat straight up in bed. I watched you; I called out to you. I think you were still asleep but you were sitting up. Your breathing was heavy. I touched your arm; it was damp with perspiration. And just when I started to turn on the lamp, you lay down and were as calm as you were before. You must have had a bad dream...a nightmare."

"Maybe. I don't remember."

Thirty-one
Night Session, Psych 1010101010101

John appeared taken off-guard by Diane's frank answer.

"I hope you don't mind my mentioning it,"

said Dr. Deauville.

"Not at all."

"I had read your book recently and thought it apropos to the discussion." Dr. Deauville was referring to her reference to John's book on the Krystal Knight show.

"I was flattered. Thanks for the plug. My publisher was certainly thrilled."

"You're welcome. As you can imagine, what happened frightened me out of my mind. It all happened so quickly. I've relived those terrifying seconds a hundred times."

The minute he walked into her office, John saw the doctor in a way he had not earlier. He instantly knew what Nicholson meant. Seeing Dr. Deauville on TV, and even briefly at P.A.B., in no way prepared him for seeing her up close. She was arresting. And it wasn't simply her physical beauty; there was an aura—a decided glow about her that defied description.

Whenever Dr. Deauville looked in John's direction, her eyes seemed to penetrate him, as if she was intercepting his thoughts. John felt vulnerable, naked. He told himself to stay focused, to ignore her aroma he inhaled with every breath.

"I've been avoiding all the news," she said. "I feel so sorry for Annette."

"Personally, it's the dead guy's family I feel for," John countered, snapping out of his trance.

"Of course. And so do I."

John was again drawn to gaze at the good doctor; tempted to drop all pretense. Instead, he resisted, consciously glancing away, at intervals. It took several more minutes before he felt comfortable where he sat; his left forearm resting on the sofa arm. He inhaled, exhaled slowly, began to relax a bit, if not completely.

"Captain Nicholson tells me you're developing psychological profiles on the four cases I mentioned," John said.

"I'm preparing a written report, but I'll be happy to discuss my preliminary evaluations and thoughts with you."

John's eyes followed the doctor as she left to retrieve a manila folder from a nearby file drawer. He visualized her naked, then condemned the thought. She was clearly an intellectual, an author, a brilliant woman. However, it was not Dr. Deauville's brain that filled out her dress, or produced such cleavage. He could no more see her cerebrum and cerebellum than she could see his.

As Dr. Deauville returned to her chair, John looked away. A faint smile on her face suggested she was aware of her effect on him. Or perhaps it was her own similar thoughts that amused her. The doctor took her seat, crossed her legs and opened the folder.

"I should tell you this report is only temporary. I was asked to produce something quickly and I did. It's not the way I normally do things. I always begin at the murder site," she explained.

"I don't understand."

"I know it's a bit unusual, but I can't begin to do what I do without being there. I try to put myself into the circumstance the victim was in: the time of day; the location; the mood, even the danger. I try to come as close to being the victim as possible. I try to know what they knew... imagine what they felt at the moment of death. I am convinced that as the spirit departs, it sees and knows all. I want to connect with that spirit."

There was sudden quiet in the room. John wasn't quite sure what to make of what he had heard. "And you haven't had a chance to do that with this case?"

"Or the others. Not yet, but I have to. Otherwise, I can't submit a final evaluation that is honest."

"I'll see you have an opportunity to do what you need to do, as soon as possible."

Dr. Deauville nodded and smiled. "I don't mean to pry but what kinds of cases brings you out of such lucrative retirement?"

"Impossible ones. Those that appear to offer the most challenge."

"You like challenges? Impossible challenges?"

"I suppose." John soon felt he was being analyzed. "May I ask you how you were chosen to do profiles on this case?"

Dr. Deauville smiled, stood, walked slowly to the sofa where John sat watching her every move. She paused. "Mind if I join you? I sit in that chair all day. You seemed so relaxed here."

"Please," said John, motioning her to sit.

The doctor eased onto the opposite end, turning slightly inward to face John, her right leg bent at the knee and resting on the sofa's edge. "Honestly, I don't know why I was asked. I'm a psychologist. I en-joy forensic psychiatry. I have a decent background..."

"You're too modest," said John. "You did your undergraduate work at Yale. Your advanced degrees—including your Ph.D.—were earned at Johns-Hopkins. You're a bestselling author yourself, an expert in your field, an advocate for women's rights and health issues."

"Hmm. I see I've left a trail of evidence," Diane smiled. "I'm flat-tered. What else do you know about me?"

"I'm here to learn much more. But, I feel that's enough to recommend you."

"Perhaps. I did learn that I was not their first choice."

"Do you know who was?"

"Yes. Park Dietz. He's everyone's first choice, and for obvious reasons. He's also a friend. He turned them down."

"Lucky for us," said John.

"Park also turned down the O.J. Simpson case. He normally declines requests for his help in cases where the prospective client does not agree to give him total, unfettered access to all the evidence and materials associated with a case. He wants nothing hidden from him. That also concerns me here. However, I agreed to come aboard."

"We're fortunate to have you."

"You may want to avoid hasty judgments," Dr. Deauville smiled. "You're accomplished, yourself. Born in Harlem. Your father was one of New York's finest. You're a NYU grad, BA in English; degree in criminology from UCLA; studied Psychology at UCLA; twelve years with the LAPD, a homicide whiz. They say you have an 'eye for beauty and a nose for murder.' You're a bestselling author... screenwriter. There's more. I could go on and on."

"Seems we've both left footprints."

There was a brief and clearly uncomfortable pause filled with warm smiles. The doctor plowed on. "About the cases before us, I don't mean to play detective," she said, "but from the evidence presented me so far, it appears there's one individual at work here. You agree?"

"Yes, from what I've seen," John said. "Except for one thing."

"What's that?"

"I'm told preliminary ballistics reports show the fatal rounds came from different guns, in each case."

"Does that necessarily destroy the single killer theory?"

"No. He could be using different guns, as a way of confusing us," John continued. "If so, the questions are: how many more killings and how many .44's can he afford."

"And so you think the killer is a male."

John paused. "For the moment, but I'm not certain. I'm not the profiler here. I used 'he' in the assumptive, generic sense. My biggest question is whether this so-called Westbound Killer, everyone has been hearing about, is our man. If he is, his m.o. seems to have changed from that reported by authorities in Pennsylvania and other states."

"And the victim-profiles?" Asked Dr. Deauville.

"They've changed as well. So have the items left at the crime scenes. Is that unusual? Is it conceivable that a serial or spree killer would suddenly change his m.o.? Asked John.

Diane shrugged a bit. "It's certainly conceivable, but not likely, except over some time. Experience shows serial killers become creatures of habit like all of us. It must be extremely challenging for you, gathering all these puzzle pieces and trying to make sense of it all. Takes a lot of skill, determination."

John smiled, tried to shrug off the compliment. "What's your current profile assessment?"

"I don't want to sound cliché but experience and statistics show most serial killers are white males, in their mid to late thirties to early forties. They tend to have above average intelligence, some with IQs as high as 120 or more. Individual, case-specific research reveals many displayed cruelty to animals...perhaps to other children in their childhood; most have psychosexual dysfunctions, unresolved anger."

"And this case?"

"Based on what I've been shown, I would certainly place this killer in this category. I'd say early to late forties... very intelligent, cunning, resourceful, deliberate. The intentional clues he or she leaves do tell us something. For example, the CDs...Sam Cooke, burned on a home computer. And your novels; he obviously reads fiction, has a favorite author, perhaps. I see an amalgam of classic serial characteristics, and some things that are not so classic."

"Are you basing most of this on statistical data?" Asked John.

"Not solely. I'm using empirical and statistical data as well. And the killer appears remarkably consistent. He is perhaps acting out of moral indignation. Most young killers aren't likely to act on moral indignation."

"Why do you say that?"

"With respect to these cases, perhaps something—probably in the killer's past—has caused him to view infidelity with violent disdain. He may have had an unfaithful father."

"Or mother?"

"Perhaps. And another thing, what if his targets are really the women?"

John looked surprised.

"You look surprised," said Dr. Deauville. "Let me guess. Because the women were unknown, you naturally conclude the targets were the men—these unfaithful men."

Dr. Deauville stood, walked casually to the wet bar and poured a glass of water. John was uncharacteristically silent.

"The possibility didn't occur to you the women were the targets and the men perhaps just unfortunate victims?" Asked the doctor.

She raised an empty glass. John nodded. She poured a second, brought it to him. He took a long sip and nodded his approval.

"I confess, you're right. Should I've considered that?"

"I'm not chiding you. I merely offer it as a possibility, not a conclusion. I'm sure an experienced detective like yourself knows the wisdom of including all possibilities, and excluding none. Correct?"

"Correct. What does this guy want? What's driving him?"

"In addition to his psychotic need to kill, his drive to covet, to possess? Recognition! And he's not getting it now. Perhaps he never has."

"What are you saying?"

"I know there have been reams of coverage about the victims, not the killer. Perhaps the victims he's chosen are too famous, too well known. In their deaths they have denied him the thing he most wanted: attention and recognition. They've stolen his spotlight. Had the victims been less well-known, the focus would more likely have been on the killer, not this lopsided focus on the victims."

"Why do you think the focus hasn't been more balanced?"

Dr. Deauville shrugged at first. "Maybe it's simply a sad commentary on our desensitized society. Could be the glut of horrific violence; crimes have to be exceptionally brutal to garner attention and outrage. We are also, as a society, more concerned about celebrity; more impressed with fame than infamy. But I could be way off course."

"If all that's true, should we expect the killer will keep killing until he gets that satisfaction?"

"He'll never be satisfied. A killer's appetite for killing is not finite. There is no magic number whereupon reaching it he retires. I certainly wish that were the case. He'll have to be caught or be killed himself."

"So you think the murders will go on. "

"Yes. They may even increase, both in frequency and viciousness. So far, the deaths have likely not achieved his goal. Therefore, increased anger and an *I'll show you* 'attitude could become a factor. Of course, if the next victim or victims turn out to be single all bets are off. We'll have to look for other motivations."

John was impressed. The doctor's brain was clearly showing now. Her body had serious competition. But John was angry with himself. He could not take his eyes off her. Despite sincere effort, he was not controlling his thoughts at all. He glanced away, momentarily, unable to hold her gaze. Something was being communicated, he thought, or was it his own guilt?

"Do you think there could be any other motive, besides the ones you suggested earlier?" Asked John. "We cops look for motive."

"What do *you* think?" The doctor asked, turning the question around.

John leaned forward, then back, stretching both arms along the length of the sofa. Dr. Deauville smiled. "I don't know," he said. "But, he's very discriminating. Most serial killers are, to a point. In some ways, circumstances lead me to think the shooter could be a woman—a wife, a jilted lover or something. It's not likely but its possible."

"Possible, but not in this case?" Asked Dr. Deauville.

"Nope. In a single case, maybe, not a serial. I can only think of one in recent history."

"Which one is that?"

"The Dana Sue Gray case in Riverside, in 1998. Here's a woman who kills a number of elderly women by garroting and bludgeoning them to death, then goes on shopping sprees with their credit cards. She waits until she's 36 years old and becomes a serial killer. And nobody paid any attention, outside of Riverside."

"I remember the case. I believe the seed—the germinated roots—were always there. However, you're right. If you ask the average person about Dana Sue Gray, they wouldn't have a clue who she was. If the murders had taken place in Beverly Hills, and her shopping had been on Rodéo, everybody in California would know who she was and is."

"I don't think our killer's female," John offered. "The killer's using a .44 magnum, the most powerful handgun made. It's not the kind of weapon a woman would choose, Rose Henley notwithstanding. But, it's like you said. Maybe he *is* after the women. We'll have to see."

"With your involvement, I'm sure we will."

"You're very good, doctor."

"I don't understand."

"You're very good—shrewd. You let me pose the questions and give the answers, too. I'll have to watch myself around you. Before I know it, you'll have me lying on this sofa, pouring out my soul, and exposing the pain of my lonely childhood."

"I doubt that. I'm sure you're a well-adjusted, red-blooded American male with an enviable background and a bright future."

"Thanks," John said with a grin. "Let's talk more about sex," he said, innocently.

"If you wish," Dr. Deauville said with raised brows. John suddenly realized what he'd said.

"Of the killer. I'm sorry. The sex of the killer," he clarified.

Dr. Deauville was amused by his embarrassment.

"If we can agree that the killer's likely male, doesn't that present a contradiction regarding the degree of consistency of women killers versus the inconsistency of male killers?"

"I agree. What we've found is that when we look at the few women serial killers we note a high degree of consistency. They tend to do the same things in nearly exactly the same way. Men are different; less consistent, more impulsive, less able to stay focused on a plan."

"We're still talking about killers, right?" John mused.

"More or less," Diane answered, smiling.

"But despite that analysis, and as an experienced detective, I must include all possibilities and exclude none," said John.

"Touché, Detective Roméo."

"I didn't intend it that way, I was just..."

"It's alright. I admire a man who can think on and off his feet."

John did not dare read anything into the doctor's comment, but found himself staring again. He looked away, momentarily.

"This isn't exactly on the subject doctor but..."

"Say whatever, ask whatever. And it's Diane."

"Okay... Diane."

"What would you like to know?"

John paused to gather his thoughts. "I've always wondered how so-called experts are selected for talk shows. How did they choose you for the Krystal Knight Show?"

Diane tossed her head back and ran her fingers through her hair. "I don't know about others, but in my case it was simple. I've been very vocal and have written extensively on women's issues. I only counsel women, and the show was about a very painful women's issue. So, they called my publicist; she called me, and I said yes. That's not to say I'm the only woman psychologist available. I don't want to sound conceited or anything. But I am very good. And I choose not to provide my considerable expertise to men."

John appeared taken off-guard by Diane's frank answer. "I suppose I did ask," he said.

"C'mon,   Lieutenant."

"It's John."

"John. Don't look so wounded. Men have such fragile egos. They don't seek counseling as readily as women. However, when you do, you have more than ample numbers of male therapists to select from. Anyway, as I said, I'm sure you're a very well adjusted American male with a firm grip on reality."

"Thanks." John stood. "I've taken up enough of your time. When do you want to visit the murder scenes, and where do we start?"

"With the Sumner case. I would like to honor Captain Nicholson's request for a final report in two weeks, if I can."

"What about day after tomorrow? Thursday? Should I call to arrange a time?"

"The deaths were placed between nine 9 and 10pm on a Thursday. Meet me at the Sumner estate at 8:30pm. And bring swim trunks. Mrs. Sumner has moved out, but I'm sure she'll agree to provide access."

John looked surprised.

"Afterwards," Diane went on, "we can drive to Cicero's, talk, have a wonderful meal, some superb wine. It's really my favorite restaurant. If you haven't been there, you'll love it."

John tried to conceal his surprise at Diane's methodology, and her directness. He had second thoughts about accepting her dinner invitation but they were fleeting. "Eight o'clock then. I could pick you up, if you like. Where do you live?"

"I'll meet you there. I'll be working late. Unfortunately, there're a lot of women who need my help."

John wondered what was going on behind Diane's beautiful blue eyes. She could have suggested they meet then return to her office after visiting the Sumner estate. Cicero's guests were always well catalogued. John was not eager to read about himself in the morning gossip column.

Diane stood, walked to him, her right hand extended. John grasped it gently for a few lingering seconds, as he was escorted past the outer office.

"Sorry you have to leave so soon," said Diane.

"Except for an earlier engagement, I'd have more time to discuss the case and get your thoughts on it. However, I've learned a lot from our discussion."

"So have I."

"By the way," said John. "Four more homicides we're investigating today could be the work of our killer."

Diane's smile disappeared. "Couples?"

"Afraid so. They were both discovered within a few hours of each other."

"Same circumstances as the others?"

"Virtually identical."

"Sorry to hear that. Anyone I should know?"

"Maybe. One was Mike Gregg. He's a... was a star Major League baseball player. It's all over the news. He and a young woman were found on the course at Hillcrest Country Club. Later this morning, the body of Judge Hunter Jeffries, and a young woman, were found. Each had taken a bullet to the head. Weapon was a .44 magnum."

Diane's face was suddenly flush. She swallowed hard. "Judge Jeffries?" His name sputtered on her lips.

"Superior Court Judge."

"I'm aware of who he is," Diane said softly. 'I hadn't heard. I've been in consultations all day. I even ate in."

"He'd been mentioned as a possible replacement on the Supreme Court . It appears you're correct."

"How so?"

"About the killer. He *is* going to keep on killing, until we catch him. And I plan to do just that."

Dr. Deauville's mood plummeted. "Please, tell me about the women," she said.

"What about them?"

"Do they have names? Do you know their names... who they are? Surely they have names and families."

John fell silent. The doctor's sudden change in disposition caught him unprepared. He was not sure what to make of it.

"Goodnight, John."

"Goodnight, Doctor."

"It's Diane. Remember?"

"Diane."

Dr. Deauville smiled thinly, and closed the door slowly.

John stood just outside the office door, staring at the brass name-plate. He was unaware of a man in a brown sport coat, dark slacks, and matching fedora with downturned brim. The clandestine observer stood watching him from the shadows at the end of the corridor. John started for the elevator, glanced at his watch. It was after 9 o'clock. He had promised Aimee dinner at eight.

Meanwhile, inside her office, Dr. Deauville, now with her shoes re-moved, and the lights lowered, was lying on her back on the sofa. She closed her eyes and massaged her lids.

Suddenly, a firm knock on her outer office door. She frowned, as she rose and walked to the door. In the corridor, the man waited.

"Who is it?"

"It's me, Diane. Open up!" The man demanded in a raspy, whis-pery voice. Seconds passed; the door opened. The man stepped inside, closed the door behind him.

"I told you to never come here," Diane scolded.

"Afraid I'll embarrass you? Who was he, Diane?

"Don't you quiz me. Don't ever! And forget about more money."

Thirty-two
Counselor In Charge, What A Dick!

Earlier - 7 PM: Captain Nicholson's Office — *"Is my client a suspect?"*

Attorney G. Gordon Smythe's sudden offer

to accompany his client, Catherine Jeffries, to P.A.B. for an interview caught Detective Gerald Li by surprise. Hours earlier, Lt. Medrano had informed him of his failure to arrange a meeting with her. Now, there they were. Skeeter was his usual cynical self, suggesting the LAPD was being set up.

Gerald was joined by the Captain, Assistant D.A., Delana Menarri; Lt. Medrano, and a uniformed Skeeter. There was some concern that the size of their contingent may be intimidating for Mrs. Jeffries, but they were underestimating her and her attorney.

Smythe was a fashion-horse, complete with his patented, plaid bow tie, three-piece tailored suit, and every hair in place. He sat next to Mrs. Jeffries at the Captain's conference table. Skeeter remained seated in an upholstered chair near the Captain's desk.

A smug, self-assured Smythe leaned forward, both elbows resting atop the oval, polished maple table, hands firmly clasped. "Captain, I am not here to argue the points I have raised, but to simply state our requisites for my client's agreeing to be interviewed, regarding her husband's death."

Nicholson appeared unusually calm and uncharacteristically unflappable. "Counselor, we have a procedure that must be followed. While we appreciate you bringing your client in to meet with us, I cannot accept the method you wish to establish for us going forward."

"We're trying to be as helpful as we can," said Smythe.

"That may be. However, we won't have you preview our questions; we will not interview Mrs. Jeffries in your offices; and we will not allow you to determine which officer gets to ask the questions. If you want to cooperate, in what is a routine procedure of interviewing the spouse of a decedent, we will use the procedure we use for everyone in such cases."

"That's what concerns us," snapped Smythe.

Delana Menarri spoke up, directing her question to Catherine directly. "I'm sure you are as interested as we are in solving your husband's murder, Mrs. Jeffries. Do you mind answering some routine questions?"

Smythe was incensed. He had not been given Ms. Menarri's title and had assumed she was a detective.

"Captain, I take offense to this officer's directing questions to my client without my permission. I don't want it to happen again."

"A simple yes or no would suffice, counsel," Nicholson responded. "I'm sure your client doesn't need a sidebar to answer. It's either yes or no. I'm sure she has nothing to hide, although I understand her right to employ her counsel as she wishes."

"Listen," Smythe continued, "If you all think we're going to be goaded into waiving rights, it is not going to happen, I assure you. What we're insisting upon is what everyone has a right to insist upon, except they don't know they can. The fact is, we did not have to come here. We have made a good faith gesture."

"Just why did you come here?" Asked Lt. Medrano.

"Let me ask you. Is my client a suspect?" Snapped Smythe.

"Not at this time, though technically everyone on the planet, including you, is a potential suspect. Now answer my question, if you don't mind, sir."

Smythe bristled. "We came here, despite my client's grief, to aid in the investigation into her husband's death."

"Then, let's get on with it."

"Under our terms."

While Lt. Medrano had been engaged in his exchange with Smythe, a light on Nicholson's phone console flashed. He answered, spoke briefly to the caller then hung up. It was clear he had heard enough. Gerald had been watching him stew, and knew he was nearing the boiling point.

"I know why you came," said Nicholson, standing. "This was part of some media public relations ploy, right? An attempt to create the appearance of willingness to cooperate, rather than the fact. Tell me something, counselor. Did you call the throng of media, camped out downstairs, before or after you called us offering to bring in your client?"

"I don't know what you're talking about."

"The truth is, you had no intention of cooperating with us by having your client consent to a general interview. We explained to you that you would be permitted to be present and could voice objections, but that the entire process would be recorded for our protection. I know how your ilk works."

"I resent your implication."

"Well, excuse me!" Said the Captain, thrusting his arms above his head, his command voice booming. "I certainly did not mean to imply; I meant to be explicit. We have a well-respected member of our community—a judge, a man who was likely to be named to the California State Supreme Court—lying in the morgue with half his brain missing, and at last check, still very dead."

Catherine dropped her head into her hands and began sobbing. "We want to find out who is responsible for that. But we're not a bunch of smart-ass lawyers here," Nicholson continued, "We're just an assorted group of hardworking, ass-busting cops with families we spend far too little time with. So you will forgive us our simplicity, our intellectual deficiencies and sub-par IQs, as we pursue the most depraved and dysfunctional among us."

Smythe was clearly set back on his heels. He adjusted his tie and leaned over to his client. The two whispered a brief exchange; Smythe stood. "Captain, that was most unnecessarily graphic and insensitive. We must bid you good evening."

With that, attorney Smythe assisted a still sobbing Catherine Jeffries to her feet and the two left.

Skeeter was not sympathetic "In a perverse kind of way, I believe having her leave here in tears is just what the sonofabitch wanted," he offered.

"She'll call us," Nicholson said, calmly. "She'll call. Contact Media Relations, have someone step outside to clean up the crap Smythe leaves on our front step with the news people."

Thirty-three
The Getaway

Next Morning. — *"Who the hell are you, and why are you trying to..."*

Except for a brief note to a still sleeping Aimee,

telling her not to worry; and a thirty minute call to Benjy, assuring him they would still get to a Dodger game before school started, John disappeared. He fell off the radar screen. He knew Gerald would have a good idea what had happened. This was part of his modus operandi—a day of immersion and communion.

John and Aimee had enjoyed a wonderful, romantic Italian dinner at Fiori's; a stroll along the Santa Monica Promenade, followed by a moonlit midnight drive along PCH to well north of Malibu. It had been far too long since they had enjoyed such an uninterrupted evening.

There were no calls. John had turned off his cell. His confession, to Aimee, that such moments were much too infrequent; and his promise that it would change, brought a cautious smile to her face. She said nothing in response. She simply placed her hand atop his and allowed the moment to wash over them.

Shortly after nine, the following morning, John gathered his brief-case; his G6 laptop; two cell phones; a broadband link, a gym bag filled with T-shirts and jeans; a shaving kit with the essentials, including a bottle of Cool Water cologne, and headed for the 10 freeway.

Traffic was a bear but he didn't care; he was in a zone. No bad dreams the night before, a good breakfast, and he was good to go. The congestion thinned at the 110 Harbor Freeway, and again after he reached the I-10/Pomona 60 split. He pointed the '71 Olds 442 east, and gave her the big foot.

The rumble of 350 thoroughbred horses fed by a 4-barrel Roch-ester carb and the essentials, all nestled under the hood with room to spare, flowed through John all the way to his fingertips. The blue chariot sported a 4:11 posi-trac rear end, a 4-speed Hurst shifter, an anti-sway bar, and a six-coat paint job with a mirror finish. Detroit had not made cars like this in decades, and likely would never again.

Less than ten minutes past the 710 exit, John moved to the right lane and exited the 60 at San Gabriel Boulevard. He made the light, turned left onto the boulevard, crossed the freeway and left again at the Motel 6, his destination. It was about as incognito as he cared to be. He felt as if he had gone a thousand miles beyond his accustomed path.

John checked in, paid cash, and was given room 237. The place was in an ideal location for his purposes. A Carrow's restaurant was in front, near the street. The freeway was a stone's throw from the build-ing. A 24 hour Mobil station/store occupied a part of the complex. Charley Brown's, a well-known steak house, offered pretty decent fare. After moving his car to within eyesight of his second floor, non-smoking room, John carried all his gear up in a single trip. Once inside, he surveyed nearly every square inch without taking a step from the front door. It was all decidedly spartan, but clean. The queen-size bed was neatly made, the headboard firmly attached to the wall.

A small Formica table set beside the curtained window, accom-panied by two industrial strength, well-cushioned chairs. The wall-mounted nightstand beneath twin, wall-mounted lamps with slightly dented shades, was just wide enough for the 70's vintage, push-button telephone.

Resting atop the nightstand was the TV's remote control. John attempted to lift it, and nearly wrenched his shoulder. It had been superglued to a metal holder and locked down into a swivel device designed to prevent theft.

John broke into laughter. "What do you want, he asked himself. Trump Plaza?" He actually found charm in what he saw. Above the door, and extending from outside to about one foot inside, was the AC unit. The thermostat was mounted to the left of the door security lock and above the light switch. He had his "$49.95 worth and more.

After grabbing a cup of complimentary coffee from the small office, John returned to his room and set up what amounted to a field office—his hideaway. Whatever he had planned to accomplish here could also be done at home. It's just that, he felt a need to avoid any and all interruptions.

It took all of fifteen minutes for John to set up his laptop, lay out a score of files and notes on the bed and floor, and power onto the Internet, via his broadband connection. He checked his several e-mail accounts. There was a message from Gerald informing him of what had transpired in Nicholson's office with Catherine Jeffries and her attorney.

John was not surprised. He delayed responding immediately, closed his mail programs and used 'Fetch' to upload a new, sleek, web site he had designed only days after his meeting with Nicholson at the morgue. Final results from the latest Dreamweaver, Photoshop, and Flash software impressed even him.

John's 1tetrabyte dedicated server—home to his xcyxcy.net web domain—had a single purpose: to provide an Internet clearinghouse for tips and leads. All personal registration info was coded. Internet pro- motion of the site through select chatrooms, blogs, newsgroups, and site submission services would not take long. John had incorporated tight Search Engine Optimization.

An hour later, John turned his focus to Colin Sumner. The 'net' proved a treasure trove of information on the late computer genius. Much of the details came from reams of data from Lexis-Nexis, Hoovers Online, and an underground site that required a healthy measure of skepticism, regarding its accuracy. He learned Sumner, against the advice of is own board, had sided with Googler, and Sun Micronet Systems against Microsonix, in the latter's recent legal battle with the government. That decision had resulted in a number of anonymous threats, though none were ever connected to Microsonix or any of their associates.

Six months before his death, and a month after being ousted from his own Sumner Technologies, Sumners received a patent for a new, innovative microchip called a "honeycomb-wafer chip." The TriCore chip reportedly demonstrated a speed capable of a hundred thousand times more calculations per second than the fastest conventional chip.

Further surfing uncovered articles covering scores of buyout attempts that ensued. Sumner had rejected them all. Shortly thereafter, a nearly fatal Oregon auto accident, resulting from a curiously damaged steering mechanism on his 960 Porsche, was never fully resolved. He recovered.

All this raised reasonable suspicion in John's mind, regarding the existence of motive on the part of unknown persons within the industry. Sumner had clearly created enemies. The question was whether the more deadly of these was the wife he had vowed to spend the rest of his life with. She too, on advice of her lawyer, refused to be interviewed by the police. The pattern, coincidental or not, had emerged. John saw it as more than a curiosity.

By noon, John had developed a database and spreadsheet that provided a tool for organizing and storing significant case facts. A second allowed a storing of more speculative analysis of his thoughts about the various cases. Still, he knew it was only complimentary.

Despite technological advances, solving murders remained grunge work. Solutions almost always resulted from old-fashioned, down in the trenches police work. He was committed to doing both.

Hours later, the temptation to go "wired" rather than remain "unplugged" came and went. John was anxious to hear Aimee's sweet voice, to have her tell him how much she missed him. It would be late the following night before he returned home.

By three in the afternoon, John had crashed, watched 'Treasure of Sierra Madre' for nearly the one-hundredth time in his life, and fallen asleep. When he awoke two hours later, it took several confused seconds to realize where he was. He was starving. The single cup of coffee was all he'd had, since breakfast. The thought of a prime rib with all the fixings was too appealing to resist.

John grabbed his jacket, and was about to walk out the door, when the phone rang. It startled him. No one knew he was there. The phone rang a second and third time. He moved uneasily to the nightstand and lifted the receiver.

'Hello." Nothing. "Hello," he repeated. A click. He held the phone a brief second, hung up, and stood near the nightstand with the door slightly ajar, wondering who had called. He was tempted to call the desk to try and learn more about the caller the clerk had patched through to his room. Was it male? Female?

After several minutes pondering his next move, John dropped it. There had to be a rational explanation. Perhaps the caller had expected to reach an earlier occupant. Upon hearing his voice he or she simply hung up. Either that, or the operator rang the wrong room.

Having rationalized away the mystery, John left the room. Hunger pangs returned with a vengeance. Charley Brown's was a welcome sight. An hour later, he was stuffed—a new man. After several minutes of staring into a brilliant night sky, he strode briskly across the parking lot back toward the motel.

With newly found energy, John bounded up the stairs to the second level, wheeled left down the corridor then stopped in his tracks. Someone was at his door. About fifty feet away, a muscular guy with a ponytail, dressed in dark slacks and sport coat—biceps bulging—appeared to be milling around his door. John observed him peering cautiously through the slightly parted curtains. The man tried the door knob then returned to the window.

John proceeded briskly, appearing to not notice the stranger. When he was roughly fifteen feet away, the man saw him coming and pretended to be searching for his room key...a key to John's door.

John continued past the man and, without breaking stride, wheeled around, drew his 9mm and aimed at the man's head.

"Looking for this?" John hissed, holding up his left hand to show the man his room key. Who the hell are you, and why are you trying to break into my room?"

The startled man raised both hands, took a couple of nervous steps backwards.

"Time's up," John whispered.

"Wait. It's not what you think," the man stuttered. "I'm just...looking for my wife. I thought she was in this room...with her goddamn boyfriend. She's been screwing around on me. I thought I'd found them."

The man seemed on the verge of tears. John said nothing for several seconds.

"Well you haven't found them. Did you call this room earlier?"

"No, I didn't. Look, I'm sorry." The man apologized. "I'm sorry."

"If you want, I'll let you look inside."

"No, no. That's okay," the man insisted. "No."

"You really need to deal with this some other way. You could get your brains splattered." John lowered his 9mm to his side but did not holster it.

"You're right."

"I'm just curious," said John. "What did you plan to do if you'd found your wife and her boyfriend?"

The man hesitated. "Can I show you?" He asked.

"That depends," said John, cautiously.

"It's okay," the man assured him.

John nodded. The man then slowly grasped the right lapel of his sport coat, and eased it back, revealing a large handgun tucked inside his waistband. John shook his head.

"You got a license for that thing?"

"I'm a cop...here in Montebello. You got a license for that one?"

"I'm FBI," said John.

The man smiled. John returned the gesture. The stranger buttoned his coat and backed away. He apologized again, before finally turning to leave. John watched—gun still in hand—until his would-be intruder reached the end of the outside corridor, cleared the corner and disappeared. Twenty minutes later, he changed rooms.

Thirty-four
Dancing With Dead – First Time For Everything

The Following Night — "Colin was shot first," she said, her voice trailing.

John Roméo's brief sabbatical was over.

The modest motel room, while replete with a cocoon quality conducive to uninterrupted work, quickly wore thin.

It was barely 8pm, when John reached the sprawling, Pacific Palisades Sumner Estate atop a leveled hill overlooking the Pacific Ocean. He eased his '442 to a gentle stop behind the dark BMW sedan parked in the circular, cobblestone drive.

Just as he opened his door, the BMW driver's door opened. John saw Dr. Deauville, in faded jeans and sweater, carrying a gym bag. He exited, strode to meet her. The two greeted each other with a pronounced embrace. The night air was a cool—unseasonably cool for May in southern California.

"Good to see you again, John. This shouldn't take long. Of course I'm always unaware of time until the experience completes itself."

John was not exactly sure what that meant or what to expect. He had known a number of profilers but most worked in the comfort of their offices, with only occasional visits to crime scenes. Diane was different. And there was definitely something different about her this night. Despite her cheerful greeting, she seemed somber, subdued, distant. Her voice was more resonant, lower in tone. He shrugged it off.

The Sumner mansion was still occupied by two housekeepers and a groundskeeper. All lived in detached quarters; no one occupied the main house. Dr. Deauville had obtained the key from Captain Nicholson, who made arrangements with Mrs. Sumner's attorney. She was told the security alarm had been turned off, and would be reactivated after her visit. Dr. Deauville handed John the key. He opened the door, returned it to her. The two stepped inside.

Soft lighting rose automatically. They were immediately swallowed up by the opulent, cavernous interior. Without the other knowing, each sensed the place not simply unoccupied; it was empty—devoid of life. John felt they were trespassing into some hallowed domain, perhaps guarded by the unseen. He had not entertained such thoughts before. It took only minutes for the two to find their way through the main quarters, up a short flight of terrazzo steps, to the entrance leading to the pool area.

The sight was breathtaking. Moonlight poured through the skylights, much as it had on the night of the murders. Diane had taken great care planning her visit. She wanted conditions to be close to what they were the night of the murders.

"Where're your swim trunks?" She asked.

"This is *your* ballpark. You don't need me ruining the spell. I'll just stand quietly over here and observe."

Diane smiled and proceeded to an open doorway leading to a small dressing room just off the deck. There was no searching, no guessing. It was as if she knew where it was. Perhaps she had studied the floor plan provided in the materials Nicholson had given her.

Minutes later, Diane emerged in a dark, one-piece swimsuit, carrying a large beach towel. Her hair was pinned in a French twist.

"Damn!" He thought, as he watched her walk along the edge of the pool. Momentarily, Diane stopped and spread the towel onto the deck. She paused a full minute, gazed out over the pool then up at the moonlight washing down onto the water. John eased a few feet closer. She turned to him.

"I should warn you. Whatever you see or hear, don't be alarmed. I'm alright."

John nodded. Then, to his amazement, Diane removed her swimsuit and carefully placed it on the deck. John assumed it was the spot where investigators found Lisa Halliday's swimsuit. She eased into the water and briefly lingered with arms outstretched along the edge of the deck.

John moved to a new position that offered him a view of her face. Her eyes were closed; she appeared to ease into a trance-like state. Minutes later, she eased away from the deck toward the center of the pool. The water level rose slowly to just above Diane's breasts. She stopped, turned in circles several times. John noticed her eyes shut tight; he wondered what was going through her mind. He moved to new position, as Diane moved even farther away.

The water was now at Diane's shoulders. Momentarily, she returned, moved closer to the pool's edge. She positioned herself, facing the direction from which police theorized the killer struck. Diane peered into the darkness that cloaked the area in front of her, She stared ahead, whispering Lisa's name over and over, then Colin's name.

John could not hear her clearly but could see her mouthing something. Diane moved closer and closer to the pool edge—closer to where the two bodies were found. She stopped. John could see her more clearly now. Again, Diane closed her eyes.

A half hour passed. John was certain something dramatic had taken place in the pool. Diane moved easily, though warily, to the change room. John waited, wondering what she had divined, if anything. When she emerged Diane said nothing. She moved once more to the edge of the pool, gazed out over the water then wheeled around to face him.

"Colin was shot first," she said, her voice trailed. "He was the one they wanted. He fell back into the water. Then, Lisa was shot. It all happened quickly, less than five seconds. Lisa saw or heard movement, right over there. I'm sure of it. There was more than one person, too. Both had been there for some time."

"You determined that, just climbing into the pool?"

"No, John. By listening to Lisa—her spirit, by feeling and sensing what she felt. None of this comes from me. It's all from listening to Lisa."

"Listening to..."

"I assure you I haven't lost my mind. I know this seems strange but..."

"Just a little unconventional. You say you gain this insight by listening to the deceased, right?"

"By listening and by feeling what Lisa saw and felt, through her spirit. I set aside my own thoughts, my emotions. I become a willing vessel, an open conduit, John. The spirits of the dead are never as far away from the living world as we choose to think."

Diane turned and walked toward the steps leading from the pool. John followed. Neither spoke until they had exited the front entrance and stood next to Diane's car.

"John, let's skip dinner, if you don't mind. I don't have much of an appetite just now."

"No problem. We can talk tomorrow."

"I'll likely visit Hillcrest tomorrow night. I'll go alone."

"Then we'll meet another day."

"I don't mind discussing the case. We can go back to my office. I have to return there anyway. I'll meet you."

John agreed. Skipping Cicero's suited him just fine.

Thirty-five
Family

Detective Gerald Li

sat next to his 16 -year old son, Ray, a high school sophomore and scholar-baseball athlete. Daughter, Felicia, 14, a freshman, was perched on a pillow pile. All were in the den of their comfortable Carson home, watching a 'Raisin in The Sun.'

No one inside the two-story, four-bedroom, brick home saw the dark-colored, Ford cargo van ease to the curb just past the front door and stop. The floodlights at the corners of the house provided the only perimeter light. The closest street lamp was more than fifty feet down the quiet street.

The male driver sat motionless, at first. A young boy on a skateboard darted past then disappeared. With the van still running, the man—of average build, dressed in dark clothing, including a dark watch cap, exited, quietly closing the driver's door.

Clutching a box in the bend of his right arm, he headed briskly up the concrete walk leading to the Li home. He reached the front door, opened the box, and removed a ream of printed sheets. He tossed several at the base of the door, around the steps then headed toward the garage and driveway. The remaining papers were scattered across the hood of Laura's Saturn, parked near the garage door. Finally, he randomly tossed the last sheets onto the driveway, and raced back to van. Once inside, he eased into gear and drove away with his lights out, until he reached the corner.

Inside, Gerald was making a valiant effort to stay awake. He still had not received an answer to his last e-mail and cell calls to John, and was just a little concerned. Laura, his wife of twenty years, and an international law attorney, had suggested he try and spend at least an hour with the kids on rare weekday nights he arrived home early. Gerald needed little coaxing.

Laura, a Houston, Texas native; University of Texas, and Harvard Law School grad, lay sprawled across the bed in the master bedroom. Legal briefs were piled around her; a laptop was set on a pillow in front of her.

Dinner was done. Preparing it was a labor of love now shared by all, especially Ray and Felicia. Gerald's normal routine, after dinner, would have been to disappear into his upstairs office, turn on the TV and pass out. Tonight was different.

"Dad!" Ray called out, having turned to see his dad's head listing nearly ninety degrees. Ray's yell startled Gerald into consciousness. He snapped his head up, and straight back.

"What are you yelling for?"

"You were asleep again."

"I'm watching the movie. You can ask Felicia. Ask your sister."

"You were snoring, daddy," Felicia said, giggling.

"I heard everything."

"What just happened, then?"

"You guys got your homework done?" Asked Gerald, changing the subject.

"Chill, daddy. You're deflecting?"

"What does that mean?"

"Daddy!" Felicia chided.

"I just want to know what your brother means."

"Changing the subject," said Ray, stifling his laughter.

"You should have said that. Don't be using multisyllabic assev-erations in discussions with your dear old dad. I'm only a cop, you know."

Ray doubled over. Felicia shook her head with amusement. "Multisyllabic what?"

"Look it up."

Just then, the movie ended. "Aw, man. We missed the end of the movie, daddy. It's your fault."

Felicia stood and walked to her father. Just then, Laura entered.

"How was the movie, again," she asked.

"Daddy fell asleep, again," said Felicia. "But we love him anyway, I think."

The kids headed upstairs. Laura sat on Gerald's lap. He threw both arms around her; she leaned over and kissed him.

"Yes, counselor."

With only a wink, Laura simply stood, grasped Gerald's right hand and started for their bedroom. The phone rang. Neither said a word as they reached the bedroom door. It rang again. One of the kids an-swered in mid third ring.

Laura closed the bedroom door and began removing papers and the laptop from the bed."

"Hey, what's wrong with the floor," Gerald asked with a twinkle in his eye. "It used to be okay."

Laura turned, both hands resting on her hips. "The only time my knees touch the floor is when I pray. So, you can have the floor if you want. I'll be here on the bed."

A rap at the door. It was Ray.

"Yes," said Laura, drawing her words out slowly.

"It's for Dad, Mom. Mr. Roméo."

Laura tossed both hands in the air and fell forward onto the bed.

"Five minutes," said Gerald. "I'll get it," he yelled to Ray, turning to Laura. "I'll take it in the den. Be back before you clear the bed and get the chocolate syrup. I promise." Laura rolled over and lay staring up at the ceiling.

Thirty-six
Under The Gun...I Passed Up That For This?

SANTA MONICA FREEWAY—INBOUND — *"No, no, no. Hell no..."*

John's conversation with Gerald

followed his brief call to Aimee. He wanted her to know he was alright, and would be home soon. She promised to wait up for him. The call to Gerald was to let him know he was out of his self-imposed exile, and would see him the next day. The conversation lasted less than five minutes. John sensed Gerald was anxious to get back to something important.

John had his own flood of thoughts to contend with. What had he witnessed at the Sumner estate? He tried to brush off the unconventional methodology of the good doctor. Whatever it was, Diane appeared deeply affected.

Once inside Diane's office, it took only seconds for John to realize the extent of her dark mood. She seemed distant, although she insisted he remain to discuss the case. It was clear she did not want to be alone. However, John's instincts took over. He concocted an excuse about an urgent cell call from Captain Nicholson. He suggested they talk again in a day or so. Diane reluctantly agreed, embracing him briefly at the door as he left.

John took the elevator to the building's *Penthouse Restaurant* for a look around at the spectacular view, and to ponder what had taken place. He considered having a drink then decided against it. He stayed less than fifteen minutes.

Shortly after leaving, he stepped off the elevator in the underground garage and headed for his car. He was only steps away from the raised concrete apron when a Yellow cab suddenly stormed onto the level. With tires screeching, the vehicle lurched to a stop less than fifty feet from him.

The cab's rear seat passenger—a disheveled man of about 33, scroungy, bearded, wearing a mangy sport coat and visibly soiled slacks—stumbled out. He tripped, nearly falling to the pavement as he tumbled toward John, yelling wildly.

"John! John!" The man screamed frantically. His speech was slurred; he waved his arms wildly, kept glancing back over his shoulder. A startled John looked up to recognize Roger rushing toward him as fast as he could. Three feet away, he stopped dead in his tracks. A look of surprise and disgust gripped John's face.

"What the hell?" He blurted.

The cab squealed away, the right front tire riding up onto the apron. In a flash, a white 4-door Maserati, carrying four men, pulled up and slammed to a hard stop. In a blink, John saw the front passenger thrust his arm out the lowered, front passenger window with an Uzi firmly gripped in his hand. Roger was only steps away. John dove toward him, taking him down. Both landed with a thud onto the unforgiving pavement. Roger tried to raise himself.

"Get down!" John screamed. "Get down!"

Just then, the first burst from the Uzi erupted. Bullets ripped into the walls, sending bits and chunks of concrete flying in a thousand directions. The reverberations filled the structure.

"Sonofabitch!" John screamed. "What the hell!"

The Uzi exploded again. John began dragging Roger behind the nearest row of cars. He ripped his 9mm from his shoulder holster and crouched. The Uzi kept spraying. Roger was delirious; he briefly lost control of his bodily functions. John brow beaded with perspiration; his reflexes were on auto pilot.

"Don't let 'em kill me! John. They followed me."

"Shut up! What the hell they want with you?"

The shooter leaped from the Maserati, took several menacing steps forward.

John cranked off a short burst from a position near the front of a car bumper. That brought a quick retreat; a slammed car door, and peeling tires, as the Maserati tore away. Convinced the assailants had fled, John stood, turned and stared at Roger with contempt.

"Bastards! They tried to kill me," Roger screamed. "They tried to kill me."

"You? What about me? They tried to kill us! What the hell was that about?"

"Sorry, John. I'm sorry."

Roger's nauseating whimpering grated on John. He holstered his gun. "Be quiet!" He yelled.

"You gotta believe me."

"No, no, no. Hell no. I don't gotta do a damn thing but get away from you. You're dangerous."

"I can explain."

"Explain my ass! You almost got me killed. And you're stoned out of your friggin' mind, or what's left of it. Who were those clowns? And why were they trying to kill you? Answer me!"

Roger was slow to respond. John grabbed his collar, shook him violently. A cowering Roger covered his face, cried like a baby. John released him and stalked away.

"You can't leave me here."

"Oh yeah?"

"You can't. They'll come back. I know they will."

"They won't find me here."

Roger ran to catch up. "I'm not high, John. I'm scared shitless but I'm not high. I probably dumped in my pants but I swear, I'm not high. You can look at me. Look in my eyes. I promise. I haven't touched a thing in... in..."

"In what? A day? A week? A month? An hour? Listen, I don't have time to stand here conducting some street sobriety test. I'm going home. Goodbye!"

Thirty-seven
He Ain't Heavy, He's Just A Load

"You're nuts," John declared.

John pulled past his gated entrance

and came to a sharp stop inside the motor court. He climbed out and waited as Roger stumbled to the pavement, barely able to close the door behind him.

With the latter trailing, the two men approached the front door of the main house and entered. They had no sooner shut the door than the Maserati, cruising with lights out, eased past the front gate. The driver paused briefly then drove on.

Inside, John exploded. He and Roger stood just inside the entry, glaring at each other, looking as if they had both fallen from a garbage truck. John stalked away, arms flailing. He wheeled around, right index finger aimed at Rogers' nose.

"I want to know how you knew where to find me. I don't want to hear anything else until you tell me."

Roger remained mute, flinching at John's every move. He was in no shape to immediately reply.

"Blame me, John," Aimee answered, leaning against the upper level railing. "I told him."

John turned his full attention to the railing at the top of the stairs. "I see, I see."

"What happened to you two?" Aimee continued. "You both look terrible."

Aimee wore a knee length, blue silk gown over a blue negligee. She had never seen John so furious; she didn't know what to make of it.

"Thanks, Aimee," John said. "Why?"

"John."

"I told you I wanted nothing else to do with... with him."

"Please, John," Roger interrupted. "It's not her fault."

John was hearing none of it. "I made it clear I needed to put some distance between me and you. Not because I want to, but because I have to."

"He's your brother!" Aimee reminded him.

"He's a taker. He drains without giving anything back. And you had no right to interfere."

A wounded Aimee walked away. Roger summoned the courage to turn to his brother again, attempted to apologize. John was in no mood.

"I don't want more apologies. They're all lies."

"I know. I've screwed up before but..."

"I've done all I can do for you. I've had you in treatment a dozen times, gotten you jobs, bought a place to for you to live, which you had the gall to sublet and allowed to be trashed. That's it."

"I can explain."

"I have to face the truth, Roger. You're a cokehead and a drunk because you want to be. You don't want to be anything else. I've tried to help you, but I refuse to be your damn co-dependent. Understand?"

"I don't want to be like this, John. And I'm not dirty, I swear, man. I had a few beers, but I'm not dirty, John. You gotta believe me."

"I don't believe a word. Correct me if I'm wrong, but that big guy with the gun—the one who tried to kill us tonight—he wasn't trying to collect on charity pledges, was he?"

"No."

"Then tell me why I almost got blown away tonight!"

Roger hesitated, infuriating John even more. "Alright. I owe them a little money. But not really."

"For what? Drugs? Gambling? Parking tickets? What? Look at me!

"They... they think I found this... briefcase with fifty-thousand dollars in it, which I didn't because Carole did. She's the woman I was going to marry. We lived together in the house you bought, until I leased it to these guys who I think must've been into drugs because... well, I kinda know they were and I think they're Russians...they sound like Russians. Anyway, they moved away overnight 'cause the cops must've been onto them from a tip I think Carole... she gave them to get a reduced charge on her prostitution and drug rap.

"Then, we went back to the house and found this briefcase in a closet. Carole took it and we... I mean she took it to the bus station and got one of those lockers, but then she skipped out on me and took the money, and I can't find her. And I found out she'd lied about where she was from, so I can't find her. And now these guys are trying to kill me. But I haven't done drugs in a year. I swear."

Roger's wild rambling finally ended. John shook his head in profound disgust. He took a couple of steps back and stared at his brother. He couldn't believe they had both come from the same womb.

"You're nuts," John declared.

Before Roger could say more, John bounded up the stairs, leaving him standing in the middle of the entry.

"They're still gonna kill me, John. They're gonna fuckin' kill me first chance they get, I swear."

"So is fuckin' killing you the same as just killing you?"

An hour later, John was awake, angry, and staring aimlessly at the ceiling. Aimee's back was turned to him, but he knew she was not asleep. He was not surprised she had taken Roger's side in the confrontation. It was in keeping with her character and personality.

"Sorry I... I yelled at you. Getting shot at with an Uzi tends to wreak havoc on one's disposition."

Brief silence.

"He's your brother, John," Aimee said, facing him. "You can never give up on your brother. You are a warm, compassionate, loving person. I know you cannot do this. He needs you. You two are all the family each other has. As many times as he stumbles and falls; as long as God gives you the strength and the means to reach down and lift him up, you have to do it. You have to. The reward for your love and attending to his suffering will come. "

John returned to staring at the ceiling. Moments later, he submitted to overwhelming fatigue and closed his eyes. Yet, sleep eluded him, for a time. John loved and cared deeply for his brother. For years he had supported him; bailed him out; hired attorneys to defend him on drug violations; gotten him countless jobs; purchased housing; placed him in job training, and more. It simply had not worked.

Roger was no dummy. He was a gifted musician, possessed a keen intellect, a brilliant mind, He graduated high school two years after John, with honors and a 4.0 GPA. A brilliant future lay before him. Roger received a four-year scholarship to M.I.T, attended one year, then self-destructed, succumbing to drugs.

John had played the *brother's keeper* role, for years. Roger had clearly taken advantage of his kindness. He used his cunning, his ability to make John feel his success obliged to accede to his brother's every whim.

After repeated consultation with drug-rehab experts, John had backed away; tried to force Roger to assume responsibility for his own condition. It had not been easy. But up until the night's events, John felt the new approach was essential for his own sanity, and Roger's salvation.

Roger remained downstairs. John was awake, staring through blurred slits; his mind flushed with memory of his mother who, on her deathbed, forced him to promise to care for Roger, unconditionally. John felt it unfair but understood. He drew a deep breath, glanced at Aimee, buried his face in the pillow and began counting sheep. It didn't work.

Unable to fall asleep, John eased out of bed and made his way to the study. He plopped down at his computer desk and, using data Gerald had provided, began keying in crime-scene data, including graphics, into a special program he had developed two years earlier.

The complex program enabled John to animate victims, perpetrators, and scene specifications in plausible scenarios. The results could be altered by changing the variables, such as: point of entry for killers; position of victims prior to their murder; trajectory of gunshots based on estimated height of shooters, and so forth.

Based on crime scene dimensions and projected time for various activities, an estimate of time spent by the killers at the scene could be estimated, as well as conjecture concerning likelihood accomplices involved. Available commercial software lacked some features he needed. So, he created his own.

Three hours later, John was still running variables through the system. Unfortunately, his efforts were being hampered by incomplete data, and growing fatigue. Several times, he found himself opening his eyes, uncertain of just when he had closed them. Realizing the futility of forcing himself on, John shut down the system and made his way back to the bedroom. This time, sleep seized him the instant his head touched the pillow.

Thirty-eight
Brother's Keeper — Yeah, Right.

Next Morning: *A picture of a police officer's badge riddled with bullet holes.*

This morning,

Tom Baswell was at the top of John's shit list. The acerbic, self-styled minister had piqued his interest by promising to offer aid to anyone accused of murdering "adulterers." The man's zealotry; his outrageous, violence-laced, unabashed race-baiting pronouncements made him difficult to ignore. His influence amongst those who viewed themselves as anti-government, true Christians-defenders of all things white and right could not be blithely dismissed.

John had heard Baswell's ranting before. During the serial murder trial of Sgt. Bolen, the so-called minister defended the officer's actions. He and his organization even contributed money to the disgraced officer's defense. Even now, Baswell was raising money for Bolen's appeal. In a recent appearance on national television, he boasted of helping the ex-cop's attorneys uncover exculpatory evidence that could free the convicted serial killer. He did not elaborate.

Fully dressed, John quietly reentered the bedroom from the bath. Aimee was still asleep; he took care to not awaken her. With suit Jacket clutched in one hand, he moved to the bed, leaned over and took a long look at her. She stirred, but did not wake.

When John reached the kitchen, he found a new Roger. His brother had slept on the den sofa, rose early, showered, trimmed his beard, and was dressed in clean slacks and silk shirt. A sport coat was draped over the back of a chair in the informal dining room. Two coffee cups were on the table—one full, one empty. Roger glanced up, saw his brother enter, and poured the second cup. A moment of acute crept past.

"Thanks for a place to crash... the borrowed clothes, everything. Hope you don't mind my fixing breakfast. I heard you coming before I popped in the toast. You still don't eat eggs, right? I couldn't find the..."

"Listen, Roger... you're welcome to the clothes; the shoes; the food, and... you can stay here a few days. I had thought about putting you up in a hotel in Long Beach for a month or so."

"That sounds... great. I appreciate it, brother. I really do."

"Hold on. I've changed my mind. I want you to stay here."

"What?"

"You can stay here...with me and Aimee... for a while."

"No, no, John. I couldn't. I couldn't impose on you two like that. You were right last night. You've done enough for me."

"Look, I can't measure it like that. I... I see that now. You're my brother. We're all each other have. I want you here. There's more than enough room. You can hide the USC Trojan band in this place. Now, there will be a few...a few expectations. But we're going to set them up together. They won't be mine alone; they'll be yours, too. First, I suggest a change in the kind of company you keep. If you truly want to get better, we'll see that that happens... together."

Roger rushed forward, threw his arms around his brother. John seemed uncomfortable with the emotional display, at first. Roger sensed the discomfiture and released his bear hug.

"I know I haven't behaved in a way that makes you proud. I'm not proud of myself. I never made Dad proud." Roger's voice was filled with emotion and contrition. "Mom died hoping I'd turn things around. I'd like to think she believed I would. I want *you* to believe in me."

John was visibly affected by his brother's words.

"I appreciate the things you've done for me," Roger continued. "And someday... some way, I'll repay you. I don't mean this to sound like some sob story. I really mean it."

"I'll call you later," said John. "And we'll see what we can do about those clowns in the Maserati. Based on what you said, warrants are probably still out on them. There aren't that many white Maseratis roaming around L.A. with a passenger packing an Uzi."

John headed for the door. But, before he could exit the dining room, the phone rang. He answered. It was Gerald. By now, the garbage strewn across his porch, driveway, car, and lawn had done its emotional damage. The crudely drawn, but unsettling, message had been discovered by Laura as she left for work.

A picture of a police officer's badge had been riddled with bullet holes. Below the image appeared the words: 'Rest in Peace.' What was worse, each sheet had been smeared with what Gerald concluded was fake blood.

Gerald quickly gathered the 'trash,' determined his children not see a single sheet. Surprisingly, Laura was not particularly emotional; that caused him even more concern. John was enraged; it got worse. Gerald suggested he open his front door. He did so. A blanket of white confetti littered a wide area of the drive and grounds, just inside his gate. For the moment, possible reasons for the events escaped them. They agreed to keep the incidents secret.

Thirty-nine

It ain't over 'til... So, where's the fat bitch?

Case Closed? — *What's in the cooler? What's in the cooler?"*

The stunning news came

in a second cell phone call from Gerald, just as John reached Sunset and Doheny. He had a particular dislike for devices protruding from his ear, so he eased his Ferarri to the curb and answered.

"It's all over. The case has been solved," Gerald said."

"What case?"

"Ours. We've got a suspect in custody."

"A what?"

"A prime suspect. He walked through the front door at Central and confessed."

"Confessed. Another one?"

"What's new is that he's being believed... being called a prime. That's all I know."

"I'm on my way."

"I'll meet you."

"Give me about twenty or so. I was planning on visiting a certain minister."

"Baswell?"

"One in the same."

"Let's do this first. I'll go with you, later."

"I'm there."

At or about 8:30 am, a 38 year-old white male; approximately 5'-10; weighing roughly 165 pounds; wearing military fatigues, soft cap, and carrying a red and white Igloo cooler, walked into Central Division. He was halted only steps inside the door by the two officers at the desk.

"Freeze!" One yelled. Both officers drew their weapons; one sprang from behind the desk. Other officers in the area drew weapons and ordered the man into the felony-prone position on the floor.

With no fewer than eight officers drawing down on "Jethro," the man, Clyde Fortier, from Lancaster, lowered the cooler to the floor and complied.

It wasn't until he was literally dragged outside, and the entire area evacuated, that officers learned reason for his being at Central. A minute more and the entire building would have been evacuated.

What's in the cooler? What's in the cooler?" Officers demanded.

"Guns. Just a few guns."

"Guns?"

"Just guns...pistols. No bomb. There's no bomb in there, just guns. I'll open it for you," the handcuffed man volunteered.

It took a few anxious minutes of trying to decide whether to call in the bomb squad, before the rectangular cooler was examined. Inside, carefully wrapped in blue bubble wrap, were six IMI .44 Magnum revolvers, each with 8-3/8" barrels.

"I did it," the man kept saying. "I did it. I killed 'em... killed all of 'em. I'm the one you want. They were nothing but adulterers and fornicators."

It took several minutes before the officers in the lobby understood to what the man was confessing. He was read his rights, placed under protective arrest, and placed in a holding cell. Lt. Medrano was alerted at HQ.

A half hour later, Sergeant Foster, accompanied by Assistant Division Commander, John Chen, and Sgt. Emory, the man was brought to a downstairs interrogation room. That's where he was when John arrived to find both Gerald and Lt. Medrano waiting for him in a small observation room. All were peering through a two way mirror and watching the show.

Inside the room, Foster inched a full-sized recorder closer to the suspect and fired off another question.

"So, who was the first person you killed?"

"The hardware guy—Talon, Sam Talon and his mistress. He'd been married thirty-two years, you know. His wife had herself a stroke, but that was no reason to commit adultery. 'Til death do ye part; that's what the Bible says; said nothing 'bout...except for catastrophic illness. I can show you. His affair started long 'fore that."

"How do you know?"

"God reveals things to his own. You saved, Lieutenant? You a 'born again' believer?"

"It's Sergeant. And just try to stick with my questions, for right now."

Gerald turned to John. "I understand Foster's been pumping him for nearly an hour. We just got here. What we know is that Foster thinks the confession has enough details to make the confession legit. He thinks the case is damn near solved.

"What about ballistics? Asked John.

"Foster's betting they'll confirm it."

"He thinks? You're shitin' me, right? Oh, well, that shouldn't surprise anyone," John shrugged.

Gerald nodded agreement. "Anyway, this guy's name is Clyde... Clyde Fortier, from Lancaster. Says he's responsible for the killing spree. Insists it was God's will."

"Let me get this. Are you saying this guy walked in...carrying a cooler with six .44 Mags wrapped in plastic?"

"Right."

"Where are the guns now?" Asked John.

"Down the hall."

"Get me one."

Two minutes later, Gerald returned with a shiny, nickel-plated .44 Mag; handed it to John—grip first, barrel down. John examined it carefully, rolled out the six-shot chamber, eyed the barrel, sniffed it, snapped the chamber back in place.

"Let's cut to the chase," he said then threw open the door leading into the main interrogation room, carrying the .44 held at his side. Gerald followed. Lt. Medrano remained in the observation room.

The sudden entry of the two officers startled all three. Foster dropped his head and clenched his fist. Emory's eyes bugged. Fortier stopped mid-sentence.

"Please, continue," said John. He and Gerald remained several feet from the table, just in the shadows, and barely out of the bright light showering the table.

Foster stood, walked over. "You been listening?"

'A little," said John. "Just got here. This our man?"

Foster swallowed hard. "I think so. Could be. His name is Clyde Fortier...lives in or around Lancaster. He has been cooperating... answering my questions."

"You mind if I pose a few?"

Foster hesitated, momentarily. "No, be my guest."

John nodded then approached the table, and a smiling Clyde Fortier. He said nothing, just aimed a laser stare for several seconds. Fortier looked away. John started pacing along the length of the table, directly in front of Fortier. The latter followed John's every move, glancing obliquely, fidgeting nervously as John stopped a couple of feet away.

"Mr. Fortier, my name's Roméo."

"Mr. Roméo. Are you a lieutenant, too?"

"Just call me John, alright?"

"Well, that's a little awkward for me, sir. We just met. I'll call you sir, if you don't mind."

"Whatever you like."

"Yessir."

"Mr. Fortier, you own a lot of guns, or just .44s? "Aah... aah, I own mostly .44s, at least I used to."

"I see. What do you do for a living?"

"Well, I sorta... I sorta sell stuff."

"You sorta sell stuff?"

"Yeah, I mean, yessir. I... I sell trinkets and... and do-dads and such... sell 'em at flea markets."

"Hmm. Business must be pretty good. These .44's you bought are expensive. Now, do I have it right? You've walked in here, on your own volition—your own decision—and confessed to the murder of eleven people?"

"No sir."

"No?"

"No sir, it was twelve. There are twelve victims. I killed twelve of 'em... killed 'em in pairs. Two, four, six, eight, ten, twelve."

"Correct. I'm sorry. Twelve. You're confessing to murdering twelve people."

"Yessir."

"Why stop at twelve? Were there only a dozen adulterers in Los Angeles? Did you rid us all of these unrighteous, hell bound sinners?" "I think you're perhaps being a bit facetious, if you don't mind me saying so, sir. You see, I simply listen and obey?"

"Listen to whom?"

"To the voice of God Almighty...through his Holy Word, sir. We are told that death is the wage—payment, just reward for sin."

"So, God told you to kill these people and to stop at twelve."

"Yessir. There's biblical significance there."

"How did you decide whom to kill, and how did you get inside the homes? For example, tell us how you gained entry to the judge's condo? That was brilliant."

Fortier smiled, cocked his head. "Thank you, sir. But I can't tell you that. They would kill me."

"They would kill you? They, who?"

"I was in Special Ops... worked for the CIA, DIA, NSA, DEA, all secret stuff.

John glanced at Foster, Emory, looked at Gerald and shook his head, turned back to Fortier. He had heard all he needed to hear but decided to go on. He could not believe Fortier was being considered a suspect. Still, he did not want to appear totally dismissive of Foster.

"Well, let's see what you *can* tell us. Describe the deck around Colin Sumner's pool. What color is it?" Fortier shook his head. "What brand of blank CD is being left at the murder scenes?" More silence. "Can't you answer my questions? The real killer would have no difficulty answering these simple questions, Mr. Fortier."

More silence.

Without warning, John dropped the .44 onto the metal table. It landed with a loud, reverberating crash that bounced off all four walls. Fortier flinched, slapped both hands to his ears, briefly.

"Did I frighten you?"

Fortier took a deep breath, and leaned as far back as he could. "It was a bit loud and unexpected," said Fortier. "Very loud. I wasn't expecting you to do that. I tend to shut down when people yell at me or make loud noises. My father yelled at me...a lot."

"Hmm. My apologies. But, if you've fired a .44 before, you must certainly be put off by the even greater noise they make."

"I use plugs."

"Plugs?"

"Ear plugs, sir."

"I see. "You want us to believe you simply plugged your ears, and used .44s—different .44s when you murdered these living, breathing human beings?"

"No sir."

"No?"

"A silencer. I used a silencer."

"Silencer? Mr. Fortier, I don't recall seeing a silencer in your cooler. Did I miss it somehow?"

"I couldn't find it."

"You misplaced it."

"Yessir."

"Pick it up, Mr. Fortier."

"Sir?"

"You heard me. Pick it up. Pick up the gun!"

Fortier flinched, hesitated a second, glanced about the room at the other officers then reached nervously for the .44 with a shaky right hand. He lifted it, seizing the non-slip grip, uneasily.

"Stand up!"

"I...."

"Stand up! Now!"

Fortier stood, slowly. John moved toward him, quickly, threateningly. A shaking Fortier stood with the pistol hanging loosely at his side.

"Point it at me, Mr. Fortier. I want you to raise the gun and point it at me. Show all of us just how you held this powerful handgun, and coolly blew the brains out of your victims. You did refer to them as victims, didn't you, Mr. Fortier? I don't usually hear killers refer to people they waste as victims."

"I'm not sure what..."

"Not sure of what I'm asking you to do? I want you to point the gun at me! Pretend I am an adulterer, and you've just found me screwing my mistress, Mr. Fortier. Show us what you did. On the count of three, ready? One, two, three! Raise your gun and shoot me, Mr. Fortier? Am I not close enough? Too close, maybe? Should I be lying in bed? Would that be more realistic for you? C'mon!"

Fortier grimaced, started to slowly raise the gun, with both hands. He brought it up just above his waist, hesitated then faltered, allowing it hang at his side. John snatched the gun away from Fortier and placed it on the table.

"You've never fired a .44 in your life, have you Mr. Fortier? I'll bet you're afraid of guns. Would I be right? Perhaps you're a bit nervous; maybe that's it. You're just nervous. Okay, I have another request. Tell me about Frankie and Johnny."

"What do you want to know?" Fortier's voice quaked.

"Whatever you want to tell me."

"It's the title of a song by Sam and Dave."

"Sam and Dave, huh? Sing it."

"Sing it?"

"Sing it! You've been leaving copies of the song at the murder scenes, right? Sing it for us... as much as you can. Don't worry about being off key."

Complete silence. A nervous Fortier stared around the room, up at the lights then at John.

"I... I don't know the song, and I can't sing...."

"That's fine. That's fine, Mr. Fortier. Just answer one more question for me.

Do you own a computer of any kind?"

Fortier shook his head.

"I need you to answer aloud."

"No... no sir."

"Thank you, Mr. Fortier. That'll do."

John had heard enough. He moved to the far side of the room and waited until a uniformed officer escorted Fortier out. A thoroughly embarrassed Sergeant Foster cast a furtive gaze at everyone except John.

Lieutenant Medrano entered the room and sat on the edge of the table. "I can't believe anyone is taking this guy seriously," he said. Look, the most you can hit this guy with is illegally obtaining handguns...false confession, maybe. I guess someone checked to see if he's got priors."

"We haven't done ballistics yet," said Foster. "First things first."

"You can do all the ballistics you want. A flash of anger swept across Medrano's face. He stood up. "It won't friggin' matter! This guy's no killer, not yet, at least not the one we're looking for. I wanna know who really put him up to this. There's no way in hell this was his idea. Anyone track the serials on those guns to see where and how they were purchased?"

Foster and Emory said nothing.

"I want a copy of the tape of this—session, please," John said then started for the door. Gerald and Lt. Medrano followed. Foster was left twisting.

Forty
Turf War , Smurf War

The atmosphere

in Nicholson's jam-packed office was tense. FBI Agent-In-Charge, Charles Peligrano, a neatly coiffed, forty year-old with a flair for the dramatic, not generally found in FBI agents—stood at one corner just in front of Captain Nicholson's desk. Nicholson was planted near his office window, arms folded and poker-faced. John, Medrano, and Gerald sat on the sofa. Commander Lister waited patiently in an upholstered chair next to Nicholson's desk. Skeeter remained standing near the closed office door.

"I realize we should have briefed you guys on this before now," said Peligrano sounding a contrite tone. "We always want to involve local law enforcement as much as possible, you understand. However, our concern is that local investigations not compromise our own. We understand the local politics. The FBI's regional offices are in local communities. We want to be good neighbors. Where we have well-defined mutual interests, we must have a singleness of focus, purpose, and effort. That is especially true in high profile cases like this."

Nicholson took a couple of slow, deliberate steps forward, stopping just behind his high-back chair. He drew a long breath and carefully chose his words.

"Agent Peligrano, I want to be clear on this. Are you suggesting we merge our efforts, or subjugate our investigation to the FBI?"

Peligrano turned to face him. "Captain, we certainly do not presume to tell the LAPD what to do. I am simply here to inform you of what we know about the man we've been tracking for three months. We also want to ask that you provide us any investigative details that may aid us. We believe we may be after the same guy. If that's so, we are not helping either investigation by a duplication of effort. I think Chief Dennis agrees."

Nicholson was not impressed. "From what our own investigators tell me, the likelihood the killer we're looking for is the same as your *Westbound Killer...* is less than remote. I must say the FBI has not opened *its* files to us before. The only similarity in these cases—likely a coincidental one—is some aspect of the timeline."

Peligrano never spoke above a conversational tone. He glanced at John then turned to the Captain. "Even more reason to review what you've gathered. We've had a pretty good track record regarding these kinds of cases. And that's not to denigrate the LAPD. It's just that we have the resources, the knowledge, and the experience."

"Does that experience also include Ruby Ridge, Waco, contrived lab results in several big cases.?" Asked Lt. Medrano.

Medrano's acid-laced question brought the only icy response Peligrano displayed. His smile evaporated; his brow tensed; he swallowed hard and turned toward the Lieutenant.

"Lieutenant, I'll make you a deal. You don't impugn the reputation of the FBI, based on the alleged failings of a few, and I won't judge the LAPD on the basis of the Eula Love case; the Rodney King case; the Steve Bolen case; the drug thefts at various divisions, and renegades at Rampart. Should I go on?"

"Gentlemen," said Commander Lister—straight-backed, pencil thin, white-haired, and replete in dress-uniform—a man known for his stern disposition and steely resolve. He now stood a few feet away from the agent.

"We all have a job to do," the Commander noted. "A circular firing squad won't do any of us any good. Setting my own personal views aside, for the moment, I want it made clear that Chief Dennis and I have unqualified confidence in our department; in RHD, and in Captain Nicholson here. We also value the involvement of the FBI," he said, turning to Peligrano." We'll do whatever we can to help...within reason, and considering our own parochial interests."

Agent Peligrano thanked the Commander and the others, said his goodbyes and left. The room remained silent for a full minute. The shocker was that John had not said a word during the entire meeting. Lister turned to face him.

"John, I hope this doesn't dissuade you from continuing to provide us your invaluable expertise," he said. "I assure you, I would have preferred things continue as they were. The fact is, we have enormous demands being placed on this department. We're taking a beating in the press and at City Hall. Like it or not, we cannot escape a certain amount of political fallout. There are those who believe we should be focusing on the suspect the FBI has been tracking."

"Let's be honest," said John. "We're in the middle of a serial murder investigation. Do you people understand that? We have nothing to indicate this *Westbound Killer* is any more responsible for these murders than that poor weasel of a man, Fortier—the one Foster wanted to declare guilty less than an hour ago."

"He was just pursuing what he thought was the right course."

"Sure. It seems all anyone wants is a warm body to parade in front of cameras. It won't solve a damn thing. Unless we nail the right bastard, the killings will continue. Look, Commander. I've always respected you. But if you, the Police Commission or the chief don't want a straight-up, honest investigation where everyone is working from the same page, then so be it. You all know me. I'll take help from any quarter. But I did not sign on to become a junior G-Man. We know this is about differences in the focus and direction of this case. I have no problem working out differences."

Lister nodded. "During my meeting with the chief and the police commissioners, the issue of your fee also surfaced. Some are concerned about what certain members of this fractured City Council will say about it all," he explained. "Things have changed."

"That's a red herring. I don't need the money. I would do this for free. State law says you have to pay me. A dollar is enough...was always enough. But there's one more thing, sir. I have a feeling part of this has to do with a certain Sergeant and his relationship with the Chief."

"I assure you, that has nothing to do with why I'm here. But I will say there are those who believe that if the FBI does commandeer our investigation, and fail, it's their nuts in the oven, not ours. I don't agree with that view, but that's the view of some."

John understood the long-knives were still flailing over a political clash a few years earlier. Disagreements pitted Chief Dennis; against the Police Commission; against the Council, and on, and on, and on. John was determined to not immerse himself in banal city politics.

Commander Lister was nauseatingly apologetic. "Sorry about all this," he kept saying. "I'm not comfortable changing the rules in the middle of the game. As it stands, we have to produce results." Lister turned to Nicholson. "Thanks, Bear."

With that, the Commander left. Nicholson turned to John. "Hold on, Roméo. I'm pissed too. We all are."

John had nothing to say. He started for the door.

"John, hold on," Nicholson called out. "The media is kicking our ass. I'm afraid to show my face. I even check the stalls when I go to the dumper. Don't walk out on us. C'mon, now."

John kept walking.

"You're right to be fed up," said Nicholson. "I don't like the fact I'm being treated like a damn potted plant. Just tell me how do you want to handle this?"

John reached the door and turned to face the captain. "Nick, I've had enough. I'm out. All this is coming from the top. My rule is, when doodoo is falling on your head, you don't stand around looking up."

Before Captain Nicholson could respond, John blew past Skeeter, who winked, was out the door and gone.

Forty-one
Reflection

FOREST LAWN CEMETERY- Same Day, Noon - Today was one of those times...

John stood in front of the crypt,

final resting place of his beloved parents, Alexander & Caroline Rose
Roméo. His decision, five years earlier, to have them re-interred had
not come easily. Alexander Roméo had little love for any place west of
New York.

    John traced his fingers over his parents' names; his eyes teared.
He turned, stepped away to a nearby bench and sat hunched—fingers
laced together. For nearly an hour, he stared into nothingness, permit-
ting his thoughts and feelings to flow without contest.

    The drive to the cemetery, just past Burbank, had taken much
longer than necessary. John crept along barely above the speed limit,
ignoring vehicles speeding past him. Many honked, even as he drove
the slow lane. This place, though close by, always seemed so far away
from Los Angeles...from everywhere, really. The green hills, the carefully manicured grounds always seemed a respite, especially from a

fleeting vantage point on the 134 Freeway, amidst the danger, dash, and desperation of everyday life.

For years now, this was one of only two places where John felt completely at peace with himself. He could think more clearly. And if he closed his eyes he could almost hear the comforting voice of his *Sweet Caroline*. Her voice had always soothed away his cares, brightened his darkest day. The other refuge was Wayfarer's Chapel, located in Palos Verdes and overlooking the Pacific Ocean.

At Forest Lawn, John could finally speak to his father without feeling he had to always say the right thing... behave in a way that would not anger him. He would often spend hours walking the grounds, clearing his mind. Today was one of those times he needed the solitude and peace more than he realized.

John felt if he could have a single wish granted, it would be for his father to see his father, and have his father see him once more. He would wish for him to see that his achievements were worthy of a pat on the back; to have a nod of approval for a son who would always be proud to be his son.

Forty-two
Remembering Keith Langhorne

Catalina Bound — *He died at the scene. There was little left to bury...*

From the bridge's center helm station,

behind the shiny, aluminum-framed Venturi shield, John held the wood-accented, tilt steering wheel. He pointed his white, 45 foot Sea Ray toward Avalon and went throttle up. Sporting a bare chest, except for his bright orange life vest, he applied more sunscreen to his arms, shoulders, face, body parts not hidden by the white deck pants.

The powerful, twin inboard, 430 horsepower Cummins engines offered an irresistible temptation to fly. He had purchased the boat in '02 from its owner in Santa Barbara. John could count the times he had taken her out of her berth in Long Beach's Marina.

For a brief while, he had a three-gull escort. The birds finally peeled away, in search of more rewarding enterprise. Except for the occasional all out sprint of a couple of Catalina tour boats, traffic was moderate to light. John would not classify himself a genuine sea urchin, although he always loved the ocean.

As for boats, he felt the larger the better. The "Sweet Caroline" was about as small a vessel as he cared to own or step aboard. It was more than suited for infrequent weekend getaways.

Once he entered Long Beach Marina's gangway 44, John was just as content to stay put, as to set sail, especially when he and Aimee's goal was to simply escape. Only Skeeter and Gerald knew about the boat. Of course, Claire knew, although, following their divorce, John relocated it from its berth in Marina Del Rey.

Following the gathering in Nicholson's office, John was determined to put the case behind him. This was a great start. All around him was the California everyone dreamed, wrote, and sang about. The blue sky, seventy-two degree temp, a soothing sea breeze—it was post-card perfect. From below deck, Jose Feliciano's stirring guitar riffs from his 'Best of' CD wafted up to the covered bridge.

From his comfortable perch in his swivel helm seat—one of two—John scanned the instrument panel: the tachometer, compass, the GPS system. All systems were 'go.' He repeatedly sounded ship's bell, just for the hell of it. And kept sounding it, like a kid just discovering a new toy. For the moment, John Roméo was ten again, and it felt damn good; he did not resist the feeling. He felt free, totally unencumbered.

Approximately ten nautical miles out, John drew up just outside of the main lanes and throttled down. From the immaculate bridge, he slowly took in a 360-degree view and spotted another yacht anchored nearby. A small boy, accompanied by a man he took to be the boy's father, was flying a kite. John watched as the multi-colored, twin-diamond soared high above the water, attracting a growing number of curious water-fowl. For a moment, John imagined he was that boy, and that the man was his own father. He was not sure just how long the fantasy lasted, or when the boat moved on.

John was feeling more calm and relaxed than he had in months, when thoughts of his late partner descended upon him like a boulder. Perhaps it was seeing the young boy and his father that triggered the thoughts.

Keith Langhorne was ten years older than John. He was a free spirit with a raucous sense of humor; a Grateful Dead fanatic; a revered homicide detective, and a great human being. More than anything, Keith loved being a husband to his wife JoAnn, and father to their only child and son, thirteen year-old Mark.

Keith was only one week from his 'Aloha Day' with the LAPD, when the horrible nightmare occurred. The Brasolla kidnapping and murder case was to be the swan song for the dynamic homicide duo. John was certain the case would not be solved before Keith's official retirement; and had argued, unsuccessfully, that his partner not work the case. True to his character and stubbornness, Keith insisted.

Only three weeks earlier, 33-year old Mike Brasolla, son of a Los Angeles Superior Court judge, was kidnapped from his Woodland Hills Law office complex in broad daylight. Keith and John worked around the clock, determined to crack the case and find young Brasolla alive.

Judge Brasolla adamantly refused ransom demands, despite his wife's tearful pleas. At 5:45pm on a Friday afternoon—a detail John would never forget—a final, angry, epithet-filled call came in to homicide. The caller, using a cell phone later determined stolen, indicated where police would find the son's body.

Within fifteen minutes, John, Keith, and a score of police vehicles, trailed by media, arrived at an abandoned warehouse on Alameda, near downtown Los Angeles. While others followed at some distance, John and Keith moved ahead, beyond the entrance and into the damp, dank facility once used for silver plating.

No more than fifty feet inside, the two spotted the nude body of Mike Brasolla slumped on the floor, near a conveyor line. Keith motioned the other officers to stay back, to preserve evidence and allow the body, and a grid surrounding the body, to be examined.

Keith took the lead, moving ahead, while John stepped back to give instructions to other homicide officers and the coroner's team. From that moment on, every second was forever engraved upon the consciousness of all who were there.

As Keith approached the body, he paused to put on latex gloves then proceeded. He walked slowly, taking note of every particle on the floor; searching for footprints, any scintilla of evidence. He reached the body, stared down at the grotesque, mutilated remains of Mike Brasolla. He noted the gouged out eyes; blood still flowing from an open mouth absent a tongue.

John's memory of the moments that followed would forever yield images recalled in slow motion. From forty feet away, he saw Keith kneel, extend his right hand to touch the upper torso, when a violent, massive explosion erupted like a nuclear bomb. The sound was deafening. A blinding flash replaced what was the image of Keith Langhorne and Brasolla's body.

In an act of inhuman savagery, the killer had wired a timing device with a pressure switch trigger, to no fewer than a half dozen sticks of dynamite placed underneath the victim. Keith died at the scene. Little was left to bury of either Detective Langhorne or Brasolla. Several officers were injured by flying debris; showered with blood, flesh and body parts,

Amazingly, the killer—a two-time felon once sentenced by the victim's father, Judge Vincent Brasolla—was apprehended sitting in a stolen car across the street from the warehouse, camcorder in hand. Apparently he had remained in the area to record the hell he created.

For John, and every officer on detail that day, there would be no forgetting. Tears could not wash away the images. No fragrance could banish the smell: the stench of burned flesh, and scorched blood. John would have given his right arm to have it not be necessary to deliver the heart-wrenching news to JoAnn and Mark. He had insisted upon doing so. Keith would have done the same for him.

Hours later, John took a deep breath, stared into a fiery sunset and turned his boat toward homeport. For the moment, every concern not involving matters of life and death faded into insignificance. Whenever he was tempted to permit selfish thoughts to creep into his day, John thought of Keith, and the hundreds of other victims and survivors he had come to know during his career and lifetime.

Forty-three
Expert Opinion

LAPD FIREARMS AND EXPLOSIVES LAB, Same Night

Denora Halley,

director of the LAPD Firearms and Explosives unit, stood hunched over a comparison microscope at a second floor, laboratory work station. John and Gerald looked on. The Captain had nearly exploded John's cell phone, and email server with pleas and assurances. It was the sounds of crying, and the gnashing of teeth that convinced him to give his old boss one more chance.

A half dozen clear plastic containers containing bullets and bullet fragments were on the bench, near the scopes. Halley adjusted the two new Leica microscopes, connected by an optical bridge. They were focused on two .44 slugs recovered from different crime scenes. She stepped back to let John take a look.

"As you can see, the markings... lands and grooves are clearly dissimilar," she said. Gerald took a peek. The process was repeated. Each pairing was photographed and cataloged.

"Conclusion?" Asked John.

"My conclusion—the conclusion of the analysis is that each pairs of victims, to date, were shot with different weapons, all .44 Magnums firing 250-260 grain, jacketed hollow points."

"Different guns, but same m.o. down the line. No way different shooters would mirror each other like that," said Gerald.

"I agree. What about that container of IMI .44s brought in this afternoon?" John asked Halley.

"We barrel tested them. None of those rounds compare to anything found at the crime scenes in this case. Other cases are being checked."

"What do you think," John asked Director Halley.

She shrugged. "You guys are the detectives. But if you ask me..."

"I'm asking.

"If all this is the work of a serial, he or she is definitely no garden variety killer. None of this seems to be tracking classic serial behavior. But again, I'm not the expert."

"You're too modest. Thanks."

John turned from the table with hands dug deep in his pockets.

"We're done," he said. Gerald nodded.

Forty-four

"Might have to call them in and kick them in the ass."

Gerald entered the second level of the garage

located atop the communications center. John had been practically mute during the entire drive in from the Lab. Only when they exited the 110 and started through Chinatown, did he bring up the Jeffries case.

Once in Medrano's office, the two began wading through the mound of material taken from the Jeffries' condo. If the judge had a personal attorney, and one would have suspected he did, he or she had not contacted police. Having heard no objections, they proceeded. All the material had been separated, boxed, dated and labeled by type and broad category.

John went straight for the box labeled "finances." More than three years of monthly statements; used check registers; investment portfolio, and loan documents were laid out. It did not take long for an interesting pattern to develop.

Gerald, who had been scouring through what appeared to be a diary, soon joined him. Both noted a sudden decline in size and frequency of deposits and average balances, leading up to three months before the judge's death. One consistent deposit for $12,000 simply disappeared from the statements.

There were no bank copies of any deposited check for that amount. The two were left to speculate, concluding the money most likely came from Mrs. Jeffries. Of course, permanent bank records would easily verify the source. Any bank deposit of $10,000 or more had to be reported to the IRS.

An entry in the judge's journal both stunned and intrigued: while entries in the five-year journal were not made daily, they were made consistently during the trial of LAPD officer, Steve Bolen. Even a brief examination revealed the judge was puzzled and frustrated by the prosecutors. He apparently felt they were not as aggressive as they might have been.

"I don't understand the gaping holes they're leaving in their case," he wrote two days after the trial began. "Might have to call them in and kick them in the ass." Near the end of the prosecutor's case, the judge scribbled:

"Bastard. I doubt he's the only one."

Gerald and John both concluded the entry had to do with   Bolen. Even the judge suspected there were others like him.

An hour and a half later, the two had hardly scratched the surface. Catherine Jeffries' name kept surfacing. What did she know and when did she know it? The subject of the 'stage production' put on by lawyer Smythe came up. John was not surprised by his performance. He had encountered the suave, debonair, slippery Mr. Smythe on previous occasions. His only question was whether or not Smythe represented any of the other surviving spouses. Gerald had already considered the possibility, and had yet to find anything to suggest the answer was yes.

A half hour more found the pair seated, staring blankly at the mounds of material in front of them.

"Could be a cop," Gerald blurted out. John sat straight up, turned to his partner. "Why do you say that?"

"Something Skeeter said."

"He suggested the same to me."

"Could be right. Crime scenes have all been too damn clean...not even a hair. It's like the killer knows what we'd be looking for. Plus, in three of the four cases so far, the victims had top security systems. Yet, they were breached with no apparent signs of entry. What does that say to you?"

"Inside job. Spouses, maybe someone familiar with security codes and defeating security systems, or all of the above."

The day had been long. John locked up, and the duo called it a night. They reached the garage, bleary-eyed and with more questions than answers.

"What are you thinking?" Asked Gerald.

"Not sure. I'm just... just trying to put an umbrella over all this. In my mind, I line up all the major elements and, one by one, drop each one into one of two containers: one, labeled *In*, the other, *Out*. Right now, the in-box runneth over. I agree with Halley. It just doesn't feel like a classic, serial murder case to me."

"What does it feel like?"

"Contrived, made up—manufactured. I take a reading of my instincts; my sixth sense kicks in without any manipulation from me, and that's what I'm feeling," said John.

"I know," Gerald agreed. "By now, we should have had some taunts from the killer: a note, a phone call; some anonymous e-mail, or letter. The thing with the different guns but with the same m.o. doesn't compute for me. We need to establish some link between the sets of killings. If we can establish a link—one outside the established facts—I think we'll make quick progress in some direction."

"Where are the usual suspects when you need them?"

John tossed his head back and heaved a long sigh.

"Felicia's got a track meet tomorrow. I'm going. She's in the 200 and 400 meters."

"You're lucky," said John. "Great kids, beautiful wife—smart *and* beautiful."

"If I only had your money to add to all that, I'd have it made."

"Don't be so sure," said John. "You're already a wealthy man."

"Thanks. You're right."

The mutual admiration fest ended. The two began their short walk to where John's car was parked near the elevator. As they approached the '57 Chevrolet, both were unaware they were being observed. Their footsteps reverberated loudly, masking their conversation from the hidden observer.

"By the way, I checked," said Gerald. "No rose petals were found at any of the other murder scenes. Why the judge's?"

"We just keep looking," said John. We look at every piece of evidence... everything. Like I said. I don't think the FBI profile and the doctor's preliminary profile are at odds."

"This session in the Sumner pool with the doctor. What was that all about?" Asked Gerald.

"That's her way of trying to somehow get a read on the killer by projecting herself into the body and mind of the victim. It's weird, but if it works, I'll sure as hell take it."

"You never said whether you agreed with Skeeter? You think the shooter could be a cop?"

John was suddenly distracted and did not answer right away. He slowed and stared toward his car. A note was stuck under the right wiper blade. He grabbed, held it carefully at corners, read it then showed it to Gerald.

The note read: "D-I-E."

"What the hell is this?" John did a quick 360.

"Somebody's jerking your chain," said Gerald.

"But I'm not laughing."

John carefully folded the note, slipped it inside his coat pocket, and resumed searching around his car. He checked underneath, shining a small pocket flashlight from front to rear. He examined the hood for fingerprints, peered inside before opening the door. Both climbed inside.

"You don't think this is a joke. You're taking the note literally."

"It was literally written."

The two sat quietly for several minutes. Several rows away, John heard someone close a car door and key an ignition. Gerald started to climb out and start for his own car.

"Let's take a little trip," John suggested.

"Where to?"

"I'm not sure."

Gerald strapped his seat belt back on, leaned back and relaxed. John started up roared for the exit. He reached 1st street but drove only a block, before pulling to the curb and killing his lights.

"What are we doing?" Asked Gerald.

John turned in his seat and looked over his shoulder. Just then Sergeant Dennis exited the garage and drove past.

"There goes the Klanmobile," Gerald joked. "You don't think he had anything to do with the note, do you?"

"This has nothing to do with the note," said John, turning his lights back on and moving into traffic. "I'm just playing a hunch."

"About what?"

"We'll see."

John followed from several car lengths back, as Dennis entered Harbor Freeway South. In less than a minute they reached Interstate-10 and the Santa Monica Freeway ramp west.

Gerald was more than curious. "How far do we follow this fool? He lives in Torrance."

"Relax."

"Don't get too close. He knows your car."

"I know."

Minutes later, Dennis took the Fairfax exit. John followed. The light at the end of the ramp was red. Careful not to get too close, John slowed to a crawl. He was being tailgated but continued at less than twenty miles per hour.

Just then, the light changed. Dennis continued across the intersection at Washington, in the curb lane, and wheeled into the Kaiser Permanente Hospital parking lot. John followed. Gerald lowered himself in his seat, as John slowed to a stop and waited.

Dennis drove the full length of one long aisle and parked next to a dark, commercial van. John turned off his lights and eased into a vacant space several yards away. The van had no plates, only a Chrysler Dealer's placard.

John and Gerald waited and watched. Nothing happened.

It seemed forever before Dennis climbed out of his car. The right side sliding door of the van opened but the van remained dark inside.

"Whoever's in the van killed the dome light," observed Gerald. "You don't do that unless you want to protect your identity."

"Okay. So, what do you think is going on?"

"Don't know yet."

Seconds later, the van cranked, began backing out. John and Gerald watched as it started toward them, headlights out. The two ducked down, and waited a few seconds before rising. It wasn't until the van reached the exit that its lights came on. John started his car, backed out, and stormed toward the exit. When he reached the street and turned west, the van was nowhere to be seen.

"They couldn't have disappeared that quickly," said John.

"What's this all about? You suspect Dennis of something other than being stupid. What is it... was it drugs, again?"

"I'm not sure. Maybe I'm just wanting to bag his weasel ass."

John turned left at the light, returned to the Santa Monica freeway and up the eastbound ramp.

"Why would Dennis leave his car parked on the back side of Kaiser's parking lot?" Gerald pondered.

"Your question, your guess," said John.

"Fine. Whatever, it has to be illegal. Wish there was some way we could search his car."

"It's his personal vehicle, not the department's.
"That old Ford is his?"
"Surplus police car... had it for years... bought it at auction.
"Great. We should bust it anyway."
"Let's keep it legal, for now," said John.

Forty-five
All Eyes

The sun beamed in a near cloudless

Los Angeles morning sky. Dozens of limousines lined the curb, stretching forever behind the black Cadillac hearse. Luminaries, including a smattering of celebrities and hordes of the political Who's Who of California, made their way into the picturesque chapel overlooking the Pacific. More than two-dozen plainclothes and uniformed officers covered the facility.

John and Gerald entered the small sanctuary and slowly made their way toward the south wall. Streams of light poured through the stained glass windows that stretch from floor to ceiling. A large, oval stained glass mural of the Garden of Gesthsemane scene adorned the wall just below the A-frame apex of the ceiling, and front wall of the sanctuary.

From their position, the duo scanned the throng, taking care to draw little attention to themselves. While a small string ensemble played, ushers seated family and mourners. In the balcony near a wooden railing, an officer recorded the services with a small, hand-held, digital camcorder.

John moved slowly forward, near the front of the assemblage, and observed Mrs. Jeffries, the deceased's wife, seated in a front pew directly in front of her husband's closed casket. Dr. Diane Deauville was seated next to her, speaking to Catherine, stroking her shoulder. Mrs. Jeffries appeared quite composed.

Gerald joined his partner. Both were surprised but careful to not react visibly. John motioned his partner toward the rear. When they reached the vestibule, Gerald turned to him. "What do you think?"

"I'm not sure," said John.

"Maybe Mrs. Jeffries is a patient. Is that possible?"

"Maybe she's just a friend."

Both men continued out and onto the cobblestone walkway leading into the chapel. Directly in front of them, Rose Henley, smartly dressed in a navy blue suit, and wearing a fresh rose in her lapel, approached with a female friend. Her diamond necklace sparkled in the sunlight.

John was surprised to see. He had no idea who her friend was. When the two reached them, Rose nodded politely, and continued up the steps.

"Friend of the family?" John mused.

"Maybe she knows the funeral director."

"Funny."

Forty-six
The Widowmaker , Again?

Later that afternoon, John sat scouring more notes,

reviewing transcripts of interviews, those of victims' relatives, pouring through more of the judge's possessions. So far, under the advice of their attorneys, none of the surviving spouses had agreed to be interviewed.

Gerald listened to the 'old school' cassette of his brief interview with Rose. The earlier scribblings and notes were still on the marker board. He pressed the stop button on the old cassette player, removed the tape, and returned it to the clear plastic storage case. Stacks of files were on the cluttered table. Rose's book was nearby. "She's tough," said Gerald. Sure as hell speaks her mind, doesn't mince words on the tape or in this book. And it's pretty clear she doesn't have a very high opinion of men. Take a look," he said, handing John a tabloid size newsletter. "Laura showed me this last night."

"What is it?"

"A newsletter, called *For Women Only*. It's also an Internet newsletter. Laura found it at a lawyer's conference she attended in San Diego two days ago. It's also mentioned as a resource in Rose's book. Check out this classified, right there," he said, pointing.

John read aloud. *"Husband Cheating? Don't Get Mad, Get Even. Send your inquiries to:* widowmaker@womenlivefree.com. "That's pretty goddamn suggestive. WomenLiveFree.com. Check out the web site."

"That address in the classified ad could be a drop box," said Gerald. "Question is, who placed the ad? You think there's a connection?"
"I'm not ruling out anything. I want to find out." John said, continuing to study the newsletter. "I'll come back to that in a minute. What else we got?"

Just then, Lt. Medrano burst into the room. A look of surprise covered his face. He held a sheet of legal pad paper containing scribbled notes."

"Captain was right. Mrs. Jeffries did call back."

"When? Who?"

"Foster. I've got some of the notes. A more detailed report is being written. Still won't do a sit down, but at least we know a little bit more."

Lieutenant Medrano began reading from the notes: "On the night in question, Mrs. Jeffries says she had a lengthy session with her therapist... got home about nine thirty p.m."

Did she say who the therapist is," Gerald asked.

"No. Not sure if Foster asked or she refused to say.

"Maybe it'll be in his full report," Medrano offered. "She indicated there were no servants around, when she arrived. No one saw her immediately afterwards, not until the next morning at about 8:30. Very cool... dispassionate, it says here in the margins. Foster also notes she had no comments regarding the fact her husband was found with another woman...shot to death. Did you know the woman? It reads. Long pause, shrugged. Then declined to comment. Conversation ended abruptly. That's it."

"Based on this, we can't clear her as a suspect yet. She had possible motive and opportunity. And she refused to identify her therapist, right?"

"Nothing indicates she provided a name," Medrano repeated.

Gerald picked up Rose's book. He turned a couple of pages and suddenly pointed. "Dr. Diane Deauville. She wrote the foreword to Rose Henley's book."

"That didn't come out on Krystal's show," noted John.

"I'll check on that full report and leave it on my desk if you're gone when I return," said Medrano, then left.

Less than a minute passed, when the door opened. A smirking Sergeant Dennis strode in—a newspaper folded under one arm. Gerald eyed John, who signaled him to not speak. John folded the newsletter and pushed it toward Gerald. He returned it to his briefcase.

Dennis took several steps and stopped. "Gentlemen. I'm glad to be working with you. I truly am. Who's gonna bring me up to date?"

"Sorry, said John. "We were both on our way out. Tell you what. I want you to take all the data we've collected, create a spread sheet—a database—plug everything into the program I put together, and let me know when you're done. I want a complete flowchart so I can track every single development at a glance. Then, prepare a written report referencing your results, got it? And I want daily updates. You'll have to work from another office. Use the one reserved for the other task force members. We keep this one closed. Lt. Medrano will only clear the two of us to be in here."

Dennis' grin evaporated. "You serious?"

"Am I serious, G.K?" Asked John, turning to Gerald.

"He's serious. See his eyes? I've never seen this man so serious," said a grim-faced Gerald.

A uniformed officer bolted into the room. "John, telephone for ya'...conference room. And Price, in Narcotics, says the warrant on the assholes in the Maserati is still hot. He wants to talk to you. Quick, like yesterday."

John thanked the officer, started to leave then turned back. "G.K., lock up for me."

"Roméo!" Dennis called out. "I spent all night thinking about this case. I need a briefing on your meeting with Dr. Deauville the other night. I should know what she said. And I thought you might like a personal copy of this." He extended a folded copy of a tabloid newspaper, the National Insider, featuring Aimee and a bearded John on the cover. John took a quick look, ripped the paper in half, tossed it back at Dennis then left the room.

Gerald turned to a smug Dennis. "Don't forget your assignment. That's an awful lot of work. And understand something. You're not running this investigation. You're here to follow orders, and that's what you'll do or you're in deep shit. Got it? You want to run your sniveling ass up to your uncle's office, go ahead. You screw up, you're dog dung. Now that we've had this nice little chat, you have a nice day."

Gerald grabbed his jacket and held the door open. Dennis sulked past without a whimper.

Forty-seven
Bang, Bang! Who's Dead?

Two Hours Later, Downtown *"You see the car the shots came from?"*

Gerald grabbed a couple of hot dogs

from a street vendor. He handed one to John as they walked along
Figueroa, near the Sheraton Grande Hotel. The two were munching,
hunched over to avoid dripping chili on themselves. Sidewalks were
packed with the noon lunch crowd; street traffic inched along. Exhaust
fumes and high decibel bus noise was enough to send urbanites scrambling for a one-way ticket to Oregon.

"Yuk! What's in this thing?" John chortled. "I just chewed something crunchy in my hot dog. That's not supposed to happen. I'm not
supposed to find crunchy in a hot dog."

"Crunchy?"

"That's what I said." John took a long swig from his Pepsi, and
tossed the rest of the hotdog in a nearby trash bin. "About that newsletter," he said. "If somebody's hiring themselves out to get even with
wayward husbands, he could..."

"Or she," Gerald added.

"Or she, could be busy for a damn long time. Of course, I'm specu-
lating, but if true, then we don't have a classic serial killer case. It's murder for hire. We have to check it out."

"You don't think we're reaching, do you?" Asked Gerald.

"Maybe. But we have to. I'm curious about whether anything like
this is happening anywhere else."

Gerald suddenly pointed to a newspaper vending machine. The
headline on the paper's front page read: ADULTERY MURDERS BAF-
FLE LAPD. The two stared then turned away.

"It's going to get worse," said Gerald.

John was unfazed. He suspected the pressure on the Department
was being compounded by mounting media scrutiny. "Don't forget to
set up another meeting with Rose Henley, "he said.

"She's still at the Grande here. I left a message, but she hasn't returned the call. I'll check back and fill you in later on," Gerald agreed.

John nodded and the two started away in opposite directions. They
were only a few feet apart. Suddenly, a burst of automatic weapons fire
exploded. Tires screeched, glass shattered; planters cracked, rounds
ricocheted. Instinct took over.

"Down!" John screamed with the first blast.

Both men crashed to the ground and scrambled for cover, as
deadly rounds whizzed around them. Screams rang out. Pedestrians
scattered. Shards of concrete showered down. The blasts lasted only a
scant three or four seconds but did their damage.

Somehow, both Gerald and John ended up behind the same group
of tree planters, guns drawn—eyes searching for the direction of the
gunfire. It had come from a passing car. John thought the vehicle was a
2002 Cadillac DeVille, but was not certain.

"You alright?" Gerald asked, inching toward his friend.

"Yeah. You?"

Satisfied the threat was over, the two rose to their feet, disheveled
but unhurt, guns still at the ready. They quickly determined no pass-
ersby had been injured.

"Police! We're police!" Gerald yelled to frightened pedestrians. John searched the crowded street north of their position. His adrenaline was at max; he was livid.

"Somebody just did a drive-by on us," he shouted. "Some crazy bastard just tried to kill us."

After calling in the attack on his cell phone, John joined Gerald searching frantically for spent casings at curbside. Within minutes, an LAPD chopper was overhead. Patrol cars screeched to a halt along the curb and just in front of the hotel. John stepped onto the edge of the street. Gerald quickly yanked him back, as a car breezed by within inches.

Several officers began redirecting traffic, preventing other cars from proceeding on Figueroa, north of Wilshire Boulevard.

"You see the car the shots came from?" Asked Gerald.

"No. But whoever it was, they're a lousy damn shot."

"Damn lucky for us."

John's cool facade quickly disappeared. Things had changed; it was personal. Someone had tattooed a target on their backs. He was no longer the hunter. While he had no way of knowing whom or why, this was a new game. The old rules of engagement no longer applied.

John ran down a quick laundry list of possible enemies. He remembered the anonymous phone caller; the curious calls on the motel phone; the guy at his door. He left no one out, including Thomas Arceneaux, the kid he slammed into those lockers outside Mrs. Washington's classroom all those years ago. It was a stretch, but stranger things had happened.

Problem was, the list was longer than he would have guessed. You don't do the things he had done for 13 years as a cop—busting heads, destroying illicit fortunes—without creating enemies.

Forty-eight
Drive-by, by Real Badasses

Less than twenty Minutes later — *The right hand seized a pair of scissors*

The white Maserati

eased onto the driveway entrance and stopped several feet from the gate of John's residence. Two unsavory-looking characters, men in black suits, climbed out and approached the speaker mounted on the gate column. The driver and front passenger remained inside the car. One of the men pressed the speaker button.

Inside, Rose Reina, John's 50 year-old housekeeper, answered before the man could speak.

"May I help you, gentlemen?"

The men glanced curiously at each other. Reina's response told them they were being observed.

"Is Roger there?" One man asked, in Russian-accented English.

"I'm sorry. No one by that name lives here. Good day."

"Excuse me," said the first man.

"There is no one here by that name," Reina repeated.

After several silent and puzzled expressions, the two reluctantly returned to the car. Once inside, all appeared to argue violently amongst themselves. Finally, the Maserati pulled away.

Miles away, in the dingy bedroom, a virtual forest of candles were arranged on the floor at the foot of the bed. As before, they gave off an eerie, flickering light that bounced off the unsightly walls and ceiling. A tabloid newspaper, *The National Insider,* lay open on the bed. Latex-gloved hands leafed through the pages then stopped abruptly. The right hand seized a pair of scissors and began cutting out the cover page featuring a picture of a bearded John Roméo and girlfriend, Aimee.

The headline read:

MILLIONAIRE WRITER HOLDS BEAUTY CAPTIVE.

WIFE SWEARS: "HE'S FORCING ME TO HAVE HIS BABY."

The silhouetted figure began cutting around the photos and banner headline. A knock sounded at the bedroom door. The interruption spawned an angry outburst. The scissors were hurled toward the door. The knocking persisted.

Forty-nine
Frame by Frame

Later, LAPD Audio-Video Lab: *"Right. John, this shit is real..."*

John sat at a bank of TV monitors,

along side Lt. Medrano, Skeeter and Don Woo, a 25 year old civilian video editor. All were viewing grainy, stop-action black and white footage from the Wilshire condominium's surveillance cameras. So far, it offered little.

"That's about as good as the quality gets, Lieutenant," said Woo. "The old line: *garbage in, garbage out,* holds true in this case. Most older, low-res surveillance systems are about the same. I've actually seen worse."

John leaned back, rubbed his eyes. "Three hours of this is about all I can take at a stretch. How much of this do we have?" He asked, yawning. "Excuse me, guys."

"Three hundred hours," Medrano answered. "Three hundred?"

"Problem is, we don't know what the hell we're looking for. Good thing is, the date shows on some of the tape, but not all," said Meddrano. "We know what the coroner determined as the likely time of the murders. So far, we haven't found tape that matches. Nothing stands out. You asked us to look for someone carrying flowers. —Nothing.

"We've looked for someone piggybacking in on another resident. I understand from the guards that many residents do that as well. It'll take time. We'll probably have to look through this first batch several times, before we glean any clue. We're noting the license plates as best we can, checking them against those of the residents. We'll also keep checking for floral deliveries, like you asked."

"Good," said John. "None of this is going to help, unless we can establish who is a resident and who isn't. And keep after management to keep searching their offices until they find all the remaining footage."

"Hopefully, we'll get tape that shows either of the victims entering the complex," said Medrano.

John stood and stretched again. "I'm outta here. Got a brief meeting with the doctor tonight. See you guys tomorrow. "

"I'll look at this stuff a little longer," said Skeeter.

"Not past 8pm though," John joked.

"Remember what I told you," said Skeeter. John nodded, He knew exactly what his friend meant.

A suddenly solemn Lieutenant Medrano accompanied John out of the room, saying nothing until they reached the elevators. "I know you're gonna squawk, but we're assigning a couple of UCs to trail you and Li. You got no choice in the matter, so don't give me a hard time. Got it? And do not try to ditch 'em."

John chuckled out loud, but not because he was amused. "No. No way," he said.

"Why not? A few inches to the left or right, and we'd be wiping two damn good detectives up off the sidewalk. Now, it's clear that someone—maybe from some old case, I don't know or care—is trying to retire you, permanently. We won't stand by and not do something. This comes straight from Nick. It will be done."

"Then I'll walk. I refuse to give in to some... some cowardly asshole who apparently doesn't have the balls to face me head on. No way. Tell Nick I'm serious. I appreciate the concern, but I have to do this my way or not at all. Period."

A long silence.

"When is your serial murder expert due in from Minnesota?" Medrano asked.

"Two weeks. He can't get away earlier. Wednesday...two weeks. I'm picking him up at LAX."

"You say his name is Sechler?"

"No. Sachler, Steve Sachler. He's a very busy man. Unfortunately, he's had his hands full the last few years. Business has been good, too damn good."

"Listen, John. The reason I came out was to pass a little warning on to you." Medrano's voice had an ominous tone. He glanced down the hallway in both directions before continuing.

"Warning about what?"

"A call came in to the Captain before you got here."

"About me?"

"Yeah."

"From whom? From where? What about?"

"From a phone booth in Chinatown. The male caller warned that if you weren't taken off this case, you wouldn't live another forty-eight hours. Said they wouldn't miss next time."

"They said *they* and not, he?"

"Right. John, this shit is real. You and Li just had someone try to take you out. Like I said, maybe it has something to do with this case, maybe not. Either way, the bullets are real. I know it's not the norm for homicide detectives to be targeted, but somebody's doing it."

John smiled nervously. He remembered the quirky phone calls; the attempt on his life only hours earlier; the bloody leaflets left on his driveway, and Gerald's doorstep. Somebody was trying to intimidate them—even kill them. No way this was some psychopath involved in serial murder. This bastard was bearing a grudge. But who, and for what?

"Like I said, the call came in directly to Nick," said Medrano. "Apparently the caller is aware of the chain of command. It was a raspy, male voice. Had a slight accent... maybe Eastern European. Could be a crank, but we can't assume that. Both you and Li were together. Only the shooter could be certain the attempt was on you. But I don't think there's little doubt."

"Who on the outside knows for certain I'm on this case? There's been no confirmation to the press," said John.

"Who knows? Are you kidding me? At least every reporter in LA, and God knows who else. At least thirty press people saw you at Hillcrest. There was plenty of speculation about you joining us, long before the Captain spoke with you. It's no secret. Besides, you can't have a shooting downtown in broad daylight and not have the media learn what's going on. You'll be all over the news tonight. I promise."

Fifty
Heart to Heart

JOHN'S RESIDENCE, same day — *"Don't do this," John pleaded. "Tell me."*

 inutes past 6 PM

a dark gray Chevy cargo van moved slowly past John's residence and continued out of view. Seconds later, John pulled past the security gate onto the motor court. An emotional Aimee met him at the front door, kissed him repeatedly, clung to him fiercely. John could tell she had been crying. Her heart was still pounding. He kept assuring her he was fine. He smiled, kissed her, held her tightly. Finally, she took his jacket, and the two stepped inside. John bounded quickly up the stairs.

"Where's Roger?"

"In the pool. Why are you in such a hurry?"

"I've got another meeting with Dr. Deauville, remember? Shouldn't take long. There's growing pressure to solve this thing, at least show we're leaving no stone unturned. That's the political side."

Aimee didn't respond. She stood near the dresser, watching John.

"How was your day?" He asked, undressing and dashing for the shower. "Fine. Other than the attempt on your life, how was *yours?*"

"Sweetheart, I'm a cop. These things can happen."

"Wrong. You're a retired cop; you're a writer, John. Besides, who would want to target a homicide detective? It's crazy. It's not like you're a...a narc or something."

"Darling, I understand how you feel. I love knowing you care. And I care about how you feel. But I am who I am. True, I am helping my old Captain, but I may also help save some lives."

"Go on and get yourself killed. Trade your life for someone else's... for lives of people who obviously aren't concerned about themselves."

John took care to not sound defensive, but understanding. He took care not to interrupt, but to wait until Aimee finished.

"There are a lot of people who aren't exactly sympathetic about the deaths of wayward husbands and their mistresses," he said. "I understand that. But, I can't decide what killers to go after based on the moral indiscretions of their victims. If I did that... If cops did that, not many cases would get solved."

John was aware Aimee found it difficult to understand his continued involvement with the LAPD, given the literary success he enjoyed. "Sweetheart, after tonight, I promise to spend every night with you until you leave for Paris," he said, softly. Aimee was not appeased.

"I can imagine how things are when you're on...on one of these cases. Already, you've changed. I remember something Claire wrote in her RedBook article. She said you sacrifice everything else. It's like a drug with you; it's an addiction. Look, I realize this is very important. Like you said, lives are at stake."

"They are. And I also know how important it is for us to spend time together. That's what I want, too," said John. A long silence followed.

"You'd better get your shower. Don't want to be late," said Aimee, resigning herself to the inevitable.

John kissed Aimee and stepped into the shower. She returned to the mirror, stood quietly for several minutes, staring beyond her image. She lifted her right hand, carefully examined her face, traced every contour—every line. She turned slowly, gazed at her profile, pressed her left hand flat against her stomach.

Minutes passed. Aimee moved to the love seat, lifted the remote and flicked on the television to the six o'clock newscast. She plopped down and began watching a story in mid report:

"Today, L.A police finally acknowledged there is indeed a connection between the series of murders we've been following. This confirms what experts contacted by KCBC have been suggesting for nearly two months. The involvement of former homicide whiz, John Roméo, referred to in our earlier story on the brazen downtown shooting, made further denials fruitless. However, Police are still not commenting on reports the shooting was an attempt on Detective Roméo and his partner, Sergeant Gerald Li.

"Meanwhile, the shocking murder of Judge Hunter Jeffries has city and state officials reeling. Jeffries, slated for appointment to the State Supreme Court was found brutally murdered, along with a female Deputy District Attorney, in a Westwood area condominium. He was buried yesterday.

"On the same day Jeffries' body was found, the body of major league baseball star Mike Gregg, and a prostitute, were discovered nude and brutally executed on a local golf course. City council President George Havilland, candidate for Mayor, charges police with ineptitude in the investigation. The mayor immediately labeled Havilland's comments as, and we're quoting: *political opportunism and grandstanding of the sickest sort.*"

Aimee clicked off the set and sat transfixed. She turned to see John in the bedroom doorway, still drying off.

"It's gonna get a lot nastier," he said.

Aimee stood just as the phone rang. She reluctantly answered. "Hello." There was no immediate response. "Hello," Aimee repeated.

"John?" Came a raspy voice.

"No. Hold on a second," said Aimee.

She extended the phone toward John. He wrapped his towel and hurried to the phone. Aimee looked on. John lifted the receiver and heard only a dial-tone.

"There's no one here."

"There was. I heard him."

"Was it a clear voice?"

"He sounded hoarse."

"Raspy?"

"Why do you ask? You think you know who it was?"

"It's nothing."

Aimee didn't buy John's explanation but let it drop and left the room. He finished dressing, headed downstairs and found her at the table in the formal dining room. She seemed reflective, distant.

"I've been doing a little soul-searching," said Aimee.

John moved to her side of the table. "Let's talk about it."

"Can't keep the doctor waiting."

"Don't do this," John pleaded. "Tell me."

Aimee hesitated for what seemed forever. "I've been asking myself... why I'm here."

"Here with me?"

"Yes."

John pulled out a chair and sat next to Aimee. "Are you having doubts about us... or just me?"

"I'm having doubts about everything: about me, about you, about my career. Somehow, there's this emptiness. I don't know what it is. I know you love me. And I love you very much."

"I do love you. You know that," John declared, leaning toward Aimee and placing his hand atop hers. "I also know I don't tell you often enough."

"I know you love me. It's just that I'm not sure at what level you love me," said Aimee.

"I don't understand."

"You go on," said Aimee.

"We can talk more...when I get home?"

"I'm leaving for Paris tomorrow,' said Aimee. "And it's not because of the phone calls or these other things. You're busy and I could use the extra time with my family...visit friends."

Aimee's bombshell caught John off guard. He took a second to let it sink in. "Aimee, please, don't do this. We'll spend more time together tomorrow... dinner tonight, tomorrow night. Whatever you want."

Aimee was unmoved. "For the past few months all we've done is eat and screw, and watch TV and screw, and...that's all fine, but we haven't made love once, or talked, not heart to heart. And this case you're on is *not* like the others you told me about. It's *not*. And we both know it."

"Aimee, please. We'll talk about it later tonight, when I get back... promise."

John stood, gave Aimee a lingering kiss on the forehead. Just then, Roger entered, headed upstairs.

"John! Damn, I'm glad you're alright, man. "

"Thanks, Roger."

Aimee gazed at John. He kissed her again, and again. "We'll talk when I get back."

Aimee smiled weakly, but did not respond. John left the room, glancing back over his shoulder.

Aimee was reaching out to him in a way she never had before. He knew if he had a brain, he would reschedule the appointment with Dr. Deauville and spend the entire evening with her. There was yet one other 'thing' pending—the meeting with Claire. Aimee had still not asked him about it, and he had not volunteered to tell her. She deserved to know and John wanted to tell her. He knew he had to, but this was definitely not the time.

Fifty-one
Night Session – Did I Really?

DR. DEAUVILLE'S OFFICE -Night— *"I've been less than candid with you."*

Dr. Deauville was at her desk

when a knock sounded on her suite's outer door. She answered. John waited in the corridor, questioning his decision to leave Aimee. The door opened. He instantly noticed a different Diane Deauville. She had an even more seductive presence; the glow in her eyes; her subtle, but distinct fragrance filled his nostrils. She stood just so, tilted her head a certain way. Perhaps he only imagined it all. It wasn't fair—her looking this way.

"John, good to see you again. Please, come on in," she said.

John inhaled deeply, exhaled audibly.

"I heard what happened." Diane's voice was laced with genuine concern and relief. "I'm so thrilled you're in one piece. I couldn't believe what I was hearing. They're saying it was a direct attempt on you and your partner. You think that's what it was?"

Diane guided John to the leather sofa. He all but collapsed into its lavish comfort. "I don't think so. I'm almost sure it was just another act of random violence. The shooter had no way of knowing we were cops. For all they knew, we were businessmen out on a lunch break."

"I hope that's all it was. May I get you a drink?" John shook his head, no. "I have a great Merlot, a Zinfandel, a Chardonnay, Evian..."

"Perhaps later. It's just nice to relax for a minute, taking in this soothing ambiance. "I Love the atmosphere. Looking around here, I imagine it's easy to forget there's a world out there...everyone rushing to get nowhere faster than the next guy."

Diane stepped closer, exuding charm, stirring visions—her arms folded just below her breasts, affording support they certainly did not need. John fought to not notice.

"I've tried to make it feel that way, experimenting with all kinds of decorating schemes before settling on this one. I wanted to create a cocoon effect...a place where one could more forget outside concerns."

"I'd say you've succeeded."

"Thanks. Listen, I'm going to change. Make yourself at home." Diane started for her dressing room then turned back. "You know, I remembered that last week was not the first time we met. The first time was five years ago in your criminology class," she said.

"Impossible. I would've remembered."

"You're too kind. I was looking rather nondescript that day."

"That's not possible."

Diane smiled, placed her right hand lightly on her right hip. "Are you flirting, Mr. Roméo?"

"Flir... flirting? No, I don't think so." John loosed a slight smile and briefly glanced away.

"I was doing research... sat in for just one class, without pre-approval, I admit. I tried introducing myself afterwards, but there were at least a dozen young women vying for your attention. I gave up and left. And here you are."

John shrugged with faint embarrassment.

"I'll only be a moment. Put on some music if you like. Stereo is over there. CDs and cassettes are on the shelf."

John watched Diane exit through a doorway leading to a dressing room just left of the wet bar. He took a deep breath and stood, made his way to the entertainment center, pressed the power button on the receiver, the CD player, and began sorting though a stack of CDs. Seconds later, he stood glancing around the office; the detective in him took over. He peered toward the dressing room door then moved cautiously to Diane's desk.

With his back angled toward the dressing room door, John carefully examined several sealed envelopes. His attention was drawn to a stack of audio cassettes next to the telephone. Glancing frequently over his shoulder, John examined several. Most had no labels.

Minutes passed. John remained at the desk. He lifted a cassette, turned it to the light to check for the manufacturer's name or logo. There was neither. But one tape caught his eye. It had a small, handwritten label with illegible markings. John could not resist. He slipped the cassette inside his jacket and returned the others.

A sudden tap on his shoulder. John wheeled around to find Dr. Deauville standing behind him, only a foot away. His heart nearly tore a hole in his chest.

"It's music for my portable player," she said. "Call me old-fashioned, but for some reason, I haven't gone the iPOD route, yet. I love to listen when I run, and when I work out."

John was momentarily speechless. The doctor stood in a soft spray of light that illuminated her in a way he had not anticipated.

"You look stunning," he said, taking her in from head to toe.

"Would you like me to play one of those tapes? They're oldies. One of my patients makes them for me. My assistant arranges to have them done . I've got Otis Redding, Jackie Wilson, Sam Cooke. I even have the "Frankie and Johnny" you've been hearing on the killer's CDs."

"Oh yeah? You say a patient makes them?"

"Yes."

"What's his name? Perhaps I could get him to burn some for me."

"*His* name? I have no male patients, John, remember?"

"I forgot."

Diane never answered the question, and John did not ask her again. No one could have blamed him for being more than a little distracted. She wore a revealing black dress with plunging neckline—a designer creation that caressed her like second skin, accenting every curve. To his surprise, Diane moved even closer—so close, only inches separated them.

John's discomfiture spiraled. He wasn't sure how to respond but couldn't conceal the natural effect all this was having on him. Diane must have noticed too. Her gaze briefly fell.

"You say these are Sam Cooke cassettes?"

"Some, not all. I just love his music. Too bad he died so young...had his whole life, and a fantastic future in front of him. Amazing, considering the success he had already enjoyed...and at such an early age."

"How do you know all about that? That was decades ago." John was impressed.

"Late sixties. He was shot to death at a motel, right here in Los Angeles. He was only thirty-three. I have all his hits. Sure you don't want me to play some of them?"

Diane's gaze was riveting, her voice wafting like silk in the wind.

"Maybe some other time," said John, his voice deepening.

"Just say when. By the way, I meant to tell you what a wonderful writer you are. I love your passion, your unmistakable literary voice that never wavers. I'm sure I have all your books, and I've seen all the adapted movies."

John blushed. He fidgeted with his hands, finally stuffed them into his pockets. "That's good to hear. I know I've said this already, but you look absolutely beautiful."

"Actually, you said stunning, but I'll accept beautiful."

"I hope its alright to say that."

"You have permission to say whatever you like."

An awkward, seemingly endless silence followed. Both John and Diane found themselves locked in a stare, unable or unwilling to break the spell. Diane was first to speak.

"I've been less than candid with you."

"How so?"

A deep sigh, atilt of her head. Diane's eyes darted about the room. John watched her, anxiously awaiting an explanation.

"I asked you here tonight for one reason—a reason that has nothing to do with the case."

"I don't understand."

"I think you do," said Diane.

There was palpable silence. Diane moved even closer; her gaze froze him. John stood motionless, as she closed the short distance between them. Her smile gave way to serious expression; her eyes danced mischievously. John was mesmerized.

Diane lingered inches away, their lips nearly touching. John first thought to leave right away—head straight for the door. The thought vanished. He could feel Diane's sweet breath on his face; he drank her aroma. She leaned forward, kissed him lightly on the lips.

John's instincts screamed for him to embrace her; to draw her in firmly, to submit to the sudden swell of raw emotion swirling around them. He kept telling himself to resist, even as he slipped his hands from his pockets. "Thanks for being so concerned the night we visited the Sumner place," Diane all but whispered, surprising him. "The experience affected me in a way I had not expected."

"No problem. It was... interesting, to say the least. Did you visit the Hillcrest site the next night?"

"Yes. The experience was quite different, but revealing. I'm including that in the report as well."

It was clear this discussion was merely a sidebar. John kept thinking of other questions, determined to keep his mind and the focus on the investigation. Diane remained only inches away. He could almost see his reflection in her eyes.

'What about the Jeffries case? You plan to visit the condo, too?" John asked.

Diane hesitated, glanced away momentarily. "I'll have to. I'll need a little more time to prepare, though? Will you go with me?"

John nodded. "Yes...yes, if you'd like," he added.

"I'd like."

Diane's voiced trailed. Then silence. John had no doubt what was happening. Erotic tension filled the room to overflowing. A rush coursed his body; he felt intoxicated, lighter than air. It was clear Diane was presenting herself to him. She stood there staring her eyes piercing him, pinning him.

Neither spoke for what seemed minutes, but were scant seconds. It was as if Diane was waiting for John to make the next move. He felt trapped between his natural, involuntary surge of masculine desire, and the voice of conscience that spoke to him in a soft, but persistent voice.

"Diane," John began. She smiled.

"That sounds very unofficial." Diane's voice softened. "Forgive me for liking the tone of it," she smiled. John returned her smile.

"Diane, I... I'm thinking," John drew out his words. "I'm thinking perhaps tonight is not such a good night for conducting business."

"I agree."

John's looming erection was now full bore. Diane took notice. "I mean, I probably should...should go."

"I'm sorry. I don't understand," said Diane with a coy smile.

"I think you do. I think we both do. And if I may speak, candidly."

"Please do."

"You are a very attractive woman, to say the least." Diane smiled, clasped her hands behind her. "You're an extremely intelligent and beautiful woman. No red-blooded, heterosexual man in his right mind could find you anything but irresistible. And my blood is the reddest there is. I am... I am sure you've noticed my difficulty in concealing my physical reaction to you."

Diane smiled, glanced down briefly, took John's hand, and led him to the sofa. She sat while he remained standing.

"It's okay," she said. "Hey, I promise not to seduce you, even though I do admit the temptation is very, very strong. Did I say very strong? And it suddenly feels warm in here."

John smiled, eased down beside Diane, determined to control the nearly uncontrollable. The fact Diane was coming on to him, in such an unexpected and unambiguous way, made her even more alluring.

"This may sound corny, certainly not vogue," said John, "but I have this...this old-fashioned attitude about being true to whatever woman I'm involved with."

"You're married?"

"No. Recently divorced. All the tabloids had a ball with it. But I... I now have this wonderful woman I'm..."

Diane smiled, and exhaled. "John, it's alright. It's really alright," she interrupted, "I respect that very much, I do. True, I am disappointed, but... but if anything, your honesty makes you even more attractive... more desirable. Despite my feelings—morally, ethically, and professionally—I'm still a woman. I find you... very desirable. You can't see my physical reactions to you, but I'm having them...even as I speak.

"And I have no problem admitting to wanting you; to have you want me only. I know that sounds sophomoric, even irrational. If you have someone you honor and respect, I'm happy for you. You are rare, indeed. And if you were mine, I would insist you be only mine."

John was briefly lost for a response. "You had no way of knowing. And I also have a practice of not getting involved with women with whom I have a professional relationship."

"A good practice. However, I could always end the professional relationship." Both chuckled. "Listen," said Diane. "I suppose I should let you go, unless you do want to discuss the case."

A long pause. Both stood. Diane was still only inches away. She smiled, realized she was holding John's right hand, released it, and took step back. Seconds later, at the door, John grasped the handle and turned back to face her.

"We've got a lot of work to do."

"We'll try this again tomorrow," said Diane. "I promise to restrain myself... be on my best behavior. It would also help if you don't wear the Cool Water aftershave; lose that silky baritone, and chill that warm smile of yours."

John grinned. Diane raised herself slowly, planted a lingering kiss on his left cheek. Now all John had to do was avoid tripping as he made his exit.

Fifty-two
Kitchen Bandits

KING RESIDENCE—An hour later — *"Better make it a long one, Dad."*

Gerald wore his *Yogi Bear* pajamas proudly.

Ray and Felicia joined him around the kitchen table, munching German chocolate cake and slurping milk. The unsettling incident of two nights earlier had not affected the Li household. The kids never saw the crap dumped on the lawn. Laura tried to conceal her own fear and anger. She suddenly appeared in the doorway, arms folded, posturing like an angry drill instructor. She still wore the blue, pinstriped business suit, minus her usual smile.

"I might have known," she said. "What in the world is this, Gerald Li? Look at all of you!"

Ray stood, stuffed the remaining cake into his mouth. Felicia stared at her mother, smiled cautiously. Gerald bowed his head, covered his mouth with one hand and swallowed hard.

"Let us all pray," he joked. Ray and Felicia snickered.

"Better make it a long one, Dad," said Ray.

Laura was not amused. "No more German chocolate cake."

"No more tonight," a contrite Gerald repeated.

"No more, period."

Gerald and the kids groaned in unison. There was little use pleading for leniency. Laura was in no mood for mercy.

"And you two should be ashamed," she scolded the kids. "You know your father is not responsible when it comes to sweets. And you let him talk you into becoming partners in his crime."

"It was my idea, Mom. I'm sorry," Felicia confessed.

Laura was not forgiving. "And a child shall lead them. Clean up in here. I don't want a million ants all over the place in the morning. Felicia, Ray... it's almost midnight. Goodnight."

Felicia had one last request. "Mom, could you please put a little more separation between the 'Felicia' part and the 'Ray' part. You make it sound like my name is Felicia Ray."

Laura couldn't help but laugh.

"Fine, Felicia... and Ray. That alright with you, miss?"

"Thanks, mom."

Ray was at the sink. Felicia, her hair in long thick braids, quietly took her plate and glass to the dishwasher. Gerald kept quiet.

"That's not enough for a full load," Laura pointed out, "Just rinse those and leave them in the sink until morning."

The children said goodnight; gave their parents a kiss and hug. Ray feigned a jab at his dad; he returned the gesture. A somber Gerald looked at them and smiled as they left the room. Laura moved to the table and, with folded arms, glared at her suddenly silent husband.

"How's the petition coming?" He asked.

"Fine. But don't change the subject. When's your next physical?" Gerald stuttered. Just then, the phone rang, bailing him out, momentarily. He eagerly answered. As he passed her, Laura grabbed a handful of gut and squeezed. He playfully brushed her hand away.

It was John. The instant Gerald heard his voice, he knew something was not right. He barely got beyond hello, before Gerald cut him off and suggested he come over. Both agreed it was best they talk face to face. Laura watched and listened. Gerald returned to his chair, wearing a puzzled expression.

"John Roméo?"

"He's on his way over."

Laura cleared her throat. "Wait. The John Roméo, I know, is coming here to Carson—tonight?"

"He's been here many times before."

"Only twice since he left the force. And for about ten minutes."

"Well, he's busy. I'm busy, you're busy."

"Make sure I'm awake to see this. Maybe I can get him to autograph my brief," chuckled Laura, as she left the room. Gerald followed.

"You make it sound as if he thinks he's too rich, too successful to associate with us peons. You can't be serious. The John who's had his feet planted under our dinner table more times than I can count? He's the kids' godfather... been my best friend for ten years. He's been here a thousand times."

"Not since he hit the big time."

"Okay. I see. You know what? It's you. It's not John, it's you, sweetheart. John hasn't changed. I think maybe your view of him—your expectations of him have changed. You know, that happens a lot when people become wildly successful. They don't change; the people around them change. It happens."

Gerald threw his powerful arms gently around Laura, and began nibbling her neck. She made a weak attempt to fend him off, but succumbed.

"Maybe... maybe you have a point," she conceded.

"Thank you, Counselor," Gerald whispered in her ear.

Fifty-Three
Soul Search

AN HOUR LATER - *"What did they find on this guy?"*

Gerald and John sat side by side,

on the porch steps, staring blankly toward the quiet street. From the curb, the two were barely visible on the stoop. Far in the distance, an ambulance siren split the cool night air. John gazed toward his car parked in the driveway. Suddenly, the entire area was illuminated by the beam from a LAPD chopper. The rotors drowned out their voices, momentarily, then moved on.

"You should have canceled the meeting with the Doc," said Gerald. John nodded agreement. "Look, I am no expert, when it comes to women and romance, and all that. But when a woman tells you she's leaving for Paris, and could be gone for weeks, you don't keep an appointment with another woman, especially one that looks like the doctor. — So, how did the meeting go?"

"Fine. I didn't stay long."

"I'm impressed at the way you're able to stay focused on your work. She's single, beautiful, intelligent, and sexy. And so is Aimee. I'm very proud of you. You're a one-woman guy. Not many of us left. But why are you here? I would have thought you'd make a beeline for home."

"Maybe I'm chicken. Besides, I needed to think... needed to talk."

"Okay. But before we do, let me brief you on the big news, in case you haven't heard.

"Foster solved our case again?"

"Don't upstage me. About an hour ago, a twenty-six year old white male, dressed in a black, ninja outfit was caught, trying to enter Lieutenant Governor Brill's Bonaventure hotel room. Could be the FBI's *Westbound Killer*, but I doubt it. He had a valid room key card, and a loaded .44 magnum, not a 9 millimeter.

"Brill?"

"Exacto. His female friend, not his wife, booked the room in her name; Brill arrived later. Hotel security nabbed the guy. Medrano got the call about 8:30. Dennis was the first from our section on the scene. He made the arrest."

"You're kidding. Who did the interrogation?"

"He and Medrano. No way the Lieutenant was gonna leave Dennis to do it alone. Foster was there, so was Emory. I didn't want any part of it. It's probably still going on, as we speak. Medrano wants to see you before anyone talks to the press. I was there for a while, but I left after the first thirty...forty minutes."

"What did they find on this guy, besides the .44?"

"They searched a black duffel bag he carried, searched his car—a '99 Maxima with Arizona plates. Damn thing was a rolling trash dump. They're still checking it. So far, all we have is the gun, a silencer, and a room key card. How he got the card, we don't know. FBI showed up just as I was leaving."

"Could be our guy?"

"We'll see. Look, go home! Go make wild, passionate, head-to-toe, monkey love to your lady. That's my advice. Just keep Aimee from leaving for Paris tomorrow. And one more thing," Gerald remembered, "I went to the *Women Live Free* web site. You should see some of the stuff I downloaded. I'll show it to you tomorrow."

"Anything else?"

"Yeah. Skeeter discovered the newly widowed Mrs. Jeffries put her estate on the market the day of the Judge's funeral. She's also booked a one-way trip to London."

John had no comment. He stood, stretched, turned to Gerald. "Thanks for the ear... and the shoulder. Say goodnight to the family."

"Sure there's nothing else?" Asked Gerald.

"Nothing. I'm just... I think I need a very long trip. Maybe to Mars or... or Jupiter or somewhere."

"Sounds like you're tired. You've been burning the candle at both ends for a hell of a long time, my friend. You are not superman, you know, despite the blue tights and that cape you hide underneath your clothes.

"You're right."

John started for his car. Gerald followed.

Gerald could sense that there was more his friend wanted to   say. They stood next to the Ferrari for several silent seconds.

"I've been keeping something from you," John said.

"Hmm. Can't imagine what that would be, unless your real name is Rupert or something?"

"I've never told anyone this." John's tone was serious. "Let's sit in the car."

Both climbed inside. John rolled down the windows, sat slouched in the driver's seat. Gerald waited, half turned in his seat."

"You know, I have this... reputation for being this, this tough, no nonsense, sometimes cocky, so-called homicide whiz."

"It's true. I mean, you do have that reputation. Hell, it's all true."

"Right. Here's another truth. For the past two years, I've been see-ing a shrink."

There was dead quiet. John waited. A wide-eyed Gerald turned to face his friend squarely.

"We all have," Gerald said weakly. "Department rule."

"No, no. I'm not talking about the periodic exchange of pleasant-ries with the damn Department shrink. I mean, on my own... personally, secretly. I got to a point where I had to do something, especially after Keith..."

"I know."

"It isn't easy talking about this."

"I'll listen to whatever you want to tell me. We're friends."

"I know. The truth is, what we do is emotionally drenching, psyche-twisting, taking nothing away from the shit street cops face everyday."

"True."

"It's not something any homicide investigator wants to admit. We tend to conceal the cumulative effect of staring at gory images, wasted lives and knowing what it does to families. I concealed what it did to me. I also ignored the...the dreams."

"You mean nightmares," said Gerald. Any one of us who says he or she hasn't woke up in the middle of the night—heart pounding, sweat beading, eyes filled with images of some murder scene pasted to our eyeballs like Velcro—is a damn liar. It's just that most of us will never admit it, especially to our spouses."

"Or ourselves."

"Spouses probably know anyway, though."

"Right. Claire asked me about it. I lied. Told her I would never go see a shrink. Actually, he came to me...on my boat."

"A shrink who makes yacht calls?"

"For years, I've had this recurring dream—a never-ending night-mare. I can't get rid of it."

"What's it about?"

John took a long sigh. "Always starts in the same place, ends in the same way. I'm in a field out in the middle of nowhere. There's...there's a carpet of beautiful flowers, swaying grass, gently rolling hills, brilliant blue skies—the kind of place you would give anything to find. I feel like I'm in some...some place unspoiled by human hands. I never want to leave it; I never want to wake up. And even though it seems so real, I know I'm dreaming. At least, I think I know.

"Then, all of a sudden—and it seems like only a few feet away from me—a corpse, the remains of a victim from one of my cases. With the skeletal structure intact, it starts rising straight up out of the ground. The arms are outstretched, the head tilted to one side. There's nothing but skeleton, but I can make out this plaintive, mournful expression on its face. I can almost hear the last pained utterance he or she ever made in life."

Gerald sat gripped by John's emotion-filled voice—a voice he had not heard before. There was little he could say. He just listened.

"Before I can react," John went on, "there's another one, then another, and another. Dozens, hundreds, maybe thousands; the whole field is full of them. It's a graveyard—a common graveyard for every victim of every case I've ever investigated; for every murder case there's ever been. I'm...I'm surrounded. Moments later, they begin moving towards me. I turn in a complete circle, and I see the same thing, as far as my eyes can see. But, strangely enough, I... I'm suddenly not afraid. I feel I should be afraid, but I'm not. I'm mesmerized—awed by what I see—but not really afraid. Seconds later, I realize why I'm not afraid." John's speech faltered. He stared straight through the windshield, out into the night and far beyond. Gerald felt as if John, for a time, was no longer aware he was sitting next to him.

"I realize why I'm no longer afraid," he went on. "I raise my hand to touch the corpse nearest me. And just as I reach out, I see the skeletal remains of my own hand—my own hand. I'm dead, too. I'm one of them. I'm one of them! It's the weirdest damn thing. That's when I become truly afraid. I can't explain the fear." John said nothing for nearly a full minute.

"I wake up, breathing heavily... sweating. I would glance over to make sure Claire was still asleep. Same has happened with Aimee. I raise my hands, put them to my face to make sure I'm actually awake. I tell myself all this is just a product of my overactive imagination."

"But you know better," said Gerald.

"Hell, yeah I know better."

"But you walked away from this gig. You got out. You put in your time. And you were the best I've ever seen. You still are. So why do you...why keep coming back? Why? You don't need this."

"I tell myself the same thing. There're two reasons, maybe three. First, I guess it's the only way I know to fight the demons—whatever it is that taunts me, tries to reduce me in my own eyes. I can't really banish them by running away. Maybe when I can conquer them, I can truly walk away. I believe that."

What's the second?"

"The ghost of my father—the one in my head. I still hear him challenging me, facing me down like he did when bullies would beat me up in grade school. I'd come home crying. One day he sat me down. And I can still see him towering over me, pointing, shaking his finger, frowning, flecks of spit raining down on my face.

"Anyway, he started teaching me how to box...showed me where all the vulnerable points were, how to attack them. Said if I ever came home crying like some girl again, he'd make me wear a dress and panties to school. I vowed to never cry again. I know he was just trying to toughen me up.

He loved me, and I loved him. But he never told me, not in those exact words. And I never told him either. I wish I had. I'm sure he did too, before he died. We only have the living years, you know. We have to get it right, during the living years."

"So you feel that your walking away...that your running from the demons is like... like crying in front of your father."

"He would think so, my father."

"Naw."

"He would. There's no doubt in my mind if he were alive he would say exactly that."

A long silence.

Gerald searched for some poignant, wise, timely remark. None came. He concluded that if he forced a comment, it would likely be something wrong and stupid.

"You've had a full day," Gerald managed. "All I can say is, we should all be smart enough to know when we need help fighting the demons we all have. Know what? I'm proud to be your friend."

John smiled, leaned back, and seized the steering wheel with both hands. "Do I have permission to leave now, Sergeant Li," he asked. Gerald smiled, nodded yes.

Fifty-four
The Long Way Home, Rodéo or Rodeo?

John's gaze was suddenly drawn to his hand.

John chose every indirect way

home he could find. He wanted to think. He needed to think. He also wanted to give Aimee enough time to work through her thoughts. There was little doubt dinner was a bust, the moment he decided to leave home. He kept thinking of what he had revealed to Gerald. No regrets, he actually felt a sense of relief, having shared the whole thing.

For forty-five minutes, John Roméo meandered along sparsely traveled boulevards and avenues. He crept along remote streets, finally entering the 405 Freeway at Century and exiting at Wilshire. He found himself slowing for red lights, rather than speeding through on cautions. Taking a circuitous route home gave him plenty of time to reflect. He contemplated withdrawing from the case. It was time he moved on, enjoyed the life his success had made possible.

John was in a deeply reflective mood. He drove farther east on Wilshire Boulevard than he had intended. At Rodéo Drive, he turned left and crept along at a snail's pace. He did not notice a Beverly Hills

Police cruiser, with two uniformed officers, ease alongside. The officers looked to their right, observed John. He noted their presence and kept driving. Shortly, the cruiser fell back, rolled up behind John and 'lit' him up.

"What the... ?" John muttered.

He was in no mood. He pulled over in front of Giorgio Armani's, stopped and waited. The cruiser stopped behind him. He could see the passenger cop on the radio. Then both officers exited the cruiser, each with a hand on his gun butt, and approached him from either side. John shook his head with disgust. The driver's side officer spoke first.

"Good evening, sir."

"What's the problem, officer?"

"License and registration, sir."

"What's the problem," John repeated.

"Sir, your license and registration, please."

John chuckled. "My license is inside my own wallet," he said, slowly and deliberately. The registration is inside my own glove box. I am now slowly removing my wallet...now slowly opening the glove-box of my very own personal Ferrari, which I personally paid for, and do personally own, sir."

John handed the documents to the officer. The officer focused the flashlight on the license, and immediately recognized the name and photo. His attitude instantly changed.

"Oh, fu... ah, Mr. Roméo. It's you. Sorry. You're, you're free to go."

John was having none of it. "I don't understand."

"There's no problem, sir. Have a goodnight."

"What? There's no problem?"

"No sir."

The officers turned to walk back to their cruiser. John stepped from his car, determined to draw attention. Pedestrians on both sides of Rodéo paused to observe.

"Excuse me, officers. Excuse me but there *is* a problem," John's voice rose. "You stopped me for a reason. Why? I'm just driving along, minding my own goddamn business and you stop me. Why?"

The first officer turned to respond, while the second beat a hasty retreat to his side of the cruiser. "We didn't know you..."

"Didn't know what, officer? Who I was? All you saw was a black face in a Ferrari, right? That's why you stopped my black ass! Well, in case you didn't know, this is Los "Friggin" Angeles." We's all got 'Ferrarises' and 'Mercedeses' now, suh."

The officer turned away, attempting to end the confrontation, even as the crowd grew.

"No, no, no. You don't get off with "excuse me, but we thought you were just some unknown Negro fitting the description. So, arrest my ass. Handcuff me like you would any other black man. Make me lie on the ground in my damn Armani suit. I don't want special privileges!"

John knelt in the street, next to his car, his hands clasped behind his back. "Just forget who the hell I am! You stopped me, so ticket me or arrest me, damn it!

The officers climbed into the cruiser, and quickly left the scene. John stood and dusted his clothes. The crowd broke into loud applause. John climbed into his car and drove on.

Fifty-five
Curse of The Gods

He rushed over, grabbed the pillow...

John pulled past the gated entrance

and was surprised to see Aimee's BMW center court, not in the garage. She never left her car out all night. He parked, climbed out slowly, walked toward the front door, peering inside the car as he passed. Only steps from the door, he stopped cold.

A large manila envelope was taped dead center. "Roméo" was penned in large, black letters in the upper right-hand corner, apparently made with a black felt marker. John stared at it, momentarily. He opened the door. It was pitch black inside. The sensor operated interior lights did not activate, surprising him. The interior security system did not respond to his wrist-mounted link.

"Aimee!"

No answer. It was deathly quiet, too quiet. John paused inside the entry. Something was wrong. He drew his 9mm, slowly closed the door. Moving laterally to the wall-mounted manual light switch, he flipped it on. The chandelier flashed on, lighting the spiral staircase.

John's gaze was suddenly drawn to his hand. Blood. There was blood on his palm. Shock sprang through his body. He turned to see the floor at the base of the stairs strewn with long-stem roses. He tossed the envelope to the floor, did a three-sixty.

"My God! Aimee! Aimee!"

John bolted toward the stairs. Several drops of blood dotted the white carpet , and the banister. He started up the stairs, gun raised.

"Roger!   Aimee!"

No response.

John sprinted the rest of the way up and bolted for the master bedroom. It was dark. He flipped on the light. The room had been trashed. Slashed pillows lay on the floor; overturned dresser drawers lay strewn across the bed. Small amounts of blood were splattered on the top sheet. Partially spent white candles formed a semicircle on the floor at the foot of the bed.

John was nearly floored by the sight. He dashed to the master bathroom, swearing aloud. It was empty. Inside his study, his computer monitor had been smashed. Papers and books littered nearly every surface.

"God, what in the..." John tore from the room, charged down the corridor to the other bedrooms. In the nearest, he slapped on the light. His focus was drawn to the unmade bed and a pillow. He rushed over, grabbed the pillow and examined a pancake-sized spot of blood. Fear and anger seized him; he stared at his bloody fingers, tossed the pillow back onto the bed. "Aimee," he whispered, bolting from the room.

Twenty-five minutes later, a half-dozen LAPD vehicles, including a white police S.I.D. lab van, crowded John's motor court. The front door to the house was wide open. A small army of uniformed, plainclothes officers and SID technicians blanketed upstairs, downstairs, the grounds, and the gated entrance.

Scouring the residence, investigators searched for clues. In the master bedroom, a woman investigator lit a new white candle and waited for it to burn down. She was trying to determine time required for it to reach the stage others were found.

A somber John sat on the living room sofa, his head buried in his hands. Gerald was next to him, holding the manila envelope and its contents: a stripped cover from John's *Curse Of The Gods,* and a cutout from the cover page of The National Insider.

An animated John suddenly sprang to his feet. "GK, I can't...I can't sit here," he insisted.

"I know. But you have to."

"Aimee and Roger are out there, somewhere... in trouble, maybe worse. I don't understand this at all. Who? Why?"

"Don't think the worst."

John was beyond consoling. "I was *here* at six. They were fine. It must have happened right after I left. It's gotta be one of those guys who were after Roger. It has to be. The bastards are part of the Russian Mafia.

"How the hell they get in? Breach your security?" Asked Gerald.

John shook his head. "I can't figure it out, Reina left early. Roger wouldn't have answered the gate for any reason. Aimee must've have gone out. They could have ambushed her when she returned. That would explain her car being left outside. Sonofabitches. The bastard's are good as dead." John's mixture of anger and fear approached melt-down."

"Listen to me," said Gerald. "I can only imagine what you're going through. But you've got to let these guys here do their thing. They're the best. If there's any kind of clue here at all, they'll find it. The good thing is, they're sure the amount of blood loss here is not enough to have caused death."

John was not comforted by Gerald's valiant efforts. Just then, Lt. Medrano approached in a rush. His face was stern and drawn.

"What is it, Paul?" Asked John.

"We just located an abandoned van about two miles from here."

"Where?"

"On Coldwater. We've got a team up there now. It's dark gray. A check shows the van was stolen a week ago from a florist in Pasadena. If there's any connection with any of this, it may explain the roses. Plates are stolen, too."

John turned to walk away. "Hold on," said Medrano.

John was adamant. "I refuse to just sit here with my thumb up my butt!"

"We need you here. I know I can't keep you out of this but we've got to plan this thing... move carefully. Maybe this van *does* figure into the disappearance of Aimee and Roger. If so, then all this likely happened only a few hours ago. It also means there was a second vehicle, and likely more than one person was involved. They sure as hell didn't leave on foot. We're checking the van for other forensic evidence."

An S.I.D. investigator called for Medrano. He excused himself. A drained John turned to Gerald. "We've got to find them," he whispered.

"We will. If this is a kidnapping, you have to expect to be contacted. You need to stay put. We'll handle this, and manage the serial case with new people."

"I'm not quitting that case."

"You changed your mind?"

"That's secondary, right now. I've got to find Aimee and Roger."

Medrano returned with the technician. "Excuse me, John. Do you happen to have any... animals, pets of any kind?"

John was perplexed by the question. "No. Why?"

"We just completed prelim tests in the lab van on two blood samples. One taken from the stairway, is definitely human blood. The sample taken from the master bedroom is either dog or cat blood."

"Dog or cat?"

"Wait, you said your brother looks a lot like you, right?" Asked Medrano.

"Somewhat, except he has a beard."

Gerald reached for the torn novel cover, held it up. He looked at John then the cover. "Wait a minute. Wait, this is you...with a beard. I remember you having that thing."

"So?"

"So how much does your brother look like this picture of you?" Medrano asked.

John took the cover, stared at it. "I never thought about it."

"Listen, could someone have mistaken your brother for you?" Asked Gerald.

Lt. Medrano reached for the cover.

"I guess so... when I had a beard," said John, thrusting both hands to his face. "Damn. Damn! They were after me? You think they were after me?"

"But why would the guys in the Maserati be after you, if they were looking for Roger? They knew what he looked like," said Medrano.

"You're right," John agreed.

Medrano stepped away, signaling Gerald to follow him. The two stepped into another room. "I don't think I can convince John to stay on the sidelines on this one," said Medrano.

Gerald Agreed. "You know him. Once he makes up his mind, nothing stops him."

"Exactly. He's feeling responsible for what's happened. I'm worried about his state of mind. Maybe you can talk to him...get him to settle down."

"Lieutenant, the only thing that's going to get him to settle down is finding Roger and Aimee. I'll try and talk to him but I can imagine what's going through his head right now.

Despite his own reasoning, John felt he had been the primary target. He blamed himself for leaving Aimee alone; for not returning more quickly. But who could have mistaken Roger for him?

Fifty-six
A Clue? Give Me A Break!

"What do you mean? 'Cause it's privileged?"

Gerald and Medrano joined John

in his media suite. All stood in front of the audio system, as he placed the nearly forgotten cassette taken from Dr. Deauville's office, into the player and pressed the rewind button.

Both Gerald and Medrano had their suspicions. But when John pressed the *play* button, they were not prepared for what they heard.

"But you *do* know. How long have you known or at least had some inkling about all this?"
Long Pause...

"From the beginning. I suppose I knew from the beginning—fifteen years ago. There were signs. There were always signs. I just refused to accept them. I simply could not bring myself to accept the obvious. I blocked it all out, to my own detriment. I would always say to myself:

Catherine, don't be silly. He loves you. Reason this out. He would not have married you; he would not be here if he didn't love you. Besides, he repeated the vows. He said the words with such fervor and

passion. You heard him with your very own ears. So, what are you going to believe? His emotional, tear-filled pledge of eternal love and fidelity... or your own eyes?

Well, he's been unfaithful from the first. And I've been tolerating it,
like a fool. I feel so weak...so stupid."

"There's no need for self-flagellation."

"I'm being honest."

"I understand. But I don't want to hear anymore of this self-blame,
alright?"

"It's just that I hate myself for loving him like I do and for not having the strength to leave him."

Another long pause... the sound of sobbing.

"Is that really what you want to do, Mrs. Jeffries—leave him?"

"I don't know. "Yes. Yes. I do."

"You seem unsure. But, if that's true...that you do want to leave
him, then what's stopping you?"

 "Actually, I'd love to kill him."

"Kill him?"

"If I had the nerve, I'd end his lying, his cheating."

The tape ended abruptly, leaving the three staring at each other.

"What's the significance? What does it mean?" Asked Medrano.

"Mrs. Jeffries obviously spoke to the doctor in great detail about
her husband and their marital problems," said John. "She wanted him
dead."

"Okay. But the woman is her patient. You'd expect them to talk
about everything," said Gerald.

"True. But then he shows up with a bullet between his eyes, his
head blown off," said John. "And now we hear this conversation. What
if we find wives of the other victims were patients of the doctor also?"

"We don't know that. It would be interesting, perhaps even dis-
positive, but we don't know that," said Medrano.

"I know. I said *what if.* And what if we find other tapes like the ones
we just listened to? I know it's a stretch, but look at what we now know.
You've got to admit it's the one possible common link."

"This is no good," Medrano said.

"What do you mean? 'Cause it's privileged?"

"Damn right. This taped conversation is between a doctor and her patient. Even if this was a smoking gun, which I'm not convinced it is, it would almost surely never see judicial daylight. Besides, you...you borrowed it, John."

"I hate to say this, but we have to search her office, said John. "

"You mean the doctor? Why?"

"The tapes."

"Because she likes Sam Cooke? What do you expect to find? The killer is leaving CDs, not cassette tapes. And even if she is protecting a patient—which we both know is wild speculation—what does that have to do with the case?"

"Maybe nothing, maybe something."

"I know how you feel. But we can't just break into some office. If you want, we'll try to get a warrant. But we've got to have a little thing called probable cause. Plus, there's such a thing as doctor-patient privilege. You can't just go rifling through some doctor's files on a whim, even an educated one."

"We act on whims all the time."

"You're not saying the doctor has anything to do with what happened here, are you? Like you said, it's probably those guys who were out to get Roger."

"I don't believe she's involved in any of this," said John. "But I think one of her patients may have something to do with the killings. Maybe that's who's behind this and the attempt on us the other day. If that's true, they want me off this case. That's clear."

"That's a hell of a stretch. What gives you that idea? And even if it's true, you just agreed that's got nothing to do with all this," said Medrano.

"What I said is, someone wants me off this case...wants us of this case. They took shots at us. Remember?"

"John. You're not making sense. And I don't expect you to, right now. Let Skeeter check things out first. It won't take him long."

John stalked away. Medrano turned to Gerald, placed a firm hand on his shoulder.

"I want you to stay with him, okay? He's not responsible right now. I want you to keep an eye on him. He goes to the dumper, you go to the dumper. He goes to the pisser, you go to the pisser."

"That's taking friendship and devotion to duty a little far," said Gerald.

"There's no other choice. He's too close to this. And you and Skeeter are the only ones he really listens to."

Medrano had no sooner finished his statement, than Skeeter ambled through the front door. He had heard what happened. But something etched on his weathered face told everyone he had another reason for being there. Skeeter spoke with John then listened quietly as Medrano filled him in. Afterwards, he took the three aside and revealed his own news, in his 'no holds barred' style.

"On my way over, I heard a breaking news story that's gonna make your friggin' heads spin. The State Supreme Court has just ordered a new trial for the bastard. It's all over the news."

Shock does not describe the reaction Skeeter got.

"You're shitin' me," Medrano chortled.

"Wish I was. Prosecutorial misconduct, they ruled. They've ordered him back to Los Angeles. He's being released on bail, but placed on a state-of-the-art electronic monitoring system. They say it's so sensitive, we'll know if he so much as farts."

"Nobody gives a damn if he farts, or shits on himself," said Gerald. "Unbelievable. Never thought I'd end up hating the damn 'Supremes.' This is screwed."

Skeeter continued. "His mother and brother live in Glendale. I've said this before; the bastard was not alone in what he did. I'll always believe that."

A grim-faced John said nothing. Just as he started upstairs, Captain Nicholson walked in. His face was drawn, etched with anger and concern. No one was surprised Nicholson had shown up. Despite their few clashes, he and John shared a mutual respect.

But it was not only John's plight that brought the Captain to Beverly Hills. He had news regarding the man arrested at the Bonaventure. Within an hour of concluding the suspect's interrogation, the FBI arrived. Flexing their muscle, agents whisked him away to the Federal Detention Center.

An hour later, the Captain was advised the Feds were convinced the suspect was not their man. However, he and his girlfriend would be remanded to local custody. A news release would be issued stating the *Westbound Killer* was still at large.

Fifty-seven
Stake-out

The sprawling garage was practically empty.

John sat behind the wheel of Gerald's unmarked car, his head planted against the headrest. Gerald was asleep, snoring mercilessly. Both were still reeling from Skeeter's revelation. He had promised to now focus on those he always suspected of having a connection to Bolen. He was not sure where the trail would lead, nor did he care.

John lifted his head, glanced at his partner, shook him slightly. The snoring stopped but only briefly. Minutes later, both were fast asleep. Skeeter and Lt. Medrano had reached a compromise with John, persuading him to satisfy his questions about the doctor; talk to her, personally, and leave the search for Aimee and Roger to others; fat chance of that. They assured him of constant communication, to keep him informed.

Gerald agreed to be his chaperone. The idea to wait in the garage was John's. From previous conversations with her, he was aware the doctor often arrived hours before her assistant or her first patient. She said it gave her time to think, to plan, even write. Already she was half-way through the fourth draft of her next book.

John's cell phone rang; he awoke with a start. Gerald stirred but only shifted in his seat. It was Medrano. He had information about the cars found registered in the doctor's name. They included a '06 BMW 760iL and a '07 Lexus LS-460. John scribbled notes on a small note-book he removed from his jacket.

The most surprising news was that three men in a white Maserati, all Russians, were pulled over in a routine traffic stop on the Ortega Highway by a two man CHP unit. When a check was run, warrants popped up. Because of the group's reputation for extreme violence, three other units arrived, plus a CHP chopper. All were arrested and taken into custody without incident. There was no news about the fourth man.

John was excited; he fired a fusillade of questions at Medrano. "What about the fourth Russian...about clues regarding Roger and Aimee?"

There were none. For John, being a bit-player in his own worst nightmare was driving him crazy. He struggled to remain calm, fo-cused, and trusting in others to find answers. No ransom call had come. The fact no one had yet called made him more convinced this was not a random snatching. He was now certain the act was aimed at him and his involvement on this serial case.

Gerald was nearly awake now, yawning repeatedly. John related the news from Medrano, and his disappointment that the fourth guy—reputed to be the group's leader—was still at large.

Gerald glanced around at what was now a sea of cars at every turn. "Where'd all these cars come from?" He asked, still rubbing his eyes and peering at his watch. It was almost nine. He opened his door, stepped out to take a look around the garage, to breathe in a dose of an exhaust fume cocktail.

"You sure she parks on this level?" Gerald asked, amidst a yawn.

John assured him she did. They waited. Twenty minutes later, both decided to head for the doctor's office.

The pair stepped off the elevator and moved quickly down the corridor toward Dr. Deauville's office. Halfway there, they observed a woman, fortyish, dressed in a dark blue business suit, briefcase in hand. She slipped her key into the doctor's office door. The duo hurried toward her, badges in hand. The startled woman turned to face them, then backed away.

"Excuse me, ma'am," said Gerald. "Don't be afraid. We're police. You work for Dr. Deauville?"

"Ah, yes sir."

"I'm Detective Li. This is Detective Roméo. And you're..."

"Dana. My name's Dana, Dana Seybold. I'm Dr. Deauville's assistant. Is something wrong?"

"May we step inside?" Asked Gerald, moving forward even as he spoke.

"What's wrong? Is Dr. Deauville alright?"

"May we step inside?"

Dana complied, entered with a cautious eye on her visitors, and placed her purse and briefcase on her desk in the reception area. Gerald closed the door. The first thing they noticed was the bank of pullout file drawers recessed into one wall. It likely contained all patients' records, perhaps the doctor's session notes. John said nothing; he continued on toward Dr. Deauville's office.

"I'm sorry, sir. That's the doctor's private office. No one's allowed in there without her permission. Could you tell me why you're here?"

"Dana? It's Dana, right?" Asked Gerald.

"Yes sir."

"Dana, what time do you expect Dr. Deauville?"

"I'm not sure. I know she planned to get in early, to complete a report for the LAPD... do some writing on her book. Later this morning, she planned to leave for Oregon...to visit her father's grave. His birthday is tomorrow."

"Oregon? What part of Oregon?"

"Eugene. That's where her family's from... or was from."

"You know her family?"

"No. I've worked for... with her for nearly five years but I never knew her family. She has a sister. She lives here in southern California, but I've never met her. What's all this about?"

"A brother. What's her name?"

"Dennis"

"Is he older? Younger?"

"Older. He's thirty-eight, I think. Dr. Deauville often spoke about their growing up; how he... Excuse me, but you haven't told me why you're here."

"We will. Ah... you were saying something about their growing up together."

"Well, Dr. Deauville says Dennis often tortured small animals and birds; he even set them afire. Officer, why all the questions? Am I supposed to be telling you her personal business like this?"

"Why wouldn't you, Dana?"

Dana was listening to Gerald, but watching as John entered the doctor's office. "I won't lose my job, letting you in here, will I?"

"Of course not. We'll look around then leave. We'll give you a number. You can tell the doctor we were here and have her call us. How's that?"

Aren't you supposed to tell me why you're here? Where's your warrant? Shouldn't you show me a warrant?"

"We're conducting a murder investigation. The doctor is assisting us. We're working together."

A wary Dana watched from the doorway. Gerald guided her away and back to her own desk, as he continued the questions.

Meanwhile, John, finding it nearly impossible to focus exclusively on the matter at hand, quickly dialed Medrano on his cell. There was nothing new to report. Detectives were interviewing John's immediate neighbors, most of whom like him, lived in estates obscured by towering fences and trees.

John put his phone away, strode across the office to the doctor's desk. The stack of cassette tapes was gone. A legal pad lay where they had been. John was certain the pad had not been there the night before. He removed what appeared to be a clean sheet, folded it and placed it in his jacket pocket.

While Gerald continued with Dana, John's attention was drawn to the desktop computer on the credenza behind the desk. He did not recall it during his earlier visits, but it must have been there.

John had no doubt there were files on the hard drive, and the zip disks stacked next to it, that were not in the hard copy files in Dana's office. He would have given anything for a chance to pour through them. He now had no choice but to ask the doctor for as much information as she would volunteer. He planned to ask her about the fact Catherine Jeffries was a patient; that she had not revealed that, even though the judge's death was being investigated.

There were more questions. Principally, if any other surviving spouses, in the cases being investigated, were her patients. He was not sure how far he would get but had to try.

John was about to leave the office, when he decided to check the dressing room. By now, Gerald stepped to the doorway, saw him approaching, and entered the main office. John continued toward the dressing room door. When he pushed against it, he met resistance; something was blocking it. Gerald observed his partner's difficulty. Finally, John was able to open it enough to poke his head inside.

"Jeezus!" He blurted.

Lying face down in a heap on the floor was an ashen, motionless Diane Deauville, still wearing the black dress from the night before. John forced his way inside, dropped to his knees. He could not believe what he saw. Her right wrist was severely slashed, but was no longer bleeding. An old-fashioned straight razor was clutched in her left hand. An empty aspirin bottle lay nearby. Blood covered the floor beneath her right arm. Several rose petals lay beside her lifeless form. John quickly checked Diane's pulse. It was faint—nearly imperceptible.

"GK!" John yelled.

Gerald was immediately behind him, peering past the door. "Damn!" John bolted for the phone, called out to Dana.

Again, John frantically searched for a pulse, and began CPR. Dana rushed to the bathroom door. She saw the doctor's body, the blood, and collapsed to her knees, gasping, covering her face with both hands.

"She's still alive... barely," John announced. "Pulse is very weak, bleeding's stopped. Get me a towel or something... pillows from the sofa."

Dana managed to stand; she struggled to steady herself. With tears streaming, she turned away. John hovered over Diane. This made no sense. He could not believe she had tried to take her own life. He suddenly felt responsible, though uncertain why she would do such a thing, or why he felt responsible in any way.

Fifty-eight
Behold, a Mystery.

"Why? Was she ever violent."

Twelve minutes later,

police and EMS personnel crowded the office suite. Dr. Deauville remained unconscious, as she was transported from the office. An IV was in place, her right wrist heavily bandaged. A solemn John watched as she was carried into the corridor, en route an ambulance parked in the garage.

Medrano, who had hurried to the scene, radioed ahead, instructing an officer Fordham to keep reporters clear of the garage and the elevator entrance. Gerald and John were quick to both console and gently question a distraught Dana. A female officer handed her a cup of coffee.

"I'm sure you want to help Dr. Deauville," said John. "We pray and expect she'll be alright. The best way for you to help is to tell us all you can." Dana nodded. "I'll be brief. Do you have any idea who would want to harm the doctor?"

"No sir. No one," Dana muttered, brushing away tears.

"Does anyone have a key to the main door, or her office, besides you and Dr. Deauville?"

"No one except the building services people. They come in every night. But Dr. Deauville never lets them into *her* office unless she's here. She keeps it locked. Her brother may have a key to both doors."

"It wasn't locked when we came inside," said Gerald.

John stepped closer to Gerald and barely whispered. "I guess that's because she came back here last night and never left. But she wasn't wearing that dress when I last saw her yesterday evening. I think she was meeting someone, then going to dinner from here."

"Do you know who she was meeting," John warily asked Dana,

"No. She made the appointment herself. But I'm sure it had to do with the serial murder profiles she was working on. I can't believe she would try to harm herself. She just wouldn't," Dana declared, tears still streaming."

There was brief silence. John pressed on. "Did Dr. Deauville tape sessions with all her patients?"

The question even caught Gerald by surprise. No one had mentioned taping during the present exchange. Gerald was concerned that fact would not escape Dana. She must be wondering how John would know to ask her about taping.

"I'm sorry. Would you not speak of her in the past tense, please?" Asked Dana, tearfully.

"I'm sorry. I meant, does she?"

"She always tapes. That way, she always has an exact record. How did you know she tapes her sessions?"

"I just... assumed. It's a common practice among psychiatrists and psychologists, I understand," said John. Dana nodded.

Gerald took a deep breath. John cleared his throat, glanced nervously at his partner. He was anxious to change the subject.

"You said there was a brother. Tell us about him. Do you know where he lives... where Dr. Deauville lives?"

"Dennis lives in Pasadena. Dr. Deauville lives in San Marino."

John's eyes widened. "So, did they get along well?"

"Not really. Dennis is extremely jealous of his sister; envious of her fame, her success, the relationship she had with her father. I think Dr. Deauville is a... a little afraid of him."

"Why? Was he ever violent."

"Not that I'm aware; not as adults, but she was violent as a child?"

"You mean, like you were telling us earlier?"

"Yes. Yes, with animals and stuff. He would torture them... sacrifice them. He was alright until she was six. That's when he found out he was adopted. He did dissect Doctor D's pet kitten, after beating it with a baseball bat."

"How do you know all this?" Asked Gerald.

'I learned most of it from Dr. Deauville, although she doesn't like talking about her childhood."

"You have addresses... phone numbers for the sister and the good doctor?"

"In my Rolodex. But..."

"But what?" John interrupted.

"The doctor has been negotiating to sell her home."

"To whom?"

"Rose Henley, the writer."

There was dead silence. This was far more information than they hoped to learn from Dana.

"Would you get those addresses for us?" Asked Gerald.

"I can't believe this," Dana repeated.

"She'll be alright," said John, hoping to calm her.

Dana left to get the information. Medrano approached. "Bingo!" Gerald blurted.

"Maybe," said John. "Maybe. This is amazing. What's next?"

"How was the doctor when you left her last night?" Asked Gerald.

"Fine. She was fine. Look, I think she'll pull through; she has to. But my overriding concern right now is finding Aimee and Roger. I've got a feeling time is running out. And I can't wait for Skeeter to finger Bolen's fellow Nazi wannabes."

There was blood in that van we found," said Medrano. "Animal and human—more splattering than anything else. They had to abandon it...blown engine. We also found flex cuffs. And the vehicle was padded inside to soundproof it. It appears this was done hurriedly. It all looked makeshift. We're doing fiber and hair analysis on specimens we found. And we're sending other split samples to the FBI lab and D.O.J. There's no telling when they'll be able to get it back to us, though. Big news is, we've got a line on that fourth Russian."

"Where? Who is the sonofabitch?" John snapped.

"Name's Sergei Yukanovich. He and his cohorts are all part of some west coast Russian Mafia, like you said. Their major operations involve bootlegged gasoline and diesel fuel tax rip-offs. Anyway, SWAT is moving in on him at this Palos Verdes address."

Medrano handed John a crumpled note. Gerald took the information but his mind was spinning. John was on the same wavelength.

Dana returned with the requested information scribbled on a sheet of legal pad paper; she handed it to John.

John glanced at the addresses, showed it to Gerald. "Dana, I'd like for you to go with us," he said. Dana was speechless. "You may be able to help us contact the sister, and there are some other questions. I assure you, you won't be in any danger. Paul, I'm going to need a female officer—plainclothes."

It took a several seconds for Dana to speak. "I... I really would rather not."

"It would help us a great deal."

Dana looked away, glanced down then nodded a reluctant, yes."

"A female officer," John repeated to the Lieutenant.

"Summers. She's downstairs. We'll have to wait for an order to search beyond the immediate crime area here, and that's not going to be easy... could take a while."

Medrano turned to Dana. "Excuse me, Miss. Do you know who Dr. Deauville's attorney is?"

"Yessir. His name is G. Gordon Smythe."

A collective sigh rose from everyone except Dana. The surprise was that Smythe had not shown up yet to monitor police presence.

"Like I said," Medrano continued. "It could take some time, and quite some doing." He stepped closer to John and all but whispered. "Don't take anything away from here that doesn't stick to the soles of your shoes,"

"I plan to be in Palos Verdes when SWAT moves in," said John. "I have a feeling that's where Aimee and Roger are."

"Let *us* find them," said Medrano. "You take care of *this*. The media's already crawling all over downstairs. This thing is blowing up in our damn faces."

John understood Medrano's pleadings. He made sense, but he could not go along with his suggestion. And he kept hoping the lieutenant would not make it an order.

"I have to be there. They're in danger because of me," John all but whispered. Medrano placed a hand on his shoulder.

"Anybody seen Sgt. Dennis?" Gerald asked.

"No," said Medrano. "He just fell off the damn radar screen after the arrest of that turd in the Lieutenant Governor's hotel room last night."

Gerald took John aside. "I know this sounds nuts, but from the description, that van could be the one we saw the other night in the Kaiser parking lot."

"Could be. I'd feel better though, if I knew where Dennis was. I don't trust his Neo-Nazi ass."

Fifty-nine
Operation: Get The S.O.B.

The restraints cut even deeper into his skin.

Gerald maneuvered deftly

Through heavy outbound traffic on the Harbor Freeway, en route to Palos Verdes, southwest of Los Angeles. No one spoke at first. The only sound was the roar of traffic and the faint strains of classical music on 91.5 FM on the car radio.

John glanced anxiously at his watch and glared straight ahead through the bug-splattered windshield. For the first time in a long while, he felt helpless. His mind kept turning over Skeeter's news about convicted Sergeant, Steve Bolen. Like everyone, John had years earlier dismissed Bolen's wild-eyed threats. The rogue cop had threatened everyone involved in his tracking, prosecution, and conviction.

With his mind awash in anger, John desperately tried to organize his thoughts. Aimee and Roger could be dead. Despite his circumstances, Bolen was somehow managing to orchestrate a campaign of harassment.

And now Dr. Deauville was possibly near death—perhaps at the hands of her brother. It sounded like a plot line of one of his novels.

The Dark Bedroom

A nude Roger and Aimee lay side by side; their wrists tied, secured to the post of the large, iron-framed bed. Both wore heavy masking tape on their mouths; blindfolds covered their eyes. Aimee trembled badly. Roger was nearly motionless. The only light came from the flickering glow of a dozen candles arranged in a semi-circle, on the floor at the foot of the bed. A putrid smell, far exceeding the usual, filled the filthy room.

A shadowy male figure stood at the foot of the bed, dressed in a long black, lace dress, staring at her captives' nakedness. Roger began writhing and twisting, suddenly awakening from unconsciousness. The restraints cut even deeper into his skin. Blood soaked into the thick cloth strips. Aimee began crying, begging for her freedom. The figure remained mute, unaffected by the mournful pleadings.

Meanwhile

LAPD Metro, including several Harbor Division members, quickly established a presence area surrounding the suspect's rented Palos Verdes home. A red Porsche 911 Turbo sat in the driveway, the driver's window partially lowered. Several SWAT officers approached, cleared the vehicle and signaled an all clear. A steely-eyed Lieutenant Reibol motioned his men into positions surrounding the house's perimeter.

On the freeway, Gerald eyes were riveted on the traffic. John stared ahead then clapped his hands, turned to Gerald, startling everyone.

"Something's not right," he yelled.

"What?" Asked Gerald.

"About the doctor," John said, half-turning.

"Dana! Dr. Deauville is right-handed, right?"

John's question drew a puzzled look from everyone.

"Yes, sir," she answered.

"She didn't do it!" John declared, shaking his head from side to side. "She didn't try to kill herself. She didn't cut her wrist."

"Dr. Deauville would never try to commit suicide," Dana declared, her voice breaking.

"Her right wrist was slashed. She's right-handed," said John. "It doesn't make sense. Think about it. If she slashed her own wrist, she would've used her right hand to do it."

"He's right," Officer Summers added.

At Palos Verdes Scene

Reibol held a cell phone to his ear and waited. Seconds passed before he turned to his deputy.

"If he's in there, he's not picking up. That's definitely his car and everything else the girl said has checked out. I'll try one more time, then we'll flash and move in on him."

"What if he's got hostages?" The officer asked.

"If he had hostages, we'd probably know it by now. Hostages would be his shield... his ticket out."

Gerald exited the freeway and wheeled into feeder traffic. His cell phone rang. He thrust his right hand into his inside breast pocket, removed it, tossed it to John then swerved to avoid a car. John answered. It was Skeeter. Gerald made a hard right onto a residential street.

"We're almost there," John announced, as Officer Summers and Dana Seybold struggled to right themselves. "If we're right about this place," John told Skeeter, "we'll secure Aimee and Roger, get them to a hospital to be examined, then head to Pasadena. Medrano can get Pasadena to have a unit standing by."

Tear gas canisters sailed through the master bedroom window of the Palos Verdes home. SWAT was poised to assault the   structure.

Reibol quickly dialed the home's number, waited several ticks. No answer.

"If he's in there, he's hanging tough," he said to the Swat sergeant standing next to him. Having given sufficient opportunity for any occupants to respond, the Commander authorized the sergeant to signal entry. On command, SWAT launched tear gas from four points around the perimeter. The assault was on.

Gerald's car screeched to a hard, sliding stop two houses up of the tape barricade. He and John jumped out. Summers took the wheel and moved the car even farther away, taking every precaution to provide safety for their civilian passenger. Gerald and John raced toward the house, stopping just behind the safety of SWAT vehicles positioned at the northeast corner of the property. Two uniformed officers met them. Within minutes, several team members began exiting the house. Reibol quickly followed. The two quickened their pace, moving anxiously toward him.

It's a bust," groaned Reibol, shaking his head. "He was here, though. Left his breakfast on the table, clothes still in the closets. We found a desktop police scanner in the master bedroom. From what we can tell, he was alone. No sign of hostages or anything. Sorry."

John, dejected and disappointed, seemed ready to buckle. He dropped to a stoop—forearms resting on his upper thighs—head lowered. Gerald stood next to him, with a concerned hand resting on his friend's left shoulder.

"I swear, we'll find them," Gerald assured him. "We'll get 'em back safe. The FBI's on this; our guys are working with them...tracking every hint of a lead. Aimee's and Rogers' photos have been released; the suspect's mug has been plastered on every TV station from here to Las Cruces. We'll find them." John stood slowly, nodded weakly, turned and started walking away. Gerald quickly caught up to him.

During their trek back to the car, Gerald suggested getting an officer to take John home. He reasoned there was no need for him to tag along to Pasadena. The likelihood the trip would yield anything significant was not great. At most, Gerald expected to find an eccentric, perhaps even uncooperative sister. Besides, he knew John's thoughts were understandably focused on finding Aimee and Roger. Despite the thoughtful effort, John insisted on joining them. Dana Seybold's description of Diane's brother gave him reason for some concern.

Sixty
The Chamber

Aimee's heart was near exploding...

John was emotionally spent.

Both he and Gerald had expected, prayed and hoped to find Aimee and Roger. They now found themselves inching along in tortuous inbound Harbor 110 traffic. Gerald had a death grip on the steering wheel. John's cell phone was pressed to his left ear.

"Pasadena responded?" He asked, his voice dripping with anger and urgency.

"They're on the scene now," said Medrano. "They've got two, two-man units waiting. How's it look where you are?"

"Bad. Have them hold their positions... maintain surveillance on the house. The plan won't work until we're less than fifteen minutes away. I'll get back to you."

John ended the call, pocketed the phone and pounded the dashboard angrily with a closed fist. As they approached the 9th street exit, traffic all but ground to a halt.

Spotty patches were all that remained of Aimee's hair. In obvious pain, she raised her head, strained to peer past the edges of the blindfold. She was startled to realize Roger had been taken from the bed. She was alone. Suddenly, three muted pops from a silencer-equipped .44 magnum broke the quiet.

Aimee came apart. She squealed and twisted; tears streamed. She struggled violently to free herself. To her stunned surprise, the cloth strip on her left wrist slipped. Aimee did not have time to celebrate. She worked feverishly to free her arm. Seconds seemed like hours. Any minute she expected her tormentor to reenter the room and dispose of her.

Then, after what seemed an eternity, Aimee finally freed her right hand. Trembling wildly, both hands now free, and trying desperately to not sob aloud, she fumbled with the remaining restraints. She quickly freed her ankles. Weak and exhausted, she rose to her feet, glancing anxiously over her shoulder.

Aimee stumbled badly, falling to her knees, striking her head on the corner of the bed frame. Now driven by unspeakable fear and sheer will, she managed to lift herself. Blood trickled down her brow; she struggled toward the door. Her heart was near exploding; tears blurred her vision. The distance to the door seemed light years away. Within a single faltering step, Aimee lunged, grasped the knob with a shaky hand, leaned against the door for support, and listened. Nothing. Not a sound.

Aimee slowly twisted the knob; it turned. Her pulse raced. All she could think of was getting away as quickly as she could, and calling for help. She took a deep breath, stepped back, and eased the door gently toward her.

Then, terror. A cold hand gripped her shoulder, yanking her backwards and down onto the dirty, damp floor. Aimee's chilling scream ripped the pungent air. Her captor, shrouded in deep shadows, hovered, gleefully glaring down at her.

Gerald sped down the old Pasadena Freeway 1, Los Angeles' very first. He maneuvered his unmarked police car through butt-gripping lane changes and near misses. This was no place for the faint of heart. A frightened Dana covered her eyes, lowered her head. John sat rigid, glancing at his watch every five seconds, biting his bottom lip. Summers was poker-faced and tight-lipped, cringing as Gerald weaved his way around slow-moving traffic, cutting off angry drivers.

"Why are we going so fast," John asked, calmly."

"I don't know," said Gerald, shrugging his shoulders and slowing noticeably. Dana heaved a sigh of relief. He reached the Orange Grove exit, bounded up the ramp, wheeled left onto the famous thoroughfare and headed north. Fortunately, the heaviest traffic was moving in the opposite direction.

A half-mile down Orange Grove nearly everyone heard the unmistakable rumble of a flat tire. A frustrated John, smothering expletives with a hand cupped to his mouth, thrust both hands to his head.

"Shit! Not now!" He howled.

Gerald wheeled the car to the right curb. John leaped out, took a quick look at the right front tire. The hiss of escaping air confirmed what he knew. With his badge held high in his right hand, John dashed to the rear of the car and into the lane, facing oncoming traffic. He stepped boldly into traffic, and began flagging down a white limousine. He dashed to the chauffeur's door. The startled man stared long and hard at the badge before rolling down the window.

"What is it officer?"

"An emergency. Sorry, we need your vehicle, sir. Would you step from the car, please?"

The man appeared dumbfounded. "Excuse me, officer?"

"Could you step out please?"

"But..."

"I can arrest you, if you like," John barked.

"Officer, you take this car and I'm fired, I swear."

Sixty-one
The Ploy

"I'm afraid I have unfortunate news for you."

An unmarked Pasadena Police sedan,

a half block in front of a marked police cruiser, sat parked on the street in a quiet neighborhood of stately old mansions. A few doors down was an old, two-story, Victorian-style mansion in serious need of repair. The lawn had clearly been unattended for weeks. A six-foot high, ornate, wrought iron fence surrounded the aging estate.

Two detectives inside the unmarked vehicle took note of a slow-moving white limousine approaching them. The chauffeur was at the wheel. John sat in the front passenger seat. Gerald and Officer Summers were in the rear, behind the partition. Dana sat to their left, in an adjacent, rear seat. The limo eased to a stop a few yards short of the address for Diane's brother. A silver BMW 760iL set in the driveway.

"There's the car... in the driveway, next to the house," Gerald noted. "Somebody sure as hell drove it here. We'll impound it later."

"Is this the house?" Asked John.

Yes," said Dana.

"Who owns this place?" Gerald asked.

"Dennis," said Dana. "Dr. Deauville gave it to him but he never maintained it. He didn't deserve it."

"I don't see any other car," said Gerald.

"Maybe there's one in the garage in the rear," John guessed. "We've got backup... down the street there." He pointed to the unmarked, police vehicle and punched in a number on his cell phone.

"This is Roméo. We're all set."

"That you in the limo?" Asked the Pasadena officer.

At John's direction, the chauffeur flashed his headlights. The signal was quickly returned. "Here's what we're going to do," said John.

Inside The Estate

The telephone rang incessantly. Dennis reached for the black, antique rotary phone resting on a small, pedestal table in the hallway outside his door.

"Hello!" He answered, softly.

"Mr. Deauville?" Asked a nervous Officer Summers.

"Yes. Who is this? And it's Dennis."

Inside the limo, only Dana, the chauffeur and Officer Summers remained. Reading from notes scribbled on a piece of paper, Summers spoke into John's phone. "Mr. Deauville, this is Nurse Phillips at Queen of The City Hospital. You *are* the brother of a Dr. Diane Deauville?"

Silence.

"Yes... Yes. Why? How can I help you?"

"I'm afraid I have unfortunate news for you."

More silence preceded Dennis' response.

"What is it?" He asked, with surprising calm.

"It's about your sister, Diane."

More silence.

"What about Diane? Is she alright?"

"I'm sorry. She's... she's suffered a serious injury; she's in emergency surgery right now."

"Emergency? How did you get my number?"

"Your sister's associate gave us your number as next of kin."

"Associate. I see. How serious is the... injury? Will she be alright?"

"We're not sure. We're doing the best we can. As I said, she's in surgery. At this moment, we have three members of our counseling team on their way over to your home. They should be there at your home about now."

"On their way here? Couldn't I just drive there myself?"

Summers was not expecting the question. She scrambled to answer. "That would be fine, except they should be there any minute."

"Could you describe them, please? Are they male or female?"

"Dr. Summers is female, her two assistants are male. Can you be ready?"

"Well, ah... yes. Yes, I'll be ready."

"Sorry to have to call you like this. I look forward to meeting you," said Summers, breathing a little more freely.

John and Gerald returned from their clandestine survey of the house's perimeter. Summers filled them in, noting Dennis never asked for details of Diane's injury. That was revealing. Dana was quickly escorted to the far side of the street to the safety of a marked Pasadena police cruiser. John, Gerald and Summers climbed back into the limo.

On John's command, the chauffeur drove slowly up to the target driveway, wheeled in and eased to a stop behind the BMW.

"Hopefully, we'll get him to talk to us here. If necessary, we'll take him downtown," he said.

Sixty-two
Face Off – What Is That?

"Sonofabitch!

The doorknocker sounded.

"Who's there?" Came a female voice.
"Dr. Summers."
"One moment."

John could barely see the outline of someone peering through the door's security glass. Finally, the heavy door creaked open. Gerald and John nearly stopped breathing. Standing before them was a man in a black suit, only feet away. Stunningly, except for being a man, he was the exact image of Dr. Deauville. Apparently, an identical twin. Jaws dropped.

Dana Seybold had said nothing about the brother being a twin. Dennis appeared to be exactly Dr. Deauville's height and weight. His blue eyes were every bit as piercing.

"Come in, please, please," he said. Even his voice was remarkably similar, only slightly lower.

"Dennis?" Asked Summers. Dennis nodded yes.

John could not stop staring, as all stepped inside. He suddenly remembered Ms. Seybold saying the brother was older. He was even more puzzled.

"I'm Dr. Summers. The hospital called about us. Are you ready?"

"Yes. I'll just get my wallet. It'll only take a second. You know, it seems unusual the hospital would send a doctor and two assistants to escort me to see a crime victim. There must be hundreds of serious crime victims in this city every month. Do you do this for all of them?"

Summers scrambled for an answer.

"Dr. Deauville isn't just any victim. She's your sister. Quite frankly, she's also a celebrity. And she's also deeply involved in a police investigation—a special victim, you might say."

"I see. I suppose I should be grateful for her celebrity. Hopefully, the special status means she's getting the best treatment possible."

"It does and she is," Summers insisted. "We'd better hurry."

Dennis excused himself and hurried from the room. The three exchanged cautious glances, as he disappeared into the hallway. Although still reeling from surprise, John had the presence of mind to quietly signal his colleagues to spread out. All drew their weapons, now held to their sides as a precaution.

Gerald started to speak. Suddenly, Dennis reappeared in the doorway—gun in hand. "Gun!" Summers yelled out.

Without firing, Dennis bolted—disappeared into the corridor. "Sonofabitch! "John blurted.

Gerald grabbed the two-way. "Move in! Subject with gun," he barked. "We're okay, no shots fired. We're tracking a white male, blonde, in black suit, armed with a .44 magnum. Make sure the rear is well covered. Get EMTs up here on standby." Gerald turned to John who signaled him to come closer.

"I'm going in. Back me up."

John took the lead, as the two moved cautiously into the semi-darkened hallway. Each heard a door open and shut. Gerald followed, carefully moving along the opposite wall.

"Keep low. Where's Summers?" John whispered.

"Back near the doorway. I think we're on to something here."

"You think? Just keep low... stay close to the wall."

John eased down the darkened hallway, his back pressed against the wall. Gerald paralleled him, slightly to the rear. When they reached a closed door, John kicked it open, quickly crouched, both hands clutching his 9mm. He backed away and motioned Gerald farther past.

On John's hand signal, Gerald moved to just outside a partially opened door. He eased the door open. John joined him, crouched just above him, and to one side. On a silent three-count with raised fingers, both darted inside, adrenaline gushing. Gerald tripped over a rug just inside, but quickly recovered. John checked him, moved past. Another door slammed shut.

The cat and mouse death game proceeded. John and Gerald were at a disadvantage. Neither had any idea where the door in front of them led. Taking deep breaths, each carefully approached, eased open the heavy door. Sweat beaded; they flinched with every sound.

Another door in this endless maze slammed shut. The duo continued inching forward. The floor was clammy, slippery, covered with a damp, gritty film. A deathly quiet hung like ground fog.

Finally, Their eyes were beginning to adjust to the darkness. Gerald tapped John on the shoulder, pointed to a door approximately ten feet away. He started for it. John followed.

Gerald reached the door, paused, and pressed his ear to its surface. Silence. Crouching again, his weapon gripped firmly in his right hand, he grasped the brass doorknob and turned slowly. It rotated easily in his hand. The tiniest crack appeared; flickering light spilled. Gerald turned curiously to his partner and beckoned. Seizing the knob in one hand, Gerald opened the door. Both moved inside on all fours.

The Shrine

The room was small, measuring less than eighty feet square. In the dim, flickering light, both saw what could only be described as a small shrine located against the farthest wall. A framed oil portrait of a bearded, greying, middle-aged man in a three-piece suit hung on one wall above an altar of some sort. Below the portrait, a single eternal candle burned brightly. John moved toward the area. Suddenly, the door behind them, and a door directly across from them, slammed shut. Each pivoted but held his fire.

Almost instantly, a cloud of choking white mist began filling the room; the source, was a mystery. A wheezing John and Gerald struggled to breathe; their eyes watered. Gasping, both men rose, stumbled toward the forward door and again fell to their knees, desperate to find breathable air. The room seemed to spin, then tilt.

John banged hard against the door. Gerald joined him, laying his right shoulder full square, with all the force he could muster. Their efforts fell short. Taking a short step back, John fired two rounds at the lock, sending knob, plate, and lock mechanism flying. Gerald kicked the door open, ushering in a gush of welcomed air.

Coughing violently, each labored to replace the contaminated air sapping their strength. The door was kicked closed, to seal the room again. Despite irritated eyes and tingling, raspy throats, both steadied themselves and moved forward into even more treacherous darkness. Following countless twists and blind turns, John reached a large, dark room dominated by a high ceiling with exposed beams. Acting as rearguard, Gerald was only steps behind.

Scant light, from a missing portion of vertical wooden blinds covering a cathedral-style window, invaded the space. An offensive stench filled the air. The musty room apparently served as a huge den or family room. Old furniture: discarded mattresses, cushions, overturned chairs, and other items were strewn about.

Hidden from her pursuers, a winded Dennis crouched behind the bar on the far west side of the sprawling room. He heard the approaching footsteps, as John moved farther into the room—his eyes darting, searching for any sign of movement. Cautiously panning left to right, he dashed to a position just behind a large sofa.

Once there, he was quickly overcome by a foul, clinging stench that stung his nostrils; he nearly vomited. John pinched his nose, forced his chin against his chest and waited for the compulsion to hurl to pass. It worked. A couple of moments later, he turned, carefully peered over the back of the sofa. A chill coursed his body; he felt flush. He was greeted by the sight of a nude, decomposing corpse of a bald, giant of a man.

Even in the darkness, it was obvious that a large portion of the man's skull was missing. Further observation revealed he had been castrated; his penis and scrotum removed. John felt a sympathetic pain shoot through his own. Certain Dennis was in the room somewhere—maybe only feet away, he fought to remain silent. He took a deep breath, slowly exhaled, and eased to a secure position behind a marble statue.

"Police!" He yelled. "Police! We know you're in here. No use dying today. We can get you the help you need. Toss out your weapon and step forward with your hands raised."

There was no response. John saw Gerald crouched low in the doorway, and motioned him toward a chair along the wall that extended behind and parallel to the bar. Just then, a scream of sirens and the whirl of a police chopper rose. John took aim at the large, ceiling-high mirror behind the bar, and the dozens of bar glasses lining the thick glass shelving.

John fired twice, striking the mirrored wall above and behind Dennis. Shards of mirror and exploding glass crashed around her. She loosed a chilling scream, as a jagged shard barely missed her head.

"Don't shoot! Don't shoot!" She yelled.

"Throw out your weapon. Do it now."

Dennis complied, flinging the gun across the floor. "I didn't know you all were police. Why didn't you say so?"

"Stand slowly, with your hands high above your head and step out. Do it!, Do it now!"

Dennis obeyed. On John's signal, and covered, Gerald advanced with his gun trained on Dennis. He located and retrieved his gun. He stood several feet away, his features partially obscured in the poor lighting.

"You should've identified yourselves," he said calmly. "We've had a number of break-ins here."

"You pulled a gun on us because you hate doctors? And I suppose that hunk of rotting flesh on the sofa was a cat burglar," said John.

Dennis lowered his head and refused to respond. Gerald now covered John, who moved quickly to cuff Dennis. While John was Mirandizing her, Gerald backpedaled to take a look at the deposit on the sofa. The stench quickly drove him back.

John continued. "You have the right to have an attorney present, before and during the answering of any questions. If you cannot afford an attorney, one will be appointed for you. Do you understand this?" Asked John.

Dennis nodded yes. He looked squarely at him. His eyes flared.

"Are you alone? Talk to me! Is there anyone else in the house?" John demanded.

Dennis only stared. John checked the .44. It was fully loaded. He showed the full cylinders to Gerald who released a loud whoosh. The latter kept staring at Dennis. "Damn," he whispered.

"I know," John whispered. "Remember, there's a dead man on the sofa with his dick missing. Check on Summers and let's get a uniformed officer in here," said John, guiding Dennis to a nearby chair. "Wait. Let's take him back up front. Smells too bad in here."

John grasped Dennis securely by the right arm and escorting him from the room.

"You all over -reacted," said Dennis.

John ignored him. "You never answered. Are you the only one in the house?"

Dennis flashed a wide smile.

Sixty-three
To Be, or Not To Be

"We... we have a slight problem."

While a uniformed officer

whisked Dennis into a downstairs bathroom, John and several other officers conducted a room by room search upstairs. The Coroner's team arrived, while news vehicles were kept hundreds of yards away. Barricade tape laced half the block.

John's mind was riveted on Roger and Aimee, as he and Gerald prepared to search the sprawling house. Police agents in every southern California County had been alerted. Serious consideration was given to getting the media to solicit the public's help. John was calling in every debt owed him—legal and otherwise; official and unofficial—to find the pair.

Keeping his mind on the immediate task proved nearly impossible. Careful to treat every square inch of the house as a potential crime scene, John, Gerald, and officers donned latex gloves and booties. A police photographers accompanied them.

The search began upstairs and moved from one bedroom to another. It was hot and muggy. If the old house was air-conditioned, it was not working. The team found the rooms empty. They were about to end the search, when John came to the next to last room. He turned the knob to Dennis' bedroom. They entered to find the old television tuned to an *I Love Lucy* rerun. The polished, bare oak floor glistened. The bed was made; everything was immaculate.

John started for the closet, when an officer in the hallway called out. He wheeled around, left the room, and dashed to where he met Gerald. The two raced several feet to a locked bedroom door. The uniformed officer launched powerful, well-placed kicks. After several attempts, the door gave way.

A shocking, gut-wrenching sight greeted them. A rush of putrid air filled their nostrils. All froze, stunned speechless. Eyes nearly tumbled from sockets. Only feet away, lying in the middle of the filth-drenched bed, a nearly catatonic Aimee languished in her own excrement. Regurgitated stomach bile stained the front of her clothing.

"Oh, my God!" John blurted. "Aimee! Aimee!"

He rushed to the bed, reached down to lift her then saw she was secured to the bed. Grimacing and swearing, John removed her hair from her face, stroked her damp cheeks, and whispered her name over and over. He feverishly struggled to remove the strips from Aimee's bruised wrists.

Gerald hurried to grab what clothing he could find in the old dresser. John frantically tried to revive Aimee. An officer's search of the closet revealed Roger. He was trembling, cuffed, on the floor and collapsed on his knees. Gerald lifted him to his feet.

John kept trying the revive Aimee "I'm here, baby. I'm here." Aimee began sobbing, uncontrollably. John embraced her passionately. Gerald turned to an officer, Sergeant DeBarge, and instructed him to summon EMTs. Another officer began taking photos, cataloguing the entire scene.

Downstairs, Officer Summers wore a curious expression, as she entered the living room. Paramedics arrived and were directed upstairs. Summers turned to Lt. Medrano. He had only arrived moments earlier.

"Lieutenant, I need to see Roméo."

"What is it?"

"Is he upstairs?" Summers insisted. Medrano nodded, yes.

Officer Summers bolted upstairs, but stopped when she saw the EMTs descending with Roger and Aimee. Gerald and John followed. Summers retreated to the base of the stairs and waited. Seconds later, she collared Gerald.

"Sergeant Li. Could you come with me please?"

Without questioning her, Gerald followed her down the corridor to just outside the restroom door. Summers turned to him. Her face was pale and drawn. He stepped closer. "You finished your strip search?"

Summers hesitated. "Yes, but it wasn't pleasant. I had Baltasora check him – he found another weapon—a single-shot derringer. "

"Where?"

"Taped between his asshole and his ball sack."

"What led him to look there? Don't answer."

Gerald stared at Summers for a long several seconds, Summers eased open the door. A still handcuffed Dennis flashed a wide smile. Gerald closed the door.

Sixty-four

Post-mortem – And?

Nicholson, Lieutenant Medrano, Sergeant Dennis,

John, Gerald, Skeeter, Foster, Emory, and four other task force members crowded the Captain's office for a post-mortem of sorts. They were recounting the bizarre twists and turns that led them to this moment. The mood was not celebratory. Everyone recognized the investigation was really only beginning. Diane remained in Queen of The City Hospital. Her attorney, G. Smythe, had not yet consented for her to be interviewed. The District Attorney was petitioning Superior Court for an order, forcing examination of any of the doctor's relevant files.

The difficulty with the D.A.'s petition was that required specifics were missing from the document. The court required the request name specific files and documents. That was nearly impossible. Without the doctor's cooperation, the effort appeared impossible.

Despite a twinge of short-lived euphoria, John could not bring himself to feel the case was truly solved. Some, even task force members, still believed the 30 year-old, Dalton Kannard, now once identified as the prime suspect in the FBI's *Westbound Killer* case, would eventually be found responsible for some, if not all the so–*called Adultery Murders*. John vehemently disagreed.

Finally, Dennis was at Windwood Psychiatric Hospital, under maxium guard and scheduled to undergo a battery of psychiatric examinations. He was, at the least, the prime suspect in the murder of the still unidentified dead man found on the sofa.

Captain Nicholson stood in the middle of the room. "Hopefully, we will get some insight into the brother's attempt on his sister. We have no confession, just his denial he murdered anyone. We still don't know what the doctor's role was in all this... how the kidnapping was accomplished. It's not exactly over, but good work, guys." John also knew it was not over.

"We're waiting on the DA and the court now," Nicholson continued. "I still can't believe the doctor was involved. The only thing that makes sense is that, unknown to her, her brother...sister, may have actually had contact with her patients. We've learned from Ms. Seybold, that he may have had phone consultations, posing as his sister. By the way, we should prepare some sort of commendation for Ms. Seybold. Without her help, we would not be where we are in this case."

Dana Seybold unwittingly helped with another crucial question: *Were spouses of the other victims all patients of Dr. Deauville?* The answer had come during Gerald's questioning her, while John was alone in the doctor's inner office. After Dana was invited to accompany them to Pasadena, he failed to recall that fact, and inform John, until the next day. He agreed, at John's request, to keep that information between the two of them, for the time being.

Gerald had asked Dana if the doctor's patient load was being affected by her work on the case. Without thinking, she remarked: "Not really. Most are just coping with the pain of losing their husbands." Gerald did not react, but did make a mental note, which he later memorialized.

"There are remaining questions regarding motive," Nicholson continued. "It sounds unbelievable. We anticipate being granted subpoenas to examine the financial records of select patients, the doctor, and anyone else we can think of. We may have to go the Grand Jury route, in order to force cooperation from these wives. That's one way of neutralizing this... this Mr. Smythe.

"We still don't have solid evidence," said Gerald "We do have that tape John *borrowed.* How else could you explain the killer being able to gain access to the victims without any sign of forced entry? "

"But remember, we can not use that tape as evidence," Nicholson remarked. "Besides, you think we know for sure that this...this Dennis person is responsible for all the killings... any of them, even the vic on the sofa?"

"We can't say yet," said Gerald. "However, I don't think the fact Dennis is a pre-op transsexual has anything to do with whathappened here. Gay, straight, cross-gender or whatever, I think he...she was and is sick. Period."

"We have to remember we've only found one gun at the house, so far," Nicholson noted. "But the evidence there is powerful. It was definitely the .44 used to murder Colin Sumner and his girlfriend. The others may have been destroyed orhidden."

Then Medrano chimed in. "Maybe we'll know more if and when we get clearance to search the doctors office, and maybe listen to some of those audio tapes she made."

The very mention of the tapes brought a pained expression to John's face. He realized the legal wrangling over access to the tapes and files could end any day. Her attorneys had obtained an injunction preventing re-entry by police until a court hearing.

The new injunction prevented the removal of the tapes. While all the cassettes, and perhaps even the CDs in her collection, were of concern to John and the department, there was only one of particular interest to him. Although he had behaved honorably, he preferred to not have a tape of his last meeting with Dr. Deauville aired on CNN, or posted on the Internet.

While there appeared to be a mountain of hard, and circumstantial, evidence against Dennis, the case was not airtight. Investigators were going through hundreds of photo negatives found at the Pasadena house. No camera had yet been located.

During the entire meeting, Sergeant Dennis had been little more than a potted plant, ignored, unable to get a word in. He finally spoke up. A slimy smirk covered his face.

"This is all fine," he began, "But the truth is, solving this case was as close to accidental as anything else. We sure as hell didn't need some overrated Prima Donna with a bloated ego. We could have done this without damn outsiders. The LAPD shouldn't be kissing anybody's ass to get them to show us how to get things done."

While Dennis chimed on, John strolled over to him. He held up a piece of paper, and a half dozen 5"x 7" black and white photos to Dennis' face. The photos had been manipulated with Photoshop, to make the subjects appear to be embracing and kissing each other.

"This is the damn note you left on my car," John calmly noted, "It has your damn fingerprints. And these are pictures of Skeeter and me at the Amtrak station; me and Sergeant Li at Cal State, and others. I found this crap in your locker."

Dennis refused to look squarely at the photos. "That's what you say," he said with a grin.

John stepped to within one foot of Dennis, stared him down. Dennis kept grinning. John lost it. He barreled into Dennis, pinning him against the wall. He clutched his shirt with both hands, ripped downward. Buttons flew; fabric ripped, exposing Dennis' chest, emblazoned with a small swastika tattoo.

The room fell silent. Eyes were glued on Dennis, now minus his stupid grin. John turned away then wheeled back, landing a crushing right to Dennis' left jaw. The latter crumbled to the floor in a heap. Blood streamed from his mouth. No one came to the Sergeant's aid.

The phone rang. Nicholson answered. It was for John. He took it. "Roméo, here."

It was Claire, calling to express concern about Roger and Aimee. John thanked her, assured her they were fine. He finished his conversation, turned to Gerald and nodded for him to join him. The two left Nicholson's office without a glance back.

Sixty-five
The Visit

Queen of The City Hospital - *"Where are you getting this?*

"I won't say.

And please don't... don't press me. I just can't," Diane insisted.

"But you could have died in that room. Attempted murder is nothing to dismiss. You're here in critical condition."

"I know."

"So, I suppose we can rule out attempted suicide, right?"

"I did not try to kill myself. But you have to believe me. Dennis had nothing to do with the murders. You've got it all wrong."

"But the gun used to murder Colin Sumner and his girlfriend was found in his house. How can he possibly explain that?"

"I don't know. It was planted. It must have been."

"He tried to kill us with it. Look, sometimes, when it's family that's involved, one can easily lose objectivity. No one can blame you for that. However, if your family commitment overrules your obligation to society, and permits a serial killer to escape punishment, that is another matter."

"Don't preach to me, John. Please. He... Dennis would never shoot or kill anyone. Tell me, did he fire at anyone?"

"No."

"That's what I mean. Can you imagine that the real killer would not have fired... not tried to kill you? It's not logical. We are desperate to solve this case, and you haven't, John...not yet."

"Then, tell me who the killer is? Your job was and is to help us answer that question."

"I don't know who. No one does. If I did, I certainly wouldn't protect him or her."

"What makes you so certain your...your brother wouldn't kill? If he would harm animals, kill pets..."

"Kill? What are you talking about?"

"When you both were young. Your brother tortured animals, dissected your pet kitten."

"Where are you getting this? Is this some cop's ploy?"

"Are you saying it's not true?"

"I am most certainly saying it's not true, not a single word of it."

"But he tried to kill you."

"I never said that. Who told you these lies?"

"You don't have to say it, doctor. He tried to kill you. He was angry because you refused to give him the money he needed to complete his operation. Is that much true?"

"It's true I did not think he was ready. And I refused to pay before he was ready. That much is true."

"And he was angry—very angry. He came to your office; you had an argument, and he tried to kill you."

"John. I will never testify to this, but I will tell you. If Dennis had wanted to kill me, he could have."

"One more thing. Why did you not tell me that the wives of the male victims in these cases were all your patients?"

"Who my patients are is confidential information, John."

"We know Mrs. Jeffries was a patient."

"How do you know?"

"She said so."

"Fine. She's free to provide that fact. But it's not my practice to re-veal who my patients are or what treatment I provide, not without an order from the court. And even then, I would have to decide whether to comply or not."

"Even if it were suspected they were contracting to have their cheat-ing husbands murdered?"

"You are really reaching, John."

"A court could order you to reveal that information, with cause demonstrated. And to turn over session recordings as well."

"Another bit of surmising? I do not now, nor have I ever taped my sessions, John. In my profession, I see it as a lazy way to avoid listen-ing. I listen to my patients. I make notes and I listen. If I taped, even as a backup, I would likely not listen as intently as I do. One cannot respond properly, in real-time, without listening. Sorry, your surmise is inaccurate on this one."

John deeply regretted the turn events had taken—a turn that now made him wonder if the doctor had knowledge of much more than she was revealing. He feared the answer was yes.

"Diane," he said calmly, "Your brother is in serious trouble. There's no way he can possibly explain his way out of this."

"John, he didn't do it. He could not have."

Just then, the door to Diane's hospital room flew open. In strode the inimitable G. Gordon Smythe. He was clearly incensed but never had a chance to utter a word.

'We're done," said John. He and Gerald left a fuming Smythe. But after the conversation with Diane, their own heads were spinning. Nei-ther knew what to believe.

Sixty-six
The Visit

After a half hour of sitting in the hospital garage,

watching his partner fire up his laptop and scour the 'net,' Gerald now found himself at the end of a rocket-ride back downtown to Diane's office building.

"You could at least tell me why we're back here. This isn't one of your novels or movies. You don't have to save some twist...some wild ending just for me. I'm your partner," Gerald rambled. "You're supposed to trust me. We're a team. I said nothing while you talked to IAS. I knew you must've been getting a report on some lab analysis. I was sure you would fill your partner in. But no! Now, please explain why we're back at the doctor's office. I am not going to do a 459 with you, John Roméo. That's not what you're about to do, is it?"

"God! You always talk this much to someone who won't answer you, huh?"

"It's not too late. This elevator goes both ways. I'm getting off here. You coming?"

Gerald relented. Both stepped off the elevator and started for Dr. Deauville's office. "How're you going to get in? You don't have a key."

John removed a key ring from his jacket pocket. It contained at least eight keys, including one with a Lexus logo.

Gerald shook his head. "You're amazing."

"It was on her nightstand," John confessed. "She doesn't need it there. Her car is down in the garage. I'll get 'em back to her."

John motioned for quiet, glanced up and down the corridor and slipped the key into the lock. With his left hand gripping the brass door lever, he turned the key slowly. The door eased open; with it barely ajar, both could see the darkened outer office. John opened the door farther; the two of them slipped inside.

Lights were on inside Dr. Deauville's private office. John moved cautiously to the door and placed his hand on the knob. It turned. He beckoned for Gerald.

"Go turn the lock on the main door there, John whispered. "I don't want anyone coming in."

John waited. Gerald returned. "Why are we whispering?" He whispered, leaning closer.

"I'm just cautious."

John gripped the doorknob and was about to open it, when they heard a noise coming from inside the doctor's office. He and Gerald hurried to the main door, and quietly exited. Once in the corridor, both took crouched positions on either side of the door, guns at their sides, and waited.

The sound of approaching footsteps grew louder. Seconds later, Diane's inner office went dark. They heard someone opening the door. Momentarily, Gerald and John saw the main door ease open. The intruder stepped into the corridor.

"Freeze!" Both yelled."

Dana Seybold screamed, threw up both hands, released the handle of the black, portable luggage piece. She nearly fainted.

"Miss Seybold," John spoke calmly, stepping toward her, his gun slightly lowered. "May we come in?"

Even as he asked, Dana was backpedaling. She nodded, yes.

"Is that a yes?"

"Yes," she answered, weakly.

"Going someplace? Taking a little work home?" Asked John.

"Lieutenant! Oh, my God, you nearly scared the wet out of me. Wait a minute. Ahh."

Dana thrust her right hand to her chest. "I'm so glad it's you." Just then, she noticed Gerald. "Sergeant. Why are you both here?"

"We were... wondering the same thing about you."

"Oh, I'm going on a...a little vacation. I...I just stopped by to get a few things to...to work on."

"I see. You know, we never had an opportunity to properly thank you for your help," John said, holstering his gun, Gerald put his own weapon away, also. "Why don't we go inside the doctor's office, have a seat and chat a bit?"

"Oh, I... I'd love to, Lieutenant. But I have to get to LAX within the next hour. My plane leaves in a little over two and a half hours."

"Where're you going?"

"Ah, San Francisco. I visited Dr. Deauville earlier. She's doing very well. She should be released in a few days. I think she should take a vacation, too."

A long pause. John's expression hardly changed. "Miss Seybold, I don't think you're going to be catching a plane. You see, I don't believe you have a reservation, at least not for today." John turned to Gerald. "Sergeant Li, would you please take Ms. Seybold's luggage and place it atop her desk?"

A puzzled Gerald nodded, and proceeded to place the heavy cart atop the desk. Dana face reflected her shock.

"Miss Seybold, I am going to recite something to you. First of all, may I open your luggage?"

"Ah, why? I don't understand why. It's just papers and things. Confidential papers about patients and stuff like that... Doctor Deauville's new manuscript and other items."

"Is that a no?"

"I... I can't say yes, without her permission."

"Of course not. I... I do understand. Ah, Ms. Seybold, you are under arrest. Anything you..."

"Arrest? Arrest? Why? I haven't done anything. I'm innocent."

"Innocent? Innocent of what?"

"Innocent of..."

"Hold on, please. You have to let me do this, for your own protection, alright? It's called a Miranda warning. I'm sure you're familiar with it. It's required. Afterwards, if you wish to speak to us, you may. Now, where was I? Oh. You have the right to remain silent. You have the right..."

It was difficult to observe who was more stunned, Dana or Gerald. After being mirandized and cuffed, Dana protested her innocence of whatever. She declined to enter Diane's office but did accept a sip of water and a chair.

"You've made an awful mistake. Why am I being arrested?"

"On suspicion of murder and..."

"Murder? I murdered no one! This is insane!"

"And conspiracy to commit murder."

"Who are you saying I murdered? What conspiracy?"

"The list is quite long, Miss Seybold. As for the conspiracy: your employer, Dr. Deauville."

"Tell me you're joking! You must be. I did nothing but work my fingers to the bone, helping Diane get where she is. I love her."

"Love her?"

"Like a sister... like a sister. " John noted it was now Diane, not Dr. Deauville. "Even though, she never gave me the credit or the compensation I deserved. But I remained devoted to her. I did nearly all her research. But you couldn't tell by looking at her book credits."

"Miss Seybold, you lied to us. You fed us bogus information about Dennis. However, even if she did represent him to you as her brother, she could not have told you all the other things you told us. And you were very careful to provide us what amounted to a very distinct profile of someone who could be a serial killer. That was no accident. I do believe that Dennis attacked his own sister. But I also know you were involved in this murder for hire enterprise?"

"That's insane," Dana insisted. Gerald did a double take.

"You're not married, are you Miss Seybold? You were, but you're not any longer. You were divorced in '01. You became a patient of Dr. Deauville's, shortly, thereafter. Correct? Your husband abused you; he cheated, he left you for a younger, thinner woman. You tried to kill him. Correct? You shot him with your service revolver—the one you had then, as a member of the Riverside County Sheriff's Department."

Dana looked away.

"Your charge was bargained down to aggravated assault. You were sentenced to time served, and placed on probation. Am I close on any of this?"

"You're dead wrong. Dead wrong!"

'You left a handwriting sample on the manila envelope tacked to my front door. It was compared to, and matched, the writing on the addresses you wrote down for us. And it was not the doctor who taped her sessions, it was you who did so, secretly. That's how you knew every detail of the patients' personal lives; about their husbands; their homes; personal data, their finances... everything. I'm not quite sure how you persuaded Dennis to get involved. I suspect it was you who promised to provide funds for her operation, and did so with proceeds from your... work you performed for some very disturbed women. Bank records will help. But you had help, didn't you? Someone approached you, and you were receptive, even eager."

"That is preposterous. I helped you... I helped you catch a killer! I didn't have to do that!"

"Miss Seybold, Sergeant Li is about to open your luggage. If I were you, I would say nothing more without the presence of your attorney. If it contains what I suspect it contains, you are in serious trouble." John gave Gerald a nod.

Dana gazed into her lap, as Gerald began unzipping the large case. John looked on, hoping he had not guessed wrongly. Gerald seemed to take forever. Finally, the bag was unzipped. He lifted the top flap with his right hand. John's eyes nearly popped from their sockets.

Inside the luggage were things even John did not expect to see. He had expected to find computer disks, thumb drives, cassette tapes, CDs, files, and incriminating files. Those items were there, but so was Dana's personal checkbook, and to his and Gerald's amazement, a large, bubble-wrapped bundle.

Gerald carefully lifted the bundle out onto the table. Even without unwrapping the package, both could clearly count five, shiny, nickel-plated, .44 Magnum handguns. Neither could do more than back away from the desk and exhale. Apparently, Dana had been hiding them in plain sight, right under the doctor's nose.

"Skeeter was right. It was a cop... an ex-cop. And how the hell did you know she was here?" Gerald asked.

"I didn't. I was about to do a 459, remember?"

"Well, what about all the background stuff on her?"

"Got a V-O-I-P call from her husband, right out of the blue. Turns out he was looking for me, even visited one of my web sites."

"What the hell is V-O-I-P?"

"Oh, I'm so sorry. It's ah... Voice Over Internet Protocol—phone number on my laptop."

"Got it. —Her husband called you?"

"Yeah. Revenge is a powerful motive. I checked him out, met with him...got the goods. He says he'll testify if needed."

John winked, turned and motioned Dana to stand.

"Dana, I repeat. I'm sure you were not alone in this. I don't think this was your idea; someone approached you. You saw it as a way to get revenge for perceived slights... make some money. Am I close?"

Dana remained silent.

"It's all gonna come out, " John continued. "You can help us and help yourself. It's all up to you."

Dana still said nothing, but appeared almost overcome. Tears streamed down her face; her hands trembled.

Sixty-seven
Dead Wrong – I Can't Do Jail time.

"I'm not running from you. Shoot me..."

John retrieved Dana's office keys;

Gerald called to inform Captain Nicholson and Lt. Medrano of the startling developments. He next requested female officers and a black and white. The two planned to escort Dana to the garage, place her in the unit, then return to secure evidence and the office until SID arrived.

John started to open the office door, when the elevator chime sounded. For reasons unknown to even himself, he hesitated then quickly moved back inside the now darkened office.

"Hold on," he said, motioning a puzzled Gerald to hustle Dana to the far side of the room. "Somebody just got off the elevator. Hold on a minute. Shhh."

"You expecting someone," Gerald asked in a loud whisper. Dana shook her head, no.

They waited several seconds. The sound of footsteps grew closer. They could hear muffled voices—voices spoken in a deliberately lowered manner. John's curiosity soared.

The steps grew even closer, then slowed. John drew his 9mm. Gerald drew his own. Dana's brow dripped with perspiration. Her breathing grew labored; she slumped onto a nearby steno chair.

"Keep absolutely quiet," Gerald warned her.

Then, the footsteps stopped at the doctor's door. John glanced in Gerald's direction, motioned him several steps back. It seemed an eternity passed. Then, the clink of metal on metal; a key was being slipped into the door lock. John stood roughly fifteen feet away, to the left of the door to avoid the spill light from the corridor.

To steady himself, John bit lightly into his bottom lip and waited. He could see the knob slowly turn. His hand tightened on his pistol-grip; his finger rested gently but firmly on the trigger. In his wildest imaginings, he had no idea who could be on the other side of the door. The answer came.

It seemed to take forever. First, the tiniest sliver of light appeared between door and doorjamb. It was soon obscured by whoever was lurking at the door. The vertical space widened. A figure—a tall man, broad at the shoulders—a gun in his hand and held waist high, appeared foreground. Another stood just behind him. John forced himself to pause until the right nanosecond.

Within five ticks—John counted them—the door eased open. The two male figures took one, two, then three cautious steps inside. Just as the trailing figure reached for the light switch, and the first lowered his gun hand, both John and Gerald screamed a stream of orders. Their guns were aimed; their free hands jabbed the air.

"Police! Freeze! Both bellowed repeatedly.

But before the first command reverberated, the first man pivoted and raised his gun hand. John and Gerald fired. A twin stream of bullets ripped into the man's upper torso, forcing him back. He teetered for a second then fell forward, without firing a round.

The second man bolted into the corridor, dashed toward the crossing corridor, just beyond the elevators. In hot pursuit, John leaped over the crumpled body in front of him.

"Check him!" He yelled back to Gerald.

Now in the corridor, John saw the fleeing assailant, dressed in jeans, dark sport coat, and cowboy boots. He could see a gun in his right hand. He dashed after him, his gun aimed at the man's back.

"Freeze," he yelled! "Police!"

The chase was on. Then, to his amazement, the man suddenly stopped. Only feet from the crossing corridor, he stopped still. With his back facing John, he stopped. Both his hands, including the right hand gripping the gun, were extended high above his head. For several long seconds, the man cast in stone.

"Drop the gun!" John yelled, moving cautiously toward him, angling to within inches of the left side of the corridor. He was thankful no tenants had ventured out, and prayed those who had heard the gunfire, had secured themselves. Again, John identified himself.

"If anyone can hear me, this is the police! I am an LAPD police officer! Do not open your doors. Stay in your offices!"

"Drop the gun. Now!" John barked to the gunman.

There was no immediate response. Meanwhile, Gerald flipped on the light and checked the first man. He was dead. Dana remained glued to the chair. She appeared catatonic. He secured the man's gun, and carefully stepped into the corridor to back up his partner.

"Drop the gun! Drop it!" John repeated. "Do it slowly! Let it fall to the floor. Do it!"

John moved forward a few more cautious steps. He saw the man begin to lower his right hand then stop. John lowered himself to a crouch. "Do it now!" John ordered.

Then, just as it appeared the man would release the gun and let it fall to the floor, he suddenly flicked his wrist, pressing the gun barrel to his own temple.

"I'm not running from you. Shoot me, Roméo," boomed a familiar voice. "Shoot me!" The man repeated.

Both Gerald and John watched the unbelievable scene unfolding before them. The man daring them to shoot; the man demanding they execute him, was Dennis—Sergeant David Dennis.

"Dennis!" John called out, "What the hell? Are you nuts? Don't do it! Drop the gun. C'mon, don't make us do this. You need help, man. Drop the damn gun. Drop it!"

Dennis pressed the gun even more firmly against his temple; his eyes flared, he turned red. "Fuck you, Roméo. Shoot me! Go ahead. I'm not afraid of you or your jigaboo friend. I'm in charge here! Surprised? I'm in control. Even if you shoot, I win. You see, I can't die, not permanently. Everything is temporary. Life and death... it's all temporary."

"I'll shoot if I have to. Don't make me do this," John repeated.

"What do we do now, Roméo? Wanna dance? May I have this fuckin' dance? I know. You think maybe I'll launch into some...some long-winded confession? Maybe I'll rollover on brother cops who feel the way I do—brother cops who have done a lot more than me? And there are many of 'em, you know. You'll never get us all. Never! So shoot me, you black bastard! How 'bout it, nigger? You'd love to kill a white man, wouldn't you," Dennis said, staring at Gerald.

John and Gerald had their 9 millimeters aimed at Dennis' upper torso. In a flash, Dennis screamed out, incoherently, then moved his gun-hand away from his temple, and toward them.

"Don't!" John yelled.

In a flash, Gerald opened fire, then John. Dennis' gun dropped to the floor; blood spurted, soaking his shirt. His eyes bulged but amazingly, the half-dozen rounds had not dropped him. Instead, he staggered forward. Gerald looked on in awe, expecting him to drop any second. John rose slowly from his crouch, glanced briefly at Gerald, then back at the mortally wounded Dennis.

Remarkably, a smile crept across Dennis' face. He kept inching toward them. Despite the temptation to empty his clip, John knew he could not fire again at the now disarmed Dennis. But he did not want him to be found dead and handcuffed. For the moment, he and Gerald could only watch.

The wait seemed to take an eternity. Finally, slowly and defiantly, Dennis dropped to his knees. He was still breathing, as he slumped back onto his haunches. He lingered for what seemed minutes, his eyes barely slits. His lips were moving, but no sound escaped. Suddenly, Dennis seemed to come alive. He raised himself to his knees then hesitated, before finally keeling over, collapsing face forward onto the hard floor, with a thud.

It was John who first walked the remaining distance. Gerald followed. He saw his partner kneel next to Dennis' crumpled body. Despite the tremendous amount of lost blood and splattered tissue, John placed his fingers to the sergeant's carotid artery. He was dead.

The shock was numbing. The moment was as surreal. Neither spoke. It was only after other officers arrived, that John returned to the doctor's office and made another startling discovery. At first, he stood staring down at the second man's face.

At the moment, he only looked vaguely familiar. Then, the light came on. John knelt for a closer look. The dead man lying on the floor of Diane's outer office was the Montebello Police detective John earlier confronted outside his motel room.

It was all making some sense, now. For the first time, he recalled Dennis' security systems background, his Navy Seal background. And as a cop, as a task force member. He had inside information no killer could get. John was now certain the murderous orgy of the past several months was all part of a sick enterprise based upon pure greed, revenge—perhaps even psychosis.

The inescapable conclusion was that the victims' spouses were involved. He had no doubt Dana would eventually tell all. Just what role each played was yet to be fully determined, but the truth was sure to come. If all else failed, the money trail would tell the story.

A shudder coursed John's body. Just then, an inescapable realization descended upon him like a boulder. There was no doubt another killer was still out there. Even the FBI would have to admit that, now. John stood rock-still for what seemed forever.

The calm outer expression John wore gave no hint of the maelstrom churning inside. Without a word to anyone, he turned and made his way slowly past investigators, past Skeeter, Captain Nicholson, Lieutenant Medrano, and into the corridor. He glanced at where Dennis' body lay covered. Gerald was still briefing Foster, Emory, and Commander Lister but saw his friend and partner enter the stairwell. He watched as the heavy metal door clanked closed behind him.

Sixty-eight

There Are No More Heroes

---

2 Hours Later, Pacific Coast Highway – *Looking for a Sunset*

The final spray of sunlight on the horizon;

thousands of small, flickering lights along the undulating California coast. John was beyond solemn, as he slipped his S600 down PCH toward Malibu and beyond. 'The Wave's' 94.7 smooth jazz, spilling from his radio, was welcomed but was no cure for what really ailed him. He lowered the volume and issued voice commands to check messages.

"Voice mail."

"Hello, John. You have two messages. First message received today at 1:22 P.M."

"Mr. Roméo. This is Lieutenant Keith Rendel, Pittsburgh P.D. Regarding the Westbound Killer case, could you call me at..."

"Save message," John interrupted.

"Message saved, John. Next message Sent at 4:13 P.M.

"John, Inspector Paul Braswell, Scotland Yard, here. Give me a ring back when you get a chance. We've got a...

"Delete message."

"Deleting message now. There are no more messages, John."
"Disconnect. Power off."
"Are you sure you want to disconnect and power off, John?"
"Yes."
"Disconnecting and powering off now, John. We will speak soon."
The radio volume rose. A male newscaster was in the middle of a news bulletin.

"Once again, convicted former LAPD Sergeant, Steve Bolen, recently released on bail, and awaiting retrial in the gruesome 'Prostitute Slayings,' has escaped, despite a twenty-four hour, manned surveillance. Reports are incomplete, but we do know he escaped, in spite of a sophisticated, ultra-sensitive monitoring device. Preliminary reports we are receiving say he did so by severing—you're hearing me correctly—by severing his right foot and leaving the device intact. Police became suspicious when no movement was detected for more than forty-eight hours. Reports from the scene in Glendale, say Police suspect Bolen had help from his brother, and that the small amount of blood found suggests he had expert medical assistance. Unbelievable. A massive search is now underway. More details as we get them."

John took a deep breath and briefly turned toward his front-seat passenger. "Radio volume up," he said. Guitarist Jonathan Butler's *"Song For Elizabeth"* rose. He slowly placed his right hand on the exposed left thigh of the leggy female seated next to him.

Claire smiled and caressed John's hand. Before them, the fading flare from the sun's flaming crown sank slowly into the blue Pacific. The remains of a day in hell, at last, gave way to another glorious sunset in 'Paradise.'

John Roméo could now see Los Angeles and environs receding in his rear view mirror. Nestled comfortably in his motorcar, he continued westward, uncertain just where he and Claire would stop. Aand that was okay. There were sensitive personal dilemmas to resolve, for both of them. For the first time in a long time, he allowed himself to exhale. All the while, he knew the respite would likely not last long. And that, too, was okay.

Epilogue

Into the Dark

Dennis wore handcuffs,

a long-sleeve shirt, and drab-grey slacks. A male nurse, a female attendant, and an armed female security guard were escorting him down a long corridor. All reached a locked door manned by a male, uniformed attendant and were waved through.

The entourage moved a short distance down a narrower corridor and stopped abruptly in front of a closed door. The nameplate read: Dr. Howard Hemphill. The guard knocked twice in rapid succession and waited. Momentarily, they were invited inside. The doctor looked up and smiled.

"I'll call you when we're done," he told the guard.

"Are you sure, sir?" She asked.

"You may leave," said Hemphill.

"Whatever you say, doctor."

"And remove those cuffs, please."

The guard reluctantly removed the cuffs. She and the others then left, closing the door behind them. Hemphill sat at his desk, perusing a file folder while a tense Dennis stood in front of him. Dr. Hemphill, 48, greying, placed the folder down and sat back with fingers laced. His eyes widened; he smiled broadly.

"Please, ah... Dennis. Have a seat. You know, you remind me so much of your sister. I know her very well."

Dennis sat in the chair in front of Hemphill's desk. The doctor stared at him, not saying a word for a long minute.

"You're accused of complicity in some horrendous crimes. Do you understand what you're accused of?"

"I'm innocent."

"Of course. Of course, you are. I understand one of the murder weapons was found at your residence."

"Are you a judge? How do you know I'm a killer? There's no forensic evidence to support that. Who made you God? Look, I admit that I am not as well as I should be. I am sure you are too, at times."

"But I haven't killed anyone."

"Neither have I. Are you listening?"

"Yes, I'm listening. Please, go on."

"I admit that at times, I wanted to be her."

"Your sister?"

"Right, my sister—my blessed sister. At times, I wanted to live my life like she does. She's always had the opportunity to be whomever and however she wants to be. When we were kids we were soul mates. I sometimes imagine being back there. Father was seldom around. Mother insisted on treating us like one person, like we were the same... made a big joke out of it. It *was* a joke to her. But that wasn't all. We both grew to hate my mother."

"Hate? You hated your mother?

"She was *my* mother. Don't interrupt me, doctor. It's not polite."

"Sorry."

"My father was a saint. My mother was an unfaithful, cheating, conniving bitch who drove him to suicide. I was only eighteen when my father took his own life. But she pushed him into it. There was no way he would have done such a terrible thing on his own. He blew his brains out with a .44 Magnum. Our mother clearly drove him to it. And she didn't even attend his funeral."

"What happened to your mother?"

"She was later murdered by one of her lovers. He was the same guy who had molested us both... from the time we were nine years old. Diane won't admit it, though. Sometimes he made us watch while he molested the other. We told our Mother. I remember the day we both told her. She didn't believe us, didn't want to believe it... got angry, called us liars—her own children. The bastard even threatened to kill us if we told anyone else. The day mother died was the happiest day of my life. End of story."

"How did *you* feel about her death?

"I'm not talking about her anymore."

"Fascinating. And I'm sorry you and your sister had to endure such unspeakable horror. You sure there isn't more you'd like to tell me?"

"I've said all I have to say, except we both feel the same way about Father. These men you think I killed were like the men who pursued my mother. They were no different in any way; they deserved to die. And the women were nothing but whores... sluts, like our mother. The world is better off. Whoever killed them deserve medals."

"So, you helped killed them and their lovers because they all symbolized the unfaithfulness of your mother and her lovers. Both of you blame your mother for your father's death?"

"You're not listening. I killed no one. I am no psychopath. If I had killed these people I would take credit. I would be glad to do so."

Dennis suddenly stood and turned away. Dr. Hemphill rose, walked around his desk, positioning himself between Dennis and the door.

"Where are you going? We're not done yet" he said. "You can't leave. I want to know more about you,"

Hemphill gently grasped both Dennis' hands and raised them and smiled. Dennis yanked his hands away and stared back coldly. He took note of the wedding band on Hemphill's finger, and took a step back.

"You're... a carbon copy of your sister, except for a few little details," he said. "I think I understand you."

"Do you really?"

"Oh, I do. I do indeed."

"Do you want me, doctor?"

"Want you? In... in what way?"

"You tell me."

"I ah... "

"You're attracted to me, in some way? I mean, I'm brought in here; you see me for the first time in your life, my dick is probably twice the size of yours, and you make assumptions and put a move on me? Really?

The doctor was breathing heavily. Dennis stepped away long enough to lock the door and return. Dr. Hemphill unbuttoned his lab coat and tossed it aside. He dropped his trousers and kicked them away.

Dennis stepped forward to only inches of where Hemphill sat perched on the edge of the desk. Dennis lowered his right hand, keeping his left arm planted firmly around Hemphill's fat neck. Before Hemphill could speak, Dennis pushed him back then thrust her right hand upward to his chest, with all the force he could muster.

A dull thud sounded. Dr. Hemphill gasped; his eyes bugged out then locked in a death stare; he lumbered backward; clutching at his chest, gurgling blood.

"You sick fuck," Dennis hissed. Dennis stared at him, as if angry that he would not simply die and be done with it. Why wouldn't he just be a man and die?

Hemphill's hands fell away, exposing the base of a steel-point note-holder. It now rested flat against the center of the doctor's chest. His eyes still bulged; his neck veins seemed ready to burst. He took a final gasp and slumped lifelessly onto the floor.

Dennis collected himself then unlocked the door. He returned, stood over the doctor's lifeless body for moment then lifted the phone and dialed the operator.

"I think Dr. Hemphill needs some medical attention," he all but whispered then hung up and stood with warms crossed, waiting.

Seconds later, a female and a male security guards crashed the door, guns drawn. They found Dennis simply waiting with both arms outstretched, palms up, and smiling.

"He shouldn't have done what he did. He's a... he was a very bad man. He really was."

More guards and medical personnel soon arrived. While an emotionless Dennis was being hustled away, a male guard stood shaking his head, staring at Hemphill's lifeless body. The doctor's wedding ring sparkled in the overhead light.

THE END?

For Readers

Purchases:

Autographed copies and free eBook versions of Gene's Cartwright's, "The Widowmaker," and all his books, may be purchased at:

falconcreekbooks.com | GeneCartwright.com

Film Rights are available:

See ReadyForFilm.com | GreenLightThis.com

Write the author:

falconcreekbooks.com/contactus

Book Clubs/Booksellers/Libraries : For Author Appearances, request info: Nancy@falconcreekbooks.com